# NO MORE TEARS

*A Father's Love, A Daughter's Cry*

*A story by Michael W. Ndiomu*

ISBN: 979-8-89570-071-6

# Foreword

My name is Rebecca Mallum, and I'm one of the 276 Government Secondary School girls who were abducted by Boko Haram on April 14, 2014, from Chibok, Borno State, Nigeria, and taken deep into the Sambisa Forest.

The memories of that day remain etched in my mind. Despite years of captivity, brutality, and unimaginable hardship in Sambisa forest, the human spirit within me refused to break. I was fortunate enough to be rescued, but the trauma lingers.

Many of my fellow captives are still missing, and their families continue to hold on to hope.

This book is a powerful testament to the resilience of the human spirit in the face of unimaginable brutality. The author's masterful storytelling weaves together the threads of our experiences, capturing the complexity of our emotions, the depth of our pain, and the strength of our determination to survive.

As I read through the manuscript, I was struck by the parallels between the narrative and my own experiences - the fear, the uncertainty, the moments of hope, and the struggle to hold on to our humanity in the face of such inhumanity.

The stories told in this book are not just about the past; they are about the present and the future. They are about the girls who are still in captivity, still suffering, still holding on to hope.

They are about the families whose lives have been irredeemably shattered, whose loved ones are still missing, and whose hearts continue to ache with grief.

They are about the communities that are still

healing, still rebuilding, and still searching for justice. I hope that this book will be a beacon of hope for those who are still suffering.

I hope that it will remind the world of the ongoing scourge of Boko Haram's brutality and the many girls and women who are still in captivity.

I endorse this book because it sheds light on a critical issue that demands global attention and action.

The stories of our experiences must be told, and this book is an important step towards healing, justice, and advocacy.

As you read this book, I urge you to remember the faces, the names, and the stories of the girls and women who are still suffering.

Remember the laughter, the tears, and the hopes of those who were affected by this conflict. Let their stories move you to action, to compassion, and to advocacy.

Let us work together to ensure that justice is served, that those who are still in captivity are rescued, and that the families who have been affected receive the support they need to rebuild their lives.

By reading this book, you'll gain a deeper understanding of the human cost of conflict and the resilience of the human spirit.

You'll be moved by the stories of courage, hope, and determination that define our experiences.

I am honored to write this foreword because I believe this book has the potential to make a difference in the lives of those affected by this conflict.

*- Rebecca Mallum*

# Dedication

I dedicate this book to everyone who has been affected by the seemingly intractable insurgency in Nigeria.

Every man, woman and child who has been killed, maimed, orphaned, kidnapped, starved, raped or otherwise deprived of the right to life and freedom.

The girls and families of Chibok, Dapchi, Kankara, Abuja and hundreds of other locations across Nigeria.

Our soldiers who have made the ultimate sacrifice and fallen in the line of duty in the fight against this scourge, like my friend Col. Kenneth Eze Elemele and others too numerous to mention.

And to my beloved country Nigeria, a country of such great potential, I dedicate this book to you, as I believe that one day, you will be great again.

God bless the Federal Republic of Nigeria.

# NO MORE TEARS

What would you do if they took your heart?
Yes, you, I'm asking you.
You see, that's what happened to me.
They took my heart,
And there was nothing I could do.

First, they took my choices.
You cannot work here,
You cannot marry her,
You cannot live here,
And there was nothing I could do.


I lived by their rules,
I did as they asked,
I gave them my will, my choice,
Yet they wanted more,
And there was nothing I could do.

This is my life,
This is my cross to bear,
This is my shame to carry,
And I have to bear it alone,
For there was nothing I could do.

I thought despair had an end,
I thought the pain would one day fade,
I hoped the hole in my chest would kill me,
Because they took Aisha, my heart,
And there was nothing I could do.


**Michael W. Ndiomu 2021**

# TABLE OF CONTENTS


**PART ONE:  APRIL 2014**......................................................1

CHAPTER ONE ...........................................................2

CHAPTER TWO.........................................................35

CHAPTER THREE .....................................................65

CHAPTER FOUR ......................................................92

CHAPTER FIVE .......................................................111

CHAPTER SIX..........................................................135

CHAPTER SEVEN ....................................................159

CHAPTER EIGHT ....................................................182

**PART TWO:  JUNE 1998**.................................208

CHAPTER NINE.......................................................209

CHAPTER TEN ........................................................230

CHAPTER ELEVEN .................................................248

CHAPTER TWELVE..................................................270

CHAPTER THIRTEEN .............................................306

CHAPTER FOURTEEN ............................................329

**PART THREE:  AUGUST 2014**.......................344

CHAPTER FIFTEEN .................................................345

CHAPTER SIXTEEN .................................................378

CHAPTER SEVENTEEN ...........................................399

CHAPTER EIGHTEEN...............................................422

CHAPTER NINETEEN...............................................440

CHAPTER TWENTY ..................................................454

CHAPTER TWENTY-ONE.........................................474

CHAPTER TWENTY-TWO .........................................491

CHAPTER TWENTY-THREE .......................................512

CHAPTER TWENTY-FOUR ..........................................536

**PART FOUR: JUNE 2021** ..............................................563

EPILOGUE..........................................................................564

Michael W. Ndiomu

# PART ONE:

# APRIL 2014

# CHAPTER ONE

The last rays of the fading moonlight filtering in through the window louvres form a pattern on the wall of Emmanuel's bedroom. It is early morning in Maiduguri, Borno State, in North-Eastern Nigeria. The large sprawling city is stirring as the early morning *Salat al-fajr* rings out over the corrugated roofs of the heavily populated Gombaru neighborhood.

Outside, the sounds of neighbors getting ready for the day's activities are accompanied by the fading darkness. April in Gombaru was hot skies and hotter moods as people laboured to keep themselves from the heat and sweat. Many of the people in this small market town could not afford air conditioners and had to rely on fans for cooling.

Emmanuel's light but muscular frame allowed him to jump off the bed with ease in a way most people couldn't and land on his feet without toppling over. Being forty hadn't taken away any of his youthful agility. He took care of his mind and body in a way that most people his age did not bother or seem to care about.

He stretched his arms and legs in his morning routine and then walked to the living room, where he found Aisha seated with a book in her hand. His daughter's quest for knowledge and academic excellence was something that both intrigued and impressed him. She lifted her head to the sound of his presence and offered him a smile that made the words in her 'good morning' more genuine.

This was not the regular father-daughter relationship where greetings were perfunctory. There was a deep connection borne of shared sorrows and quality time. He nodded and smiled in return.

Emmanuel moved closer to her to get a better look at the textbook she held in her hands. *Essential Government for Senior Secondary Schools* was one she had read completely before.

"You're reading this for the second time, I see."

"No, chief. I'm reading it for the *fourth* time. You lost track a while back."

He laughed with the hearty ease of a man whose daughter didn't call him the usual *"Daddy"* or *"Papa,"* but instead used the affectionate, and slightly unusual, title of *"Chief"* when she spoke to him. *Chief* was the name his mother called him, and his then two-year-old daughter had taken to it at once.

The moment her mouth had been able to form the word was the beginning, after which there had been no stopping her. She had continued to call him by that appellation through the years, even though that wasn't something a father should eventually get used to. Maybe he wasn't supposed to get used to it. Maybe the warmth that came with it was supposed to be a constant reminder of the bond that existed between them, a bond that could not be severed by circumstances.

"Do you know when my next paper is…?" she asked, head tilted sideways, a mock stern expression on her face, daring him to forget.

"Oh, God! It slipped my mind. It's today, isn't it?"

She laughed as he floundered and raised his hands in mock surrender.

"I don't have any paper today, but I need to go to school, nonetheless. Would you walk with me?" She eyed him as if daring him to refuse.

He could see the taunt in her eyes, daring him to say the wrong thing. It was obvious she was ready for banter this morning, and Emmanuel had to find an intelligent way to counter her arguments.

"Is there a rule that says every girl must bring their dad today?"

"Every girl must bring *her* dad, chief. Not *their* dad. Singular nouns give birth to singular pronouns. I thought we settled this last week?" She feigned exasperation, pulling her mouth into a slight pout.

The taunt was still in her eyes, glistening from the light bulb's reflection in them. She had him right where she wanted him and was expecting him to make a move. An intelligent one. Intelligent by her standards, not his.

"Okay, Ada. You're already doing good this morning. You win."

"You're already doing *well* this morning, not *good*. The word 'good' is an adverb while the word—"

"Chairlady!" he exclaimed, feigning anger, "If we are to speak like this, then no one I know would talk for a minute without interruption."

He had to laugh as he finished saying this to show he wasn't trying to belittle her efforts at verbal dexterity. She responded by looking at him with her right palm on her chest and her mouth open in mock disbelief.

"Did my Chief just shut down his professor? Outrageous! Ludicrous! Preposterous! Atrocious! Insufferable! Nefarious!... Uhm…," she groped for more adjectives to use.

"Why are you stopping? You must finish the dictionary today. Oh, insceptilous! Amphibious!" he continued, making sure the travesty in his choice of words was apparent. He was almost bursting with suppressed laughter.

She laughed at his poor attempt to mimic her.

"What is *insceptilous* now?" She laughed, humour softening her countenance.

"Ada. Leave me alone, oh. I don't need big words to get my job done in the office. My life is fine like this."

They both laughed. As their laughter died down, his eyes caught a picture of her mother, his beloved wife Zainab, on the wall, and he felt a faint stab of guilt. They had not laughed like this during the last two years when Zainab, his wife, was with them.

Even Aisha had moved carefully around her mother and was more formal with him in those days, though he knew that deep down, she wanted to be expressive, to relate with her mother in the same way she did with him.

Unlike him, Zainab was not very expressive and internalised her pain, putting a wall between her and the world as she fought her private demons. A woman who used to be full of life and exuberance, she had, over the years, withdrawn into herself and almost become a different person.

Thus, she was quite stern and taciturn with Aisha, and her inability to be open had caused a rift between them that he was never able to bridge. He did his best, but he just could not get through to her, so he buried himself in his work and his daily routine.

Until that fateful day, a day just like any other day. The sun was out; people woke up and went about their normal day's endeavours. The cocks crowed, the taxi horns blared, and people greeted each other on the streets as they hurried off to their jobs, schools, or businesses. No dark and ominous clouds in the sky, no black cats sitting outside the house or on the windowsills, no black crows sitting on the roofs, nothing to indicate the darkness lurking in the shadows, just waiting to creep into their lives.

It was a bright and sunny Tuesday, and it was Emmanuel's turn to take Aisha to school. They both hugged Zainab as usual and ran off to get a bus. At the junction of their street, Emmanuel turned to catch one last glimpse of his wife, smiled, and blew her a kiss, which she strangely had not returned. Unknown to him, that was the last time he would see her.

The first inkling he got of the coming darkness was when he got a call from Aisha's class teacher informing him that she had not yet been picked up. In confusion, he called Zainab's phone, which went straight to voicemail. He called a few more times as he got more worried until the number was switched off.

In confusion, he left work and rushed to Aisha's school, picked her up, and rushed home only to find an empty house. Assuming she had just gone out and forgotten to charge her phone, he went around the neighborhood asking if anyone had seen her. All their responses were the same; they had not seen her leave, and they saw no one come to the house during the day.

He waited anxiously for hours, and with each passing moment, his unease deepened. By evening, he had really started to panic. He begged a neighbor to watch Aisha for a while and went out into the night to look for his beloved. He went to the market; he went to the

Police Station; he went to the school again, all to no avail.

In desperation, he went to the home of Zainab's parents only to be chased away by her brothers. Emmanuel roamed the streets in desperation; his mind filled with images of all possible horrors his beloved wife could be facing. The more his imagination raced, and the more powerless he felt, the more desperate he became.

Days passed, and he went from confused to shocked, to desperate, and all shades in between. There was no help from the police or the community apart from a few sympathizers who stopped by occasionally to commiserate with Emmanuel and Aisha.

He prayed for her return.

He went back to being a devout Catholic and did everything he was advised to do to gain the favor of God and the Blessed Virgin Mary.

As the day turned into weeks and the weeks turned into months, his faith began to dwindle.

By the second year, he had lost all hope of finding Zainab alive again. He believed that their love was so strong that there was nothing in this world that would make her stay away from him and Aisha for that long if there was life in her body.

By the third year of her disappearance, he had gotten to the point of acceptance and prayed that she had had a quick death and that whatever had befallen her, she had not suffered for long. It was his way of finding a little consolation in his desolation.

The only thing that kept Emmanuel sane and functional during this period was having to take care of Aisha and putting up a brave face for her.

He sometimes still felt her presence. He looked to the parts of the house where she mostly used to be and took solace in the imaginative smell that was hers and hers alone. Nights were when he felt her absence the most. His hands would roam around the surface of what used to be her side of the bed. He would imagine she was there and clench the bed cover so tight. It was easy to think up a non-existent intimacy that had begun to fade long before her disappearance.

Even now, he thought he heard a laugh that sounded like hers. Zainab had been filled with youthful exuberance before everything changed, and her easy nature had receded to somewhere far that couldn't be reached.

Coming back to the present, he left Aisha in the living room and went to check his report for the contractors at work. He had drafted it and gone through it last night, but if there was one thing he had learnt from his daughter, it was never to be too sure about a thing if you had the opportunity of cross-checking it. And that was what he was about to do. He had to be thorough; he couldn't afford to make mistakes. He was meticulous that way.

As the Lead Engineer at Ngala Local Government Headquarters, it was his responsibility to oversee all engineering-related requirements of contracts, and this one had a lot of those. Yunusa and Ibrahim, the other members of his team, were the last people any person would want to delegate vital responsibilities to because of the amount of effort they put into it, which was practically zero. They had their jobs because of the people they knew and not because of what they could do. He, on the other hand, was only relevant because of what he could do. The moment he stopped doing that, it would be the end of the journey for him.

So, he had to be the responsible one and shoulder most of the tasks, not that he was complaining.

"Ada, what was that thing you said about not ending a sentence with a preposition again…" he called out to Aisha, loud enough to be heard in the living room.

She didn't answer the question, and he tried to ask again when, with a soft knock, she came into the room.

"Yes, you can't end sentences with prepositions because their function…"

"No need to explain further," he said without raising his head from the sheets on the table to look at her. "Is the word 'to' a preposition?"

She dimmed her eyes and squinted for some seconds in a bid to recall something, and finally spoke.

"It is a preposition sometimes, an adverb at other times, and it…"

"Okay, okay. Just help me look at this report. I can end this sentence with 'to', right?"

She took the paper from his hands, looked at it for a bit, and nodded.

He smiled in a way that allowed her to see that he was impressed and thanked her. She asked if she should make bread and eggs for breakfast, and he agreed. It was not the best of breakfasts, but it would have to do. It would also mean she would spend less time preparing breakfast and more time studying. He liked that.

As he went through the contract, he noticed one thing: a group of numbers wasn't aligning with the ones on the report that Mallam Abdullah, his boss, had asked him to input. The disparity between these numbers meant only one thing: money was being siphoned by the Admin Department, and by presenting the report, he too would technically be a part of it, even though he didn't receive any 'settlement.'

They left him out of those dirty deals. He was an upright man who wouldn't be moved by a bribe.

He remembered the case that involved Idowu two years ago. Mallam Abdullah had made a deal with some of the people at the Ministry of Agriculture, and as usual, a lot of money got lost in transit between the two offices. Idowu, the Lead Engineer then, had suspected the deal and had probed into it to find out the reason for the discrepancies.

This led him to Mallam Abdullah and the accountant from the Ministry. Idowu reported the matter to the State Auditor General's office, and Mallam Abdullah was queried.

Idowu, however, lost his job two months later in questionable circumstances. He ended up being accused of doctoring contract figures and fired for fraud.

Everyone in the office knew the truth—he was paying for the 'crime' he'd committed against the boss. No one crossed the boss and got away with it.

Emmanuel looked at the figures one more time before arranging the sheets and putting them back in the file.

Office corruption was a terrible thing for one to turn a blind eye to, but a father neglecting the welfare of his daughter simply because he reported a crime perpetrated in the office and losing his job was worse.

Though honorable, it was a stupid move, and Emmanuel didn't consider himself a stupid man in any sense of the word. He would ignore the stealing; he just wouldn't take part in it.

****

Aisha watched as her father left for work that morning. She was dedicated to every area of her academics, and her father showed the same passion in his work. Everyone who knew him around called him *Injiniya* (Engineer) or *Mai rada* in response to the abilities he exhibited daily at his office.

But for her, he was simply Chief—a name that, despite its oddity, had found a way to her lips and a place in her heart.

The bond she had with him was what she had wished for with her mother during the silent years. As a child, she had yearned to get closer, to be seen and understood, but it seemed the more she tried, the more she was shut out.

It pained her, left her questioning what she was doing wrong—but over time, she tried to get over it, tucking the ache away like so many other things she never said aloud.

She tried not to worry too much about her mother's disappearance these days, even though she knew her father did. He would go off into a world of silence every time something happened to remind him of her mother. He missed her so much that it was obvious. He would stare for long at her picture or her favourite chair, and his eyes would moisten. He would avert his eyes when the emotions surged through him, but nothing escaped Aisha's notice.

It wasn't like Aisha didn't miss her too; she did, so much, but there was nothing she could do about it. There were days when she missed her more. Days when the memories of her would dampen her spirits and have her wishing she were there. Her mother hadn't shown much affection for her, but she knew that she loved her. There had been times she caught glances of her mother staring at her. The silence they shared sometimes brought them closer, mother and daughter.

Today, she had made bread and eggs for breakfast, and he had teased her after he discovered she had gone a little off with the salt in the eggs. But he still ate it, not minding it. He was like that. He never took offense at anything she would do.

"Nana would have thrown the eggs away if she had been here," she said, and regretted it as soon as the words left her mouth. It had become somewhat of an unspoken rule to never speak about her mother.

Her remark about her mother had drawn a brief cough from him, a glance at her, and he retreated into the world of solitude of men who had lost their wives to bizarre circumstances. She didn't blame him. His life had been built and centred around her mother, and it almost came crashing down.

He had loved her so much, everyone knew that. When she had gone missing, he had nearly gone mad.

For months, he had withdrawn into a shell dominated by grief and regret. Grief, because he missed her so much. Regret, because he felt he had lost out on the most important parts of their lives. He believed he hadn't been able to make her happy. He had folded in on himself. For him, his whole world had collapsed. She believed it was because of her that he didn't get lost in his grief. She, as a spark of light, during a period where a rayless sun thrived, had given him hope for the future, made him hold on.

Aisha cleared the dishes and went to pack her books in her bag before heading for the bathroom. There was a sense of ease that came from being organized first before hitting the shower. One would let the water touch their skin and settle, knowing they didn't need to worry about loading things and inviting heat.

It was the time of the year when people relished the coldness of the bathwater on their bodies while it lasted because, by the time they stepped out from under their roofs, the sun would be waiting to continue heating the earth as if it had a grudge to settle with its inhabitants. Maiduguri's sun cared nothing for the people it contained.

She walked with measured strides from the bathroom to her room and dressed up for school. Since today was just pre-exam tutorials, she could choose to wear any of her clothes apart from the school uniform. She chose a cream- coloured gown in hopes that its silk nature would reduce the heat trapped beneath it. She picked up a black veil decorated with pink flower patterns. Even though black was a poor choice in this weather, she couldn't afford to mismatch her dressing colours.

She was conscious of her dressing to a fault, and her

father sometimes teased her about it.

She stepped out of the house and was welcomed by the harsh sunlight. Even though it was still early morning, Maiduguri's weather had a mind of its own. The glare of the sun threatened to scorch her skin as she hastened her steps.

Mamman Zaliya's shop was her next stop. She needed to get the final set of examination materials and sweets for her friend, Mairo.

The fifteen-year-old Zaliya, who was manning the shop, already had sweat beads making their way down her neck to her chest. The shop's opening faced the direction of the sun, making it an unfortunate position for the teenager for the next three hours. Her question made the girl snap out of her morning reverie.

*"Akwai biro da pencil? Ki ba ni ko wanne guda uku."*

*"Wani kala?"*

*"Blue."*

Aisha didn't need three pens and three pencils, but she

was too careful to be a victim of unforeseen circumstances. The young girl looked through the stacks of items on the shelves for what Aisha wanted. Even though she was a year older than Aisha, she was almost a head shorter. Most people her age were not as tall as she was. The face and frame of her mother and the height of her father dominated her genes.

After a lot of stretching, the girl brought down the pack of ball-point pens, selected three, tested them on a piece of paper, and handed them over to Aisha. With that, Aisha flagged down a commercial motorcycle and headed to school. She relished the wind that rushed past her face as the motorcycle sped off. Even though the wind was a bit hot, it had a redemptive feel to it.

Mallam Nasiru, their Government Studies teacher, had set a final revision class for tomorrow's exam in school. She preferred her lone reading method over the man's impossible teaching style and would not have gone if not for the fact that she wanted to meet with Mairo.

The conversations she had with her best friend were nothing short of spectacular. Mairo had a way of making a *Turtle and the Rabbit* kind of story sound like a climactic chapter from Harry Potter if her audience were willing to pay attention. And Aisha had always been her audience, listening with rapt attention, her 'oohs' and 'ahs' serving as extra fuel for Mairo's signature: 'Come, let me gist you something.' Her friend would make a great actress.

As the motorcycle sped along the dusty streets, Aisha remembered the first time they met. She was in Junior Secondary School 2 (JSS2), and the students of Federal Government College Maiduguri had deemed her unworthy to be associated with by the end of the first term of JSS1. She had been on her own for the rest of the year; the product of a Fulani Muslim mother and an Igbo Christian father. The teachers didn't seem to mind, but her classmates did, so they took advantage of every opportunity to show their prejudice.

When Mairo came at the start of the term in JSS2, she didn't mind the unsettling stories she had heard about Aisha. It was only Aisha she spoke to for the first two weeks, until someone threatened to beat up Aisha.

Mairo, even though a new student, had confronted the girl and put the fear of God into her.

Word soon spread about how Mairo had promised to strip the girl naked and flog her with *ciyawa mai ƙaiƙayi*—the stalk of a plant that caused itchiness. She didn't say that, of course, but anything that would keep others off their backs was a welcome embellishment.

The motorcycle dropped her at the school's entrance, and she walked towards the Senior Secondary section of the school. Mairo was standing at the door of their class, talking to a group of fellow students. Both had come a long way since their junior secondary school days and now relate with a lot of their mates, but not all of them, though. Hassana, with her hoop of hags, was the exception. Mairo stood tall amongst the other girls, but would be dwarfed by another's height the moment Aisha joined the group.

Her friend wore a blue gown that accentuated the buxom curve on her hips, making her look much older than she was. It was unlike her wide school skirts, which covered everything. Their school uniforms were deliberately made to hide the very parts of their bodies that had developed in recent years. The cuts and expansive spaces were made to strangle the voices that spoke sensually of their bodies as young girls.

"Yeesha! The yet-to-be-crowned queen of SS3 Art class!"

Mairo didn't even let her step on the concrete pathway that connected different classes before she started tossing complimentary remarks. Aisha smiled and shook her head as each of the girls in the group hugged her. Even though she was the youngest, she had a presence about her that made sure every unspoken antagonism remained hushed. There was a quiet strength in the way she carried herself—an elegance that needed no words.

Today, they sat on the last seat in the classroom, something Aisha wasn't used to doing. Mairo was jumpy and looked like she couldn't wait to let out whatever it was that she had kept in that mischievous mind of hers. She always had something to tell. Even if it didn't turn out to be significant, her friend's dramatic gestures would have been sufficient to set the day's mood.

"Hey Yeesha, come let me gist you something," Mairo said with an expression that screamed gossip. Aisha smiled at the familiar phrase.

"What is it that's getting you all flustered like this, Maya?"

She always called Mairo—Maya. A name formed by combining the first syllable of her first name, Mairo, and her surname, Yakubu.

"Keep 'flustered' aside; we will talk about him later," Mairo responded with a dismissive wave of the hand.

It wasn't that she didn't know 'flustered' was an adjective; the personification of the word was her way of setting the mood for a non-academic conversation, which would be dominated by sarcasm and anything that was on the opposite spectrum of a philosopher's lecture. She liked this about Mairo—the ability to switch between her Shakespearean and Patience

Ozokwor personalities. Her friend was the perfect model for the average street girl with the mind of a scholar, and Aisha relished it.

"Yeesha, the time has come for you to flourish. I have just uncovered the mysteries of the times."

"That President Yar'adua didn't die as we were told, or what?"

"No, crazy girl. Joshua Ndua… Nduagwi…"

She sighed exasperatedly as she said, "Nduaguibe."

"Yes, him. See, your tongue is even comfortable pronouncing his last name … He is in love with you, girl. The boy is already in—"

"Maya … How do you know this?"

Lines of sweat had gathered around Aisha's neck by now, and her heartbeat seemed to pick up pace. The focus of Mairo's gist had intensified the heat that hung in the air. Despite the open windows and the flapping of shirts of passers-by, the air outside the classroom held to its own as if it had no contract of delivering comfort to the people in the class.

"Yeesha, I'm very serious. My source is reliable. You know I don't joke with my information."

"Okay, Maya. Even if what you're saying is true, what am I supposed to do with that information? It's not like I can just walk up to him and express my feelings." She knew exactly what she was supposed to do: jump for joy, because she harboured a massive crush on Joshua.

"I suppose not. But that's why I am here, is it not? I'm here to smooth the path."

*"Kina dai so ki hada ni da yaron nan ko ƙarya na ke yi?"* - You just want to hook me up with this boy, right?

Aisha rarely spoke Hausa to the people close to her, apart from Maya. There was a depth that it brought to their conversations. And she suspected that Mairo was more interested in the idea of her being in a relationship with one of the coolest boys in school than in what she, Aisha, wanted. But she couldn't deny it; she did have a crush on Joshua.

Even when he didn't seem to see her, let alone reciprocate her feelings, she didn't put the brakes on her emotions. She allowed them to linger in her heart, vicariously relishing the possibilities.

*"Amma kina son shi da gaske?"* Mairo asked.

Of course, she loved Joshua, or she believed that what she felt was love, but it was not reason enough for Mairo to intervene and force them together. To Mairo, however, the end justified the means. Aisha had been uncomfortable with this trait in Mairo at first, but after a while, it became part of their friendship.

Before they could proceed with the conversation, Mallam Nasiru, or Mallam Nas as the students called him, walked into the classroom with his usual stern expression. However, despite his strict demeanor, students seemed to be the worst under his tutelage, and his class was always the noisiest. It was almost like his strict demeanour had the opposite effect on his students.

"Keef kwayet (Keep quiet)… I will not repeat myself."
He uttered in his heavily accented English.

The truth is, he repeated himself so often that Aisha thought that it made up one-fifth of his lesson time.

He settled in and wasted no time in starting his lectures for the day. The two girls listened with rapt attention at first, just like the other students in the class. But after a while, everyone got bored and continued with what they were doing before he came to the class. Aisha began to wonder why they came to school in the first place. Maybe they, too, like her, just wanted to hang out with their friends instead of spending the day at home.

She and Mairo continued to talk about Joshua for a while before Mallam Nas walked to the back of the class and interrupted them with a question.

"What iz zha dipperence between Autocracy and Monarchy?"

It was an easy one, but Aisha and Mairo let the question linger to create a dramatic effect. After they were sure the man was beginning to conjure up a reason why they couldn't answer the question, probably because they were talking, Aisha got up gracefully to answer the question. Mario had allowed her to answer questions like these, not because she didn't know the answers herself, but because she claimed that answering too many questions made people look at her weirdly, and she wasn't ready for that.

"Eben ip you know zha ansa iz not mean you will be making noise and disrupting zha class."

Mallam Nas made sure his warning was delivered before he proceeded to the front of the class to continue with the teaching. Both girls started giggling the moment he turned his back.

"I wanted to get you sweets, but I forgot. *Yi haƙuri. Wallahi*, I had it in mind."

Mairo shook her head and gave Aisha a smile that wasn't unfamiliar to both. Aisha knew she would have to make it up to her friend somehow.

By the end of the class, Aisha had had enough of Mairo's talk to decide what she wanted to do about Joshua. She liked him, but she wasn't convinced that being romantically involved with a boy at her age was a smart thing to do. Sure, he made her heart race. She had her exams to worry about, her future. She didn't want to risk distraction—or worse, heartbreak. He wasn't like the other boys, loud and unruly. Still, she wasn't convinced this was a path she should take. Not yet.

She waved Mairo goodbye and headed home through the back gate. She often wished that Mairo's house were in the same direction as her house so that they could walk home together and continue their never-ending conversations.

But every day, they had to go home in opposite directions. Well, not perfectly opposite, but who cared about geometric accuracy when friendship was thrown in the mix?

She walked away from the blocks of classes, conscious of her steps. According to Mairo, carriage was everything when it came to putting on a show for the boys in school. She allowed their stares to follow her with interest. She wasn't concerned about their interest as much as she was concerned about hers. Her interest was schooling, getting the best grades, and graduating with the best grades she could. This was an investment, and she was about to make a profit to build her future. That was the kind of interest that dominated her mind.

As she headed towards the gate, she thought she heard a whisper. Someone called her name in a voice that was soft enough for others not to hear but just loud enough to pick her from the crowd. She turned around to see who it was, and her shock was immediately overwhelmed by shyness.

It was Joshua, and he was wearing one of the warmest smiles she had ever seen. Or was it her emotions magnifying it? Either way, seeing him caused a rush of strange sensations in her belly, a warm flurry that spread up her body to her face, and for the first time that day, the heat felt dominant enough to overwhelm

her.

She smiled back, and he waved.

Somehow, the wave seemed to make it official. Joshua liked her, and he wasn't afraid to let people know!

She had a new spring in her step as she walked towards where he was standing.

# CHAPTER TWO

Emmanuel got to work earlier than his co-workers, as usual. The time on his wristwatch was 8:15 am, but he knew his watch was set a half hour early. That way, he always made sure to be early to work.

In the light of the early morning, the buildings still gleamed with dew as the heat of the sun had not fully dissipated it. The compound consisted of the large main office block and several smaller buildings connected by covered cement walkways. The main building was much older than most of the other buildings, which had been added at different times by different governments without a coordinated design or plan. As a result, even though the main building was quite large and imposing and must have been a masterpiece at the time it was built, the juxtaposition of the newer structures gave the compound a confused look, which was quite disorienting to first-time visitors.

To make matters worse, the entire complex was not

adequately maintained, so most of the buildings had not been painted in years, several broken-down vehicles littered the open spaces, and there were stacks of crates of machine parts that had somehow ended up gathering weeds.

When he arrived, the cleaning staff were rounding up their sweeping and cleaning of the offices, and the night security guard had just been relieved by the security man on the day shift. *Dan Yaro,* as he was fondly called, looked like he had spent the night smoking cannabis as usual.

After several attempts to educate him on the dangers of smoking cannabis, Emmanuel had given up when his words always seemed to fall on deaf ears.

*"Yana bada bala'in karfi ne, maigida,"* – It gives me strength, sir - he would retort in Hausa.

A man who did not take his job seriously, Dan Yaro, would often bring some of his friends there to play cards. He swore they did not gamble but were just having "card exhibitions," the kind of leisurely pastime common among idle men in the heat of the Gombaru afternoons, to while away the time. Today, Dan Yaro looked like he had taken more than the usual amount of weed because he struggled to make his way into the one-room building that served as the security quarters. He presented a sorry sight, and Emmanuel almost felt pity for him.

Emmanuel turned away from the gatehouse and kept on walking to the main office building, holding onto the file. He hoped his boss would approve the contract report he had drafted, given that the man never appreciated the effort he put into doing proper documentation. It had taken him all evening the previous day and assistance from Aisha, checking and rechecking the report, both the numbers and the prose. He did his best even though he knew that Mallam Abdullah did not care about grammatical correctness, nor did he have a head for numbers; he doubted if the man even knew the difference between adverbs and adjectives. The man behaved like someone whose only educational certificate was that of secondary school at best. This notwithstanding, Emmanuel was committed to putting his best foot forward as much as possible.

No one could tell where this attitude might take him next. It brought him here, and it would be proper to continue with it. He was one for putting brilliance into work, and it showed in all his endeavours.

Unlike his previous boss at the Secretariat, who read through all that Emmanuel presented and made significant amendments where necessary, Mallam Abdullah simply flipped through to the pages where the figures were and ignored the rest.

Sometimes, it baffled Emmanuel how the man rose to his current position. But he knew the drill. It all boiled down to the influential people you were allied with, your networking skills; here, hard work did not matter as long as you remained loyal to the higher-ups who had placed you there. It was the same with the other members of his team, Yunusa and Ibrahim.

For most of the workers, the only motivation for their actions was money. Emmanuel continually witnessed this in the work habits and livelihood of his colleagues, with most of them involved in one scheme or another. He didn't know whether to blame them for indulging in corruption or to reason with them amidst their mostly self-inflicted predicaments.

Take his co-worker Yunusa, for example. He had three wives and ten children while working a job that paid him Forty Thousand Naira per month, which was less than Fifty US Dollars. In the Gombaru neighbourhood, in this dusty corner of North-Eastern Nigeria, such choices were not uncommon. Here, wealth was often measured not in savings or property but in the number of children a man could boast of, for children were seen as a man's honour, his legacy, his labour force, and his insurance for old age. Yunusa claimed it was his right as a Muslim to take up to four wives if he so wished, quoting the Qur'an as if it were a shield against any practical objection. Yet Emmanuel could not help but notice how the same scripture also placed the burden of fair provision upon the man, a duty Yunusa was clearly failing to meet.

The very idea of family planning was anathema to him, as it was to many men here, who considered it a foreign intrusion meant to weaken their lineage. And so, he lived under constant financial pressure, forever stretching his meagre salary over the endless needs of his household, relying on loans, favours, and the occasional 'arrangement' to keep afloat. Emmanuel could never understand it—how pride could override reason so completely.

Kande was the first to arrive after Emmanuel. A recent graduate undergoing the mandatory one-year National Youth Service Corps scheme, she showed dedication and passion for her work, taking an interest in areas that were not even directly related to the tasks assigned to her. Being a government office where gossip was rife, people speculated that she was either doing it for recognition with the hope of being retained, or she was just a hard worker and was doing it out of passion. Because very few people worked for the passion these days, the consensus leaned towards the former reason.

Kande dropped her bag on her table and walked towards him with a smile on her face. It seemed to Emmanuel that she always had a smile ready for him. She always treated him with more respect than she showed to the other staff. It had started with deference due to his obvious competence and natural leadership abilities compared to the others, but recently, even Emmanuel had noticed that maybe she harboured some sort of affection for him. He found this quite unsettling. Apparently, other people in the office had noticed the gradual change in her behaviour towards him and had begun to question him about it.

*"Me ka ke yi ne da wannan yarinya ke sauraran ka?"* one of his colleagues asked in Hausa.

This had happened some weeks back when the other men in the office questioned him about the seeming reverence that Kande had for him. It had been that noticeable. Ibrahim, the younger of his two team members, had begged Emmanuel to set him up with Kande, but he refused. He didn't want to be involved in the personal affairs of his colleagues and definitely not in their personal lives.

Apparently, Ibrahim had feelings for her, and he didn't take Emmanuel's refusal too well, accusing Emmanuel of wanting Kande for himself. Of course, it wasn't true, but he didn't bother wasting his time trying to refute the claim. He responded instead by keeping things strictly professional and keeping to himself, cutting off anything that could lead to personal entanglements.

Keeping to himself was how he got out of the troubles most men in his office seemed to get themselves into, and he wasn't about to put himself in a position where he could be caught up in a noose because of a woman.

As a result, he rarely got into trouble. He never got past his boundaries, either. He knew not to make an input on a matter that didn't concern him, something most of his colleagues at work were fond of. Most of them believed it was all pretence on his part, the holier-than-thou attitude, but it didn't faze him. He left them to their gossip.

Fifteen minutes later, Haruna walked into the office

complaining about his wife and her lack of appreciation for his efforts. As soon as he stepped into the office, he went to the switch and turned on the fans. As usual, the old fans screeched in protest through several turns before they settled into a moderate buzz, pushing the tepid air around in the room.

"Good morning, Mr Emmanuel. Kande, *ya ya ki ke?*" —he greeted, his tone carrying the easy familiarity of everyday exchanges.

Emmanuel and Kande both responded to his greetings and settled behind their tables in their corners.

Apart from money, Haruna talked about his wife the most, almost always negatively. The man was quite awful himself. It was a wonder the woman was still stuck with him. He was an abuser and a philanderer who had been known to try to have his way with girls young enough to be his daughters.

No matter that Emmanuel tried to stay away from

delving into other people's affairs, he could not help but overhear the rumours that dominated many conversations with Haruna being the subject.

"I won't be surprised if this woman poisons me one day, wallahi, " he had said at one point.

It had become normal for the others to listen to Haruna without trying to explain to him where he was wrong. Several people had tried in the past, but it didn't amount to much as the man continued on his trail of matrimonial negativity.

The sound of Mallam Abdullah's Toyota Hilux announced his presence in the compound. From the window, Emmanuel could see the man talking on his phone as he stepped out of the car. Mallam Abdullah walked into the office, nodded to their greetings, and made his way to his office without saying another word. Judging from his demeanour, Emmanuel felt that it would not be the best time to go to him with the report, so he waited. The pungent smell of his perfume dominated the office, so strong that Emmanuel struggled not to sneeze. Emmanuel always wondered why the man insisted on using such strong perfumes.

"I heard that they're transferring Mallam to another place."

When Haruna wasn't talking about money or his wife, he was busy gossiping about other people in the office. His ability to magnify simple discussions and opinions into larger-than-life themes that needed urgent attention was one of the few 'skills' he possessed.

Like most of the people there, he knew someone who knew someone who knew someone else. He didn't need to have any useful skills or qualifications; he just had to know the right people and be willing to accept the job offered to him. With respect to the job, many staffers, most of the time, did not even bother to pretend to be working.

Neither Kande nor Emmanuel responded to Haruna. Emmanuel had made it clear he didn't engage in office gossip, and he assumed Kande was also keeping to herself until her time in the office elapsed. Haruna continued speaking, nonetheless.

"Some people upstairs don't want Mallam here any longer. Maybe they will take him to a better place or a place where they will show him pepper." He whispered in a conspiratorial tone. Emmanuel noted that he said this with a sly undertone, knowing that the phrase meant trouble, not the fiery bite of chilies, but the slow, deliberate process of difficulty in a man's life, as if seasoning it with hardship until he burned from the inside out.

"Haruna, that's none of our business. It shouldn't be your business, too."

Emmanuel's comment was met with an unfriendly stare. Haruna didn't like to be shut down like that, and especially not by Emmanuel.

Mallam Abdullah came out a minute later and walked to his car. He still didn't say a word to any of them. Through the window, Emmanuel could see him talking to Dan Yaro, and the two seemed to be coming to an agreement on something, probably the grass

Mallam Abdullah was pointing to, which was on the east side of the compound that needed to be levelled.

Dan Yaro was too lazy, and Emmanuel knew the man would probably ask for an inflated fee for the work and pay off some boys from the area a meagre amount to do the job for him.

As Mallam Abdullah came back, he summoned the staff to his office, and all three followed without hesitation, Haruna with false diffidence and Emmanuel and Kande with blank faces and open minds. They grabbed a chair each in front of the desk as indicated by their boss, but Haruna chose to sit at the back on the long bench along the wall.

*"Ka matso kusa mana Haruna."* Mallam Abdullah said, motioning for the man to sit in one of the chairs before him, and he quickly complied.

Emmanuel didn't know why the man chose to speak in Hausa to some of the staff. They were all capable of communicating in English, and this was supposed to be an office that dealt formally with staff. He kept his eyes on the man as he spoke to them, regardless.

"As you may have heard, I will be leaving the LGA Headquarters for another place. It was supposed to be later, but the people in charge had deemed it necessary that I move earlier."

*Was that a hint of sadness in his eyes?*

"So, I will be leaving this office today. Emmanuel, are you done with the report?"

"Yes, sir. I have finished everything."

Emmanuel reached into the file that he had brought with him and handed over the sheets that he had worked on.

"I'll want you to make sure those two under you are part of this work. No excuses, *ka ji ko?*" he added.

"Yes, sir."

"Where are they, by the way? I did not see them when I came into the office."

Just as he was speaking, Emmanuel's team members, Yunusa and Ibrahim, walked into the outer general office, engaged in good-natured banter. They did not know that a meeting was going on, but stopped short when they saw the others gathered through the door of their boss's office. Mallam Abdullah motioned for them to come in and join them. He then scanned through the documents Emmanuel had given him, signed and stamped them, and gave them to Kande for processing.

Addressing the staff, he reiterated what he said earlier about leaving and urged them to behave well. Emmanuel knew the man didn't care if they turned the office upside down. He imagined the man would wish for that to happen. After speaking with a solemnity that seemed more practised than natural, he sent them back to work. As they left his office, the rest of the staff members arrived for work.

News of Mallam Abdullah's sudden and imminent departure set a strange atmosphere around the office, even though work went on as usual. People were trying to tidy up and present a respectable image for the next man in the seat. It was a wise move to be in the good books of a new boss, even though most of them had been negligent during Mallam Abdullah's tenure. Emmanuel hoped that the new boss would be stern enough to set off a more work-oriented environment.

Around noon, Mallam Abdullah packed the remainder of his personal belongings and had the cleaners carry them to his car. As he said his final goodbyes to the staff and headed towards his car, he motioned to Emmanuel to walk with him. Emmanuel was surprised, but he did not let it show.

"You are a very smart man, Emmanuel." Mallam Abdullah said in a low tone as they got close to his car. *"Na san ka ga abubuwan da aka lissafa a contract da na ba ka?"*

Emmanuel wasn't sure whether he wanted to have this conversation with his boss. Of course, he had seen the discrepancies in the figures. But it wasn't something one confronted his boss with. Now that he was being offered a piece of the pie, he didn't know how to respond to that.

Outrightly refusing to collect what he was being offered was another way of telling the man that he was a corrupt man and he, Emmanuel, a righteous one. That tactic was not known to be effective and had been known to backfire seriously. Deciding to collect, on the other hand, made him an active accomplice in the corruption.

Seeking a neutral stance, Emmanuel just smiled and thanked him, not for offering to 'settle' him, but for all the years of service he had given in the Headquarters. Eight years as a boss was no joke, even if the boss was not someone who was inspiring or added value to his subordinates.

Back in the office, talk of who the new boss could be had started to fly around, and Haruna was at the centre of the discussion. No one knew who the person was, but everyone had a theory of who it might be. Some had more than theories; they went as far as claiming to have 'credible' sources.

"It's Isyaka Bada that is coming to this office," Sadiya said. She was the clerk in charge of documentation.

"Which Isyaka Bada? *Wa zai ba shi irin wannan wurin?*" —Who would give him such a position?

Maryam always seemed to oppose everyone. Like Haruna, she too had a knack for gist and spreading rumours.

*"Farouq Yazid za a kawo mana. Shi zai zauna a kujeran nan."*

Her Kano accent contrasted with the North-Eastern accent that most of the people in the office had. Her claim that Farouq Yazid, a notorious Administrator, was the one who would occupy the boss's seat wasn't completely unfounded. After all, Maryam had a lot of connections with people who should know. Her information was usually validated.

Emmanuel left the group and walked out to the compound. The sun shone with ferocious fury—the kind that made even the chickens and goats embrace the shade that the mango trees provided.

He didn't care who would replace Mallam Abdullah; he just hoped that they wouldn't be as criminally corrupt, incompetent, and partial as the man had been. He felt guilty for thinking of the man who gave him his job in that manner, but it was the truth. The man had thrown his prejudice in his face several times.

Even though he was discriminated against due to his religion and ethnicity, he carried on quite well. Over time, he learnt to focus on his job and ignore the jibes, taunts, and the sometimes-blatant tribalism.

On the rare occasions when arguments broke out that could have deteriorated to a physical altercation, Emmanuel always held on to his temper and chose to walk away.

The budgetary allocation to the Technical Department has increased over the years in line with the Local Government budgets. However, the number and quality of the projects executed had reduced instead of increasing, and there was only one person responsible for this: Mallam Abdullah.

Projects were grossly inflated, and no one could do anything about it. Those who were loyal to him were compensated, and the others were kept in line with subtle threats; hence, no one dared go against him.

Emmanuel watched as the gateman opened the gate for a very clean Honda Accord, which drove into the compound and parked in front of the main building. He didn't recognise the woman who came out of it. He had never seen any of Mallam Abdullah's wives, but he wasn't sure this woman fit the profile of the wife of someone like his boss. Ex-boss, he reminded himself. His wives were sure to have an aura of ignorance about them, and this woman seemed quite the opposite.

The woman approached the main building, everything about her exuding confidence. She was tall and walked with long strides. Her clothes were formal but simple and elegant at the same time. She had the air of a woman who could hold her own anywhere and knew it.

As she approached the entrance, Emmanuel stepped

forward to greet her.

"Good afternoon, madam. Are you looking for someone, Hajiya? How may I assist or direct you?"

The safest form of address to use in the north for someone of a reputable standing was Alhaji (for a man) and Hajiya (for a woman), and Emmanuel knew that all too well. This little bit of information and practised wisdom had kept him from trouble and granted him favours in places that were uncertain before.

The woman responded to his greeting and asked where the Technical Department was. Emmanuel offered to take her. As they walked into the outer office, they came upon his colleagues still debating who their new boss would be.

"Do you work here?" she asked Emmanuel.

"Yes, Hajiya." He replied.

She then turned to face all the staff.

"Good morning, everyone," she greeted politely yet

loudly enough to be heard over the office chatter. Her voice was commanding, her carriage was authoritative, attracted respect, and drew attention, nay, demanded it. Everyone immediately stopped what they were doing and focused on her.

"My name is Mrs. Hadiza Abdulaziz. I'll oversee this office from now on."

No dilly-dallying, no beating around the bush, just a brisk and straight-to-the-point introduction.

Emmanuel didn't know what aspect of the new boss impressed him so, but he knew one thing: they were in for a journey none of them had embarked on before.

The new boss seemed like she meant business, and that was going to be bad for most of them in the office, but he didn't mind. Maybe it was a good thing for him after all. Change had finally come. They had no choice but to embrace it.

****

Aisha didn't know what it was about Joshua that caused her knees to grow weak. The wobble in her limbs was a very alien feeling and made her conscious of every step she took. And then the feelings in her belly. She now knew what "butterflies in your belly" meant. As she walked away from him, she felt like she would misstep and fall, so she flagged down a passing motorcycle to take her home. Throughout the ride home, her mind was overwhelmed with thoughts of Joshua.

It was the beginning of new things, and she had no idea what the next few weeks held. Heck, she had no idea what tomorrow would bring. But one thing was for sure: her encounter with Joshua had changed something within her.

The trip home seemed shorter than usual, and she hopped off the bike and almost forgot to hand the man his money. She handed the notes to him and walked into her house with a spring in her step. She felt lightheaded, and her emotions were all over the place. She smiled sheepishly, recalling what had transpired between her and Joshua. The thoughts filling her mind felt inappropriate, but she couldn't stop.

Her mother would have rebuked her for this stupidity if she were here. "That's not the girl I raised you to be" would seem like the proper response to her daughter's childishness now. But all this didn't faze her.

What about her decision to stay away from relationships and boys entirely until she was through with her studies? That seemed like a thought fuelled by naivety. What mattered now was for her to be happy, and thinking of Joshua made her feel that way. The thought of his face aggravated her squishy insides some more.

He had asked if he could meet with her after their paper tomorrow, and she had hesitated a bit before agreeing to his request. It felt like the right thing to do, even though she had wanted nothing but to scream 'yes'. She didn't get that kind of attention, and she had to put on a show of hesitating before agreeing.

She picked up her phone and dialled Mairo's number. Her friend needed to know what had happened. She was almost exploding with the news, and she needed an outlet, someone to share it with. It felt so wrong and so right at the same time. It was true what they said about teenage girls. They were all firm and fine until they weren't. She was so excited that she had to sit down to steady herself.

"Hello, Maya. Let me gist you on something," she said using her friend's usual opener to start the conversation.

Mairo, as always, was there, ready to listen to what her best friend would say. She could sense that Maya already knew what she wanted to tell her, but she still played the part of the friend who was about to be surprised.

"Joshua asked me to meet after the papers tomorrow."

"Eh, he did? And what did you say?"

This was Mairo's way of making sure Aisha didn't mess things up by turning down the request. Aisha paused for dramatic effect before she answered, but just before the words rolled off her tongue, the door opened, and her father walked into the apartment.

She froze with the phone in her hand like a child who had been caught doing something wrong. She suddenly felt guilty and started rethinking the whole thing. Aisha had never hidden anything from her father before. They were very close, and she spoke to him about anything and everything. He was the one who explained puberty to her. He went so far as to monitor her monthly menstrual cycles and buy her sanitary pads during her periods. Her dad knew exactly what to do. He paid so much attention to the details about her that even she sometimes forgot. He played his role as her father and mother so well, and she didn't want him to be disappointed in her. He had so much confidence in her as it was.

"I'll call you later, Maya. The chief has just come back. Welcome, sir. How was work?" she said, ending the call and getting up to greet him while trying to keep a straight face. She kept from pacing restlessly.

*He wouldn't pick up that she was hiding something, or would he?* She would soon find out.

"Afternoon, Ada. You call me *Chief* when talking to your friend?" he asked, a bit surprised.

"Y..yes. It's easier like that." She almost said something else, but clamped her lips shut. She hoped he did not notice her nervousness.

"And what do you call Mairo's father? Uhm… Sorry, her mother?"

Aisha's father had a good memory. *Was it a gift, or was it because he cared about people so much that he remembered such details?*

She had told him sometime back that Mairo's father had left them and gone away with another woman because her mother refused to become a Muslim. But that was about four years ago.

"Well, we call her T-woman."

"What?" her father exclaimed, unable to hide his

shock. "I bet it was your idea."

She kept from giggling at her father's perplexed expression.

"No, it wasn't. Mairo had always wanted to call her that, but she just needed a partner, and boom, there I was."

"So, she doesn't call her T-woman to her face then?"

"Haba! No, she doesn't."

"Ah! Okay, oo."

She smiled and watched him from behind as he walked into the bedroom. Her father was careful to make sure their relationship was easy and relaxed, devoid of any rigidity, like the situation with her mother.

He was playful when he needed to be, serious when the situation called for it, attentive whenever she had something to say. And always, always, had the best advice to offer and the best solution to any problem she was facing.

"What are we eating?" he shouted from the room.

"I don't know. Rice and stew?" she replied.

"You and rice ehn. You treat that food like a husband."

Her body froze at the mention of the word *husband*. *Yikes! Did he suspect already? But how could he know?* She didn't want to keep the news about Joshua from him, but she had no idea how he would react, especially during the period of her final examinations. She needed time to think, to find her bearings in the strange land she had allowed herself to travel to.

Aisha got up and walked to the kitchen, still thinking about the matter. She indeed loved rice, but it paled in comparison with what she felt for the young man in her class.

If it was what she suspected—fleeting emotions— then she didn't need to worry about it too much, but if it persisted, she would have to share it with her father at some point. She had to. If she didn't, he would find out one way or the other, and she didn't want him to feel bad that she kept something like that from him.

But for now, what was most important was that she started preparing lunch, and she pushed the thoughts of Joshua to the back of her mind.

# CHAPTER THREE

Aisha set out for school the next morning, the day she had Government Studies exams. She didn't study as much as she would have two days back because of the thoughts of Joshua in her head, but she managed to go through the *SSCE/WAEC Government Questions and Answers* the previous night.

She woke up feeling on edge. Her sleep had been restless. She had tossed and turned in bed, swamped by thoughts of Joshua. She wondered how bad it could be, giving in to Joshua's request.

She moved about the house silently and prepared breakfast for herself and her father. He had his head buried in a file, and it seemed he didn't want to be disturbed. It was on the tip of her tongue to tell him all about her newfound feeling of love, but she reckoned it wasn't the right time. Their usual morning banter was absent as her father seemed a bit on edge. Maybe it had to do with the new boss at work, whom he had told her about yesterday.

He had seemed excited as he spoke about the woman. Her father was passionate about his job, quite alright, but it was rare to see him talk excitedly about anything concerning his work or his colleagues. He had told her the arrival of a new boss meant a new beginning for the office, and he was glad about it.

He asked her how prepared she was for her exams, and she replied in the affirmative. But, in truth, she wasn't sure. For the remainder of the morning, her nerves felt jittery.

The yam chips and eggs she had for breakfast settled uncomfortably in her stomach. She was not sure what exactly was causing her stomach to be unsettled, but she put it down to exam jitters. She would just have to fight through it, though. Today was not the day to be distracted by an upset stomach or nerves. She made sure everything she would need for her exam was complete.

This morning, Aisha took more time in front of the mirror than usual. She checked her cornrows and smoothed some errant hair strands, smiling as she watched her reflection in the mirror. She caught herself and shook her head, realising ruefully that she was taking extra care of her appearance because of Joshua.

As she packed her things and headed for the door, her father shouted from his room.

"No goodbye, Ada?"

She rushed back into the house and went into his room.

"I wish you the best of luck today. Go and make me proud."

"I will, Chief."

He got up and hugged her, and she slid off his arms when she realised he was beginning to get emotional.

"I have to run to school. We won't want me to go late and be unsettled, would we?"

He let go of her, and she stepped out of his room and out of the house. As he watched her leave, he was once more overwhelmed by how much she reminded him of her mother, especially during the early years. His thoughts dragged him into the past, and he thought of the last days with renewed pain. He consoled himself with the knowledge that when Aisha finished her exams, they would make plans to leave Maiduguri and start a new life elsewhere.

****

When Aisha got to school, she found Mairo in class with a group of other students, noses buried in books, revising. Her friend spotted her as she made her way to the seat they shared. She grinned as she stood up to allow her to move in to sit.

She greeted the other girls and replied to Mairo's question, "How prepared are you?"

"Well prepared," she replied, her eyes darting around the classroom, seeking out one person: Joshua. She saw him conversing with some boys in a corner of the class.

He looked even more handsome than he did the

previous day. He must have sensed her gaze because he looked in her direction and smiled at her. She looked away quickly, hiding her sheepish smile.

Surprisingly, her usually nosy friend didn't seem to notice the brief exchange. She was even more surprised that she wasn't greeted with the routine "Let me gist you something." Her friend's concentration was on the book before her. The students were all revising.

Unlike yesterday, today's atmosphere was quite sombre as students in their green and white uniforms clustered in small groups in final preparation. Exams had a way of stirring up restlessness in students, but this wasn't just any examination. This was the Senior Secondary School Examinations, the one that defined destinies and set paths for the future.

The tense atmosphere in the class only served to increase her nervousness. She checked her materials again to ensure everything was in place: her pens, pencils, school ID card, eraser, rulers, and anything that had the potential of playing a role in her success today. Satisfied, she joined in revising alongside the other students.

The class was set for exams, and everyone sat straight, nervousness etched on their faces. Aisha was not left out. Her nervousness stemmed more from the person seated beside her than the exam itself. They were seated in alphabetical order of their surnames, which was why Joshua was seated beside her, Aisha Nweze, and Joshua Nduaguibe.

She turned to look at him occasionally. His mouth was set in a grim line, as if he were not so sure of his readiness for the exams. She wished Mairo were beside her. Her presence would at least calm the flutters of her heart.

The examination papers were brought in, and the mood in the classroom got even more tense.

As the papers were distributed and the students were instructed to start, Joshua gave Aisha a sideways glance and winked. Or maybe he didn't. Maybe her mind was conjuring up imaginary things. She took a deep breath to steady her nerves, then opened the question paper and glanced through the questions. As she did, Aisha visibly relaxed, seeing that the questions were a piece of cake. Her concentration, however, wavered intermittently, no thanks to Joshua's presence so close to her.

Halfway into the theory section, she heard whispers of her name. At first, she thought it was Joshua, but on hearing it a second time, she realized they were female voices. She spared a look backwards and saw Jamila and Nabila, trying to get her attention. She knew what they wanted, and she quickly turned back to her paper, ignoring them.

They wanted her to give them answers, answers she wouldn't give them. As the bullies they were, they felt entitled to whatever they wanted, including answers during exams, and dared anyone to cross them. They formed a posse of similar girls, intimidating and bullying other students. When the invigilator at the front of the hall called out that they had an hour left to the end of the paper, the whispers became more insistent, but Aisha continued to ignore them. Then the threats started. At one point, Nabila nudged her hard with a pen. Aisha paid them no mind.

"Wallahi, we will deal with you after the exam. Just you wait! *Yar iska kawai,*" one of them said, the insult—useless girl—spat out with the kind of contempt that needed no further explanation.

The others hissed viciously. Aisha became unsettled. She wanted to call the attention of one of the invigilators, but she thought better of it. That would land her in much more trouble.

They continued to threaten her, thereby distracting her for the rest of the paper. Joshua finished before her, and her eyes trailed him as he went to submit. Aisha turned back to her paper and hastened to complete it before time ran out.

After the paper, she quickly got her things and started to leave. As she walked outside, she saw Nabila and Jamila in a group of girls with Hassana. The group stood near one of the major exits out of the compound, obviously waiting for her. As she stopped and wondered how they had gathered so quickly,

Hassana walked forward, and the others trailed behind like a pack of jackals.

She turned and headed for the canteen, but was intercepted by another group of girls before she could make headway.

They had received word of her 'insubordination,' and they wanted to deal with her accordingly. There was now a total of eighteen girls, but Aisha stood her ground, refusing to cower in fear. She looked around for any help, but Mairo was nowhere to be found. Maybe she was still in the hall writing her exams.

The girls had quickly formed a circle around her, jeering and spitting at her. She tried to run, but they closed ranks, making it impossible for her to run away. The looks on their faces said it all; they were going to give her the beating of her life.

Gripping her bag in front of her to defend herself as best she could, she clenched her fists and prepared for the attack.

Just as Hassana rushed forward, a teacher who had

observed what was happening came out of a classroom and intervened. She pulled them apart and enquired about what was going on. Aisha tried narrating what had happened, but Hassana kept interrupting, claiming Aisha had insulted her mother, and the other girls supported her. After going back and forth and getting nowhere, Miss Amina, the teacher, got enraged and asked them to kneel and raise their hands as punishment. She did this to all of them, including Aisha.

"But that's not fair! They attacked me!" Aisha protested.

"See here, better kneel down before I report you all to the principal, and your exams will be cancelled. See how you girls have disturbed the other students who are still writing their exams?" The other girls quickly knelt, sniggering.

Aisha felt powerless. As she stood defiantly with the teacher glaring at her, she realised that she had no choice if she did not want the issue to be escalated. In defeat, she knelt, her eyes filling with hot tears of frustration.

Just then, Joshua walked by and saw her kneeling in punishment along with the group of notorious girls. Their eyes met, and he stopped, looking at her first in surprise, then disappointment. As he turned away from her, Aisha's heart broke.

*He must think very poorly of me now; he must see me as unserious and wild,* she thought to herself. She wanted the ground to open and swallow her. She reckoned he'd stop talking to her after today. And whose fault was it? She couldn't blame him.

While her heart was breaking into a thousand pieces, the girls continued in their threats and taunts. No remorse, Aisha thought sourly.

After about ten minutes, the teacher released them with a caution, and Aisha stood up, her knees wobbly. She thought to bolt before the girls would gang up on her again, but then, she caught sight of Mairo approaching her. She exhaled in relief.

Mairo had somehow gotten wind of what was

happening, hence the reason for finishing her exams quickly to save her friend. She got upset when Aisha told her what had transpired.

"Don't worry, I'm fine," she said to her friend in a bid to reassure her. "Look, I'm not hurt," she twirled about for her friend to examine her body.

"But you have bruises on your knees," Mairo said, anger lacing her voice.

Aisha tried to stop her from going after the gang, but Mario would not be dissuaded. She practically dragged Aisha with her to where the group of girls stood gathered.

*"Ku kale ni nan 'yan iska,"* Mairo stood in front of the group, literally screaming, *"In ku ka bar ni na kama daya ku ko…,"*—if I catch that girl, ehn…—she said, letting the words hang heavy in the air. *"Sai na cire mata idanu, wallahi!"*—I swear on God, I'll rip her eyes out!

The threat to break their bones hadn't been enough for Mairo, but that second promise—ripping someone's eyes out—hit home. Fear flickered across their faces. The girls backed away, shocked by Mairo's ferocity. Even Hassana, who normally thrived on the pack's aggression, looked unsettled; without her crew's full confidence, she wasn't about to risk having someone like Mairo lurking, ready to strike.

*"Mu tafi."* Hassana said to her crew—Let's roll. They turned and walked off. "We will get them another time."

Mairo then escorted Aisha to the gate, where she would get a motorcycle that would take her home. Aisha thanked her friend for this protection and hopped on the motorcycle that Mairo had stopped.

They waved each other goodbye as the motorcycle zoomed off.

٭٭٭٭

Aisha got home feeling agitated. The day had not gone as planned, and her mood had taken a downward turn. She took off her school uniform and went to take a shower. She needed to get rid of the day's humiliation.

She thought of Joshua and the look on his face as he

turned away, and her heart began to ache anew. She was sure he would not want to see her anymore.

*But did he truly like me, or was I just some pawn to him?*

She needed to be sure, but how? She liked him; that much was true. *But did he like her in return? What if this was all just a game to him?*

After her bath, she went to the kitchen and started preparing lunch.

She sat to eat but kept picking at her food, her mind not entirely settled. Perhaps it was time to tell her father what was going on with her. She needed words of wisdom.

She nibbled at her food some more and gave up eating entirely. She took it to the kitchen and covered it to be eaten later.

There was only one other person she could talk to. Mairo would know what to do. She picked up her phone and dialled her friend's number, but there was no response.

She tried two more times before calling Mairo's mother's number. It rang twice, but she didn't answer her phone.

She couldn't watch television because there was no power in Gombaru for a while now, and they only used their small generator at night, so she lay down on the couch, lost in her thoughts for a while.

When her thoughts seemed to be circling about, going nowhere, she went to the room to get her clothes for washing. She wanted to appear neat and crisp for school tomorrow.

*"For whom?"* A voice taunted in her head.

"For nobody!" She snapped out loud.

****

Emmanuel started off his day pleasantly at work with his new boss, Hajiya Hadiza. When he arrived in the morning, he found Dan Yaro in a sober mood. He didn't know what was more amazing, that the man was calm and lucid, or that he was on time. Emmanuel shook his head at the magic before his eyes. However, he didn't inquire about the cause of the newfound attitude. He just assumed that Dan Yaro was like this because Hajiya Hadiza had had a word with him.

The woman seemed to be restoring things to their proper place very quickly, and that obviously included the previously carefree gatekeeper.

As he walked further into the compound, he noticed the boss's car parked. She had arrived before him, and that was something he was impressed by. His former boss never arrived early to work until the very day he was to leave the office for good. Such a contrast.

Before he reached the door, two of his colleagues also arrived for work—Kande and Maryam. The Kano lady had never been to work on time as far as he could remember. It was unusual, a novelty. While he still thought about it, three others walked in through the door of the general office. There was no smile on Haruna's face, or Sadiya's, or Ustaz's, but there was a willingness to appear hardworking. That was a good start.

They wanted to impress the new boss. The everyday chatter that had become more of a tradition in the office was absent that morning. This was indeed a new beginning for them all.

While they went to their desks, Hajiya came out of the office, looked at her wristwatch, and got everyone's attention by clearing her throat. Authority.

"Good morning, people."

They responded with "Good morning, Hajiya" and "Good morning, ma" from different corners.

"Let's get down to business, then. I want every member of the department to come to my office with a written report of their work in the last three months."

Some people began to murmur, but stopped when they realised it wasn't a good sign at the moment.

"I want these reports to be presented to me by the end of the day." The place was silent.

'Stern' was the word that had been absent in the former boss's demeanour. This new boss wouldn't be so easy to work with for the rest of his colleagues, but Emmanuel was loving it.

****

*"Maigida, Injiniya…"*, Both of his team members stood in front of Emmanuel's desk, looking pitiful. Emmanuel knew why they were here, and frankly, he had been expecting them sooner or later.

Yunusa and Ibrahim begged him to do their reports for them since they had not done much work in recent times, and Mallam Abdullah had never asked for a progress report, so this was alien to them. Knowing that there was no way they would be able to do proper reports, and realising that if they did reports, it would reflect badly on their team, he agreed to do their reports in return for them going to the automobile spare parts market to buy parts for the office vehicles, a proposal they happily accepted.

The office was in a frenzy of activity as everyone was working to ensure they presented their reports to the new boss, even the ones who had not done any work.

The chatterboxes of the office had quietened down in the face of the activities that day. There was no peddling of rumours by Maryam. No Haruna talking ill of his wife, or Ustaz talking about how President Goodluck Jonathan was letting the country down. Everyone went about their activities with a pretended zeal. Emmanuel loved this new work environment.

At the end of the day, everyone submitted their reports, and the boss asked them to stay back and present those reports.

*"Wane irin abu ke nan kuma?"* - What kind of thing is this again? - Aliyu, the driver, complained. His tone carried the weariness of someone already half out the door.

It was obvious that someone else had drafted it for him. Emmanuel wondered what the person had asked in return. Here, people rarely did things for free and for good reason.

Unfortunately, Emmanuel's teammates and a host of others couldn't defend their reports at the presentation, which caused the boss to inquire who drafted those reports for them. No one was foolish enough to admit that they had gotten someone else to do their reports, so nobody spoke. Hajiya nodded and smiled, more to herself than to the group of workers.

"You all can leave." Hajiya Hadiza ordered. The staff members hurriedly got up to leave.

"Not you, Mr Nweze." Her words stopped him, half standing with his reports in his hands. He slowly straightened himself fully upright and waited while the others filed out.

"Shut the door."

Emmanuel complied and then came back to stand in front of the desk facing her. She observed him in silence for a few minutes before she spoke.

"I know you did their reports."

At this point, Emmanuel realised that it would be pointless to deny it. Worse, it could sour his relationship with the new boss and may negatively affect his career, so he decided to come clean.

"Yes, ma'am, I did."

"Why?"

"Most of the staff are hard-working if pressed, ma. It is not their fault that things were being done in a certain way before you came. The truth is that they had never been asked to do a report before." He wanted to sound apologetic, but it seemed to be coming out wrong. "Ma, some of them simply do not know how to write reports, so there was no way they would have done it."

"Okay. You can go."

Emmanuel heaved a sigh of relief as he walked out. *That was not so bad,* he thought to himself as he walked to his desk.

He had barely sat down when Hajiya Hadiza's office door opened, and she walked out. Everyone was still at their desks, even though it was almost 5 pm. Before now, they would have all been in their houses by this time.

"I'll be setting new rules of engagement in this office, and I'll have it put on the board by the door for all to see." She met their gaze and continued.

"From now on, no one is to draft another's report, even though I expect you to work together and produce unprecedented results."

Emmanuel liked the sound of the word, *unprecedented*. He glanced at the faces of his colleagues and saw looks of suppressed anxiety. They were anxious because they knew that now they had to put in more work than they did before.

The day ended on a positive note for Emmanuel. He packed up at work, whistling tunelessly. The boss was still in her office. The light was on, and the shuffle of papers could be heard.

As Emmanuel packed, his mind went to Aisha. He could feel that she was keeping something from him, but he wasn't going to push. He would let her come to him when she felt comfortable, not by compelling

her.

****

While Emmanuel got home from the office happy with the way the day had turned out, he was also concerned about Aisha. It was exam period, and the weight of it might be getting to her and causing her to withdraw. But it felt like it was more than the exams. Aisha had never really been troubled by tests or exams before. Quite the opposite; she had relished such moments.

This was something else, and Emmanuel wanted to find out about it sooner rather than later. She might not feel comfortable right now, but it might be the best thing for her. With that in mind, he pushed open the door and entered his house.

Aisha wasn't in the sitting room when he came in, so he called out her name and she answered from inside her bedroom. He went straight to where she was and found her sprawled on the bed, a book in hand. He smiled.

"Reading for tomorrow, eh?" he asked, a smile stretching his face.

"Chief, welcome," she greeted him, getting to her feet. "Did work go well today?" she asked as she took his bag from him, leading the way to his room.

"You didn't answer my question," he reminded her.

She rolled her eyes. "Chief!" she called out, stifling laughter. "You know I'm only revising. I've done the whole of my reading weeks before," she said, turning to face him.

"Well…. isn't 'revising' still 'reading?" He asked, feigning meekness. Aisha burst out laughing.

Aisha sat on his bed, watching as he removed his wristwatch. "You look tired, Chief."

"Yes, I'm tired," he answered. "We had to present a progress report for the last three months. Hajiya didn't come here to joke, o. The woman means business."

"You like work too much. See how you're sounding happy even with tiredness."

"I am happy, Ada. Work is getting better." He smiled, recalling the day's events. Then he noticed her knees. "That," he pointed, "what… are those bruises on your knees?"

"Oh, this? I got in trouble with some girls at school, and we got punished for it," she shrugged.

"What did I tell you about staying out of trouble? I'm going with you to school tomorrow," he declared.

"What? No. You don't have to. The issue has been resolved."

When he didn't respond, she tried one more time. "Come on, chief," she cajoled.

"Don't patronize me," he warned. "We talked about this, Ada. I spelled it out for you. Stay. Out. Of. Trouble!"

"I know you said that, but I couldn't avoid this one, I swear." She flinched when she realised that he reacted to her swearing, and she quickly apologised.

"I am sorry for swearing, but listen. There was a group

of girls who wanted me to give them answers in the exam hall, but I refused. They ganged up against me, and that was when the teachers intervened, and one of them asked us to kneel."

"Including you?"

"Yes."

Emmanuel became unsettled. His daughter wasn't the kind of girl one associated with trouble, but that didn't seem to calm him.

"Why didn't you report to the invigilator when they were asking you for answers in the exam hall?"

"And risk the wrath of the entire class? No."

She had a point, but he was still not comfortable. He didn't want his daughter getting mixed up with troublesome people.

"I'll be going with you to school tomorrow." he said, not giving her room to argue with him.

He knew she didn't agree with his decision, but this

was not the kind of thing that needed her consent. He was her father, after all.

And he would not allow anything to happen to her—she was the only thing her mother had left behind. His little girl was too precious to be left at the mercy of life's wahala.

It was his duty to care for and protect her, even if it meant confronting the bullies in her class or having a proper talk with the schoolteacher about how they handled quarrels among children.

# CHAPTER FOUR

The next day started with a rush of activity. Hajiya Hadiza had called Emmanuel to come in earlier than usual.

There was a Toyota Coaster bus that had been parked in the compound for a year now, broken, and Hajiya needed it to be fixed. There was a very important State function taking place soon at the State Government Secretariat, and Hajiya wanted the delegation from the District Office to go with the official bus, instead of individually. Mallam Abdullah hadn't bothered to fix the bus and had left it in that state for thirteen months.

He had been a little disgruntled by the call because it meant he had to cancel his plans to go to Aisha's school to register a complaint about the events of the previous day. However, he did not dwell on it. This was his job, after all. It had been a while since he had done any major mechanical work on the office vehicles.

Hajiya had inquired about the state of the bus the

previous day during his report presentation, but he had not known she intended to do anything about it. So, when she called asking why it had been left there for so long, he told her what the problem was and explained that the office had refused to provide money for the repairs even after he had submitted the request.

They had just left it to rot. No matter how hard he had tried to convince Mallam Abdullah that it could be fixed easily, the man had ignored him at every turn. He preferred to use the money for transport upkeep on inconsequential things. After the continued refusal, he had stopped appealing to him at some point. Since he wasn't in a position to change the situation, he left it as it was.

He took a quick bath and prepared for work. He had slept early the night before after an early dinner and a brief discussion with Aisha about her exams. Once he was done arranging his bag, he knocked on Aisha's bedroom door.

"Come in," her still sleep-filled voice said.

Of course, she was up. He wasn't surprised. She was lying in bed, book in hand. His daughter never ceased to amaze him. He had faith that she would ace her exams. After all, she was a smart girl just like her parents. Her enthusiasm for reading never failed to impress; he was sure she would go far in life. He had high hopes for her. If only her mother were here to see her, to love her the way he did. He believed she, too, would have come to cherish their daughter as deeply as he did now.

 "Chief, you're up early. What's happening?" She asked.

"Ah! No 'good morning'?" He teased.

She rolled her eyes, "I'm so sorry it escaped me. Good morning, Chief."

He laughed heartily. "I have to leave now. There's an issue of importance that requires my urgent attention."

"Oh!? You're not going with me to school then?"

He could see the beginnings of a triumphant smile forming at the corners of her lips.

"Well, no. That doesn't mean I won't still go with you, but not today." He said simply.

"Well, well, don't you have to run along, Chief?"

It sounded to him like a line from one of her favourite movies. If he were another father, he might have found it quite disrespectful that his daughter told him to 'run along'. But he wasn't that type of father. He could picture Zainab's face in a frown at this father-daughter exchange.

He smiled and nodded, making his way out of her room.

"Aren't you forgetting something, Chief?" She called.

He went back and stuck his head in the door frame ridiculously. "Do well in your exams. Read well, too."

"Aye, aye, captain!" She saluted and laughed. He gave her a thumbs-up and headed off to work.

On his way to work, he called Yunusa and Ibrahim and asked them to come in early too. Both men complained about how early it was, but Emmanuel wasn't having any of it. His team members were way too lazy. Not their fault, though, the former boss had indulged them too much.

On getting to work, he went straight to the store where the automobile tools were kept and got to work. There was a newer bus which they had been using, so he wondered why the new boss insisted on fixing the old one. It wasn't like the new bus couldn't contain all of them.

*Or was it to be used somewhere else?*

She had her reasons, he thought.

He went through the tools in the shed and picked out the ones he would need. He checked his wristwatch and shook his head at the lateness of his team members. None of them had arrived.

Given the circumstances, they were supposed to arrive before him. Both lived closer to work than he did, but they always had an excuse for coming late. It had already been an hour since he called. He would have to commence on his own.

Emmanuel changed into his overalls, grabbed his toolbox, and walked to the vehicle. Just as he reached the vehicle, Yunusa came into the compound on his motorcycle—a battered white *Wayo Kudina*. The motorcycle sure needed changing, but the man wasn't in the least bit bothered by the battered state of it.

He didn't know what his colleague did with all the corrupt money he made, but he suspected that having three wives was enough to bankrupt a man like him. Yunusa parked his motorcycle and walked towards Emmanuel, with a frown on his face. He evidently resented having to come in early.

"What is wrong with this Hajiya? Why can't we use the bus that is working? *Mata suna da wahala, wallahi*"—women are troublesome, I swear. "She thinks that because she has been appointed as the new boss, she can do anything she likes. *Na rantse ba na son ta*"

"Watch what you say, Yunusa." Emmanuel cautioned.

Yunusa was an unrepentant male chauvinist. He believed women were beneath him, no matter their education or status. He had no problem with a man of even lowly status, but he would degrade women at every turn.

Reluctantly, he went into the shed and changed into his overalls, too. Emmanuel couldn't remember the last time he had seen Yunusa wearing one. He laughed as the lanky frame of his partner walked toward him with resentment in his steps. Yunusa glared at him in return and murmured something about Emmanuel getting what he had always wanted. Emmanuel continued to laugh.

The engine compartment of the bus was filled with dirt as Emmanuel opened it up for inspection. He asked Yunusa to change the battery and try and start the bus. The man turned the ignition, but the engine did not crank. It had been left for too long.

"What did you do to it the last time?" Emmanuel asked curiously.

"Uhm… *Bari in gani*—let me see, I changed the oil filter and the fuel pump," Yunusa replied, refusing to meet his eyes.

"Did you check the ignition system?"

"Yes, I got the electrician to change it."

"You condemned the entire system without first being sure whether that was the problem?" Emmanuel asked, incredulous.

"Err, well, when the bus still did not start, I said to myself, 'Maybe the ignition is bad, ' so I changed it. Anyway, we had several in the store, so it was not a problem." He still was not meeting Emmanuel's eyes.

"How can you change the entire ignition system without first checking that other things are not bad? This is a waste of money, Yunusa. I've told you people several times, you need to check properly before changing complete parts. What if we didn't have these parts in the store? What would you have done then?"

He kept from raising his voice. What he wanted was to bash the man on the head.

Yunusa looked at Emmanuel with an expression that

told him he wasn't sorry and would probably do the same thing again if the opportunity presented itself.

"See now, the ignition was not the problem, which means you had simply wasted time and money and a perfectly good ignition system." Emmanuel continued. "This is such a waste, Yunusa. Such a waste. Haba!" He looked at the man in irritation.

"But it is government money. Why all this wahala?" he mumbled loud enough for Emmanuel to hear.

"Yunusa, we could have used these parts for another vehicle at another time when there was a real need, not this waste. You just don't get it."

He paused to get his emotions in control. "Where are the old parts you removed?" he asked.

"I threw them away," Yunusa replied with a defiant look. The man didn't even show any remorse.

Emmanuel caught himself just in time before he lashed out. He knew Yunusa was lying; he had obviously sold the parts. That was the real reason he kept changing vehicle parts that were not bad. The man was a crook.

*Well, those days were over.* With Hajiya's leadership and support, things were going to be different. He would hold them accountable going forward.

He saw Ibrahim walk into the compound from the corner of his eye. The man didn't even behave like he was late for work. It was the typical attitude of most workers in the civil service.

Only a few of them stood out, like his present boss, Hajiya. Well, they were in for a surprise. He had resolved to follow in Hajiya's footsteps and be stern with them from now on. He pretended not to see Ibrahim and concentrated on his work with Yunusa.

"Did you check the injector nozzles? What about the piston rings?" Yunusa shook his head at both questions.

He sighed and refrained from swearing. "Okay, let us open the top cylinder and dismantle the injector system."

"*Mu canza shi gaba daya ko?*"—Should we replace it entirely?

Emmanuel sighed again. The man still expected them to replace it, ask for money for a new one, and 'discard' the old one.

"*Ba za mu canza kome ba,* Yunusa,"—We are not going to replace anything, Yunusa—Emmanuel replied

"Good morning, Oga Emmanuel. *Ina kwana,* Yunusa." Ibrahim said as he joined them, wearing his overalls.

Emmanuel wondered why the man greeted him in English but Yunusa in Hausa, when he knew that Emmanuel spoke Hausa fluently.

Or did he do it to show that he, too, was as educated as he was? Or just his way of rubbing in his face the fact that he was not a Hausa man and, as such, would always be an outsider to them?

He sighed and turned his thoughts back to the task of fixing the bus. "Ibrahim, hold this for me. Yunusa, pull that apart. No, that other one."

His passion had been revitalized by Hajiya Hadiza, and he hoped to force that attitude on his colleagues. Shoddy workmanship upset him. Being able to accomplish much with as little as possible was a skill he had honed for a while now that put him ahead of the rest.

By this time, other workers had started arriving. First, it was Kande and then Haruna and a group of women. People were surprised to see Ibrahim and Yunusa already at work this early and actually working! It was a rare occurrence indeed to see them working ardently like this.

Emmanuel remembered the days when people in the office would gather and watch him work as he cajoled the vehicles, speaking to them like the metal parts could hear him. That was how he got the nickname, *Mai Rada*, The Machine Whisperer.

At first, he took offence at the nickname, but as time went on, he not only accepted it but began to enjoy the mystique it gave him. He actively began to propagate the myth by putting on small performances when fixing difficult faults.

It had soon become something of an office tradition in the Transport Department that when a particularly knotty vehicular problem was being resolved, the whole office gathered to watch Emmanuel work his magic. The longer a vehicle had been dead, or the worse the state of the vehicle before the repairs, the more it seemed that Emmanuel must have used some spiritual powers to bring it back to life.

And when the vehicle finally 'woke up' and responded with a roar, the entire office broke out in raucous applause and cheering. They even had a name for this tradition: *Falkawa*—The Reawakening. He worked magic, everyone said.

Emmanuel continued to work on the vehicle as the onlookers increased in number. By this time, Hajiya had arrived and briefly joined the crowd. Someone explained what was happening to her, and she smiled, nodded, and went to her office, telling them to carry on. The three of them took the injector system apart and cleaned the nozzles, valves, and intake ports using injector cleaning fluid.

 Once they were done cleaning off all the gum residue from the parts, they spent the next few minutes reassembling the engine parts. After a few checks, they were ready to test the outcome of their work.

People rushed into the offices to spread the word that *Mai Raɗa* had returned and was ready to perform, and the passageways quickly filled up with people. Even Hajiya Hadiza seemed to have caught the bug as she joined the crowd. Emmanuel motioned for silence and, in full view of all the onlookers, started talking quietly to the bus. Touching, cajoling it to come to life.

He was communicating his thoughts to the bus, so it seemed.

Emmanuel walked around the bus, talking and touching parts of the bus. He made one revolution and stopped at the front. He looked up at the sky as if he could discern something in the cloudless sky.

He then cupped his hand over his right ear and leaned on the front of the bus, nodding as if he was listening to the bus speak. The anticipation built as Yunusa put the key in the ignition and got ready to start the engine. He waited for the signal from Emmanuel, who now placed both hands on the front of the bus and whispered to it.

"*Mai Raɗa ku ke ji*!" Haruna said with an excitement that looked alien to him. He was one of the most enthusiastic people at Emmanuel's displays.

"The *Injiniya* himself! *A zo a ga falkawa. Iyawa a jini ta ke! Pesin wey sabi sabi!*"

Haruna kept singing Emmanuel's praises and turning to inform the people beside him what was about to happen, even people who had witnessed it several times.

"Haba Haruna! We've seen this demonstration before," Maryam snapped.

While they were still arguing, Emmanuel cocked his head to one side, closed his eyes, and then raised one hand with his palm outwards to signal Yunusa to stop. He shook his head slowly, signifying that the bus was not yet ready.

There was an audible groan from the crowd, and even Hajiya smiled, obviously enjoying the show as much as the others.

Emmanuel leaned closer to the bus, pretending to listen intently for a few moments. Silence filled the air as the people held their collective breath. It was as if the birds in the trees nearby were in on it as well because they, too, stopped chirping. Emmanuel nodded and turned to the expectant crowd and said in a sing-song voice.

"The bus wants the touch of a woman."

The females in the crowd shrieked in joy and started jostling for position as Emmanuel, pretending to be under a trance, put one hand on the vehicle and started pointing to the crowd.

As he pointed to each of the females in turn, he would ask the bus:

"Is she the Chosen One?" He would then shake his head in mock dismay as he announced the verdict: "NO!"

The tension built as he pointed from one to the other, and the chorus continued: NO! NO!

The women paid mock obeisance to the bus in a bid to sway 'her' to choose them.

Still, the response was: NO!

The women made gestures to be chosen and feigned disappointment when they weren't.

"*Ita ƶaya ƙara ƶaba.*" — He will still choose her. Haruna said mockingly, indicating that all Emmanuel did was a ruse and that he would eventually settle on Kande.

On hearing this, Emmanuel twirled his finger for dramatic effect and then moved to settle on Hajiya Hadiza. At this, there was an uproarious approval by the crowd, and he bowed, pointing towards the bus, and motioned for her to take the driver's seat.

"Hajiya, it seems that the bus has chosen you this time.

Both of you seem to have a connection," he cajoled.

The boss smiled, walked to Yunusa, took the keys from him, and climbed in.

As she settled into the driver's seat and put the key in the ignition, Emmanuel raised his hand sharply, telling her to stop.

Hajiya was startled and raised both hands away from the steering wheel, and a hushed silence fell on the expectant crowd. Emmanuel pretended to be listening to instructions from the bus, nodding intermittently.

With a final nod, he raised one hand towards Hajiya and made a motion of turning a key.

She then gingerly gripped the key in the ignition and turned it. The engine turned over once, a second time, then roared into life as she floored the accelerator.

The crowd erupted in joy, pent-up anticipation finally finding release in shouts, congratulatory backslapping, and high-fives.

"MAI RADA! MAI RADA!"—The Whisperer! The

Whisperer!

They cheered, voices rising above the noise as they chanted his nickname over and over. People jostled to get closer, clapping, calling out, and grinning as though they were witnessing a celebrity at work. He bowed in appreciation as they chanted his nickname, and Hajiya stepped out of the vehicle with an expression of amazement on her face. She regarded him with renewed respect.

"You did well, Emmanuel. All of you...," she reluctantly added, "Yunusa. And you too, Ibrahim," she said, and then turned to the crowd, "We are grateful to our engineers for this wonderful work!"

Emmanuel had set the mood for the day's work in the office, and everyone went back to their work, talking about the old vehicle drama brought back to life, but more importantly, they talked about how their new boss had reacted to their show.

A new cycle of rumours was about to begin with him as the main object. He could not be bothered.

# CHAPTER FIVE

Aisha's sleep the previous night had been intermittent, and she would wake up at intervals. Afterwards, she would stay up for about half an hour before drifting away again. This happened three times. On the second or third time, she wasn't sure which, she dreamt that her mother took her to a wedding ceremony of a young lady who used to work at the business centre opposite their house. The veiled bride danced to the music with her group of friends, while the families and other guests looked on.

When it was time to unveil the bride, her mother urged her to move closer and see how it was done, and she could see herself walking towards the centre of the gathering. As the groom stepped forward to lift the veil, she caught a glimpse of the lady behind the veil. It was her, Aisha.

One moment, she was walking up the stage, and the next, she was the bride. Her mother walked up to her and wiped the excess lipstick with a follow-up warning, "I told you never to touch my things? *Kina wasan banza da ni ko?*"

With that, she woke up to a not-so-brilliant morning. As she sat in bed thinking about the dream, she heard her father's voice in the sitting room. Who was he talking to at this time of the morning? His new boss must mean business.

As she walked out, she realized it wasn't Hajiya he was talking to because he was speaking Igbo. To the best of her knowledge, Chief only spoke Igbo to his family members.

"... *Ọ bụ ndị Boko Haram... ee... ee...*"

As she listened further, she realized her dad was talking on the phone with her grandparents about the recent state of unrest in the northern part of the country. These were one of the few times they called him since they left Maiduguri for Aba ten years ago. They cared for her and her father after all.

The news of Boko Haram's attacks was all over the news—from Kano to Kaduna to Abuja. They perpetrated their evil on police stations, mosques, churches, schools, and government buildings with no sympathy for their victims.

"... *anyi di mma,* "—we're fine—she heard him say between fast-paced Igbo words she couldn't make out. "*Ada dị kwa mma. Ị na -echegbu onwe gị nke ukwuu.*" – My daughter is fine, no need to worry so much.

Her grandmother, *Ahịa mama,* as she was called, had taught her Igbo when she was around. The woman had refused to speak English to her granddaughter on any occasion, and Obi M, the name she called Aisha, had to learn fast.

Aisha did extremely well with the Igbo language while her grandmother was around, but lost her touch when the old woman and her husband moved back to Aba. *Well, Mama wasn't that old.* She could understand Igbo when it was spoken slowly, but would lose the hang of it the moment the speakers picked up speed.

After her father assured her grandparents that he and his daughter were fine, she watched him as he sighed deeply. He was anxious about something, and she needed to know what it was.

"Is everything okay?"

"It's...," he hesitated as if he had made a mistake by agreeing to answer her question.

*"Daddy?"*

She didn't call him that unless she was scared or angry, and she tried to show him that she wasn't afraid to be told. After much thought, he agreed to tell her.

"You know Matthias... uhm... You won't know him. You were too young."

"Gloria's dad?" She asked, hoping to continue the conversation.

"Yes, him. The police officer, right? The station where he works was attacked yesterday by insurgents, and he and two others were shot in a crossfire. He didn't make it."

Aisha couldn't place the man's face anymore, but she

remembered his daughters, Gloria and Phoebe. They had lived a few houses away from them, and Aisha would sometimes go out to play with Phoebe before her mother would send her back to the house to read her books. *Nana* didn't want her socializing with the neighbours because she didn't want Aisha learning bad habits.

But growing up, she realized that that was her mother's attempt to protect her from being labelled an outcast. "Did this happen in Maiduguri?"

"No," her father responded. "Matthias moved to Kano when he left Gombaru. That was where it happened. Maiduguri is safe. The Nigerian Army has secured all the points of entry; that is why Boko Haram moved to other states."

"Okay." was all she could muster. She didn't know why her father's words weren't reassuring. They always used to be.

"Are you still coming with me to school?" She could feel the fear pulsing through her.

"No, Ada. I have work to do this morning, but I'll come before the end of the exams and speak to your teachers."

That wasn't why she wanted him to come with her; she didn't try to inform him so that she wouldn't appear apprehensive or fearful.

"Okay, chief."

She watched him as he left for work that morning, and for the first time in a long time, she said a silent prayer for him.

****

The news of the latest Boko Haram attack in Kano had spread through the office by the time everyone had settled in. Emmanuel's colleagues shook their heads in sympathy at the unhappy stories of the victims narrated by one person or another. Even Hajiya seemed to have allowed a level of respite among the people at work.

"They said that 180 people died in Kano," Haruna

said, getting up from his chair and moving over to where Maryam and Ustaz sat. "That's like 500 people, *kenan*. The news people have a way of reducing the casualties of this kind of thing."

It was true. Emmanuel feared that the numbers reported were but a fraction of the actual number of casualties.

Work continued at a slow pace throughout the morning, and the afternoon seemed like a distant future. Shuffling papers, office chatter, and the sound of the rusty fans punctuated the work.

By 2 pm, most of the staff were in the canteen having their lunch.

A short while later, Ibrahim quietly left the canteen and got into the driver's seat of the Toyota bus that he, Yunusa, and Emmanuel had fixed the day before, started it, and then proceeded to drive out of the yard quietly. No one paid him any attention because it was assumed that he was taking the vehicle for a road test to detect any other faults before their long drive over the coming week or simply running an errand for Hajiya.

Emmanuel and the others continued eating and chatting, all oblivious of the carnage heading inexorably into their lives.

Suddenly, from the direction of the gate came staccato sounds, like a series of cars backfiring, and they all paused their eating.

"*Wanene ke wasa da banga?*"—Who is playing with firecrackers? —someone asked.

Emmanuel frowned, thinking that it did not sound like firecrackers. Could it be …

Then Dan Yaro came running and screaming, "BOKO HARAM! BOKO HARAM!"

There was a brief pause, and everyone was frozen in shock. Then the silence was shattered by what they now realised was the signature sound of AK-47 assault rifles coming from *inside the compound!* Then someone screamed, long and loud!

Pandemonium ensued.

Workers scattered and started running in all directions. Emmanuel and those in the canteen ran out and took off frantically towards the main building. As they ran, armed men wearing the insignia of the dreaded Boko Haram Islamic sect had taken various positions in the compound and were shooting at people indiscriminately. A bullet hit someone running beside Emmanuel, his head exploding and splattering gore on him. Emmanuel ducked and kept running, as bullets whizzed past him. He saw someone in front of him being hit in the back and flung sprawling onto the dirt. He jumped over the twitching body and ran into the building and a side hallway, making for the farthest office. He and a few other workers rushed in and started barricading themselves in with desks, chairs, and filing cabinets.

Emmanuel peeped through a window and saw that the open space in the compound and car park had become a killing field with dead bodies littering the ground. The terrorists were going through the buildings, dragging people out and shooting them. Another group was checking the bodies on the ground, indiscriminately stabbing and shooting. In shock, he saw his colleague, Ibrahim, leading the second group of insurgents who were killing off the injured. Gone was the sometimes-diffident civil servant. In his place, a grotesque twisted killing machine, fuelled by religious fervour and pure evil.

People were running all over the place as the Boko Haram members kept on shooting. From the office where they hid, they could hear the screams of others in the compound and nearby offices.

There were seven of them in the office: Emmanuel, Haruna, Yunusa, Ustaz, Maryam, Jamila, and Nasir. Emmenuel prayed that the makeshift barricade would hold. As they cowered in fear behind some desks, there was a loud and frantic banging on the door from outside. It was Amina, a girl from the Accounting Department, begging to be let in.

"Please let me in," she screamed as the sound of gunshots rang in the air, getting closer and closer.

"Please, don't let them kill me."

Emmanuel rushed towards the door and started removing the barricades. Once the others in the room realized what he was doing, they all rushed at him and pulled him away from the door.

"*Innanillahi! Za ku sa a san muna boye a nan.*" —For God's sake! You will make them know we are hiding here—Haruna whispered fiercely as the other men struggled to pull Emmanuel away from the door.

"We have to help her; we can't just leave her to die," Emmanuel replied as he struggled with them.

"If we open that door, we will all die," Ustaz said through clenched teeth.

As they argued in hushed tones, the gunshots got closer and closer, and Amina's frantic screams and the banging on the door became louder.

There was a shriek from the other side. The killers had found Amina. They heard her muffled pleas.

"*Don Allah, don girman Allah, kar ku kashe ni.*" – Please,

for the love of God, don't kill me!

They heard a man asking her if she was with anyone else. That was Ibrahim's voice. She seemed to have answered in the negative because he continued questioning her and threatening her.

From outside, Amina started screaming, but her voice and her life were cut short by a burst of gunfire. Jamila sat by the corner, whimpering, and the noise she was making was beginning to get out of hand. Emmanuel was afraid she would alert the men outside to the presence of people within the office.

Then they heard a body or bodies throwing themselves at the door in an apparent attempt to break into the office. There were several tries, but they were all unsuccessful. Then another burst of gunfire erupted, but this time aimed at the door. Pieces of wood flew off the door as the bullets hit it.

Haruna, alongside the women inside, began to scream while the others gasped in fear. Emmanuel rushed forward and started throwing more furniture on the existing pile at the door in a bid to stop the killers from gaining entry.

Meanwhile, Haruna got up and moved towards the window, struggling to open it and make an escape.

Emmanuel turned round and dragged the man away.

"What do you think you are doing!? Do you know if there are more of them outside? Do you want them to come in through the window and kill us?"

Haruna crumpled into a heap, sobbing in fear.

The other people in the room were huddled in a corner on the floor, a mix of fear, shock, and panic, while Emmanuel tried to maintain a semblance of calm.

There was a short pause in the sound of gunshots from outside. Suddenly, from afar, they heard more gunshots, but these sounded more controlled and targeted instead of the prolonged and scattered shooting that had been before.

The tension in the air changed as there seemed to be a battle going on between both sets of sounds; the long, scattered shots seemingly shouting for dominance, and a quick, short reply of controlled bursts counteracting the former.

*It seemed like… could that be … YES!* The security forces had arrived.

The battle raged for a while as they cowered in the office, the sounds of bullets hitting the walls and windows. Eventually, the guns fell silent.

The seconds ticked into minutes as the people in the room who had been cowering in corners began to rise from their positions when they heard different voices outside.

Emmanuel and Yunusa looked out the windows and saw the compound filled with armed soldiers and policemen, with several terrorists dead or sitting in small groups on the ground, disarmed and handcuffed.

The group of workers led by Emmanuel, Nasir, and Yunusa removed the barricades blocking the door and led the procession to the outer office and into the compound.

As they stepped outside, the first body they saw was that of Amina, sprawled on the floor and still bleeding from several bullet holes. The women wailed while the men gasped in shock.

Almost on cue, several cries and screams broke out from different parts of the compound as the survivors came out of hiding to see the bodies of their colleagues in the offices, hallways, on the grass, in vehicles, and all over the compound.

As Emmanuel reached the door of the office, he saw another body covered in blood, half visible through the open door that led to one of the inner offices. He walked towards it, avoiding shards of glass scattered all over the floor. It was Hajiya Hadiza.

She was lying sideways in the pool of her blood with limbs cut off. Emmanuel held the door panel to try and steady himself at the gory sight, and he immediately felt sick. He turned away from the scene and moved out towards the compound where the military was gathering the survivors.

They were still on very high alert and were restricting free movement as they continued to sweep the compound. Emmanuel picked his way towards the entrance of the building and out into the compound, encountering a group of soldiers on his way. On seeing him, the soldiers shouted at him with guns raised:

"STOP! Identify yourself!"

"He is one of us, don't shoot!" One of his colleagues shouted. Emmanuel was too dazed to speak.

The soldiers searched him and then released him. Stepping into the yard, he was confronted with the full extent of the devastation as emergency workers ran around trying to save the wounded while the dead were lined in long rows on the ground outside.

The bodies were identified, tagged, and loaded into ambulances while more bodies were being brought out from the offices.

He saw Ibrahim's body on the ground, bleeding from

several bullet holes. Emmanuel then noticed the bus parked in the middle of the compound. It became clear to him that Ibrahim had used the bus to convey the terrorists into the compound to get them in undetected.

The cries of the people around him felt distant, and Emmanuel allowed the numbness to wash over him.

Emmanuel wrote his details in the impromptu register of survivors and was cleared by the medical staff. He looked back at the office and the men who carried the dead bodies of his colleagues and his boss, took a deep breath, and quietly made his way home in a complete daze.

****

The examination invigilators moved along the rows of students seated, scribbling their way through the Economics paper before them. If they were 'appeased' as Mairo had claimed, they didn't show any signs of it. Aisha watched as their eyes roved from one end of the hall to the other, probably looking for someone to use as an example.

Economics wasn't a tricky subject for her, but Aisha had not fully settled into her exam rhythm due to the unease she had been feeling all morning. She would flinch and get distracted by the slightest sound or signs of movement. They were an hour into the exams already, and Joshua was neck-deep into his answer sheet. She chuckled at the realization that he wasn't like the other boys who would stretch and turn, hoping to catch a glimpse of her work.

She felt bad again for the incident from the other day and had agreed with Mairo that she ought to explain to Joshua the reason she was kneeling with the rest. She had to make him see she wasn't that type of girl, and it was a noble thing that landed her in that position.

The quiet in the hall was interrupted from time to time by the rustling of papers as students turned over a page to continue or pretended to turn over a page to distract unsuspecting exam supervisors. She wondered if the supervisors knew the tricks and methods in the exam playbook of students.

"Okay, you have one hour and thirty minutes left to go," the woman in the orange *ankara* dress said, pointing to the clock in front of the hall.

Aisha had already gone halfway through her paper and was getting more confident. She had completed the multiple-choice section and was reading the essay questions.

*What is the definition of Economics according to Lionel Robbins? Explain.*

Economics is a science that studies human behaviour as a relationship between ends and scarce means, which have alternative uses.

*Human wants are unlimited.*

Like her mother's. She remembered the fight with her father over money spent on things he considered excessive. She was just eight years old, but she understood what he was saying when he complained that *Nana* wanted to have everything in life and was spending their money to support her lifestyle. What he didn't know was that Aisha also wanted a lot of things, but couldn't ask him since he complained so much about how things weren't as easy as they used to be. The fact was that her mother had grown up rich and hence was used to a certain standard of living which her father clearly could not afford.

*Resources are scarce and limited.*

Her father always made sure they knew that. Especially after her mother's disappearance, Aisha had been reminded time and again that she couldn't have all she wanted because there wasn't enough money to finance those desires, and she would have to wait.

"I'm working hard here, Ada. Money disappears as soon as it comes. I'll see to that when I collect my next salary."

And that was that. Their hopes and desires depended on their father's monthly income.

*Resources need to be used efficiently.*

When the money came, the most important things had to be done first: food, electricity, household necessities, and everything else he deemed necessary at that time. If there was some left, then she could have a few delightful things.

A few minutes into the essay questions, the exams were interrupted by a commotion outside. Armed soldiers walked to the examination halls and ordered everyone out.

The students looked at the supervisors, wondering what to do. They, in turn, were as bewildered as the students who looked to them for direction. After a few seconds of exchanged looks, the supervisors went outside the classroom to meet the soldiers who were now in the hallway. The students looked on, trying to understand what was happening.

Aisha couldn't make out what they were saying, but it seemed that the soldiers were insisting that the students stop their exams and move out of the hall.

A minute later, the supervisors came back into the hall and asked everyone to submit their papers and quietly walk out of the class. In a different situation, the students would have complained that they hadn't finished their work, but that wasn't the case.

The presence of the armed soldiers in full combat gear was enough to persuade even the hardiest of souls that this was a dire situation and that an F in Economics would be the least of their concerns if they didn't do as instructed.

Aisha joined the queue as they moved forward to submit their papers. The soldiers were getting agitated and urged that they move faster. The students picked up the pace and quickly stepped outside as soon as they had handed over their papers. Aisha could see Mairo at the end of the queue, and her friend motioned as if to ask what was happening.

Outside, the glare of the sun added to their disorientation. Students from other halls were gathering outside, adding to the confusion. Before her eyes could adjust, the girls were separated and hurriedly shepherded towards a line of large trucks parked and facing the school exit gate.

One of the teachers stepped up to the soldier who

seemed to be in command and asked why they were taking the girls alone and not the boys, men, or women in the school. The soldier told him they would return and pick up the others, but they needed to move the girls to their base for safety quickly because of a security threat.

As they walked towards the vehicles, one of the girls checked her phone and saw news of the attack on the Local Government Headquarters. She quickly told others the news, and confusion spread like wildfire. Aisha was thrown into panic and tried to explain to the soldiers that her father worked at the LGA office, and she needed to go.

"How would you help him?" he said in Hausa. He told her that the Nigerian Army had been sent to respond to the attack.

Of course, *she* couldn't do anything for him now other than remain safe with these soldiers, so she and the girls in her group climbed into the nearest truck.

The teacher who asked why they were taking only the

girls sensed that something was not adding up and insisted on seeing some identification. As Aisha and the girls watched, he started arguing with the soldiers, and then one of them pulled out a gleaming machete and, with a giant swing, cleaved the man's head open. As the blood spurted and the man's lifeless body fell to the dirt, the girls started screaming. People now realized that these weren't real soldiers, and they started running. Then the assailants opened fire, spraying their victims with bullets. Aisha and the girls in the truck watched in horror as the bodies of people were scattered around in a pool of blood.

Still, the sounds of AK-47s overwhelmed the shrieks of people who had lost their sense of direction and were running into each other. Some ran directly at the assailants and were shot dead before they got close.

An insurgent wearing a chain of bullets around his neck stood in front of their truck and fired repeatedly at the crowd. He turned occasionally to make sure none of the girls moved. His unspoken instruction was crystal; no one moved.

# CHAPTER SIX

Emmanuel's journey home was in a trance-like state. He felt numb, detached from the horrors of the day's traumatic events. As a resident of Maiduguri, he had, of course, heard about the atrocities of the Boko Haram terrorist group, seen pictures and videos on the news and social media. Still, nothing could prepare him for living through an attack. He had believed he empathized with the victims, but the gruesome acts of today made him realize how wrong he had been. You could never truly know it without having experienced it, and that was something he was coming to understand.

The *okada* man taking him home sped along the roads, raising dust and upsetting the people by the roadside. Typically, Emmanuel would have cautioned him to slow down, but today, he revelled in the speed and wind as he realised the futility of life, there one minute and so easily snuffed out the next.

The man dropped Emmanuel in front of his house but

refused to collect the money Emmanuel offered him.

*"Allah ya daidaita, maigida. A hannun sa muke."*

*We are all in God's hands!?*

Emmanuel stood and stared at him, incredulous. Where was God when those people were being massacred? Didn't the fundamentalists claim that they were committing these atrocities on behalf of their God? Weren't they trained to slaughter all who didn't believe in their way? He didn't have a reply for the man, so he just thanked him and walked away.

He tried to fit his key in the lock, but his hands were so unsteady that it kept slipping. The more he tried to force it, the more frustrated he got until, out of exasperation, he turned and leaned his back on the door and slipped downward gently until he was seated on the floor with his head on his knees, overwhelmed by a rush of delayed grief.

"Emmanuel? Emma?"

It was Mama Fidelia, one of his neighbours, but her

voice felt like a distant buzz in his head.

She made her way to where he was seated and placed her left hand on his knee and her right hand around his shoulder.

"Oya, get up from the ground, Emma. Please get up."

She helped him up and called out to her son, who was standing at a distance with other neighbors, to bring the white plastic chair that she had been sitting on. As he brought it out, the others came with him and helped Emmanuel into the chair, accompanied by a chorus of sympathy. They had all heard of the attack at the Local Government where they knew he worked.

After a while, one of them found Emmanuel's keys and helped him unlock his door. He whispered a "thank you" and entered his house. Understanding his need to be alone, they wished him peace of mind and left him with his thoughts.

Inside the house, Emmanuel started making his way through the sitting room to his bedroom, taking off his blood and gore-stained shirt. As he got to the door, the lights came on, and the TV came on in the sitting room. From outside, he heard the neighbours shout: "UP NEPA!"

What awful timing! Aisha would be more excited than he was.

Oh God, Aisha! He had forgotten about her in the rush of events of the day. She would be worried sick about him. He had to go and get her. His heart started beating faster as he searched for a shirt to wear. One part of him didn't think the school would be in danger now that the Army had arrived, but he needed to make sure.

As he dressed, he heard a familiar voice on the TV.

"We didn't know, they just came in and started shooting… had to hide… rescued by the soldiers…"

He went out to see what was going on and saw it was his colleague, Haruna, being interviewed by a reporter about the attack on the office. He could see some of the other staff in the background; some were crying while others looked dazed. As he watched, a breaking news item scrolled at the bottom of the screen.

## "168 STUDENTS OF FEDERAL GOVERNMENT COLLEGE, MAIDUGURI KIDNAPPED BY BOKO HARAM!"

Emmanuel uttered a scream and ran out of the house. He didn't bother to lock the door.

Mama Fidelia called out to him as he ran through the dusty streets. He didn't look back. In his rush, he almost collided with a motorcycle. He apologised curtly without giving a second glance at the man and continued running.

He could hear the motorcycle following closely behind him, probably angry at the fact that Emmanuel had given him a stiff apology. He called out to Emmanuel as he rode beside him. Emmanuel turned and tried to wave him away, but stopped running when he recognised him.

*"Maigaida, wannan hanzarin kuma fa?"* – Where are you rushing off to? – The man asked.

It was the same man who had brought him home not too long ago. How long ago was it? He couldn't discern. He tried to tell the man about what had happened at his daughter's school, but couldn't form complete or coherent sentences, so he just kept shouting "my daughter".

As if he understood, the *okada* man motioned for him to get on the bike, and they headed for the school with Emmanuel giving directions.

On getting to the school compound, they were confronted with a line of military vehicles and scores of irritable soldiers and policemen forming barricades and frisking people. The security forces were in a state of heightened alert due to the dual attacks in the city. As the news of the attacks spread, fear had gripped the city.

Even though there had been other attacks over the years, the terrorists mainly targeted police stations, military patrols, and outposts on the outskirts of the city. Never before had they so brazenly carried out not one but two attacks, and in the heart of the city, on the same day.

Emmanuel thanked the bike man and made his way through the crowd, pushing and pulling to get to the school gate. Upon arrival, he was immediately stopped by a group of soldiers. He identified himself and was let into the compound, where he joined the crowd of parents in various stages of grief, disbelief, and panic.

Parents, guardians, and relatives of the students were arriving, and those who were lucky enough to find their children alive and well, or even injured, were happily reunited with them, taking them and leaving the school premises. Those who were seriously injured had already been evacuated to hospital. This, however, was not the case with most of the parents who came to the school, their disbelief and fear quickly turning into raw pain and grief.

One mother was rolling on the ground, screaming. Her clothes and hair were covered in dust. Some parents were sitting around sobbing quietly, eyes bloodshot, lips trembling.

Emmanuel walked from one group to another, seeing

a reflection of the deep despair, and his fear mounts.

There was a hastily set-up information desk near the end of the football field where a teacher, with the assistance of two military personnel, had written down the names of the affected students as best he could. The dead were listed based on the ID cards found on them, and their bodies were taken to the morgue. Another list had the names of survivors, both injured and non-injured.

Parents crowded the teacher, shouting and pushing, trying to get any information about the condition of their children. The soldiers tried to get the parents to form an orderly line to no avail. This only infuriated the parents even more, and a fight ensued, which resulted in the papers with the list of students being torn to shreds.

One mother angrily grabbed a soldier, but the shocked soldier pushed her away, and she tripped and fell on the uneven surface. Other parents and bystanders attacked the soldier, and a mini-riot broke out. The other soldiers had to fire their weapons into the air to scare the parents and restore order.

Unable to get any answers, Emmanuel looked around desperately and spoke to one of the soldiers, who directed him to check the medical tent.

There was a makeshift medical tent set up on the left side of the football field, which was being used to provide first aid to victims of the attack as well as to house the students who were not abducted until their parents came for them.

Emmanuel rushed over, looking around for any sign of Aisha. He approached a group of girls sitting in a huddle protected by several soldiers and tried talking to them.

"Please, have you seen my daughter Aisha? Aisha Nweze?"

The girls were still in shock and were generally unresponsive. One shook her head slowly with a blank stare.

He walked down the line of the injured, looking for

Aisha. Even though their injuries were not life-threatening, the hall was filled with weeping as the survivors relived the horrible experience. He got to the end of the line of beds and found nothing. There was no Aisha.

In desperation, Emmanuel started asking each person in the beds, "Please help me, I'm looking for my daughter, Aisha Nweze?"

Some of the people there started raising their voices at him and complaining that he was disturbing and wouldn't let the victims rest. The doctors and the other parents asked him to leave, but he refused, so they called the soldiers to take him out as he was beginning to disturb the patients.

Coming out, he saw that one of the soldiers had restored the Information Desk and was taking down the information of the affected parents, so that they could be contacted by the Army if there were any new developments. He joined the queue of parents and wrote down his name and phone number.

In a last-ditch effort to get answers, Emmanuel left the school premises and headed for the hospital. Either Aisha was among the seriously wounded, or she was… Emmanuel could not bring himself to think it.

Outside the school gate, the bike man from before waved him over. Had he been waiting for Emmanuel all this time? Maybe he remained there to watch the unfortunate events like the other people who were crowded around the gate, trying to see what was happening within.

*"Ka ga diyar ka?"*

He could sense the concern in the man's voice, asking if he had seen his daughter. He shook his head, and the man asked where they were headed next. Emmanuel told him to ride to the hospital, and the man didn't say a word to him throughout the ride. He seemed to know when to talk and when not to.

Upon arriving at the hospital, Emmanuel joined another group of parents trying to get information about their children. This was a repeat of the scene from the school, simply better organized. He quickly ran through the list of the injured people that were brought to the hospital, but did not find Aisha's name.

"I'm sorry, Sir, but you may have to check the morgue as there were a lot of bodies brought in from the attacks," the attendant said to him, turning and trying to attend to other parents and guardians who were all in a state of agitation, seeking news of their loved ones.

Emmanuel made his way to the morgue, following the signs posted in the hospital hallways that smelt of potent antiseptic. He got to the ante-area of the morgue and was hit with a surreal scene.

Naked frozen bodies were stacked in piles on the floor against a wall with the air-conditioning at full blast. The smell of formaldehyde was so strong that Emmanuel almost choked, while the staff were walking around looking unperturbed.

A cleaner was busy mopping blood off the floor, but the blood seemed to keep seeping from the inner door.

Emmanuel had to take a minute for his head to stop spinning before he approached an official carrying a notepad and checking the bodies.

"Please excuse me, Sir. I want to check for my daughter." Emmanuel said hesitantly, wanting to know if she was amongst the dead, and yet dreading the possibility.

"Describe your daughter, please," the man replied. The name on his ID was Ibrahim Gambo.

"She is… tall, dark, about five feet, six… or seven inches tall, with… with… long braided hair." Emmanuel stuttered as he imagined his daughter being one of the bodies in the piles stacked in the room's corner.

"Was she wearing a school uniform?" Dr Gambo asked.

"Yes," Emmanuel replied, adding for no reason, "She is only 14 years old."

Dr Gambo looked up at Emmanuel from his notepad,

as if noticing him for the first time, then looked down at his notepad and ran his finger down a list.

"Go into the main mortuary room and check Section One on the left. The entire row is young people; the fresh sets that were brought in today."

With his heart in his mouth and choking from the cold and the thick smell of formaldehyde and human remains, Emmanuel entered the morgue proper, a large room, the walls covered with rows upon rows of refrigeration chambers containing bodies.

There were some bodies on the floor still bleeding, and two workers in white hospital gowns with plastic waterproof aprons, thick gloves, and eye protection, going through the rows, emptying out bodies that were already frozen and putting in the new bodies, as they had run out of space.

Emmanuel moved through the rows, starting from the left, opening the drawers one by one and looking at different bodies with all manner of bullet and machete wounds. He got to the end of that section, but he did not find his daughter's body.

He turned round and looked through the bodies that were just loaded, and he still couldn't find her. With renewed hope and determination, he went out to the outer room and grabbed Dr Gambo by the arm.

"She's not here. Is there anywhere else I can look? I can't find her, she's not there."

He was excited that she was not dead, but also concerned as to what that meant. There was renewed hope in him that he would find her. Alive!

"No, Sir. If she is not here, then I can't help you. I have no more information for you." Dr Gambo said as he extricated himself from Emmanuel's grasp and moved away.

Emmanuel left the morgue and hurried towards the exit of the hospital. He sat down at the reception to collect his thoughts and decide his next course of action. Aisha was not in the school, and Aisha was not among the dead. That meant that she was alive, but where? Could she have run away and been hiding somewhere?

He noticed the clock that hung on the wall of the hospital reception area: 7:42 pm.

He walked out of the hospital and saw the commercial motorcycle rider waiting for him at the entrance. In the wake of the commotion, the pungent smell of chemicals and the gruesome sight of dead bodies piled up on one another, Emmanuel had completely forgotten about the man. He was grateful the man had waited.

The ride home was not as troubling as Emmanuel thought it would be. He felt a bit guilty as the thoughts of his dead boss and colleagues were pushed to the back of his mind and replaced by a combination of happiness that Aisha was not among the dead and worry about her whereabouts.

As they stopped in front of his house, Emmanuel reached for his wallet only to discover that it wasn't there. The bike man realized what he was trying to do and told Emmanuel not to bother.

*"Taimakon Allah shi ya fi ai."*

Emmanuel frowned momentarily as the man mentioned God again. What did he mean by God's help was greater? He thanked the *okada* man and bade him good night. As he walked towards his house, it occurred to him that he had not asked the good Samaritan what his name was. Well, he was appreciative of the immense help the man had given him. He couldn't understand how the man believed in the same God that the insurgents believed in. The religious paradox.

Mama Fidelia was seated at the entrance of Emmanuel's house holding his house keys. She had waited all these hours for him to come back.

Ever since his parents left, she had done all she could to help, but she did that from a distance. After Zainab disappeared, she had drawn closer and helped him a lot with Aisha during those years. It was partly because of Mama Fidelia that he made it through the worst periods of depression. She didn't complain, she just helped.

"Thank you, ma."

She just shook her head and patted him gently.

"Can I use your phone?" he asked, remembering that he couldn't find his and that he hadn't tried calling his daughter throughout the aftermath of the day's events.

"Here," she said, handing it over to him.

He dialled Aisha's number, and it rang for a few seconds before his call was rejected. He tried again a couple of times, but her number was now switched off.

Then it hit him.

She was not among the dead. She was not among the injured. She was not back home or with any of the neighbours.

That left only one other option: Aisha was alive. She must be among the girls kidnapped by the Boko Haram terrorists.

****

The girls were huddled together in the back of the

truck as the convoy drove at speed through the bush. They had gotten off the tarred road a while back and were now bumping along, weaving and swerving. It was dark inside the back of the truck as it was covered entirely in a large tarpaulin.

As her eyes adjusted to the darkness, Aisha realised that there were no insurgents with them in the back of the truck. She assumed that they didn't bother since escape was futile. None of the girls had spoken a word since they left the school premises, apart from the sobbing. They realised their cries were futile after some time.

"Where are they taking us?" A voice spoke out fearfully in the darkness.

Nobody answered. A strange question borne out of desperation, hopelessness, and shock. Aisha was still in shock herself, but realised how easy it would be for them to be killed and dumped in the bush. Trying to calm herself as much as her fellow captives, she started whispering.

"These people must be Boko Haram. They…" A cry of despair spread across the truck as she mentioned the name of the insurgent group. "They would probably take us to their hideout. There's nothing we can do now to…," a fresh wave of whimpering ensued, and Aisha allowed it to die down before continuing. "We would need to cooperate with them for now and not try to act foolish if not—"

*"Za su kashe mu ne!"* — They are going to kill us! — One of the girls shouted, deepening their despair, and several girls started crying again.

The same thing had occurred to Aisha, but she stilled her fears by thinking that if they wanted to kill them, they would have done so at the school. They wouldn't drive them along this long route just to kill them. There had to be a purpose, and Aisha was counting on that as a measure of hope for her and the others.

As they sat in darkness, a phone rang out, and the others rushed and rallied around the girl in desperation. She quickly picked up the call, but she couldn't hear the person on the other end, and then the phone died, sending the girls into renewed panic.

"Does anyone else have their phone here?" someone asked, with renewed hope, but there was a chorus of whispered "No's."

Aisha suddenly realised that her phone was still with her. As she took it out, the other girls crowded around her, increasing the panic and causing her hands to start shaking.

"There is no network here," she whispered.

"Send a message. Say they want to kill us!" someone urged. "They should send soldiers to rescue us."

"It's okay!" Aisha said, almost shouting, "I know what to send."

She typed a short message to her father, knowing he would do anything in his power to seek out help for them.

*"WE'RE IN A TRUCK IN THE BUSH. TAKING US SOMEWHERE WE DON'T KNOW. HELP US"*

Her hands shook as she composed the message. She hit send, and it showed "sent" even though she knew it wouldn't be delivered immediately. She put away her phone quickly when she heard the trucks pull to a stop.

The back of their truck was opened by one of the men, but it was already dark so that Aisha couldn't make out his face. He was holding a torch which was pointed in their direction.

"*Ku miko wayoyin ku!*" The man shouted.

The girl with the phone gave hers to the man, but Aisha tried not to look in his direction. He ordered that *all* the phones be handed over to him. The other girls all turned in Aisha's direction, urging her with their eyes to relinquish hers. She hesitated, as it was their only means of communication and maybe a last hope for rescue, but the fear of what would happen if it was found on her or if one of the girls sold her out was too intense. She used her thumb to switch it off and handed it over.

The man collected the phone and maintained his gaze

on her for a while, shining the torch in her face. She looked down, avoiding his gaze.

He then ordered all the girls down from the truck. They were reluctant to get down, and some girls pushed others to go in front. Aisha moved forward and stepped out of the truck first.

They were in a village that looked abandoned save for the fires from the huts in the distance.

They were ordered to move in single file towards the group of huts. She could make out different images in the dark. As they moved, they were joined by the other girls from the other trucks.

The night was filled with silent cries of girls who had left home that day, intending to return to their parents and sleep on their beds. But that didn't happen.

Instead, they were led to an uncertain future in a place none of them could recognise and with men who had chosen not to be part of normal human society.

As the girls walked, the darkness enveloped them,

bringing a crushing feeling of despondency that led to increased wailing, and then the line stopped moving. One girl had stopped walking and just started screaming. As the terrorists ran towards her, she suddenly took off and started running into the darkness. The night air exploded with the sound of a gun firing, and her body was flung forward onto the dirt.

On seeing that, the others panicked and started running in different directions. The terrorists responded by repeatedly shooting into the air to stop the girls and rounded them up.

Aisha noticed that the girl whose phone had rang earlier was not with them anymore.

She had escaped.

# CHAPTER SEVEN

Emmanuel did not get much sleep that night because thoughts of Aisha and the horrors of the day overwhelmed him. He was now convinced that she was one of the girls kidnapped and hence was still alive. He couldn't lose her the way he lost her mother. He wouldn't survive this if he did. He needed closure. This was the first night he had spent in the house without his daughter since Zainab's disappearance.

Dawn came slowly. It felt like forever. All night, he tried unsuccessfully to think of a solution for his predicament. He continued to lie in bed, wondering where she was, how she slept, what they gave her to eat, and what they had done to her. Those bastards! If they touched his daughter, he would kill all of them! Every bloody last one of them!

He could feel his breathing become intense and his heart begin to beat faster. He ground his teeth in frustration.

As he thought over the situation, he heard a knock on

his door. He checked his watch beside his bed and saw that it was 8:15 am. Who was disturbing him this early in the morning? He didn't want sympathy. He needed to find his daughter, and he didn't feel like wasting his time with anyone who couldn't help him find her.

"Who is there!?"

"*Injiniya*, it's Haruna. Pls open the door, *don Allah*." He unlocked and opened the door.

Haruna and a man Emmanuel didn't recognize walked in. They stood for a while before Emmanuel gestured to them to sit. After offering their sympathies over the unfortunate event surrounding his daughter, Haruna handed over his phone to him.

"It was among the office items they gathered," Haruna said, looking intently at him. If he expected Emmanuel to break down and cry, he was disappointed. Emmanuel maintained his calm demeanour.

"Thank you, Haruna. I'm grateful. How is the state of things in the office now?"

He couldn't speak about Hajiya Hadiza or any of the others. The horror was all still too fresh.

"Everything is fine except…," Haruna sighed heavily, "…we can't find Kande. She is not at home, and her body was not found with the others."

Emmanuel felt a renewed pang of pain. This wasn't the kind of news one wanted to hear in these circumstances.

"This…," Haruna said, pointing to the man he came with, "…is her brother. He had been staying with her for some days now. He came to look for her in the office, and no one knew where she was. No one even remembered seeing her during the shooting."

For a lot of them, the events of the past day were a blur. Those who were questioned on the day of the attack by the security agents were too dazed to give them any helpful information.

Emmanuel looked at the young man in his sitting room. He looked like he was in his early twenties. What was going through the young man's mind? Did he think his sister was kidnapped? Or worse, dead? Then his mind went back to Aisha.

Emmanuel shook his head as if to clear the negative thoughts. This startled the other two into inquiring if he was alright. He assured them that he was fine and stood up, indicating that he wanted to be alone, and they left. Emmanuel switched on the phone, and immediately a barrage of messages flooded his phone. The first one he opened was from his mother. She texted to see if he was alright after complaining about why his phone was switched off all day.

He saw two more from his sister and Idowu, his former head of department. They all were praying that he was safe and out of harm's way. As he was reading his sister Oluchi's text, he saw the one from his daughter.

The words hit him like a sledgehammer blow.

*"WE'RE IN A TRUCK IN THE BUSH. TAKING US SOMEWHERE WE DON'T KNOW. HELP US."*

She had sent him a text all this time, and he wasn't even aware. He closed his eyes as a sensation of intense pain filled his head. His hands started shaking, and the shaking spread to the rest of his body. He had to help her! He didn't know how he was going to do it, but she needed him, and he had to do something to save her. But what could he do?

In anger, he quickly threw on a fresh pair of trousers and a shirt and rushed out of the house. When Emmanuel got outside, he was surprised to see the *okada* man who had helped him get around the previous day.

Emmanuel greeted him, thanking him once more for his help. He asked the man his name.

"*Zalla.*" He answered.

Emmanuel had never heard that name before, but he reckoned it was one of the uncommon *Kanuri* names. When he asked the man if it was, he nodded and said he was Hausa and that his name meant 'only'.

Emmanuel didn't dwell on the strange name or the

meaning, so he asked the man if he could take him to his daughter's school. The man readily agreed, and like before, Zalla rejected Emmanuel's offer to pay for the ride.

****

The school premises were again swarming with people, parents, family members, and other onlookers, all milling about. There was also a heavy security presence within and outside the premises.

Emmanuel approached one of the soldiers stationed there and showed him the text message he had received from Aisha. The soldier took him to another soldier, a senior officer, with Captain D. ISYAKA on his name tag. The man seemed like a veteran of the protracted war on terror in the North-East. He was young, but the lines on his face and the look in his eyes spoke of someone who had seen and maybe done things that only happened in the nightmares of most regular people.

"Good day, Sir. My name is Emmanuel Nweze, a staff member at the Local Government Headquarters,

Gombaru. My daughter Aisha was one of the girls kidnapped yesterday."

At this, the captain softened a bit. Emmanuel continued.

"I am a survivor from the other attack during the day at the Local Government Headquarters, where I had misplaced my phone. I just got it back this morning, and when I switched it on, I got this text from my daughter."

He handed the phone to the captain as he spoke.

The captain went through the text message. As he read it, his initial excitement was abated. A slight frown of disappointment replaced the initial look of expectation.

"Mr Nweze, I'm sorry, but there is no new information in this text. We already know how they left Maiduguri and the route they took." He handed the phone back to Emmanuel.

"I don't understand, Sir," Emmanuel replied in shock,

thinking that the soldiers would be mobilizing to start rushing to give chase. "You already know which route they took, and you're not in pursuit?"

"That is not how we work. We must get our orders and rules of engagement from our commanding officers before going out, as well as equipment and supplies." The captain said, somewhat apologetically.

"You mean you will stay here and do nothing because you are waiting for orders? You realize these girls could be…," Emmanuel choked on the words. He was overwhelmed with shock, anger, and fear, and he was enraged at the soldier.

"Look here, I answered you because of your situation! There is a protocol for military deployment." Captain Isyaka said, beginning to get testy.

"What rubbish protocol?" shouted Emmanuel. "These murdering Islamists kidnap my daughter, and you are talking about protocols!?" In anger, he had grabbed the arm of the captain.

On seeing this, several men, who had been standing

around the soldiers, jumped in and accosted Emmanuel.

*"Ka ji dan iskan nan!"* — *Listen to this bastard!* One of the men insulted Emmanuel.

Taken aback at first, Emmanuel quickly recovered, stood his ground, pushed the man back, and retorted in a matching tone, "You are all the same. *Ta yaya zan san ba kwa cikinsu?"*

Emmanuel's accusation that they were the same as members of Boko Haram angered them, and several other men rushed at him, and in the blink of an eye, a fight broke out.

As blows started flying, an Imam who had been on site to comfort the grieving parents rushed in to try to separate them, but in the melee, Emmanuel's elbow struck the Imam on the temple and knocked him out cold.

Screams of *"La'illah!"* and *"A'uzibillah!"* filled the air.

The mood immediately turned deadly as several of the

men drew daggers from underneath their clothes and tried to stab him. The soldiers had to intervene, led by Captain Isyaka, who had to fire his weapon into the air to calm things down.

Even at that, it was a herculean task restraining the men who wanted to kill Emmanuel, as the matter had gone from a simple fracas to an attack on a revered teacher of Islam, an unforgivable sin.

Eventually, the soldiers restrained Emmanuel and the men and revived the Imam. They then called in the Police, who proceeded to arrest Emmanuel for starting the fight by "insulting Islam" and assaulting a cleric.

He was driven to a nearby Police Station, where he was booked and locked up, all the while protesting his innocence. His protests fell on deaf ears, and he was asked to keep quiet on multiple occasions.

"*Kulle mana dan iskan nan!*" — Lock up that bastard, the officer-in-charge of the people who had brought him in said.

The others did as they were told, stripped him down to his boxers, and locked him in a cell with five other people.

As night fell, Emmanuel started banging on the bars of the jail in desperation and caused such a ruckus that everyone in the station was caught up in the commotion. The policemen on duty, in anger, then spread word to the other inmates that Emmanuel was an infidel who assaulted an Imam.

The men who had ignored Emmanuel earlier on now rose to their feet and circled him like a pack of hyenas. As they attacked, he tried defending himself as best he could, but there were just too many of them.

They punched him till he fell, and they continued by kicking him repeatedly. He curled into a foetal position to protect his face and genitals. Eventually, they got tired and left him bloodied on the floor.

As he lay there with his injuries, he started crying softly. He thought about what Aisha was going through at that exact moment, what suffering her kidnappers were putting her through, hoping against all odds that she was alive and in a better condition than her father was.

As he drifted off into a pain-filled sleep, he sank into despair, a darkness filled with pain, blood, piss, and faeces.

****

Emmanuel was woken up in the morning by a kick to his side. He screamed in pain and opened his eyes to see a policeman standing over him with a small bucket of water.

*"Tashi, dan iska!"* — Get up, you bastard! The policeman screamed at him.

As he struggled to get his bearings, the policeman poured the bucket of cold water on him. The shock of the cold water jolted him fully awake and brought him back to the reality of his current condition. And with the wakefulness, his body was flooded with the pain of the beating he had received the previous night.

From his head, his face, neck, shoulders, arms, torso,

and legs, the fire of the pains that had been numbed by unconsciousness went from smouldering to full-blown rage. He tried to move and screamed in pain as he fell back to the floor.

"I'm trying, I'm in pain, I need a doctor." He said fitfully as he gritted his teeth in pain.

"*Dan iska!*" the other inmates shouted at him, laughing gleefully "*Tashi tsaye, kai kafiri.*" – You bastard! Stand up, you infidel!

As Emmanuel continued to struggle, they began to gather round him like a pack of jackals.

"*Na ce tashi!*" The policeman screamed at him again, reaching down and grabbing Emmanuel by the arm.

As he pulled him up to his feet, one of the other inmates punched Emmanuel in the lower abdomen. Emmanuel's bladder immediately gave way, and he wet himself. As the hot urine trickled down his legs and pooled on the floor at his feet, the other inmates saw it and erupted into guffaws. The policeman put his hands together, handcuffed him, and led him out of the cell.

In pain, shame, and embarrassment, Emmanuel half-walked and was half-dragged out of the cell by the policeman, hotly followed by the jeers of the inmates.

Upon arriving at the counter, Emmanuel sat down on the bench provided for visitors, with his head in his hands, while the Desk Officer processed his discharge papers. As the man looked through the documents on the counter, his anger slowly changed into a scowl and then into a look of confusion. He looked up from the papers and turned to face Emmanuel.

"Eh, Mr Man, no be you wey dem say assault the Imam?" He barks at Emmanuel.

"It was an accident," Emmanuel replied weakly.

"*Yaya?*" – How? - The policeman asked, incredulous.

Emmanuel then looked up and realized that this policeman was not the same one who had booked him the previous night. His name tag read Sgt. Gofwan M. Emmanuel sat up a bit straighter and tried to explain.

"My daughter was one of the girls kidnapped two days ago."

"Oh my God!" Sgt. Gofwan's expression immediately softened.

"My only child!" Emmanuel continued. Several people who were at the station turned towards the direction of their conversation and started expressing condolences and offering words of comfort.

"*Za a same ta, da yardar Allah.*"

"Yes, she will be found, God willing."

"*Insha Allah!*"

"*Nagode. Nagode Sosai.* Thank you," Emmanuel replied to them, drawing hope and strength from their words.

For a few seconds, they remained silent, pondering the current situation in the country in general and in their beloved state. How and when did the security situation deteriorate to the point when terrorists became so emboldened that they would mount such brazen attacks on a major city like Maiduguri, which had a very large army base and large contingents of men and material?

"I went to the soldiers to show them the text my daughter sent me." Emmanuel continued, emboldened by the show of solidarity he felt from those at the station.

"*To me suka yi?*" – What did they do? - One of the people there asked.

Another asked if the soldiers had gone after the insurgents.

Emmanuel shook his head again, feeling the weight of his helplessness. "*Babu.* Nothing at all!"

The people stared in disbelief.

"The soldiers at the school said they already knew the route they took, but that they were waiting for orders from above before they pursued."

"*Allah ya tsine masu!*" They exclaimed in shock, cursing at the soldiers.

The Divisional Police Officer (DPO) in charge of the Police Station had come out from his office and overheard the last part of the conversation.

"So, it was when I was arguing with the soldiers that a small fight started, and the Imam came to intervene, and my hand accidentally hit him. That's how I was arrested and brought here."

"Remove the handcuffs," the DPO said to the Desk Officer as he walked forward and took the files from Sgt Gofwan and started flipping through them. "Where is his charge sheet?"

"It's here, Sir," Sgt Gofwan said, pulling out a sheet of paper from the file and handing it to the DPO. He then walked over to Emmanuel and unlocked the handcuffs. Emmanuel got up from the bench, wary of the pain all over his body, and gingerly shuffled towards the counter.

"*Wannan ba daidai bane…*" The DPO muttered in a low tone.

"Sorry, Sir?" Emmanuel asked him, assuming he was speaking to him.

"I said this Charge Sheet is not correct," he said and turned to Sgt Gofwan. "Why is the name of the complainant blank? Where is Aminu?"

"He is not on duty today."

"And he used this rubbish to lock someone up?"

As Emmanuel observed this exchange, he began to have hope that he might be released soon.

"Yes, Sir, I didn't do anything, Sir!"

"You get someone you fit call, make them come bail you?" the DPO asked, in a bit of a quandary. He clearly wanted to release Emmanuel, but he was worried about a possible backlash later if anything went wrong. Careers had ended very dramatically in the security services when people were seen to be "aligned to the other side".

"No, sir, I no get. Please, na your hand I dey now. I need treatment for all my injuries."

"These injuries ... you got ..."

"In the cell last night, Sir. The other people said I attacked their Imam, so they almost killed me. Na God save me."

"Hmmnn." the DPO looked from Emmanuel to Sgt Gofwan and back. He then straightened his back as he made his decision. He turned to Sgt Gofwan.

"Give him his things and release him. You can take down his home address, office, and phone number so we can reach him if needed. Let him go and take care of himself."

There was a spontaneous chorus of "thank you" from the people at the station.

*"Na gode sir, na gode sosai!"* —Thank you so much! Thank you so much! - Emmanuel said to the DPO with both hands clasped together in gratitude.

Sgt Gofwan brought out Emmanuel's clothes and the few personal effects that had been collected from him when he was brought in the previous day.

Emmanuel dressed as quickly as he could and

collected his watch, phone, wallet, and necklace. He put his phone in his pocket, but hesitated to put his wallet in his pocket.

"You can count your money and other items in the wallet." Sgt Gofwan said to him, realizing that Emmanuel was worried about whether his money was intact, but afraid of opening the wallet to count it in the presence of the policemen, in order not to be seen implying that they would steal his money.

"Ah, no, Sir, I was just worried whether my ATM card fit don fall out with all  the wahala yesterday," he replied.

"Check and confirm if the card is still there then."

"Okay, Sir."

Emmanuel opened the wallet and, while checking his ATM card, surreptitiously counted his money. Satisfied that all was intact, he closed the wallet and put it in his pocket. The DPO looked on, smiling to himself.

"*Na gode sir.* I'm really grateful."

As he turned to leave, the DPO called him back. "Wait a minute!"

Emmanuel, who had been walking towards the outer door of the station, stopped, heart beating fast as he feared what could have gone wrong. He turned round to see the DPO walking towards him with one hand reaching towards his side.

Emmanuel's eyes followed his hand movement, and he saw that the DPO was both right-handed and that his sidearm was in a holster on his right hip. He took a nervous gulp as the DPO approached him. Instead of reaching for his pistol, he slipped his hand into his pocket and brought out a small wad of cash. Emmanuel's eyes widened in confusion as the DPO split the money into two and handed him one portion.

"*Ga wanan.*" – Here, take this.

Emmanuel hesitated, caught off guard by this show of generosity from the policeman.

"Take it. Buy food, treat yourself. Just take it." Emmanuel slowly took the cash.

"Thank you, sir. God bless you, Sir."

"It's okay, *Babu Matsala* (no problem). You can go, you hear?"

Emmanuel walked towards the gate of the police station and saw Zalla resting on a stone underneath a tree with his motorcycle parked nearby.

Emmanuel asked him what he was doing at the police station, and the man's response confused him.

*"Na zo in d'auke ka in kai ka gida ne."* - I came to pick you up and take you home.

Emmanuel didn't know if Zalla had waited for him outside the school to take him back home. If he did, he might have seen the police arrest him and take him away. That would explain how the man knew where he was. But why would he come to take him home, still leaving him perplexed? He appreciated the help, but the man's generosity was beginning to make Emmanuel suspicious.

Emmanuel asked him why he cared about what

happened to him that much that he was willing to go out of his way to ensure that Emmanuel was alright. He also asked him why he refused to take the money.

*"Ba'a gardama da nufin Allah, maigida."*

Again, the man said it was God's will. Emmanuel could never rationalise how people could commit such terrible atrocities in the name of God—from al-Qaeda to the Taliban, ISIS, and Boko Haram. He wasn't interested in any conversation relating to religion, as the clerics use it to brainwash their followers.

Despite this, he couldn't help but be grateful for this man's actions. He didn't know what to make of it in its entirety, but he was sure it wouldn't last, and the man would soon get tired when the fuel or money ran out.

Emmanuel got on the bike as Zalla drove him to his house.

# CHAPTER EIGHT

After dropping Emmanuel off, Zalla turned his motorcycle around and headed home. In the past, he would never have felt such pity for a stranger, especially one who was neither Muslim nor Hausa. Emmanuel was Igbo, and this deeply troubled Zalla, leaving him concerned about where this foolish man's journey would ultimately lead him. Yes, he had become a fool. It wasn't something his brothers or friends would be proud of, but he didn't have to tell them.

It had been six years now since the death of *Shibarid*. Sometimes, he woke up from terrible dreams where he saw the man preaching to a crowd and then suddenly disappearing. *Shibarid* had been his guiding light in those dark days. He had seen the struggles of a young man who was captured by very bad choices. Even now, he still felt the weight of what happened on that day.

Zalla turned a corner when he reached the intersection

that led to the market and the Government School on the right, and he took the path that led to where he stayed with his friend Lado. They had been childhood friends, and for a while, he had given Zalla a place to stay when he returned to Maiduguri.

Zalla zoomed past a couple of women who were trying to flag him down, but he wasn't interested in business today. He just wanted to get back home and rest from the activities of the last two days. His eyelids protested as he tried to keep them open. He had not shut them in a while, and the weight of his body had started becoming a burden due to the lack of sleep.

He knew Emmanuel thought it strange that he, Zalla, a Hausa-Muslim man, would go through all this trouble to help him. Emmanuel would even believe by now that he was a good man. If only he knew who he was and the atrocities he had committed in his life.

Zalla passed a couple of shops that were closing because the occupants had to go and pray. Was it past noon already? He had lost track of time.

He screeched to a halt before the group of shacks he now called home. Lado wouldn't be home by this time, which was a good thing. He needed to sleep without being disturbed.

He got off the bike and pushed it into the small space covered by rusted corrugated sheets. The shed served as both a makeshift veranda and a garage where he and Lado parked their motorcycles. He could smell Mama Sadiya's cooking from the nearby *buka* and was reminded of the fact that he had not eaten. He tried to decide between sleeping and eating, but his rumbling stomach made the decision easier. He removed the keys from his bike and pocketed them before heading towards the woman's kiosk.

He walked past some children who were trying to lift a girl out of the open sewage drain where she had fallen into, a common occurrence of life in the rural parts of northern Nigeria. For most people here, Zalla included, a lack of basic amenities was all they had ever known.

He grew up here in the nineties, and nothing much

had changed. It was true that they had more to eat then, but the quality of life in other areas had practically been the same. He would go outside with his siblings after a meal and play beside the dirty gutters. He had fallen in them several times himself.

Seeing the children brought back memories of his own childhood—a time of simplicity and innocence. Now, life was too complicated to describe, but he knew that he was more of a terrible man than a good man.

The girls washing dishes outside Mama Sadiya's *buka* greeted him as he made his way into the serving area and found an empty bench. There were three other people inside, and one of them had just finished eating and was on his way out. The other two had just been served. Zalla ordered his food, and a short while later, Sadiya served him.

Sadiya helped her mother in the shop when she wasn't in school. Unlike him, Sadiya had real prospects. She had concluded her secondary school education and was now enrolled in the city's polytechnic. Even though his heart beat faster when she was around him, he knew better than to express his feelings to her. He didn't deserve a girl like her, and he wasn't going to risk the shame of rejection. Still, he allowed his heart to wallow in unexpressed romance. It seemed even someone with a soul as dark as his was capable of feeling love.

He ate his meal with practiced patience as the other men rambled on about the attacks that had occurred in Maiduguri two days ago. They spoke about it with the emotional detachment of spectators who weren't affected. They argued about modes, techniques, and motives. Doctrine, morality, and the number of casualties were added to the mix as well.

As usual, he stayed away from these kinds of conversations and pretended not to be listening to them. They were wrong on many fronts, but he wasn't going to tell them that.

He paid for his meal and gave Sadiya one more glance before walking to his room, which was a few dozen paces away. The sound of a satisfied belly accompanied him all the way to his door.

He yawned as he stepped into the dimly lit room. He didn't need any light to know where he needed to lay his head. He just needed an extra step from the door. He took off his shirt and stretched, making a mental note to check on Emmanuel after he woke up.

He didn't feel the lump that was on the bed until he tried to lie down. He was perplexed at first because the door had been locked from the outside, and he didn't see Lado's bike parked. He went to the door and lifted the curtain to allow more light into the room. It still wasn't enough, so he opened the single window in the room, and that was when he saw it properly—Lado's body sprawled on the bed with his throat slit.

****

At home, Emmanuel stripped off his soiled clothes and threw them in a pile in a corner of his room. He grabbed a towel and a bucket, got water from the drum at the back of the house, and went to his bathroom. He was in such pain that he spilled some of the water on the linoleum floor covering as he brought the bucket back into the house.

He examined himself in the mirror, trying to decide how severely injured he was. His face was badly bruised, and there was a cut over one eye. That would likely need a stitch.

There was a throbbing pain in his right side, his arms, and his hands from trying to protect his face and head during the beating. He tried to twist his head to look at his back in the mirror, but the pain in his neck became too intense and he gave up. Whenever he moved suddenly, he felt a sharp pain in his left side, and he was worried that he might have a cracked rib or two.

He knew that he could not bathe himself properly due to the pain of his injuries, so he had to settle for a hybrid bath, washing only the parts of his body that he could reach without an excessive amount of pain. He ended up washing his face, his torso, and his thighs. However, he could not properly wash his back or his feet.

He dried himself with a towel, pulled on a short-sleeved button-down shirt and pants, and walked to the pharmacy on the next street. It was barely more than a dispensary, as there was no actual pharmacist, just a guy who sold drugs and could do extremely basic first aid.

After getting what treatment he could, he left with assorted painkillers and ointments to be taken and applied as prescribed.

Since he had not eaten since early the previous day, he stopped by a roadside seller of food and bought enough food for lunch and dinner, knowing he had no cooked food at home and that he may not get back to a normal life anytime soon.

After eating, he washed the dishes and sat down in a pensive mood, thinking about his next move. He opened his phone and read the message from Aisha again. As he read the message repeatedly, his mood started to change.

He was overcome with sadness at his daughter's plight, wondering what she must have felt while sending the message.

His frustration at the military's response only deepened the ache, compounded by the helplessness of being unable to do anything for her.

It was the job of the government and the military to secure the lives and property of the citizens.

He could not understand how such atrocities were allowed to continue.

"No way!" he said out loud, getting up with a fresh resolve to go and confront the military again and get them to do their damn jobs!

****

Emmanuel arrived at the school, went through the reduced security checkpoints, and walked briskly up to the most senior officer he could find.

"Good day, sir!" he said, rather brusquely.

"Yes? Identify yourself!" came the equally curt reply.

Emmanuel looked as if he wanted to continue his belligerence, but on seeing the hard, square jaw of the officer and the set of his shoulders, he decided against it. Adopting a more conciliatory tone, he brought out his ID card and handed it to the officer.

"My name is Emmanuel Nweze, a staff member of the Ministry of Transport." The officer looked at the card and handed it back.

"My daughter Aisha was one of the students kidnapped from this school a few days ago."

The soldier relaxed and looked at him with pity mixed with a touch of resignation. Emmanuel continued.

"I was here yesterday with Captain Isyaka, and I showed him the text message that my daughter sent to me as they were being taken into the bush by the kidnappers, but he said there was nothing they could do. Is there any other information now, please?"

As he spoke, he looked around at the scores of other parents just sitting or standing around in different states of grief and hopelessness. A woman was lying to one side with a small bag for a pillow, and it looked like she had cried till there was no strength left in her.

Another woman knelt beside her, speaking softly, trying to coax her to get up and eat something. She pleaded with gentle words, her voice trembling with pity, but every entreaty fell on deaf ears. The woman on the ground only turned her face away, lips pressed tight, as if food or comfort were meaningless in the shadow of her grief. Her silence spoke louder than any wail, and her refusal to be comforted left those around her helpless, watching sorrow consume her.

"Let me see the message," the senior officer demanded. Emmanuel handed him his phone with the message open.

The officer, in a series of moves reminiscent of Captain Isyaka, quickly scrolled through the message and handed the phone back to Emmanuel.

"Nothing new here. In any case, the information is dated."

"But there must be something that you can do? You are the Army!" Emmanuel had started getting worked up again. He just could not fathom the reluctance of the soldiers to do anything concrete instead of standing around with their guns at the school.

"Look here, we have our chain of command, and right now, our orders are to maintain a security corridor at this school and other priority locations." The officer retorted, beginning to get irritated at being questioned by Emmanuel, who was a civilian.

Under normal circumstances, Emmanuel would have given any soldiers he came across a very wide berth because of their disdain for civilians. However, Emmanuel was in a not-so-normal situation. If anything, he was in the most unnatural situation a father can find himself in. So, he reacted to the officer in a manner borne out of his anger, frustration, and total helplessness.

"You are to remain here while my daughter is held by those animals in the bush," Emmanuel responded with anger and visible disdain.

"You have guns. You have planes. You have armoured tanks. And you stay here while the terrorists are out there?! How on earth does that make any sense?"

As he spoke, his voice had been rising until he was now shouting.

"My friend, who do you think you are? If it weren't for the fact that your daughter was abducted, I would have had my men throw you out now. How dare you address an officer like that? Do you know who I am?"

"I don't bloody care!" Emmanuel screamed at him, shaking in anger, fists clenched, stopping just short of laying hands on him.

"Oh, so now you want to fight me? You want to assault an officer of the Nigerian Army?"

The demeanour of the officer and his men had clearly changed towards him, and at any moment, things might escalate to the point where he would be manhandled by the soldiers, some of whom were already walking towards him.

Emmanuel was past caring. His daughter was being held by a gang of murderous animals who raped and killed without an ounce of humanity, and these people just stood around day in day out doing nothing and just offering inanities! No, he had had enough, and he was not going to just stand here and let these people continue to take his life and that of his daughter for granted.

In a fit of unbridled anger, he rushed forward, but had barely taken one step when the ground beneath his feet suddenly shifted, and the people and the buildings were suddenly upside down. Before his mind could catch up with his body and understand what was happening around him, he had come crashing down violently.

As he lay on the hard, dry, dusty ground with the wind knocked out of him and trying to come to grips with reality, the soldier who had tackled him from behind was now standing above him, with his rifle in his hands, waiting for Emmanuel to make his next move.

As the initial shock cleared, Emmanuel realized exactly how powerless he was. All he wanted was for someone, anyone, to make real, concerted efforts to find his abducted daughter, and here were the people who had the power to do something about it using that power against him instead. He wasn't their enemy, just a defenceless victim, an ordinary civilian.

Overwhelmed by a crushing feeling of shame, Emmanuel started sobbing. Low moans of emotional and physical pain grew in intensity until he was bawling his eyes out. As his cries filled the air, the officer motioned his men to move back and leave him alone.

"AH GOD, WHY?" Emmanuel cried. "WHY? WHY? WHY? AH, GOD!"

As he cried, Emmanuel started to bang his forehead against the hard earth, raising the concern of the soldiers and the other bystanders, including the grieving parents. One of the soldiers moved to stop him from harming himself, but in a desperate move, Emmanuel got on his knees, grabbed the barrel of the soldier's rifle, and pulled it against his head, screaming, "Kill me, please just kill me. I can't bear this anymore!" and he started to wrestle with the soldier for the gun.

Emmanuel felt a sharp pain on the back of his head; it was quick and precise. Then the earth shifted, and the light from the sun blurred into darkness as he passed out.

****

Emmanuel slowly came to. How long had it been—one hour, two? He wasn't sure. He tried to sit up, but the world tilted and blurred around him, forcing him to steady himself with shallow breaths. He held on, willing his strength to return. Only then did he realize his hands were bound tightly behind his back; the ropes bit into his skin as he struggled.

He tried again to rise, but a sharp pain shot through his body, forcing him back down. A sob escaped his lips, followed by a heavy heave as he fought against despair. His thoughts went unwillingly to his daughter—his little girl. What were they doing to her now? What must she be enduring? His poor daughter… The weight of not knowing pressed against his chest until it broke him, and another sob tore its way out of his mouth. After some moments, he forced himself to breathe through the tears, the silence around him only amplifying the torment in his mind. Finally, after a bit of struggle, he managed to sit up and call out for help.

One of the soldiers looked to the commanding officer for instructions, and he nodded.

The soldier walked over to where he was and unbound Emmanuel's hands and helped him to his feet.

"Mr. Nweze, that was a very foolish thing to do." The officer said. Emmanuel nodded but remained silent.

"Is this how you want your daughter to remember you? What would she gain if you died? When soldiers die, their death has meaning in that they fight for the country. What do you fight for?"

Emmanuel couldn't reply. His eyes were downcast, and his tears started to flow again.

"Are you really willing to die like this? Or are you able to live and fight for her? You see, dying is easy."

The officer removed the magazine from his gun and ejected one bullet. He extended an open palm towards Emmanuel, showing him the single bullet.

"Just one bullet to the head or the heart and it's over." Emmanuel's gaze was fixed on the bullet.

"And then six feet deep. No more pain and grief. But what then? What happens to your daughter when she returns?"

Emmanuel looked up with tear-filled eyes and sniffed amidst the stirring of renewed hope.

"Dying takes away your responsibility. But it does not wipe away your obligation to those who depend on you. Do you have a wife?"

Emmanuel shook his head in response to the officer's question.

"Any other family members? Anyone you can be with during this period?" Again, Emmanuel shook his head.

The officer paused for a few moments before

continuing.

"Mr Nweze, you need to take some time off and allow us to do our work. There is nothing you can do here. Please, go home. I can have my men drive you anywhere you want to go."

 Emmanuel nodded in resignation. "Thank you…" he said to the officer.

He looked around one last time and then started walking slowly out of the compound, accompanied by a soldier. They got into a vehicle and drove off, with Emmanuel giving him directions.

As they left, Emmanuel stole one last glance at the school and the memories flooded him once more.

****

The truck dropped him off in front of a large, imposing compound with the gate and high walls covered in Arabic inscriptions. There was a group of *Almajiri* children seated outside with sticks and bowls, waiting hopefully for a meal from the home of their benefactor.

Emmanuel stood outside the gate for a few minutes as if contemplating whether to go in or not. Finally, he made up his mind, hunched his shoulders, and approached the pedestrian entrance at one side of the gate and started to knock. Before his knuckles hit the metal the third time, the door was flung open, and an antagonistic mallam stood there and barked at him.

*"Wanene wannan? Kar ka ɓalle mana ƙofa mana."*

Emmanuel identified himself and assured the man that he had no intention of breaking down the door. That didn't seem to faze the man even a bit. He just kept on with his sour mood.

Emmanuel told him he was the husband of Zainab, Alhaji Attahiru Mansur's daughter. This did not get the reaction he hoped for, and the man continued to stare at Emmanuel without moving from the opening.

He told the man he needed to see Alhaji urgently because Zainab's daughter had been kidnapped.

This finally got a reaction from the man.

He motioned to Emmanuel to wait, went back inside the compound, and closed the gate behind him. As his footsteps receded, Emmanuel sat down on the floor outside the gate in the sweltering sun, trying to shield his face from the windswept dust, and reminisced about the last time he came to this compound. It wasn't a blissful experience.

"*Nyamiri!*" — Igbo scum! The voice of the guard jerked him out of his reverie back to the present and the reality of his current predicament.

He was not sure what to expect from Zainab's family. In fact, he expected a cold reception at best. Better a cold reception than a bloody one, he thought to himself as he stepped into the compound.

He was confronted by the all-too-familiar imposing view of the interior of the large compound, beautiful landscaping, numerous buildings, and a fleet of cars parked to one side. A lot had changed since the last time he was here. As he took in the view of the garden, he looked towards the main building, and his gaze fell upon a group of well-dressed men standing in front of the main door.

Emmanuel glanced back at the pedestrian gate, which had been shut and bolted by the guard, summoned up his courage, and walked towards the main building and the group of men, unsure of the proper greeting for the moment.

"*Ina yini, Alhaji.*" Emmanuel finally said, addressing the oldest man in the group as he prostrated on the ground in a show of respect. The group of men seemed surprised that Emmanuel could speak Hausa.

"*Tashe tsaye, don Allah,*"— Stand up, please, for God's sake—they said, urging him not to prostrate before them. Emmanuel took that as a sign that the ice was beginning to thaw and stood up hesitantly.

On a closer look, Emmanuel realized that the man he had addressed was too young to be Alhaji Attahiru Mansur, his wife's father, but he maintained his respectful posture nonetheless and continued the interaction.

He nodded courteously at the other men, some of

whom were still glaring at him, and thanked them for seeing him.

Maintaining his physical distance from the group, he continued.   He told them how his daughter was kidnapped by the insurgents who attacked her school and how he had tried everything within his power to ensure he got her back, but had failed. The men continued to simply stand and look at him with no change in their demeanour, no reaction. In confusion, he repeated himself, and his narrative took a higher tone this time around.

*"Kar ka zo ka yi ihu a nan!"* One of the younger men retorted harshly at Emmanuel's nerve to raise his voice. The man took a step forward and continued, *"Kai mahaukaci ne?"*

Emmanuel ignored the "mad man" label he was tagged with. He had readied himself beforehand for the insults he was likely going to receive here.

*"Kwantar da hankalinka,"* The older man said, restraining the others and urging them to calm down.

"Who do you think you are, coming here and talking anyhow? And so what if she was kidnapped? What does that have to do with us? We do not know any Zainab. If your daughter were kidnapped, go and find her. You think you are very wise, and we are fools, ba?"

Apparently, the older one also had an issue with Emmanuel.

"Haba, Sir, I did not mean any disrespect," Emmanuel responded, quickly kneeling. "I just need to see Alhaji to ask for his help, please!"

"And what do you expect Alhaji to do for you?" came the sarcastic response.

"Haba, sir! Alhaji is a very powerful man, very influential in this country. Just a phone call from him to the Army Commander, and they would rush into the bush to find his granddaughter..."

At this, the belligerent young man rushed forward suddenly and struck Emmanuel across the face with a vicious backhand slap.

"*Shege banza*!" He screamed, eyes bulging in rage.

The slap took Emmanuel by surprise and sent him to the ground butt-first. He recovered quickly and rose to his feet, seething, his hands clenched into fists.

"You want to die today, ba!?" the young man who had assaulted him responded while pulling a dagger from his belt.

On seeing the dagger and realizing that he was outnumbered, Emmanuel stepped back and tried to de-escalate the situation.

"Please, I don't want any trouble."

"Then get out of here now!" screamed the young man. Emmanuel looked to the others for some kind of assistance or intervention, but only met blank or angry faces.

"I said leave here now!" the young man shouted again, this time pushing Emmanuel in the chest towards the gate with his left hand while holding the dagger with his right.

At this point, Emmanuel had come to the realization that he was not going to get any help from Alhaji and his family.

So, he turned and started to walk towards the gate. The belligerent young man followed him and hurried him on. On getting to the gate, the gateman joined in pushing Emmanuel out of the compound.

Emmanuel picked himself up, dusted his clothes, and walked away in a state of absolute dejection.

# PART TWO:

# JUNE 1998

# CHAPTER NINE

The streets of Maiduguri were busy as usual, people bustling about for their daily bread. Potiskum Road was especially busy as students of the Ramat State Polytechnic hurried to and from classes.

Emmanuel and his friends left the newspaper stand at the entrance of the school and walked into the premises. They were as excited as little boys who were about to receive new toys. It was football. And anywhere there was football, there was Emmanuel, General, and Abubakar.

The city of Maiduguri was agog with excitement about the upcoming 1998 FIFA World Cup, and Emmanuel and his friends were talking about the group fixtures. He was confident that the Super Eagles of Nigeria would perform very well, even far beyond their historic run at the previous World Cup tournaments. He was also looking forward to seeing Brazil's Ronaldo shine again on the world stage, but Abubakar and General didn't think the South Americans were taking this one.

"Who would stop Ronaldo, eh?" Emmanuel spoke as they navigated their way through the blocks of lecture halls and towards the school's shopping area.

Ramat Polytechnic had little to offer in terms of entertainment, but the boys had different ways of making up for that. They could cross the street and take *fura da nono* —a local drink made of fermented milk and millet balls —walk to the field to watch football games between different districts, or gather in one of the houses in town that had a big television to watch football. Fun was everywhere; one had to know where to look.

"Have you seen Zidane play? Have you!?" General retorted, shaking his head in disbelief.

"General, I go with Italy winning this one. They have a formidable team." Abubakar said, looking at the General. As if to solidify his point, he turned towards Emmanuel and added, "It is true, Manny. Ronaldo is a great player, but one player cannot win the trophy.

It is teamwork that counts here."

Emmanuel laughed, checked the location, and motioned to the others to follow him. He was hungry, and he knew where they needed to go.

"Forget all that teamwork talk. Ronaldo on his own is already unstoppable, period. And then Brazil is also a formidable team."

They continued to banter as they approached the woman selling hot buns and *zobo*. Emmanuel ordered the drinks for them, paid with a crisp twenty Naira note, and she gave them the drinks tied in the ubiquitous small transparent polyethene bags.

They found a sitting space on some concrete slabs in the shade of some trees.

The drinks were cold were a welcome relief from the dry heat that ravaged Maiduguri. They gulped one pack of zobo after another—finally permitting an interruption to their football banter—as the sweat on each of their heads found its way to their shirts.

"What time is Mr Adaku coming for his lectures again?" General asked.

"The class rep said that he won't be coming today because his wife was … I think sick or something like that," Abubakar replied. "But he'll be coming tomorrow, and we'll have the practicals when he comes."

Abubakar didn't have much in common with Emmanuel or General. But looking back, they had all come a long way since their first encounter. The two had befriended him because he was very studious, and they needed him to help improve their grades. Most of the students were Muslims, and they did not typically want any close friendships with non-muslims. It was during this process that they discovered he loved football and had great prospects after school. This strengthened their friendship.

"I'll have to go and pray now," Abubakar said as the sound of prayers was heard from the mosque on the campus.

The other two nodded in agreement as he left them and headed for the mosque to join the other Muslim students.

"Manny… there is a fellowship in the chapel this evening," General said to Emmanuel in hopes of finally convincing his friend to come with him.

Emmanuel mumbled a few words in response, indicating refusal. He wondered why his friend continued to try to persuade him to join the Christian community in school. He had ceased being religious for some years now, and General knew this all too well, but his friend kept asking. Emmanuel changed the topic.

"Please, if you meet with Abubakar later, collect my assignment from him and use it to check for the outline. Don't copy my work o, I mean it. Simply use it as a guide."

General nodded. Even though Emmanuel knew his cautionary words wouldn't have the effect he desired and that his friend would copy him verbatim for the most part, he couldn't help but allow him to take it.

He'd have to be much more assertive one of these days. General would turn out worse if he didn't do anything about it.

"Okay, Manny. I'll need to go home now. I'll catch up with you later in the day."

"Okay, General. Stay safe. And please don't forget to come along with the assignment."

"I won't. Thanks for the *zobo*."

With that, General walked away and left Emmanuel seated alone on the concrete slab, wondering where to go next. He didn't want to go back home. Normally, he would have gone to his boss at the workshop, Baban Aliyu, to see if there were any jobs he could take off his hands, but he didn't feel like it today. So, he decided to go to the market in town to use the money he had to buy parts for the project he was working on. He collected his ten Naira change from the zobo seller and headed out.

****

Zainab had left home without the knowledge of her father, the renowned Alhaji Attahiru Mansur. Almost everyone in town knew who he was. His reputation preceded him. Today, she didn't want Garba, the driver, or Bilyaminu, the housekeeper, to accompany her as she navigated through the market, so she had asked them to stay with the car.

It was a very busy day. The shops on either side of the market were full, and mobile hawkers and stationary vendors thronged the walkways, forcing people to shove and push and step on each other's toes. Market regulars expertly maneuvered their way by spotting slight openings between moving people and jostling to get to their various destinations, all under the unrelenting afternoon sun. The stalls were brimming with all manner of produce, their vibrant colours and smells filling the afternoon air.

*"Ga doya mai arha, Hajiya,"* A hawker called to Zainab, carefully turning all sides of the yams for potential customers to see. Every trader claimed their wares were cheap, but Zainab ignored the man. That wasn't

what she came to buy today.

She came to get fruits for the special fruit drink she liked to make and share with her father's *amarya*. Radiya was Alhaji Attahiru's fourth wife, but she was just a few years older than Zainab. Unlike in most polygamous families, where the first wife and her children treated the new wives and their children with disdain, her mother, who was the first wife, had encouraged her and her brothers, Zayyad, Junaid, and Sai'd, to treat the other women and their children with warmth and mutual respect.

Zainab had long suspected that her mother had been influenced by her uncle's teachings. Mallam Ashiru's moderate doctrine and interpretation of the faith had been described as 'soft' by a lot of people. Even her father, his younger brother, had described it as 'too tolerant.' She didn't know what to make of the man's teachings, but she loved the concern for others his words espoused.

Radiya had cautioned Zainab not to go out whenever she liked, but she ignored her stepmother's pleas that day and left the house regardless. After all, her father wasn't in town, and none of her brothers gave two thoughts about the things she did. They just went about their businesses.

Zainab navigated through the different sections of the market from memory. She loved the hustle and bustle of the market but hated physical contact with people, so she moved in such a way that avoided any collision. She hung a left at the grains section, a path that led to the fruit section of the market.

She finally made it to the fruit section and Halilu's store. He never lacked fresh fruits, and unlike his companions, he never sold bad fruits to make a quick profit.

*"Ina kwana, Hajiya Zainab,"* - Good day, Hajiya Zainab - he greeted happily on seeing her.

She responded to his greeting and asked for the fruits she wanted. He was also the only one in the market who knew about strawberries. The other store owners had been perplexed when she had asked them for strawberries a few months ago. They had just shaken their heads and offered her an alternative. One even gave her a sack of peaches. Funny and disheartening.

It wasn't until she had given up and was about to leave the market that someone directed her to Halilu's stall. He seemed too intelligent to be selling fruits for a living. He knew what strawberries were, but apologized for not having them at the time. He explained that they did not stock it due to low demand. He then offered to get it for her if she could return in a week's time. True to his word, exactly one week later, he had fresh, juicy strawberries waiting for her, and he didn't charge her an exorbitant sum for the 'foreign delivery' like other traders would have done. Ever since that day, she had become a regular at Halilu's stall.

Today, she asked for the fruits she needed to make her smoothie, and Halilu carefully packed them into one of his special brown paper sacks.

After paying him and leaving a generous tip, she thanked him before heading toward the vegetable section of the market.

She had only gone a short distance before reaching a point where the path was blocked by a thronging mass of people jostling and shoving to get through the narrow space. Zainab had no intention of allowing herself to be manhandled by the sweating crowd, so she stood by the side and waited for the crowd to thin out.

She smiled ruefully as the irony of her situation hit her. She had insisted that she was an expert in the market, yet she could not go through the market as Garba or Bilyaminu would have done, shoving, pulling and pushing through the crowd to create a pathway for her but she had insisted they remain with the car and not come into the market with her and now she was on her own.

Zainab laughed aloud at her predicament, and that was when she saw him from the corner of her eye, staring at her.

****

Emmanuel had been standing for a while, looking at the girl holding the brown paper bag. He didn't think he would ever see her again. At least, not this soon. The last time he saw her was several weeks ago in the market. She and her bodyguard? He wasn't sure. But the man with her had literally shielded her from everyone, including Emmanuel, as he led her through the market.

She had been trying to get strawberries and wasn't making headway. He had tried to tell her where to get them, but her bodyguard wouldn't let anyone near her, so Emmanuel waited for the perfect opportunity— when the bodyguard wasn't looking his way—and directed her to Halilu's shop.

As he watched her, he doubted she would remember him. He looked around to see if he would see her bodyguard nearby, but he couldn't see him or anyone who looked like security. She just stood there like a girl lost in the market with no idea where to go next.

He decided this was his moment to go talk to her before her bodyguard reappeared. It was at that moment that he saw the man sneaking up to her, with obvious ill intent, as he looked around furtively and then started moving his hand towards her bag.

The thief used the noise and constant movement of people to mask his own movement as he wrapped his fingers firmly around the strap of her bag.

Emmanuel was too far away to intervene, and he realised that shouting would do no good because of the noise level in the market. However, Emmanuel quickly looked around and realised there was only one route the thief would have to take after he had snatched the bag, and so he quickly made his way to block the thief's egress.

He arrived just in time to witness the thief violently snatch the lady's bag, pulling so hard that she lost her balance and fell, her head striking the ground with a small thump, before he spun on his heels and bolted down the street. Just as he had predicted, the man came rushing straight in his direction. Planting his feet firmly, he threw himself at the thief, tackling him with full force and dragging him to the ground in a rough struggle. They rolled in the dust for a moment before he managed to pin the thief down. Realizing he was cornered and had no chance of escape, the thief finally released his grip on the bag, shoved himself free, and scrambled to his feet before taking off in another direction, empty-handed.

The moment the market crowd witnessed the incident, shouts rang out, and several men broke into a chase. Feet pounded against the dusty ground as voices urged them on, and within moments they caught up to the thief and dragged him back.

Emmanuel turned towards the direction of the lady, and he saw that she was on the ground. She had fallen over, and the fruits she bought were scattered on the ground. Emmanuel rushed to her side and knelt behind her. She was on her left side, slightly woozy from her fall. As he gingerly put his left hand under her head to help her up, she turned around, and her hijab came loose. They came face to face with their eyes just two feet from each other.

Time seemed to stop. The sounds of the market and

the ruckus around the thief seemed to fade into silence. Emmanuel could only see the beauty of her eyes, the bridge of her nose, the line of her mouth with her lips slightly parted, and the sound of his heartbeat thumping in his ears. They stayed locked in that position, frozen in the chaos, transfixed for what seemed like minutes, though it could not have been more than a few seconds. Then the spell broke. A sudden roar erupted around them as the crowd found its voice, screaming for blood. Shouts rose from every corner, raw with anger:

"KILL HIM!"

"BARAWO!" — Thief!

"THIEF!"

The air shook with the fury of dozens of voices, a mob surging with rage, demanding justice right there in the dust of the market. Maiduguri was not a place where thieves caught in the market were taken for a formal trial, and Emmanuel knew that the man's chances of survival were next to nil.

He turned his attention back to the lady, helped her to her feet, and handed her bag to her. As he did, their hands touched, and she smiled at him. He felt his heart constrict with an intensity of feelings he never knew existed. He quickly released the bag to her and stepped away. Without taking her eyes off him, she fixed her hijab.

One of the market women helped her clean her gold-embroidered *jellabiya* while Emmanuel gathered up the fruits and put them back in the sack.

She thanked him profusely, looking at him again with eyes that couldn't hide the tumult in her heart. Emmanuel maintained her gaze as he responded. He knew she felt it too.

"Don't worry. I promise I'll be fine," she kept insisting as he reached out to steady her.

"I'm not worried, Hajiya. I just want to help."

"Please, don't call me Hajiya."

"Okay. So, what should I call you?"

She hesitated and then spoke. "My name is Yusrah."

Emmanuel had a feeling she lied about her name, but said nothing. "Okay, Yusrah. My name is Emmanuel."

If she responded weirdly to his name, he didn't notice. Most girls with her background might have flinched at the mention of his name. It was the kind of incident that he was accustomed to.

He was Igbo and a Christian. He wasn't devout, but most of them didn't know that or simply didn't care. His name was enough for them to immediately shut down and start treating him like garbage.

After much persuasion, she agreed to let him walk her out of the market. He could see her discomfort throughout as they walked, but he caught her stealing sideways glances at him.

"Your Hausa is very good," she said to him after he greeted some folks and spoke to some others along the way.

"I suppose so. I was born here, in Maiduguri."

"Oh, I see. Still, your Hausa is good for an Igbo person."

Emmanuel almost bumped into a group of women as the shock from Yusrah's words got him lost for a moment. How did she realize he was Igbo? He didn't have an Igbo accent even when he spoke in English. "How do you know that I'm Igbo?" he asked her.

"I thought it was obvious. Your complexion and some of your mannerisms. You're a strange sort of Igbo, though."

"Wow. You also don't speak like a Hausa lady."

"Because I'm not really Hausa. I'm Kanuri. I know most people can't tell the difference, especially southerners. My mother is Hausa, though, and…"

She stopped herself mid-sentence as if she had just realised she was talking too much about herself to a total stranger. She didn't say another word till they got outside the market, and she led him to a 504 Peugeot parked at the side of the road. The driver perked up when he saw her, came down, and relieved Emmanuel of the things he had helped Yusrah carry. The man put the bags in the trunk and opened the door for Yusrah. She stood with Emmanuel.

"I want to thank you, Emmanuel, for all you did for me today. I'm very grateful for your help."

"It's alright. I did it with all my heart."

*I did it with all my heart.* That wasn't the Manny his friends would have expected. The Manny they knew didn't get flustered talking to a woman, but here he was trying so hard to keep his composure.

The initial shyness in Yusrah's face had disappeared, and she was looking at him with a smile.

"Do you remember me? I was the one who told you where to… the other day you were in the market with your bodyguard… I was the—"

"I remember you, Emmanuel. I didn't at first, but it came to me eventually when you started greeting shop owners. I knew I had seen you before, but I couldn't place where or when."

The driver was beginning to get fidgety.

"So…?" Emmanuel ignored him, putting his hands in his pockets.

"So, what, Mr Emmanuel?" He could see she was teasing him. She knew what he was up to, probably what he was thinking, too. Damn! She had him down to rights.

"You think I can see you again?"

"Why would you want to see me again, if I may ask?"

"To get to know you, perhaps. Is it a bad idea?"

"I don't know, Mr Emmanuel. Is it?"

Now she was out right toying with him, and he had no comeback for her. This was embarrassing. But somehow, he was comforted by a strange realization that she didn't intend this conversation to be a show of mockery but a light jibe between two strangers who weren't sure if they were still strangers. He hoped he was right, though.

"I'll have to go now, Mr Emmanuel."

"Okay, Yusrah. Take care of yourself."

Emmanuel stood and watched as she got into the car. He waited till the car was out of sight before heading back into the market. He hadn't bought the parts he came for yet. As he walked, he heard a car honking behind him. He turned round to see her car coming back. As the car pulled alongside, she slipped him a scribbled note through the open window.

*We can meet at Halilu's shop on Tuesday at 11 am. I hope that time works well for you. And I'm sorry, my name isn't Yusra, it's Zainab.*

*Have a good day, my hero.*

The last line sent Emmanuel into barely suppressed euphoria. She called him her hero. If this wasn't the start of something memorable, Emmanuel didn't know what else it was.

# CHAPTER TEN

Zainab went home full of excitement. Yet mingled with that joy was a new, unfamiliar weight of fear and sadness pressing on her heart. Excitement because she had met a man who, in a single afternoon, had made her feel noticed, cherished, and somehow different from the girl she had always been. Fear because the obstacles standing before them—ethnic differences sharpened by prejudice, religious divides that cut deeper than either of them could bridge—felt like walls too high to climb. And sadness, quiet but certain, because she already sensed that whatever happiness she was tasting now would come at a cost, that these tender feelings blooming in her heart carried with them the shadow of pain and inevitable heartache.

Zainab tried to ignore the fact that he was Igbo and a Christian and rather focused on the flood of warm emotions she felt when she thought of him. She felt guilty for lying to him about her name at first. What if that had put him off? Zainab bit her lips at the thought of him not wanting to see her again.

"What are you thinking about like this?" Radiya, her stepmother, asked, holding a pack of cereal. Zainab jumped at the sound of the woman's voice. When did she enter the kitchen? Zainab wondered as she watched the woman pour some cereal into a bowl.

"Nothing …" Zainab responded without lifting her head to turn towards Radiya. She turned back to the fruits and closed her eyes, praying to Allah to stop her stepmother from probing further. The woman had the quick mind of a detective!

"Is it Halilu that is making you so distracted?"

"Halilu? No!" Zainab snapped.

She tried to suppress the tone of disdain that had accompanied her words. Why would Halilu even be in Radiya's mind? He was just a fruit vendor, and she wasn't attracted to him in that manner. *In what manner?* The question caught her off guard.

And how did Radiya know about Halilu in the first place? As far as she could remember, she had never gone to his stand with her stepmother. But the woman had a way of finding out about things, down to the smallest details. She had probably probed and gotten her information from either the driver or the housekeeper. Garba and Bilyaminu weren't the most trustworthy individuals. For someone of her stepmother's status and intelligence, getting information from them would have been a piece of cake.

Zainab's eyes met Radiya's. The woman pursed her lips and watched her with a quizzical look. Then she grabbed some sugar from a cabinet.

"Zee, I know it's a man that's causing this."

Radiya continued. "Look at the way your eyes are shining. You have been acting confused, and you didn't even notice when I entered the kitchen. I wonder why you're hesitant to share his identity with me. I don't hide things from you."

Radiya did not hide her disappointment. Zainab knew that the woman wanted her to relate to her as she would with her own mother, and she tried to do that as often as possible, but not today.

"Radiya, there is nothing to worry about," Zainab said, turning on the kitchen tap and washing the fruits, in hopes that Radiya would give up on the topic.

"How is business?" She asked, changing the subject.

"*Haba Zee, haka za ki bar ni?*" — Come on Zee, is this how you'll leave me? — "I just want you to be free around me. Share your issues and concerns with me." Radiya dropped her bowl and held Zainab by the waist.

Every time Radiya wanted to appear endearing, which didn't feel different from her being manipulative, she would switch to speaking in Hausa. And if that wasn't enough, she would go further to wrap the syllables she spoke with in delicateness. It bothered Zainab, but she had never figured out how to evade that tactic. It was a struggle for her. A struggle for love and space.

"Okay. I'll tell you when I'm ready," she said.

Radiya was the only one in the house she could feel safe talking to. She often wondered how a lady so intelligent and exposed ended up marrying a man old enough to be her father. What was more troubling was that Radiya had never seemed disappointed or uncomfortable with the arrangement. The woman flourished in her marriage with Alhaji Attahiru and didn't see it as something a young woman should be ashamed of. Zainab was glad she had such a good relationship with her stepmother, unlike some children in other polygamous families.

The first few weeks were problematic, but after the first few months with her, Zainab found that it was quite easy to settle in with Radiya once she gave her a chance. Her stepmother didn't fit the stereotype of new wives in her culture.

Rather than being arrogant, she was mysterious. Rather than being imposing, she was inquisitive. Her intelligence compensated for her weird traits.

"Was it in the market? That's where you met him, right?" A teasing smile appeared on Radiya's face. The woman just wouldn't give up.

"Why all these questions?"

"I care about your happiness, Zee."

"Well, if you're wondering whether I met a rich Alhaji whose first three children are older than me, then no. So, I guess you shouldn't be worried."

Radiya laughed heartily. But Zainab didn't. She felt guilty for reminding Radiya that she had married her old father instead of someone younger. But she was up against a wall, trying to deflect, and this was all she could come up with right now. She was precise with her words. It was petty, but she enjoyed getting to Radiya some of the time. Especially in times like this, when she was trying to get the woman to keep quiet and leave her alone.

And contrary to what she expected, her stepmother laughed.

"You're trying to throw me off the scent. It won't work. My eyes are on you, *yarinya*." She said that last part while using two of her fingers to point to her eyes and then at Zainab.

"I have nothing to hide, " Zainab caught herself saying. Why did she have to say that? It wasn't like she was trying to get Radiya to believe her. She shouldn't care what her stepmother thought, should she? Besides, she still wasn't sure about what she felt for Emmanuel.

"Only people who have something to hide say that."

She smiled at Zainab as she spoke, allowing the effect of her words to linger before adding milk to her cereal. Radiya was good at playing with people's emotions, especially Zainab's.

"So ... tell me what—"

"I said I will tell you when I'm ready!"

Zainab had lost patience and sliced through the watermelon to the point of cutting her thumb. She dropped the knife and held her blood-stained hand.

"*Auzubillah!*" She said in between gritted teeth.

Radiya dropped the bowl, and in a second, she was holding Zainab's hand. She dragged her to the dining table and made her sit down.

"Let me get the first aid box!" She rested Zainab's

hand on the table and hurried to the kitchen cabinet.

"All this because of a man." Radiya giggled as she returned with the box.

She was really having fun with the situation. Zainab was now annoyed, especially with herself. How could she have lost control to the point of cutting her finger? She hated the thought of having to nurse the wound. She hated seeing raw flesh. And Radiya was making things more difficult for her. Who laughs at the sight of blood?

Radiya soaked some cotton wool in methylated spirit and got to work on Zainab's hand.

"But really, Zainab. Tell me why you were so lost in thought when I entered the kitchen. I can't remember ever seeing you so lost that you didn't even notice I was here with you. Who is he?"

Zainab lifted her head and looked at Radiya in disbelief. There was no point trying to convince her to forget about it.

"Can I trust you?" She asked, hoping that this trick would work.

Radiya didn't reply, but the disappointment in her face could not be mistaken.

"All right, then," she said, wrapping the dressed wound with a plaster.

"You can talk to me about him when you are ready. But please talk to me. There are things that you would need me to help you with on this journey of yours, lover girl." Radiya touched her cheeks, giving her a warm smile before she grabbed the first aid box and walked towards the kitchen cabinets.

She had every right to make friends with whom she wanted, regardless of what others might think about it. Right? She closed her eyes and rubbed the plaster on her wounded finger, remembering tragic stories of people who were ostracised by her people for associating with the likes of Emmanuel.

It was a dangerous path to tread, but it was just a harmless crush. It wasn't like she was going to marry him. The thought brought a sudden rush of warmth to her face, though, and she smiled to herself as she fought back the sinful thoughts that swarmed her mind. She was the maverick of her family. Her cousins saw her as the model of feminine individuality they secretly craved but were unable to voice publicly. But it was one thing to be outspoken about politics, business, and social norms. Having a personal friend like Emmanuel was a whole other thing altogether, and she knew that her family would never approve. She had won their hearts with her studies and chaste character, and it would be foolish to risk her father's wrath by fraternising with Emmanuel, but the way he looked at her made her giddy with excitement.

Her father had warned her and her siblings not to associate with people like Emmanuel, even as mere friends. According to him, it was better for two people with the same beliefs to walk together, to avoid a lot of disagreement. But everything felt different with Emmanuel; the way he talked, the look in his eyes when he looked at her, his physique, the way he walked, so fit, handsome, and brave. Zainab felt light-headed just thinking about him.

Zainab's thoughts shifted to her mother. She certainly would not approve of Zainab's impure thoughts. A young woman shouldn't think of a man in that manner. But Zainab knew that there was a lot of hypocrisy in those words. Her aunts flaunted these same words to their daughters, but she knew their secret conversations. And she didn't think of anything impure in the right sense. She was only reacting to something attractive. And she was sure that it was normal with ladies, but she didn't dare tell her mother that. Because when her mother said something, it was final. Maybe that was the reason why it was easier to talk to Radiya.

It wasn't like she was sinning against Allah, right? Or were these *Shaidan's* thoughts disguised as hers? Did she need to make prayers to cleanse herself of these evil thoughts?

She sighed. Maybe she needed to talk to Radiya about it.

She admitted her shortcomings as a sinful mortal. It didn't feel right, at least from her mother's perspective, to feel this way towards a man. A man who didn't even believe in the greatness of Allah. But she still felt drawn towards Emmanuel. She pushed back the chair and took long strides to the living room to find Radiya before she changed her mind.

She saw Radiya engrossed in a show on the TV. She felt it would be disrespectful to interrupt her, so she turned to walk away, but before she moved, Radiya called her.

She turned back and gave her a nervous smile. "I didn't want to interrupt your programme," she said.

"Oh! No, dear, come, come. *Ki zo mu yi tadi!*" — Come, let's chat! — Radiya sounded excited.

How did she even know that Zainab wanted to talk about Emmanuel? Before she could think too much, Radiya walked towards her and dragged her to the couch with her.

"Tell me." She waited.

Zainab smiled to herself. At least there was still a fire of youth burning in Radiya.

"Okay. Okay." She lifted her hands.

"I met someone at the market…"

"I knew it! I knew I was right!" Radiya squealed.

Zainab laughed at her reaction, and it gave her the confidence to tell her all that had happened.

She told Radiya about her first encounter with Emmanuel and how he had led her to Halilu's shop; how he had rescued her from a thief, and how he patiently protected her in the market until she was ready to go home.

"He must be a wonderful person." Radiya smiled and rested her chin on her palm. "Tell me more. What does he look like? Is he educated? What's his name? Tribe?" She asked.

"*Ki tsaya mana!*" — Wait, come on! — Zainab said, urging her to stop while laughing at her eagerness.

"He is not Hausa, though." Zainab bit her lips and

waited for Radiya to rebuke her, but nothing happened. The woman just kept waiting for her to say more. That gave her hope.

"Radiya, you must promise me you wouldn't tell anyone about this." Zainab held Radiya's hands with a plea in her eyes.

"I won't, dear. *Kin san ni sosai ai.*" — You know me very well —Radiya assured her.

Zainab inhaled deeply, and the words came out with an exhale.

"His name is Emmanuel, and he is Igbo by tribe."

Radiya's face changed immediately. The excitement that once sat there gave way to fear and despair.

"You are joking, right?" She asked.

Zainab could feel the hotness in her throat at the sound of Radiya's voice. All the hope she had came crashing down. She bit her lips again, waiting for Radiya to say something. Radiya sighed and held her hand more tightly.

"Zainab. I know how you feel. It is obvious that you really like this boy, but I'm afraid for you."

"What do you mean?" Zainab asked. She knew what Radiya wanted to warn her about, but maybe she needed to hear it again. Maybe it could snap her out of a dream that was impossible in real life.

"Your father would never support your relationship with an Igbo man, Zainab. Worst of all, your mother. You know this!"

Zainab knew all too well what Radiya was talking about. She had heard her parents talk against a muslim marrying someone like Emmanuel. They even called it an abomination.

What was she thinking, trying to hope for something that she knew she couldn't have?

"It's obvious that you like him, but I think you should stop yourself before you get used to him and begin to find it more difficult. Love grows, and this one is obviously beautiful, but it would just frustrate you, dear."

Radiya's eyes were apologetic. And Zainab understood. It was pointless to hope to be with a man who could never be approved by her family.

"Okay. I understand. Thank you," she said. Radiya hugged her and excused herself to go and settle the dispute they could hear rising from the voices of some of the workers outside the house. Zainab was left alone with her thoughts.

She felt her heart sink. She had looked forward to seeing Emmanuel again, but she wasn't sure anymore. She knew Radiya was right. It was better to kill the budding emotions coursing through her before things got more complicated.

But then again, it would be rude to ignore Emmanuel without giving him reasons why she changed her mind. Maybe she should meet him and tell him she wasn't interested in being friends anymore.

"No, Zainab. That would be stupid!" She held her forehead and rubbed it. Her head was throbbing with pain. But she still felt like she needed to give him a reason at least.

Zainab frowned at the thought, and it wasn't just her head that was aching. Her heart also. She lay down on the sofa and curled up. Maybe they could be friends, but she would have to make it clear that she wanted only friendship. She would be seeing him on Tuesday. Even though it was just a few days, Tuesday felt so far away, and she knew she was going to count the days. For now, she had just her thoughts to keep her company. She just wanted to think about him a little more. Her thoughts might be impure, but she wasn't hurting anyone, and Allah knew her weaknesses as a human, as a woman. Besides, nobody would get hurt. It was only in her mind, and she would make sure it stayed there.

She stayed a little while in a prone position on the sofa before finally getting up. She took the bowl of unfinished cereal her stepmother had left in the sitting room and headed toward the kitchen. Her stomach growled, and she laughed at how she starved herself because of a man, just like something Radiya would say.

The thought of that made her embarrassed.

But she was more embarrassed that she had confessed her feelings to Radiya. How would the woman talk to her without making her remember that she was thinking of doing something foolish? Zainab laughed at herself. She would meet Emmanuel on Tuesday and make everything right. She would relate to him in a way that would send a message of pure friendship. That's what she would do.

# CHAPTER ELEVEN

It was a hot day as usual, and Emmanuel was both excited and slightly anxious as he waited for Zainab. Quite nervous, he walked around the market wondering why she hadn't come yet. She had picked the date and time, and he was there on time, waiting.

He stopped pacing, not wanting to sweat. He walked over to a shop opposite the spot where her driver had parked his car the last time and sat on a bench in the shade.

As he waited, he read her words again:

*We can meet at Halilu's shop on Tuesday at 11 am. I hope that time works well for you. And I'm sorry, my name isn't Yusra, it's Zainab.*

*Have a good day, my hero.*

Emmanuel smiled to himself as he began to think of how things had turned out that day. It meant that she liked him. Of course, she liked him. Why else would she ask to meet him again? Emmanuel's smile broadened.

He looked down at himself and rubbed his crisp white shirt and black jeans, checking his appearance. Yes, all looked to be in order. He then checked the road again to see if he could see her car, but she had still not arrived.

He frowned and began to worry that he might not get to see Zainab, because he had been waiting for what felt like an hour since he arrived at the market, though he arrived thirty minutes early.

*"Yadda kake duba kan ka a madubi, Yarinyan nan ne ta ke sa ka kayi haka ko?"* - The way you look at yourself in the mirror, is it that girl making you do that?

Emmanuel turned to see the elderly shop owner giving him a teasing smile. Emmanuel chose to feign ignorance. He wasn't particularly thrilled at what the man was implying. He didn't want anyone prying into his personal affairs.

*"Ban san abin da ka ke magana ba, Mallam."* — I don't

know what you're talking about, Mallam. — He replied, turning away to face the road again.

"You don't know what I'm talking about, ba!? But I saw her with you at this same place the other day. You helped her carry her food to the car. *Ko ba haka ba?*" – Is that not so? - The man inquired.

Emmanuel felt embarrassed that he was so transparent to a total stranger. He thought of leaving, but then what if Zainab showed up? Deciding to stay and endure the man's sly looks, he told the man he was just relaxing from the heat and nothing more.

The man burst into laughter. Emmanuel's embarrassment began to turn to irritation. Why would the man not just let him be?

"And why exactly are you laughing if I may ask?" Emmanuel asked, his irritation now palpable.

"I'm just laughing at a young man who wants to involve himself in a journey he is not ready to embark on." The man laughed again.

A journey he was not ready to embark on? What was

the old man talking about? Emmanuel's irritation turned into confusion, and whatever the old man meant by that, he needed to get him to explain because he knew the man was referring to Zainab.

"What do you mean, Mallam?" He asked, glancing at the roadside again before moving closer.

"Oh! So, you want to talk now? *Kai! Matasa!*" — Oh, these youths! —The old man shook his head.

"Okay, I will tell you about your princess." The man came out of the shop and sat on the other bench across from the entrance of the shop.

The man was quiet for a while, as if he was gathering his thoughts and measuring his next set of words. Then, he spoke.

*"Za ka sa kan ka a cikin wahala in baka bar yarinyan nan ba."*

Emmanuel felt a mixture of pain and confusion. Why would the man tell him that he would be in trouble if he did not leave Zainab alone? His intentions for

Zainab were purely innocent, and knowing her religious and obviously wealthy family background, he wasn't going to try anything foolish.

"Why do you say so, Mallam?" He rubbed his sweaty forehead as he waited for the man to explain further.

The old man sighed. "You do not know her father? Alhaji Attahiru?" The man asked.

Emmanuel looked puzzled. Why was the man asking him about Zainab's father? He had just met her, and it was impossible to be associated with her father. Suppose anyone knew that, it should be the old man. But why was he asking?

"No, sir. I do not know him. Who is he?" Emmanuel asked.

"He is one of the most influential men in Maiduguri, and his brother, Mallam Ashiru Mansur, is a well-respected scholar in this society."

Emmanuel had heard about Mallam Ashiru and that he had a brother, but he didn't know him, and he certainly didn't know that he was Zainab's father.

He wanted to ask the man why he was telling him about Zainab's father, but he was running out of patience. He looked towards the road again, wondering if he should take a stroll and check some other parts of the market. Maybe he should go to Halilu's shop to check if she was there.

As if sensing his impatience, the man leaned forward, and his expression became sombre.

"If it is love you seek with that girl, forget it. Her father would never permit someone like you near his daughter, let alone give her hand to you in marriage."

Emmanuel knew that what the man said was the truth, but he had convinced himself that all he wanted with Zainab was friendship, not a romantic relationship, and hence, there was no risk of falling afoul of her family's wishes. He just saw a lady that he was attracted to and was trying to get closer to. The old man's words brought him back down to earth.

"*Alhaji Attahiru baya wasa da ya'yan shi.*" — Alhaji

Attahiru does not joke with his children. — The old man warned, then he rose and walked into the shop.

Emmanuel thanked him and remained there for a while, thinking about what the man had said concerning Alhaji Attahiru's care for his children. After a few minutes of waiting, he decided to go to Halilu's shop. That was the only way he would know if she was in the market. Maybe they had parked their car at a different spot.

As he stepped into the sun, the heat pounced on him, and it was accompanied by a slight headache. Emmanuel held his head and sighed. Maiduguri was a hot place, but this day was worse.

Emmanuel took out his handkerchief and wiped his face and neck. He walked to the entrance of the market to check again if he would see Zainab. When he didn't, he walked into the market.

He didn't even take note of the crowd of people that haggled prices, the sellers that tried to get people to buy their foodstuffs, and the buyers who searched for what they wanted, while they moved from one stand to another. All he knew was that he was going to Halilu's shop, and he knew the route like the back of his hand. His mind was preoccupied with what the old man had just told him. He pushed through the crowd of people, checking his pockets from time to time to make sure that his wallet and other belongings were safe. The market was filled with hustlers, and pickpockets seemed to be the greatest threat. Ever since the incident with the thief who attacked Zainab, he had been more cautious in the market.

On getting to Halilu's shop, he stopped, frowning. Zainab wasn't there. Why didn't she come? She had promised to be here in the market by eleven, and he was sure it was past one already.

He moved to the shop and saw Halilu shooing away the flies that tried to perch on his fruits.

*"Sannu da zuwa, oga. Mainene za'a baka? Akwai abarba da mangoro da lemu. Ga gwanda ma."* — Welcome, sir. What should I get you? There's pineapple, mango, and orange. There's also pawpaw. — Halilu advertised the fruits to him.

For a second, Emmanuel forgot that he had gone there to inquire about Zainab. He marvelled at the man's warmth to him. It was obvious that it was one of the reasons why he had so many repeat customers. And the man was neat, too. That made him want to buy some fruit. At least it wouldn't look too strange that he had only gone there to ask about a girl.

"*Nagode, Mallam Halilu.*" He smiled. Then he looked at the fruits and pointed at some oranges that were arranged in a tray.

"How much is this one?" He asked.

"Oh, that one is two Naira."

"Okay, let me have them."

Emmanuel paid for the fruits, and the seller put his oranges in a black polyethene bag.

"*Nagode.*" He said. Then he scratched his head sheepishly and asked, "Mallam, have you seen Zainab today? The slim, dark-skinned lady who comes to buy fruits from you."

Halilu seemed lost. His eyes grew distant as Emmanuel spoke. He was obviously wondering who exactly it was that Emmanuel was talking about.

"Alhaji Attahiru's daughter," Emmanuel added.

"Oh! Zainab?" Halilu's face brightened.

"Yes, sir."

"I haven't. She was supposed to come today, but she didn't. I don't know why." Halilu said, his face creased by concern.

"Okay then. *Sai anjima.*" Emmanuel thanked the man and turned around.

He felt deeply disappointed. He had been so sure she would come and had already imagined what it would feel like to see her again. There was so much he wanted to talk to her about. He wanted to hear her talk about her dreams and aspirations, her likes and dislikes. He wanted to know what she thought about the country, but the most important thing he wanted to know was what she thought of him.

He strolled slowly and hardly greeted the few sellers who knew him.

When he got to the main entrance of the market and still didn't see her, his disappointment deepened. Why would Zainab tell him to come if she wasn't going to show up?

He turned towards the road to his home and began to walk, but he stopped at the sound of his name. When he turned around, she stood there, smiling at him.

****

Zainab was upset, and she kept glancing at the big clock in the living room. It was already 12:30 pm, and Garba was not yet back.

He had complained that the car needed some repairs. Zainab had tried to convince him that they could manage it for the day, but he refused. He was experienced with his work, and she knew that if he insisted that the car was in bad shape, it really was.

She stood up from time to time, pacing around the room. She was worried that Emmanuel might have waited for her and left.

If she wasn't already so attracted to him, she would have forgotten about the whole thing and taken a nap, but she couldn't. All she could think of was him. It was scary that she was so restless. Wasn't she supposed to be thinking of how she would make it clear that they could only be friends?

*"Kai! Ina Garba ne?"* - Hey, where is Garba!? - She asked the empty room and stood up again.

She would make sure he regretted wasting her time. Zainab hissed in anger; her brows creased in anger. She hated how she had to wait for a driver to take her to the market. That was her parents' standing instruction, and she had no choice but to go with it, but she hated it anyway. She felt so impatient and angry because she thought that she was going to miss her time with Emmanuel. He would not be happy. And he might not trust her again. That thought alone made her want to cry.

She began to pace back and forth again when Radiya

walked into the room.

Zainab walked back to the couch and sat on it, hiding her shaky hands beneath her brown hijab. Radiya walked towards her and stood beside her, looking down.

"Zainab, I thought you were supposed to go to the market? I didn't see any food in the kitchen. What happened?" She asked.

Zainab didn't look at her. "It's Garba. He left the house since morning with the excuse that the car had some issues. And he's not back yet!"

Zainab could hear the anger in her voice. She tried to suppress the anger before Radiya would figure out why she was so angry, since she was the only one who knew about her and Emmanuel.

"Okay. Don't worry... I will just go and che…"

"No! Don't! I will go."

Zainab said the words before she could stop herself. There was no going back. She knew that she would have to explain why she reacted that way.

"What is wrong, Zainab? You seem upset. Are you hungry?" Radiya asked.

Zainab didn't know what to say at first, but the words just came out of her mouth. "Yes. I mean, no. I just don't want you to stress yourself. Besides, you are free to leave the house anytime you want, but not me. You know that this is an opportunity for me."

"Oh!" Radiya laughed. "Now I see why you have been impatient. Don't worry. Garba will soon be here. Let me go do some chores."

Radiya began to walk back to the kitchen, but she stopped.

"Wait. I hope it's not because of that boy? *Ba na gaya miki ba? Ki fita hanyan yaron nan."* — Didn't I tell you? Stay away from that boy. — Radiya warned.

"Oh no, Radiya. It's not him. I wasn't even thinking about him." Zainab marvelled at her lies and made a mental note to check her emotions and utterances, especially around Radiya.

Just then, there was a knock on the door, and Garba walked in, his apology written all over his face.

"Ha, Garba! Where have you been? Do you want us all to starve?" Zainab barked, ignoring Radiya's suspicious look.

"*Ki yi hakuri. Makaniki ne ya bata mun lokaci.*" — Forgive me. The mechanic delayed me.

Zainab hugged Radiya and walked out with Garba in tow.

On their way to the market, Zainab prayed with all her heart that Emmanuel would still be there. She knew that it was unfair of her since she had already wasted over two hours of his time. He had every right to be angry with her, and if he was, she would apologize sincerely.

When Garba entered the road to the main entrance of the market, Zainab could see him in the distance walking away. She could tell that he was angry from the way his shoulders were hunched.

She was overwhelmed with relief and hope. *"Kara gudu, Garba."* — Drive faster, Garba. — She tapped Garba's hand, trying not to sound too desperate.

She could see how Garba looked at her from the corner of his eye and how a small smile was playing on his lips. But she didn't care. If there was anyone who covered for her in her household other than Radiya, it was him. So, she knew that her secret was safe with him.

When Garba parked the car, she quickly got out and hurried towards Emmanuel, then she called his name. When he turned around, she couldn't help but smile. He looked so sad. It wasn't that she was happy because he looked sad; rather, she was happy that she had that effect on him. It was good to know that she wasn't the only one dying to see the other.

Emmanuel's face changed immediately when he saw her. He walked towards her with a bright smile that made her feel butterflies in her stomach. She even struggled to stand. Her breath ceased from the fear of having to hear what he had to say about her lack of punctuality and nervousness from thinking too much about what to say to him. All of a sudden, she was light-headed.

"I thought you would not come!" Emmanuel said as he stood in front of her. He looked so happy to see her, and for some seconds, she kept her gaze on him, not wanting to take her eyes off him. Then she remembered her resolve to keep their relationship platonic and looked away, trying to avoid contact.

"I'm so sorry I kept you waiting. We had some challenges with the car, and I couldn't come—"

"It's okay, Zainab. I understand. I'm just so happy that my waiting wasn't in vain." Emmanuel said with a smile that accentuated his jaw.

If Zainab wasn't attracted to him before, she was now. His smile melted her insides.

She folded her sweaty hands behind her back and looked around. She still needed to get some fruits from Halilu and then some other foodstuffs before going back home, but she would surely spare Emmanuel some minutes.

"Can you escort me into the market, please? I need to buy some things."

"Of course, my lady. Anything for you." Emmanuel waved his hand, motioning for her to take the lead.

Zainab smiled and walked ahead of him. And walking had never been as difficult as it felt that day. Whenever they stopped to buy foodstuffs, sellers would beckon to them to come and look at their wares in hopes that they might make several purchases. Most of them looked at them with foreboding expressions, probably wondering what she was doing walking so jovially alongside Emmanuel. And occasionally, her eyes would meet his eyes. Zainab loved the feeling, and she wished that it would never end.

When they got to Halilu's shop, the man smiled at them. He had already gotten used to Zainab, and she could see that he was getting used to Emmanuel, too.

In the process of choosing her fruits, she touched a bunch of bananas, and it shifted, pushing some oranges to the ground.

"Let me get them," Emmanuel said before she could even think of pursuing the rolling fruits.

"That boy is such a gentleman. I've watched him for some time now. Is he your friend?" Halilu asked.

Zainab felt her cheeks flush. "Yes, he is. We just got to know each other."

"Okay, dear. That's good." Halilu said. "But you know that he is neither a Muslim nor a northerner. How has your father allowed you to be his friend? Even seeing that he is an Igbo boy?"

Zainab froze. Of course, she knew that he was not a Muslim. And even though she had just found out that he wasn't committed to Christianity either, it was still the same thing. Her family would not welcome a friend who wasn't a Muslim, especially if it was a man. An Igbo man.

"My father would certainly not be comfortable with him around me, but even you can testify that he is a good person, yes?" Zainab asked.

Halilu smiled at her and continued to arrange his fruits.

"Just don't get both of you into trouble." He spoke without looking at her.

When Emmanuel came back with the fruits, she gave Halilu a pointed look, and he nodded in acknowledgement of her unspoken request. He was not going to say a word about their brief conversation.

Emmanuel arranged the fruits while Zainab paid for hers and told Halilu to give Emmanuel the fruits of his choice with the change. After protesting unsuccessfully, Emmanuel agreed to collect them, even if just to please Zainab. It gave her joy to be able to do it. She could see that he looked embarrassed, but she wasn't the type of person to try to make him feel embarrassed, and she wished she could get him to understand that he was safe with her.

As they walked out of the market, her heart sank. They

were about to part ways, but she didn't want him to go. The time they had just spent together buying food felt too short, way too short.

"So…," She started, but petered out.

"I guess you have to leave now." Emmanuel completed the sentence for her, looking forlorn.

"Yeah…," She didn't know what else to say. She had it in mind to spend some extra minutes with him, but she wasn't going to ask. She didn't want to look desperate. She badly wanted him to stay, but she wasn't going to throw herself on him. So, her heart leapt when he asked.

"Will you spend some more time with me? Even if it's just thirty minutes. Please?"

The plea in Emmanuel's eyes was real. She didn't even know when she said yes. And in her mind, yes meant: Carry me wherever you want, I'm here for you, I want to be with you! But she simply said yes.

Emmanuel led her towards the bicycle repair shop

near the entrance of the market. He greeted the old man and led her to a bench beside the shop. They sat and talked and talked, about anything and everything.

And they laughed a lot. Her laughter sounded like music to him.

After spending over an hour with him, she summoned the strength to drag herself away from him and go home. And on her way home, she ignored the thought of the scolding that Radiya would give her. All that was in her head was the man she was falling in love with.

After that day, they met more often and soon, they were head over heels in love with each other.

# CHAPTER TWELVE

Emmanuel had not seen Zainab for over two weeks now, and he was losing his mind. He knew she felt the same way about him that he did about her, no doubt about that, but her culture, upbringing, and religion hindered her from expressing her feelings openly.

"Emmanuel, you and I know that this thing between us would never work. My father will never let me be with you." Zainab had said to him on the last Saturday they had been together.

She had refused to meet his family. And he didn't blame her. It was probably because she didn't want to start a relationship with him and then have to disappear. He knew she still struggled with the decision to be with him.

His mother had a small trading business in the city, but he hadn't introduced Zainab to her because Oluchi, his sister, had advised him not to. According to her, their mother would neither understand nor support him. Also, Alhaji Attahiru could easily make life difficult for them in Maiduguri. But at this point, all Emmanuel could think about was Zainab and how she made him feel.

He was in the market running some errands for his mother when he noticed a familiar Peugeot 504 parked near the entrance to the market. He didn't even know when his legs had started moving towards the car. Maybe Zainab had come to the market to buy some foodstuffs. His heart was racing as he got to the car and looked through the open window.

The car was empty.

*"Kai! Mai ka ke nema a nan?"* — Hey! What are you looking for there? — Someone yelled from a nearby shop.

Emmanuel looked up and saw that it was Garba, Zainab's driver. He was accompanied by another man who Emmanuel assumed was Bilyaminu, Zainab's housekeeper.

*"Matsa daga motar nan!"* — Get away from the car! — Bilyaminu said menacingly.

"He's a friend of Zainab," Garba answered him on recognising Emmanuel.

"*Ku yi hakuri dani.*" — Please forgive me. — Emmanuel begged. "I was only checking to see if Zainab…"

"Zainab is not here." Garba interrupted him.

Emmanuel looked at Garba for some seconds. Knowing that Garba saw himself as Zainab's protector, he carefully chose his words.

"Garba, I know you can help me talk to her. I just need to see her, please."

"*Me yasa zan taimake ku? Kun san irin matsalar da kuke jawowa?*" — Why should I help you? Do you know the amount of trouble you always cause? — "If Alhaji catches you, *wallahi* you will hate your life!"

Emmanuel stepped forward. "Please, Garba. If you have ever loved any woman, you would know how I feel. I beg of you to just help me get in touch with her. Please."

Bilyaminu stepped towards Emmanuel in anger, but Garba stopped him. Bilyaminu turned to Garba with a questioning look. Garba nodded to him, indicating it was okay and that he was going to handle the situation.

As Bilyaminu walked away, Garba grabbed Emmanuel by the arm and pulled him away.

"Zainab has been busy with school. But Emmanuel, you are looking for trouble! Alhaji will not spare you, fa." Garba warned.

"I know, but I can't stand not seeing her. Dan Allah, Garba, do me this favour. At least let me write a note to her." Emmanuel said, pleading.

Garba looked at him for some seconds, weighing the gravity of the decision he was about to take. Then he shook his head and opened the car. *"Yaron nan bai san Alhaji Attahiru ba."* - This boy does not know Alhaji Attahiru. - He said as he gave him a pen and some paper.

Emmanuel wrote down a simple note that contained

the most important words out of the many he wanted to say to Zainab. He thanked Garba for his help and went back to running his errands with a new spring in his step.

****

Zainab had been studying for hours, and she was exhausted. Her exams were due in a few weeks, and she hated being unprepared. She was one of those students who liked to study repeatedly to boost their confidence.

She drank the remaining juice from the glass beside her bed. She then decided to take a break from studying and stretch her legs for a bit.

When she stepped out of her room, she heard voices from the kitchen. Her mother and Radiya seemed to be having an animated but light-hearted conversation. She felt jealous that she wasn't there with them, but the jealousy was quickly replaced with endearment. Her mother was hardly ever around. She was usually going around Maiduguri and other states on business with her husband or looking to expand her own numerous business interests.

"I see you are both catching up from where you left off," Zainab said with a broad smile. Though she was preparing for an exam, she tried to seize every moment she had with her mother, because she could be gone on another business trip tomorrow. Zainab sometimes wondered how she had the strength.

"*Ina yinin ku. Sannu da aiki.*" — Good afternoon. Well done with your work. — Zainab greeted. She moved towards her mother, who had already opened her arms.

"*Yar auta ta.*"  - My youngest daughter. - Sadiya hugged Zainab.

Zainab took in her mother's smell. She had missed her. "How are you?" Her mother asked, releasing her.

"I'm fine, umma. I have missed you so much." Zainab hugged her again.

"So, I'm the one who is not fit for a hug, *ko*, Zainab?" Radiya said in mock anger at Zainab.

Zainab laughed and grabbed Radiya. "*Kin san ke*

*mutumiyata ce aii.*" - You know you're my person, right? - The three women laughed.

"So... what are you two up to?" She asked, craning her neck to investigate the pot on the stove.

"You just wait and see." Her mother replied and pushed her away. "Go and do something else. Go and watch something on TV."

Zainab tried to say something else, but thought better of it. She turned and walked out, leaving her mother and Radiya, who were giggling.

"May Allah be with us and keep us alive to see the great woman that my daughter would become!" She heard her mother say as she stepped out of the kitchen.

"*Amin!*" Radiya responded.

Zainab felt her heart skip. Thoughts of Emmanuel flooded her mind at her mother's words. Something she had struggled to suppress for the past two weeks.

She had intentionally avoided him because he was a major distraction to her. Radiya had warned her about the way she came home late anytime she went to the market. When it had gotten on her nerves, she had threatened to tell Sadiya about Emmanuel.

Zainab had pleaded with Radiya to spare her. She knew that her father would not only stop her from going to the market, but he would also look for Emmanuel wherever he was and have him severely dealt with. Zainab didn't want that.

But she couldn't deny the fact that she missed him terribly. Every day, she had to stop herself from thinking of how it felt to be with him. How he whispered sweet words to her and how his eyes brightened when he looked at her.

When Zainab entered the living room, she saw Bilyaminu cleaning the center table.

"*Ina yini*, Hajiya Zainab." He said, bowing his head slightly in respect as he greeted her. Zainab couldn't help but laugh softly at his politeness, the warmth in her smile easing the formality of the moment.

"This must be the tenth time you are cleaning this table

today, Bilyaminu. *Kai ka so wahala ne kawai.*" — You just like suffering. — She teased him.

Bilyaminu's shy smile made her laugh again. She watched the way he explained how much his work meant to him. When he was leaving the room, he turned around and walked back to her with a smile on his face.

"I almost forgot to give you this." He looked around to be sure they were alone in the room, then removed a piece of paper from his kaftan pocket and handed it over to her.

As if he knew what she was about to ask, he spoke in a low tone. "It is Emmanuel that gave me and Garba to give you," he said.

Zainab felt a mixture of relief and joy. She unfolded the paper and read it with shaky hands.

*Zainab, my love. I have missed you, and I have waited every day for you to show up, but you don't. Garba told me that you are preparing for your exams. I honestly wish you the best. But I want to ask you for a favor. Please meet me just this once. I will be at our usual spot on Tuesday morning waiting for you.*

Zainab read the letter repeatedly, pushing back the tears that welled up in her eyes and the swelling in her chest.

She missed him so much. Every day before going to sleep, she would think of him and wonder what he was up to. She would wonder if he missed her. But she had to avoid him if she wanted to focus and pass her exams, and if she wanted to avoid trouble with her family.

But she had gotten a new kind of strength after reading his words for what seemed like the fifth time. And she knew that she wanted to see him, too. Somehow, she felt like it would help her gain more sanity and stability. When had Emmanuel even gotten to that special place in her heart?

Zainab shook her head. She sighed and walked back to her room with the letter. She was going to see him in two days, but for the time being, she had to go back to her books.

****

Emmanuel looked down at himself and smoothed down his shirt. He waited at the entrance of the market and checked for Zainab's car from time to time.

After a few minutes, he saw the car coming, and he could feel his joy overpowering his sense of reason. He walked to the car and hugged Zainab as soon as she was out.

Zainab looked embarrassed. "Let's leave this place, please." She said and motioned for Emmanuel to join her in the car.

On their way out of the market, Zainab gripped his hand tightly and smiled at him. She didn't say anything, but Emmanuel could read every word her heart spoke.

She had arranged with Garba to take them to a quiet place on the outskirts of the city, and Emmanuel was thankful. It would save them from the possibility of being seen together and possibly incurring her father's wrath. Emmanuel cared about that, but he was more thankful because he could have her all to himself.

They finally settled for a shady spot near a small

stream. Zainab asked Garba to bring out the things she had put in the boot of the car. Emmanuel wondered what she was talking about, but his confusion was promptly cleared when Garba started by bringing out a big basket filled with different things. Emmanuel's heart skipped when he saw the things that were inside the basket. Drinks, snacks, sweets, bread, food. She had prepared a large picnic basket.

Zainab smiled at him and grabbed a mat from the boot. She was about to spread it when Emmanuel caught her by the hand.

"Allow me," he said.

She handed the mat over to him, and he chose a good spot and spread it. When he lifted his eyes, he saw her staring at him.

"What is wrong?"

"Nothing." He said. But the obvious thing about Emmanuel was how he didn't know how to pretend. He knew that it was pointless to hide things from Zainab because he was truly in love with her, so he decided to speak up.

"I didn't know that you had arranged for all of these, Zainab. You have spent so much, and I didn't even contribute anything to make this special. I really feel bad."

He tried to maintain eye contact with her, but he couldn't. What responsible man would be comfortable eating all these delicacies without contributing anything? Zainab walked to him and put her arms around his waist.

"Emmanuel. You should know that I'm not like other girls. I didn't do this to make you feel bad, my love. I just wanted us to have a good time." She looked up to him.

"Why didn't you tell me at least?" he asked, embarrassed.

"I just explained to you that—"

"I'm a man, Zainab. I should have provided something at least." Emmanuel said sharply, his embarrassment turning to anger as he turned away from

her.

Zainab was startled by his reaction. Her face immediately fell, and her eyes filled with tears as she stood there in confusion.

"I'm sorry. I thought I was being romantic, but I didn't know that it would upset you so much. I don't want us to fight, please!" She waited for a bit, and when he did not move, she started packing up.

Emmanuel didn't turn to look at her, but when he heard movement, he turned and saw that the basket was already half full. Her cheeks were stained with tears, and it broke his heart.

"Garba! Come over and help me take these things to the car." She said.

Emmanuel only then realized how much he had hurt her, and it made him angry with himself. What was he thinking? How could he be so ungrateful?

"Zainab, I'm sorry." He moved towards her and held her from behind. She struggled to free herself from his grip, but he didn't let her go. He buried his head in her neck and sighed.

"I'm really sorry, Zainab."

He turned her around and wiped her tears. *"Ki yi hakuri."* — Forgive me. — "I should have been grateful before telling you how I felt. I'm so sorry." He held her tight, winking at Garba, but the man was acting quite fidgety as he leaned on a nearby tree.

"My love." He held Zainab's chin and lifted her face. When she tilted her head up, their eyes locked, and they looked deeply into each other's eyes. Her anger melted away.

"I'm sorry too." She sighed. "I should have told you what I was planning. But I had no way of reaching you, and I didn't know you would be upset. I only wanted to make you happy." Zainab smiled shyly.

Emmanuel hugged her. "It's all right. Let's enjoy ourselves." He released her and dragged her towards the mat. They had barely started eating when Garba walked towards them.

"Zainab, Radiya *ta aike ni*." — Radiya sent me. — "She sent me on an urgent errand for Alhaji. We have to go now. I'm sorry." He pleaded.

Emmanuel turned to look at Zainab. They were just settling down to their first proper date, and Garba was about to take her away.

"You can't leave now. We just got here." He looked longingly at Zainab.

Both men waited for Zainab, whose eyes grew distant. After some time, she looked to Garba. "Go and run your errands. We will wait for you here. Come back and pick us when you are done."

"Ah! Zainab! *Ki na son Alhaji ya kore ni ko?*" — Ah! Zainab! Do you want Alhaji to fire me? — Garba panicked.

"Ah ah! I will tell my father that I insisted on going with you." She said.

"Zainab. Alhaji is—"

"Please, Garba. I promise you that she is safe with

me." Emmanuel pleaded.

Emmanuel could see the fear and caution in Garba's eyes. The man looked at him for what seemed like forever, then he reluctantly got into the car and drove off.

Emmanuel hugged Zainab and kissed her forehead. "Now I have you all to myself." He winked. He loved the way Zainab's face flushed when he touched her.

After they had finished their lunch, Emmanuel stood up and started walking away.

"Where are you going?" Zainab asked behind him.

"Catch me and see." He teased her and took off. Zainab sprang up and ran after him. He zigzagged between trees, staying just out of reach. She stopped after a while when she could not catch him, panting for breath.

"I can't go on. Come back!" She called, but he laughed and moved away and hid behind a big tree, waiting for her to find him.

"Emmanuel! Where are you?" She called as she searched for him, starting to get worried. When she got closer, he jumped out from his hiding place.

"BOO!" He started laughing when Zainab flinched, obviously startled. He grabbed her, and they both fell to the ground laughing.

"That was scary!" Zainab hit him on the chest as he held her close. After lying together for a short while, they got to their feet and walked deeper into the bush until they got to an open space that had a big tree beside the stream.

They stood by the tree and looked at the flowing stream. From the look on Zainab's face, he could tell that she loved the view.

"I love you, Zainab. And I want to keep loving you forever." Emmanuel leaned on the tree and drew her to him.

"I love you too, Emmanuel." She buried her head in his chest, and they stayed like that for a while. Emmanuel could feel raw emotions torturing him, and he wondered if Zainab felt the same way, too. When she lifted her head and he looked down at her, he could see it.

She pulled his face to hers and planted a kiss on his lips. She moved backwards to see if he was upset, but he grabbed her and covered her lips with his.

Pressing her body to his, she held onto him. After a while, he gently pulled back and looked into her eyes. "We shouldn't be doing this, Zainab. I don't want to hurt you."

"You are not hurting me. I love you. And I want you to love me also."

She then removed her hijab and spread it on the ground. She looked into his eyes as she unbuttoned his shirt and helped him take it off. His heartbeat raced as she took off her dress. She pulled him to her, encircling her body with his arms and guiding his hands to the clasp of her bra. As he undid her bra and took it off, she looked and smiled coyly as he saw her body in all its glory for the first time, and his eyes filled with desire. Her long, graceful neck tapered into smooth shoulders, the quiet strength of her posture softened by the gentle rise of her chest. Her breasts were full and round, stirring with the rhythm of her breath. The cool air, mingling with the rush of her own excitement, teased her nipples into firm peaks, a tender reminder of the heat simmering beneath her skin. Her flat stomach tapered down to the V of her pubic hair and flared into luscious hips and long legs, almost daring him to explore further.

She pulled him to the ground as he hurriedly took off the rest of his clothes. He lay beside her, stroking her face, then he leaned in and kissed her deeply. She moaned as he moved on top of her, his left arm sliding under her neck to cradle her head while his other hand pulled her even closer. His mouth trailed from her lips to her jaw, then lower, tasting the curve of her throat. She shivered, fingers tangling in his hair as his tongue teased the hollow of her collarbone. His hand skimmed down her side, lingering over the curve of her hip before sliding up again to cup the swell of her breast, his thumb circling until her breath caught. She writhed beneath him, her body aching with want, her every nerve alive beneath his touch.

Only then did she arch her back and open her thighs, wrapping her legs around his waist.

"Are you sure?" Emmanuel asked, pausing to be sure as he looked longingly into her eyes, barely able to control his throbbing desire.

In response, she reached down between her legs, held him lovingly, and guided him into her. He paused as he entered, waiting for her to adjust, her soft nod giving him the silent permission he craved. As he pressed closer, his lips found hers in a slow, lingering kiss, tongues brushing, tasting, and seeking reassurance. He moved no further until she let out a small, encouraging sigh, and then, sliding fully into her, their bodies locked in intimate pleasure, not wanting the feeling to end. As he began to move, she moaned and slowly gyrated her hips to match his movements.

He pressed against her, their bodies so close they

seemed to move as one, writhing and shifting together in rhythm, each touch igniting shivers through her. His hands traced her curves, exploring with care, sending sparks through her chest and stomach. She buried her face in his neck, inhaling his scent as her body trembled in response to every brush of his skin. Their hearts raced together, caught in the heady current of longing and desire, lost to the world outside, lost in the sensation of being intertwined. Every movement, every brush, drew them closer, until they were suspended in the shared, overwhelming intensity of the moment.

He moved faster and deeper, she wrapped her legs tighter around him, and buried her face in his neck to stop herself from screaming in pleasure until they both erupted in the flaming throes of ecstasy.

After lying for some time to catch their breath, Emmanuel sprang up and grabbed Zainab's hijab and dress. He handed it to her and helped her put it on, and he dressed himself hurriedly.

"Garba must not see us like this." He hugged her. She

was shivering. "I'm scared."

"Me too." He hugged her again, then he lifted her chin. "Whatever happens, we'll face it together."

He saw how her shoulders relaxed, and he felt relieved, too.

After Zainab left with Garba that day, he began to prepare his mind for what was coming. And he knew that it would be a tough one.

****

For over a month, Emmanuel did not hear from Zainab. He checked the market sometimes, and other times, he left notes for her with Halilu. Halilu had told him that he had given her the notes when she was at his shop to buy fruits, but Emmanuel doubted that, because he had not gotten a reply from her.

It made him worried, and he started having sleepless nights. He wondered what the problem was. Did she hate him for what they had done that day by the stream? Did Garba tell on her? Did she get into trouble with her family? Or was she just busy with her exams? He looked so worried that his sister had asked him if he was sick.

He decided that he would leave another note with Halilu at the market. He had completely fallen in love with her, and forgetting about her seemed impossible.

The next day, he went straight to Halilu's shop, hoping that he would hear different news. He suspected that Halilu knew the reason why Zainab was not replying to his messages, but he didn't ask, out of fear of offending the man.

He met Halilu, who was arranging his fruits as usual. The man whistled along with the music that played from his radio. When he saw Emmanuel, he laughed heartily.

"Emmanuel, Emmanuel! *Na san za ka zo yau.*" —I knew you would come today. — He laughed again.

Emmanuel didn't find the situation funny. He felt like he was searching for his soul.

"She did not give you any message for me?" He asked.

He was already feeling angry that she would abandon him that way.

"She left a note for you. And she said it's urgent." Halilu handed him the note and got back to work.

Emmanuel's heart skipped. He had not heard from her for weeks, and the only time she could talk to him was when something urgent came up. He didn't unfold the paper in the market. He needed a quiet place.

When he got home, he went straight to his room and unfolded the paper before sitting on his bed.

*I'M PREGNANT AND MY FATHER WANTS TO SEE YOU IMMEDIATELY.*

The words seemed to scream at him from the paper. Emmanuel read the words carefully, hoping he hadn't made a mistake the first time. When he was sure that he had read it correctly, his vision began to blur, and there was a ringing in his ears. The heat that he felt before had doubled, and soon, he found it hard to breathe.

Zainab was pregnant with his child. A sudden feeling of regret hit him. What had he done!? What was he thinking, going as far as sleeping with her? Her, Zainab, the daughter of one of the most powerful men in Maiduguri? He was an Igbo boy who could barely take care of himself. Terror gripped him. What would his father say? What was he going to do?

Emmanuel wrapped his arms around himself, started rocking back and forth on the bed in abject fear and confusion as the ringing in his ears continued unabated.

****

BANG! BANG!! BANG!!!

Someone was banging angrily at the door of their apartment. Emmanuel rushed out of the bedroom into the living room and towards the door hesitantly, knowing it could only be Alhaji Attahiru's men looking for him.

"Who is that!?" His mother responded angrily, getting up to confront the person who dared to assault her home in such a manner.

"Mama, please don't open the door," Emmanuel begged. Oluchi, his sister, stood by wringing her hands in dread as the banging continued. His mother turned to face him.

"Emma, what have you done? Who are they? And why are they looking for you? Answer me!"

Before he could answer, the door was forced open, and three men burst into the flat. On seeing Emmanuel, they rushed forward and grabbed him.

"You idiot! You had the guts to sleep with our sister. We will teach you a lesson you will never forget!" One shouted as he punched him in the face.

"*Mu kai shi wurin baba!*" — Let's take him to father! — One of them said.

They dragged Emmanuel out of the house, kicking and fighting, ignoring his mother and Oluchi, who begged to know what was going on. They pushed Emmanuel into their car and sped off to Alhaji

Attahiru's residence.

When they got to the compound, they dragged him out of the car and pushed him towards the entrance of the main house. Even in his situation, he could not help but be impressed at the opulence of the buildings, the numerous expensive cars in the compound, and even the landscaping. Everything reeked of wealth and power. He was brought back to reality by a swift kick to his back.

"*Sa'id, ka bar shi a nan.* He is not worthy to step foot in the house." The man who kicked him shouted angrily.

"Where is Zainab?" Another one shouted.

Emmanuel kept pleading with them, but they would not listen.

"Where's the fool?" Emmanuel turned to see a man in his sixties coming out of the main house. He was escorted by four women. The last woman dragged Zainab with her. They were all very angry.

Zainab was crying and begging the woman to forgive

her. That must be her mother, Emmanuel thought to himself. He was filled with shame. When he turned to his left, he saw Garba looking at him. The man's eyes were cold, but he didn't say anything.

"Please. I beg of you—"

"Zayyad! Junaid! Bring that fool here." Alhaji Attahiru ordered Zainab's brothers. They dragged him to where Alhaji Attahiru and his wives stood and pushed him to his knees.

Zainab's mother dragged her towards Emmanuel and stood. When he lifted his eyes to look at her, she slapped him.

"How dare you disgrace my family like this?" She started to kick him when Alhaji Attahiru stopped her.

"It's okay, Sadiya." The man stepped forward.

"I'm sorry. Please forgive me. *A yi mani hakuri don Allah.*" — Please forgive me, for God's sake. —Emmanuel pleaded.

"Sorry? For what you had already done?" Alhaji

Attahiru spoke. The anger in his voice was obvious.

"You are a fool without self-control, and what you and Zainab did is an abomination." He turned to Zainab, "I'm disappointed in you, Zainab."

Zainab just stood there crying and pleading.

"You will not produce an abomination in this house. You'd better be prepared because you are aborting this pregnancy. I will not have—"

"*Don Allah*, Baba. Have mercy!" Zainab joined Emmanuel on the ground to plead with her father.

"I will take responsibility for the child. Please don't kill my baby." Emmanuel begged.

"Shut up!" Sa'id shouted and kicked him again. Radiya stepped forward and looked at Alhaji.

"Alhaji, please have mercy. You would be putting Zainab's life in danger if you make this decision. Please." She begged.

Alhaji Attahiru looked at the young lovers for a long time, then he turned towards the door. "Get this fool out of my sight."

They dragged him out of the house and locked him out. Emmanuel banged and begged, but they didn't open the gate.

He sat there until it was dark. As night fell and he lost hope of them letting him back in, he slowly made his way home. His parents and sister were in the compound waiting for him. When he arrived, his mother screamed at the sight of him. He was covered in blood, and his whole body ached.

They dressed his wounds, all the while being berated by his irate father, after which he went to bed. But he couldn't sleep due to the pains from his numerous injuries and the shame and worry the unexpected turn of events meant for him and Zainab.

For the rest of the week, Emmanuel kept going to the house to beg, but the security guard would not let him in. He waited at the market to see if he would see Zainab, but he didn't. He tried to leave some messages for her with Halilu, but Halilu chased him away. The news had spread, and attitudes towards him had changed.

Emmanuel decided to go to Alhaji Attahiru's residence one last time. That day, he begged the security man to allow him to see Zainab, but the man swore that he wouldn't.

After some time, he stopped going. Once, he ran into Radiya at the market and begged her to tell him if Zainab was fine at least. After much pleading, she told him that they had allowed her to keep the baby, but Alhaji Attahiru had said that Emmanuel would never know the child.

It saddened Emmanuel, but he was glad that at least Zainab and the baby were fine. It was pointless to keep trying to see Zainab when he couldn't, so Emmanuel went to work with Baban Aliyu in his auto mechanic workshop while he awaited his clearance from the polytechnic. There, he focused on repairing cars while he waited for a job. At least if he showed Alhaji Attahiru that he could take care of Zainab and the baby, he might change his mind and allow him to see them.

Months passed, and Emmanuel kept hoping to see Zainab. He worked hard and gathered some money. He bought some gifts and baby materials in preparation to visit Alhaji Attahiru again. And when he had heard that Zainab had put to bed, he asked his father to accompany him to Alhaji Attahiru's house. Very reluctantly, his father agreed.

When they arrived, the security guard told them to go away. Emmanuel begged him, but he refused. In desperation, he pushed the man aside and forced his way into the compound.

As he ran towards the main house shouting her name, he came to an abrupt halt on seeing her. Zainab was sitting outside, under the awning of the carport. She held a child to her chest and encouraged the child to suck, while Radiya kept touching her face and calling her Aisha. They had named his baby Aisha.

He turned and began to move towards them when Garba stopped him.

"What do you think you are doing? Didn't we warn you not to come to this house again?"

Zainab quickly arranged her clothing, and she and Radiya stood to their feet and walked towards them.

"Zainab. I'm sorry." Emmanuel moved towards her. Garba tried to prevent him, but Radiya stopped him.

Emmanuel could see pain in Zainab's eyes. He didn't know how to begin to plead with her.

"I tried to keep in touch, but the security guard would not let me. I came—"

"As you can see, Emmanuel. Aisha and I are fine. My father had let me keep the baby, and he was the one who even named her Aisha. He named her after his mother."

Zainab sounded cold, and it broke his heart.

There was no way he would have abandoned her and his baby. He still loved her, and that love was extended to his baby. He stepped forward and took the baby from Aisha. When he looked at the baby, a flush of emotions overwhelmed him. Tears spilled down his cheeks.

"My child." He looked at Zainab, who was struggling to hold back her tears.

"Our child." He rocked the baby who stretched in his arms.

"I promise you, Zainab. I will love you and this baby forever. I will do my best to be there for you and her, and I will protect this baby forever."

He turned towards his father and tried to give him the child, but his father declined. Then he turned back to Zainab.

"I have come to take you and the baby with me."

"You must be joking!" Junaid, one of Zainab's brothers, had come out at this point and grabbed the baby from him.

Emmanuel's eyes widened in anger. He tried to collect the child back, but Junaid quickly moved back, and

Garba stepped between them and ordered him to leave. Emmanuel tried to push past, but when Garba stopped him, he punched Garba. As a fight broke out, Sa'id and Zayyad joined Garba and started beating him up. Zainab quickly took the baby, and she and Radiya ran inside the house.

His father walked out of the compound quietly, head bowed in shame.

# CHAPTER THIRTEEN

"What kind of stupid son are you?" Emmanuel's father, Chinwetalu, screamed at him, the veins in his neck bulging. "You have brought such disgrace to our family." He said through gritted teeth, hands clenched into fists at his sides.

They were in the sitting room of his father's apartment. Emmanuel knew that his father was angry with him, but the look on his father's face broke his heart. It was as if he detested him.

"Papa—"

"Don't Papa me!

"Papa, I'm sorry," Emmanuel begged. He hated to see his father angry. His father had worked hard to ensure his children were educated. By now, Emmanuel should either be earning money in a steady job or assisting in growing his father's business. Instead, he had only succeeded in bringing shame to the family.

He turned to Oluchi and his mother, Evelyn, pleading with his eyes, but they turned their faces away, not wanting to be caught in the crossfire.

He turned towards his father again and knelt. "Papa... I know that I have disappointed you. But please forgive me."

After a while, Chinwetalu looked down at him, and his look softened.

"Stand up." Chinwetalu helped Emmanuel up, but he held up his hand when Emmanuel tried to hug him. Emmanuel felt a sting of pain.

Chinwetalu walked away while Evelyn and Oluchi followed behind. Emmanuel stood alone in their modest living room.

It greatly upset him that his family was against him. The people who should have been by his side when he was facing the biggest challenge of his life. But he knew they were right to be angry. He had messed up in a major way. He hoped that they would eventually forgive him, especially when he'd bring Zainab and the baby to live with him. Emmanuel had already made up his mind that he would let things calm down, and then he would go back to seek Zainab's hand in marriage.

Unfortunately, his actions had done so much damage that it had strained his erstwhile great relationship with his father, and try as he might, after this incident, he was never able to redeem himself in the eyes of his father.

****

Sometime later, Emmanuel helped his mother carry some food items to her store. He stayed with her for a while, waiting for Oluchi to come before he would leave for Baban Aliyu's mechanic workshop.

"Oluchi is taking so much time, mama. Ah ah! *Mainene haka?*" —What's going on? — Emmanuel turned around and searched the street with his eyes.

Evelyn, his mother, chuckled.

"So, you think you know how to speak Hausa?" She asked.

"Ah ah! Mama. I've lived here all my life. Do you expect me not to?"

"No, oh. You are free to. After all, I love hearing your fake Hausa." They both laughed.

Emmanuel was still laughing when he caught sight of a distinguished-looking man getting out of a Mercedes-Benz salon car.

The man was dressed in a white kaftan, and he held his *Misbaha* prayer beads while he walked down the street.

The way people greeted him with respect made Emmanuel curious. He watched as the man walked gracefully, with a smile on his face.

"Who is that man, Mama?" Emmanuel tapped his mother.

"Oh! That is Mallam Ashiru. He is a teacher of Islam. He is Zainab's uncle! Yes. I remember now." Evelyn's eyes widened.

Emmanuel bit his lips. The man looked humble, but Emmanuel was sure that the man also hated him, so he hid himself when the man passed by their store.

His thoughts drifted to Zainab. He wondered if she now also hated him. As far as he knew, she hadn't done anything to make him think she still wanted to be with him. She confused him with the way she spoke to him the last time he was at her house. He hoped that it was because she feared her brothers, because it would break his heart if he found out that she really didn't want him anymore.

Whatever happened in the future, Emmanuel was sure of one thing: he would continue to visit Zainab's house until Alhaji Attahiru agreed to let him have her as his wife.

****

Taking care of the baby took so much from Zainab. The baby would either cry until Zainab was tired of petting her or she would refuse to eat. Sometimes Zainab would pretend she couldn't hear little Aisha crying.

*"Kai Aisha! Ki ci abinchin nan."* — Hey Aisha, eat this

food. — "I want to work oh!" Zainab scolded the crying baby and tried forcing her to eat.

*"Haba, Zainab! Ki na so ki kashe yarinyan nan ne?"* — Come on, Zainab! Do you want to kill the girl? — Radiya scolded.

Zainab turned to see Radiya by the door, smiling at her. Radiya walked into the room and took the baby.

"I thought I showed you how to handle her." Radiya sat on the couch and cradled the baby for a while, rocking her gently back and forth. After getting the baby to calm down and stop crying, she collected the feeding bottle and fed the baby gently.

Zainab watched with awe. She didn't know how Radiya was able to do the magic, but she didn't mind so much if she was able to finally have some peace of mind.

She grabbed a stool from a corner and sat beside them, watching as the baby's eyes closed gradually. When Radiya was done, Zainab picked up the baby and placed her gently on the bed.

Aisha was a beautiful baby, and Zainab loved her, but thinking about how she came into existence brought Zainab a kind of pain she hated.

"So… how are you?" Radiya asked.

"I'm fine." Zainab took a deep breath and gave Radiya a long look.

"I'm still in love with him, Radiya. What my father is asking me to do is impossible. I cannot move on. Emmanuel is the only man I have ever loved."

"But do you think that this is best for you and your baby?" Radiya was worried, and Aisha could understand that, but how would keeping the baby from her father be good for her?

"Would you rather have me bring my child up alone?" She asked.

Radiya stayed silent, obviously struggling within herself. The truth was that she barely had any say in the matter. That was for Zainab's mother to decide with Alhaji Attahiru.

"I just miss him." Zainab sighed and sat down. "Would Baba keep chasing him away every time he comes? He has as much right to the baby as I do."

"But do you want to be his wife? Do you want to spend the rest of your life with him?"

Zainab tried to imagine what being Emmanuel's wife would be like. She didn't want to struggle with winning the hearts of his family members or bending to their way of life. All her life, she had known the teachings of the Quran and the teachings of an Imam. How was she supposed to blend with a man who was Igbo by tribe and from a Christian family? Then it dawned on her. If she was able to love him that much when they were dating, she could do it again.

She knew she had been hard on him for months. And she knew that she could do something to change her father's mind, but she didn't know if she was even ready to be married.

"Zainab. I want the best for you." Radiya held her hands. "I know this is very difficult for you."

"Thank you, Radiya. You've been nothing but kind to me since all these problems started. May Allah bless you." Zainab couldn't hold back her tears as they hugged.

To Zainab, it was better to marry Emmanuel and have their child grow up in a healthy environment, because she didn't want the baby to grow up thinking she didn't have a father.

But she was scared. She hoped that the people of Gamboru would not make things worse for them by reminding them of how different they were or how odd it was for them to be together.

Alhaji Attahiru made that clear again the last time they talked. Zainab knew that her father loved her and wanted to protect her. But he just had to let her go away with Emmanuel. She had not said anything to him for a while, but she badly wanted to be with Emmanuel.

Radiya rubbed her back and turned to look at the beautiful and innocent baby. "I will be in my room if you need me."

Radiya left Zainab to the silence of the room and the baby's soft breathing.

****

Emmanuel was tired of trying. Months had passed, and he was still treated like a traitor in Alhaji Attahiru's house. All he wanted to do was see Zainab and the baby. Then they could talk about getting married later.

He had done something wrong, but was it right to keep punishing him this way? He needed to do something about it. While thinking, Emmanuel felt a hand on his shoulder. He turned to see that it was Evelyn, his mother, smiling pitifully at him.

"My son. It is not your fault that things are happening the way they are right now. Even though you made the wrong move first."

Emmanuel turned to his mother and glared at her. "Mama. Is this supposed to make me feel better?"

"Chief, I'm not trying to make you feel bad. I'm just telling you that you made a mistake, a very big one."

Emmanuel did not respond as he knew she was right. Evelyn kept quiet for some time. Then she sighed.

"You remember that man you saw at the market the other day? Mallam Ashiru? Alhaji Attahiru's brother?"

Emmanuel turned to his mother and gave her a questioning stare. "Yes, what about him?"

"I think that you should talk to him. Who knows? He might be able to help you."

"Hmmnn! Why didn't I think of that? I have nothing to lose at this point anyway." Emmanuel jumped up. He felt more energized than he had been for months.

"Biko, don't go and mess up, oh. Just make sure you can convince him with your words. Men like that are sensitive with words." Evelyn rose to her feet and walked away.

Emmanuel didn't even respond to her when she said goodnight. He just kept smiling. He finally had a possible solution to his problem.

The next day, Emmanuel set out to look for Mallam Ashiru. He dressed up in a brown kaftan and slippers, looking the part of the simple Northern man. When he stepped out into the street, people stared at him, surprised that he, an Igbo boy, could dress like a Hausa man. But he needed to look the part to easily gain access to Mallam Ashiru.

He got some information from Halilu on where to find Mallam Ashiru. According to Halilu, the man was either addressing the students in his Islamic school or he was at his farm, overseeing his employees.

Emmanuel was worried about visiting the school, so he went to the farm instead. It was a bit difficult to reach the farm as it was at the outskirts of the city. But when he got there, he was awed by the work that Mallam Ashiru had done. The man had not seemed like someone who cared about anything other than his Islamic school and his teachings. But it was obvious that he was a good farmer and businessman. To Emmanuel, the farm was huge, and workers hustled back and forth, machines loading large bags of produce onto trucks. The whole place looked busy and thriving, and this was just the entrance.

As Emmanuel stood at the entrance, taking all this in, a man came towards  him to ask if he needed a job or if he was there to see someone.

"I'm here to see Mallam Ashiru, please." Emmanuel, now quite nervous. "Is he expecting you?" The man asked.

 "N...no. I... It's an emergency."

"Okay, let me tell him that you're around. What's your name?"

"He doesn't know me, but my name is Emmanuel Nweze."

The man looked at him for some seconds. It was obvious to Emmanuel that the man was not sure what to make of him. But he eventually left to inform Mallam Ashiru.

After some time, Emmanuel saw the man beckoning him to come over. He hurried towards the door where the man was standing as he ushered him through an interior hallway into Mallam Ashiru's office.

When Emmanuel saw Mallam Ashiru, it took a lot of strength for him not to falter. He was suddenly filled with doubt and became very fidgety. What if Mallam Ashiru ends up treating him in the same manner that his brother had treated him? He was seated at a large desk. The office was well furnished with cabinets containing rows and rows of books and box files.

Even though there were seats in front of the desk, Emmanuel opted to remain standing.

"*Ina yini Mallam.*" — Good afternoon, Mallam. — Emmanuel greeted and bowed his head in a show of respect.

"*Sannu da zuwa*, Emmanuel." — Welcome, Emmanuel. — "What can I do for you, young man?"

"Mallam, I have come to you because you are the only hope I have right now. I made a stupid mistake and I'm paying dearly for it." Emmanuel paused.

Mallam Ashiru did not reply. He just waited for Emmanuel to continue.

"I am the man who impregnated Zainab, your niece. I shouldn't have done that, and I'm truly sorry. We insisted on keeping the baby when Alhaji Attahiru wanted it to be aborted, but for months now, since the baby was born, he has not allowed me to set my eyes on them."

Mallam Ashiru took a deep breath and looked at Emmanuel. "You realize that my brother is a difficult man, don't you?"

"Yes, sir. And that's why I need your help. Please. I'm in love with Zainab, and I would like to take care of her and the baby."

Mallam Ashiru got up and started pacing the office. He rubbed his chin and grunted, obviously struggling with his options. Seeing this, Emmanuel became more hopeful and pressed on.

"*Don Allah*, Mallam. I know I was stupid, but I've learnt from my mistake and I'm ready to take responsibility for it."

Mallam Ashiru stopped pacing and looked at Emmanuel pensively. Then he seemed to come to a decision.

"I will be at Attahiru's house on Friday morning. Convincing my brother to let you have Zainab and the baby will not be easy, but I will try. You were wrong to do such a thing, but for how long should we hold it against you? Come to Attahiru's house at noon. That way, he will not suspect that you had talked to me." Mallam Ashiru waved him away, and Emmanuel knelt, thanking him, then got to his feet and left.

On his way home, Emmanuel imagined taking Zainab and his baby with him. He made a mental note of what he needed to do to get himself ready for their arrival.

He didn't have much to offer, but he would do his best to cater to them and make them feel loved.

Emmanuel greeted everyone he met on the streets with joy as he made his way back to his father's house with a new sense of hope.

****

Zainab was in the living room with her mother, her father, and Fatima, his third wife. Radiya had to go to the market. The baby was sleeping peacefully on Zainab's knees. They were watching a popular TV programme, laughing from time to time. Zainab started to laugh, but was interrupted by the cries of the baby as she awoke. She moved the baby from her knees to her shoulder and tried to pacify her, but the crying continued.

Zainab looked up to see her father glaring at her. "Go into your room and feed your baby. You're distracting us."

Zainab felt her anger flaring up. She wanted to retort, but just then there was a knock on the front door. Deflated, her mouth seemed to close of its own accord. She sighed, thankful that she stopped before saying something she would regret. But he wasn't being fair to her either.

She held the baby close to her chest and retired to her room. As she fed the baby, she looked down at her peaceful face.

"You deserve to be loved, my child. You are not a mistake." Zainab rocked her back and forth.

After feeding the baby, she went back to the living room and met Mallam Ashiru talking with her father.

"*Sannu da zuwa*, Mallam." Zainab greeted him, squatting in deference next to him.

Mallam Ashiru quickly stopped her. "You're squatting with the baby." He chuckled. "How are you and the baby?"

"We are fine, Mallam." Zainab forced a smile and took a seat next to him. He looked at the baby, smiling, and then turned to her father and continued their conversation.

The women excused themselves and went to the kitchen to prepare some food. When they were done, they served the men who continued conversing while eating.

Afterwards, just as they were settling down, there

was the sound of a commotion outside.

Her eyes met with her father's. He stood up and marched towards the door, followed by Mallam Ashiru. Soon, everyone was outside.

Zainab stepped out to see what was happening. There, on the ground, lay Emmanuel.

He had obviously overpowered the gate man again to gain entrance to the compound, but why was he lying down on the ground?

Emmanuel began to beg her father.

"Alhaji, have mercy. I want to see my child, and I want to marry Zainab. I love her. Please give me this chance. I know that I did wrong. But I need my family—"

"Shut up! Who is your family? You must be stupid to think that I would allow my daughter to marry a wretched fool like you."

Zainab winced at her father's words.

Mallam Ashiru put his hand on Alhaji Attahiru's arm,

urging him to control his temper.

"Please, sir. Give me a chance to make things right. I love Zainab, and I want to take care of her and the baby. Please, Alhaji."

Mallam Ashiru pulled his brother away. Zainab couldn't hear what they were saying, but she knew that it was more of an argument. Her father's tone was angry, while Mallam Ashiru was softer and conciliatory. Everyone waited for them to be done.

She turned to Emmanuel and saw him staring at her. He smiled at her, and she smiled back, but slightly. She hoped that the future held better days for them, but she anxiously waited for the outcome of the heated conversation between her father and his brother.

When the men came back, Mallam Ashiru stepped back and allowed Alhaji Attahiru to speak. Emmanuel could see that he was struggling with what he was going to say.

"Mallam Ashiru thinks I should allow my daughter to marry you." Her father heaved a deep sigh and continued. "I don't agree because I think it is a bad idea. A very bad idea." He stressed the last sentence.

As long as she could remember, her father had never turned down his brother's request. Unlike his other siblings, Mallam Ashiru did not cower at Alhaji's feet because of his money or status. He still saw him as a younger brother who needed to be taken care of. He had been responsible for sending her father to school after the death of their parents. Even now that her father was wealthy, his brother still sent fresh produce from his farms to them. And her father always felt indebted to his brother, a debt that could never be repaid with money. In addition, Mallam Ashiru was an Islamic cleric, highly respected for his conservative teachings. It was difficult to disagree with him, and he rarely asked for anything.

Her father looked at Emmanuel for a long time, allowing his gaze to work the magic of inflicting the fear that he was known for, before continuing to speak.

"You can take them with you, but if I hear that you are not treating my daughter well, I will not fail to deal with you. You can come with your family, and we will discuss on the day you are to take them with you."

With that, Alhaji Attahiru turned and walked back into the house. The others followed her father, leaving Zainab with Emmanuel. Emmanuel rose to his feet and drew closer.

"Zainab…"

Zainab held the baby and hugged him, leaving enough space in between them for the baby not to be squashed.

"I'm sorry—"

"No… I'm sorry, Emmanuel. I was too angry to reach out to you. I had blamed you for everything, but it was me who dragged you into this. Forgive me." She held him tight.

Emmanuel cupped her face with his hands. He looked at her and then the baby.

"You two are my life now. How could I be angry with you?" He wiped the tears on Zainab's cheeks and kissed her forehead.

"I promise, Zainab. I will love you and I will protect our baby. Even with my last breath."

The future was blurry. Zainab didn't know what it held for Emmanuel, the baby, and her, but she was not ready to think too much about that. All she knew was that they would take it one day at a time.

# CHAPTER FOURTEEN

Zalla hurried into the large building, which housed over a hundred students. He had been late for the first session of Mallam Ashiru's teachings for the day, and he didn't want to be late for the second.

He peeped into the room to see if Mallam Ashiru, their *Shibarid,* was inside and was relieved to see that he wasn't and the students were seated in groups having conversations with one another.

*"Zalla! Zo nan gun!"* — Zalla! Come over here! — It was his friend Lado who called him to come over to the side of the class where he sat with a group of boys. Zalla knew only two of them—Dan Tala and Zubairu. He had seen the other two around but didn't know their names or why they were part of Lado's group today.

He held his book tight and looked down as he moved towards them. He was shy and did not exhibit the confidence of most of the other students, and he expected Lado to start mocking him again, but Zalla was determined to ignore his snide remarks. Lado had tried to help him overcome his shyness, but gave up after the last attempt.

One of the boys eyed Zalla as he took his seat as the sixth boy in their company. Zalla had never had a reason to talk to the boy, let alone sit with him, but Lado attracted strays like corpses attracted flies.

*"Wannan aboki na ne. Sunan sa Zalla."* — This is my friend. His name is Zalla. — Lado said, introducing him to the boys. They looked at him with subtle discomfort but didn't speak to him.

Lado didn't bother to introduce them. He treated them not as friends but as necessary but temporary companions to push his agenda, whatever that may be for now.

*"Ama kun san Shibarid ya goyi bayan auren yar gidansa ma wani kafiri ko?"* —But you know Shibarid actually supported his daughter marrying an infidel, right?

It was one of the boys who spoke, and Lado didn't

hesitate to slap him hard. Zalla didn't think Lado slapped him for accusing Mallam Ashiru of supporting his niece's marriage to a Christian. It was either that Lado slapped him because he said it a bit too loudly or because it wasn't his right to have said it since he wasn't the convener of the "meeting".

Nonetheless, Lado nodded in approval to what the boy said and henceforth took over the direction of discourse. He spoke bitterly about how people in town were speaking against *Shibarid* and how the students from the other schools were making a mockery of them.

*"Za mu taru da yamma a kasuwa yau mu ci uwar yaran nan. Sai sun gane kuskuren su."* — We will gather this evening at the market and deal with those kids. They will learn their mistake.

Zalla was surprised to learn that Lado had planned to ambush the students from the other Islamic schools that made fun of them. Even though Lado didn't agree with their teacher, he wouldn't let others disrespect them. Typical of him.

The other four nodded in agreement while Zalla sat there thinking through what the consequences of their actions would be. It wouldn't be good in the slightest.

It was as if Lado sensed his hesitation because he asked Zalla if he was in or not and warned him not to cower when the time came to act.

The other students got up and left just Lado and Zalla. Of all the group, they were the two who were truly friends. They had been friends since they were toddlers, or so Zalla thought. The others would go around the school and spread the word that they would be fighting with the other schools later in the evening.

*"Ba sai mun yi haka ba, Lado."* - We don't have to do this, Lado.

Lado was extremely reckless and held very strong views for a thirteen-year-old. Zalla hoped he would reconsider the planned attack. He had a feeling something bad would happen. And again, it was against the teachings of *Shibarid* in every way. The other factions had mocked them, but wouldn't it be foolish to fight someone who opposed your views by violating the same views you claimed to protect?

Even after much persuasion, Lado wouldn't budge. He held to his plans and insisted that it was what was good for the students. In his opinion, allowing your competitor to look down on you was a sign of weakness and a lack of faith in your cause. It felt right when put like that, but Zalla knew in his heart that it was wrong.

Right there, he decided that he would report the planned attack to *Shibarid*. If Lado wouldn't listen to him, he would have no choice but to listen to their teacher.

****

As they all stood before *Shibarid,* Lado kept staring at Zalla. Somehow, his friend had figured out that he was the one who told on them.

Shibarid's countenance was stern, and his words were forceful and firm.

*"Za ku je faɗa da wa'yansu a kan me?"* - What are you going to fight with them about?

He allowed his disappointment to settle in every syllable. He turned towards one of the boys and asked which of them masterminded the plan. No one spoke out initially, but after he became fiercer, one of the boys, the one who looked uncomfortably at Zalla in the hall, pointed towards another boy.

Zalla opened his mouth as if to protest, but shut it as quickly as he opened it. He knew it wasn't the boy who was pointed out. They all knew it was Lado who was the mastermind, but somehow, they were more scared of what Lado would do to them than they were of *Shibarid.*

The boy cried out in protest, but soon enough, other hands began pointing in his direction. With so many accusing him, there was no way he would have convinced their leader that he wasn't the ringleader. He seemed to realize his fate even though he still made weak gestures to protest his innocence.

*Shibarid* called one of the other teachers to take the boy away. He would be dealt with and forced to recite multiple *Hadiths* during the week. It was a stiff penalty, but he knew his fate had been sealed and the matter settled. *Shibarid* released the others, and they quietly dispersed.

As they left the main building, he noted how Lado and the others looked at him. They couldn't possibly have proof that he was the one who ratted them out, but they seemed to know that he was the only one who would go to their leader with this kind of information. After all, all of them were on board with the plan except him.

Zalla took a deep breath and headed to the courtyard of the school, and settled into one of the benches there.

The air wasn't as hot as it was yesterday because it had rained in the morning, and he was thankful for that. He wished his friends would be mild on him as well.

He folded his legs and began to meditate on *Shibarid's* last teaching. It was about the desires of Allah and the desires of men. Their leader had said that not all desires that seemed good were from Allah. Sometimes, men must desire suffering so that Allah's will might be evident in their lives and in the lives of the people around them.

Most of the time, *Shibarid's* teachings were as hard as some people say they were, not because he used big words and complex descriptions, but because they seemed too difficult to follow. Other times, however, his teachings were straightforward.

He didn't have the vigour in speech of some of the other mallams in town, but his words still pierced a person's heart. They were words of truth. People like Lado had not fully understood these words, these teachings of a practical life. They were more concerned with fighting the cause than allowing the cause to fight the vileness in their hearts. This was what Islam was truly about—Allah's fight against the evil that resided in men's hearts.

All the outward activities like ablution, fasting, and the holy war were simply representations of the inward truth of Allah's intention for man. Many people didn't like *Shibarid* for saying that. The other scholars believed that he thought he was a better Muslim than they were, but that wasn't true. Of all of them, he was the only one who confidently spoke of his weaknesses and his dependence on Allah to help him overcome them.

*"Allah ba ya cire kasawar mu daga cikin mu, sai dai ya taimake mu mu cin karfin kasawa."*

These words had always been Zalla's pillar of hope. They were *Shibarid's* words to him on the day he was caught stealing another boy's ration of food. The man didn't seem as angry as his other teachers. Zalla had cried and stayed indoors for days, praying to Allah to take away this evil in him. When *Shibarid* had found out what he was doing, he called him into one of the classes and told him this:

*"God does not remove our shortcomings from us, but He gives us the strength to overcome them."*

The words seemed like a paradox to Zalla, but soon they became his solace whenever he felt like he was losing himself to the evil that lurked within him.

While he was still lost in his thoughts, Lado walked up to him and tapped him on the shoulder. He asked Zalla if he was the one who reported them and demanded that he answer honestly. It was funny how Lado sought honesty when it benefited him.

Zalla ruefully confessed to being the one.

Instead of getting angry, Lado laughed so hard that he was almost in tears. "*Ba karamin duka Jamilu zai sha ba.*"

He was excited that the other boy, who was wrongly accused, was going to be dealt with. Who reasoned like that?

Zalla turned away from Lado and looked in the direction of the classrooms where a group of five to seven-year-olds was being led into a class.

After looking at them for a while, he turned in Lado's direction and tried to warn him about the consequences of being a troublemaker. One day, he would get himself into big trouble—big enough that it would be difficult to escape from.

****

The last of the day's classes were rounding up, and the students were eager to leave to go outside and play. Evenings were always the most fun part of the day for them.

As he left the class, he noticed in the distance a young couple carrying a baby who were standing and speaking with *Shibarid* at the entrance of his home.

He didn't recognise them, but whoever they were, they seemed very important to him, as they followed him into his home. Zalla had a feeling they would be there for a while, so he postponed the questions he had prepared to ask his leader for later in the evening. As important as they were, the man wouldn't take it kindly if he interrupted his meeting with these guests.

With that in mind, he ran to join the other children outside the compound.

Lado, Dan Tala, Zubairu, and two other boys were seated on concrete slabs near the entrance to the school. By now, he knew the names of the other boys—Faisal and Mohammed. Mohammed was the one who falsely accused Jamilu. Zalla knew why they fingered him. Jamilu was always picking fights with Lado, and he needed to be dealt with.

He joined them and immediately joined their conversation. They were talking about the couple and the baby who were with their leader. Lado said that it was *Shibarid's* niece and her Christian husband. He said the word 'Christian' with contempt.

Zubairu asked what they came to do, and Lado told him that they came to give him money to show appreciation for what he did for them.

Zalla knew his friend was lying, but didn't object to Lado's submission. He was just curious about who they really were and what was happening in their lives.

****

Emmanuel and Zainab left Mallam Ashiru's house, bidding him farewell again. They walked together towards the compound gate, heading out towards the main street.

Mallam Ashiru had warned them of the scorn they would face in the town for making the choices they made and even suggested that they leave Maiduguri for somewhere like Kaduna or Jos. But Emmanuel didn't want to leave his parents alone in Gombaru, and Zainab also wanted to stay close to home.

Emmanuel glanced at the group of boys who sat at the entrance to the school. These must be some of Mallam Attahiru's students. The boys looked at him with a sort of interest that he couldn't place.

Mallam Ashiru walked them out to a short distance before informing them that he would have to go back to attend to some pressing matters. Emmanuel and Zainab thanked him again and continued to the end of the street. Emmanuel felt bad that he made Zainab walk. He knew she had been used to being driven around in the comfort of her father's cars, but now, because of him, she had been reduced to walking on the dusty streets of Maiduguri.

Just as they were about to turn a corner, Emmanuel caught sight of a boy running towards him with his hands outstretched. He recognised him as one of the boys who sat at the entrance of the school.

The boy handed him his wallet.

*"Ya fadi a gaban kofar makaranta."* – It fell in front of the school gate. – He said.

Normally, these boys would have taken the wallet for themselves, yet the reason they didn't was clear. They had clearly imbibed the integrity of their leader. Emmanuel thanked the boy and offered him a little money in appreciation, but the boy looked shocked at his gesture and quickly shook his head, backing away. He didn't want Emmanuel's money. That was a rare sight. Emmanuel had obviously underestimated Mallam Ashiru's impact on his students.

He insisted that the boy accept his generosity, but the boy declined again. Whatever it was that Emmanuel intended, whatever gesture of appreciation he had extended to the boy, the boy didn't see it that way because he bowed his head, turned around, and took off back towards the school.

Emmanuel shook his head, collected Aisha from Zainab's hands, and held her hand as they continued walking. He might not have a car now, but he promised himself that he would do his best to take care of his family and would never abandon either Zainab or Aisha. They were his life now; his breath was intertwined with theirs. For him to survive, they must survive and thrive.

He looked his baby girl in the eyes and smiled. She looked up at him, and his heart swelled with joy and hope. He would never let anyone take her away from him ever again.

# PART THREE:
# AUGUST 2014

# CHAPTER FIFTEEN

Aisha took a step forward, face creased in pain. The cramp in her stomach was almost unbearable as she walked with difficulty forward in the queue at the food stand. She hadn't eaten since morning, and it was already evening. She had been forced to go without breakfast and lunch as punishment for talking back at one of the men who was assigned to watch over her and the other girls. She would have missed dinner too if Junaidu, one of the leaders, had not intervened.

When it was her turn, she stretched her shaky hands holding her plate, waiting for the woman before her to put food into it.

The woman eyed Aisha and poured a spoonful of overcooked beans into her plate. Aisha waited for the woman to add more, but the woman gave her a questioning look.

"More, please!" Aisha said belligerently.

The woman ignored her and shouted to the next

person, motioning them to move forward, but Aisha stood her ground. When the woman saw that she wasn't going to move, she added a little to her food and commanded her to go. The girl behind Aisha pushed her to the side and moved forward. Aisha looked at the woman in disbelief before walking away with her food.

"Cursed fool." She muttered under her breath as she looked for a place to sit.

It had been roughly four months since they had been kidnapped by the Boko Haram terrorists, and life had been hard on all the girls. Normally, a person was supposed to get used to the life they were forced to live, but every day came with a new trouble.

Aisha looked at all the girls scattered at different parts of the camp, gobbling the food that had been given to them a few minutes ago. Some had already finished theirs and were licking their plates like refugees at an IDP camp. This was worse than an IDP camp, though.

Aisha swallowed a lump in her throat and looked at the

food on her plate. She didn't like beans, but she had no choice, so she wiped her hand on her skirt and started eating with her fingers. When she was done, she wiped her mouth with the back of her hand. Four months ago, she would have thought it unconscionable to lick a plate, but now her pride was gone, beaten into submission by the hunger that she felt, so she joined in the licking.

Suddenly, the quiet of the evening was shattered by the noise of a commotion coming from the food stand area.

She stood to her feet and moved together with the other girls to see what was going on.

One of the girls was lying on the ground. She was crying and begging Junaidu to have mercy on her.

"*Shegiya kawai!*" Junaidu barked as he kicked the girl.

He turned towards the girls who had gathered, waiting to see what they would do. He stared them down till they looked away. Nobody wanted their faces to be marked by one of the dangerous men in the gang.

"This is what will happen to any girl who refuses to follow simple rules!" He raised his voice so that they could all hear.

Apparently, the girl had been so hungry that she had gone to meet the woman serving them food to demand more. When the lady refused to give her more, she grabbed the spoon and tried to help herself. That had caused the woman to draw Junaidu's attention. Aisha marvelled at the girl's audacity.

When the talk had died down, she joined the rest of the girls to wash her plate. The girls were subdued, hoping that the kidnappers would not take offence at anything they would say or do, as they were punished for the slightest perceived infractions.

Aisha struggled daily with the urge to scream her defiance to their faces, but she didn't want to be in Junaidu's black book. As it was, they had to work for lengthy hours every day to make sure that the camp was more conducive to habitation.

Aisha went into the makeshift tent she shared with

some of the girls and lay on the mat using her arm as a pillow. When she closed her eyes, a picture of her father appeared in her mind. On the day that they were kidnapped, she had overheard the terrorists talking about a second attack on the Ngala LGA headquarters. They were rejoicing that it had "gone very well". Aisha almost screamed out in terror at what that meant. That was where her father worked.

Aisha didn't know what to think. Was her father still alive? Did he escape, and was he looking for her? She prayed fervently that he was. She had no way of knowing, as they were completely cut off from the rest of the world, and the not knowing had kept her in a state of constant panic. There were days when she thought she would lose her mind.

Today, a familiar feeling of nostalgia hit her. She missed him. Her father, her chief. How he had worked diligently to see that he could provide her basic needs. How he had cared for her, daily encouraged her, pushing her to be better, motivating her, and helping her dream of a bigger and better future. Now all of that was gone.

She had not been so grateful for the life he had given her before. She realised now that, like most people, she had taken her life for granted. However, in the state she was in, she would trade the life she had now for the life she had with her father a million times. She did not open her eyes, but tears spilled from her eyes. Her stomach churned, from hunger and probably from eating bad food.

The girl beside her was a terrible sleeper. She was snoring and would occasionally fling her leg, hitting whoever was sleeping next to her.

When her leg landed on Aisha, she slapped the leg and pushed it away. The girl just grunted and continued snoring. A short while later, Aisha began to smell something bad in the air.

"*Ya Allah!*" She moved her head as she struggled to catch her breath. She sat up and looked at all the girls, annoyed that she was the only one who was awake and dealing with the smell of the horrible fart.

Aisha needed fresh air, so she stepped out of the tent and took deep breaths. She would have preferred to sleep outside if not for the mosquitoes. She yawned and stretched. The night was filled with the sounds of crickets and other nocturnal animals. She walked around a bit and again thought of the possibility of escaping, but she knew that she didn't have the courage.

Talking about courage, she remembered Mairo. Her friend had been among the other group of girls who were summoned outside by the soldiers. Aisha was so busy asking about her father that she didn't watch out for her friend. She did not know whether her friend was even alive or dead.

She felt guilt mixed with nostalgia. As she walked between the tents in the dark, she hoped for the umpteenth time that her father and Mairo were safe. When she got to the last tent in her row, she started turning back to hers but stopped at the sound of whispers coming from a short distance away.

She walked stealthily towards the voices and hid

behind one of the tents.

*"Wa'yansu 'yan matan nan sun isa aure."* One of the kidnappers said.

*"Kuma sun fara fada da mu. Ya kamata su samu mazan da za su dinga hanasu. Ko ba haka ba?"* Another man said, and the other men murmured in agreement.

In shock, Aisha covered her mouth with her hands. The kidnappers were talking of forcefully marrying some off the girls, and Aisha knew that she was surely going to be among those unfortunate girls. Almost all the men had their eyes on her because of her defiance. They had already done a lot to dehumanise her.

"What do you think about that girl, Aisha?" One of them asked.

"That stubborn girl? I will not even think of picking her, but I will be happy to kill her when I'm permitted to." Another answered.

Aisha gasped. She turned around and tried to flee, but tripped and fell. As she struggled to rise to her feet, she heard sounds coming from the tent. The men had obviously heard her. If they caught her, she would be in very big trouble, especially as she was on their blacklist.

She started running towards her tent.

"*Tsaya nan!*" – Stop there! - The men were running and shouting.

Aisha kept running. Stopping would put her in trouble, and not stopping would put her in trouble. Being so exposed could even get her killed, so what was she going to do?

Now in a state of panic, she turned towards the line of trees and continued running. She tripped, fell, jumped back up, and kept running. If she was going to die, those terrorists had to earn her life. The other girls in the tents had already started coming out of their tents on hearing the commotion.

At full speed, Aisha dived into the woods and kept running. She saw flashes of torch lights behind her and heard the men yelling at her to stop, as they pursued her.

As she ran, she glanced backwards and saw that her pursuers were getting closer. Her chest was already burning badly, but she was going to be punished seriously and even killed for running, so she was left with no choice but to just keep running.

She increased her pace, breathing heavily, sweating, and flinging her hands and legs in the air as she ran in the darkness. Soon, her vision started getting blurry, and her head ached. She tripped again, and as she fell to the ground, her head hit something hard on the ground. She tried to move again, but her limbs would not obey her. Tears spilled from her eyes before she finally closed them. At least she tried.

****

Aisha slowly regained consciousness and tried to sit up. She groaned and massaged her head gently, wincing in pain.

"Stand up. Now!" A man's voice whispered harshly at her.

Aisha jolted in fright. The man grabbed her and pulled her to her feet. "You must be stupid to think that you can escape."

Aisha didn't reply. She couldn't make out his features in the darkness, but she knew she was one stupid comment away from certain death. As it was, she wondered who the man was and why he hadn't killed her yet. Maybe he wanted to torture her before killing her to make an example.

She whimpered as he grabbed her hand. *"Bari in fada maki wani abu. Mutane na baza su yarda ki kai gobe ba in sun gan ki a nan."*

Aisha's eyes widened. Of course, she knew certain death awaited her on capture.

"Who are you?" She asked.

As she looked more closely at him, she gasped. "Junaidu!" She couldn't believe it. Of all the men to be captured by! "Why have you not killed me? Are you not one of them?" Aisha asked, defiant in the face of certain death.

Junaidu shook her. "The men are searching for you in the tents right now. You will do what I say, or you die. We will go back to the—"

"I don't want to go back there. I want to go away from here. I want to—" Aisha was now whimpering and trying to pull herself away from him.

"Young girl! I'm not asking you. Do as I say, now! Would you prefer to die instead?" Junaidu asked, shaking her angrily. "You need to get to your tent before they discover that you are the one who is missing." Junaidu began to walk back to the camp, dragging Aisha with him.

"But I don't want to do that," Aisha begged, straining against him. Junaidu didn't answer her. He just continued to walk and dragged her with him. When she realized that fighting him was futile, she gave up and started to follow him. He was walking fast, and she almost had to run to keep pace with him.

When they had gotten near the camp, he motioned for her to be quiet as they looked around. Aisha's heartbeat increased when she saw that the men were doing a headcount, and they were getting close to her tent. She could see her tent mates looking among themselves and probably wondering why she wasn't with them.

Junaidu grabbed her hand and dragged her towards the back of the tent. Then they waited for the men to get distracted. Luckily for them, one of the ladies was still struggling with sleep, so her clumsiness made them focus on her. She kept mumbling something unintelligible, and one of the men angrily pushed her, and they laughed as she fell. Two of them then dragged her to her feet and pushed her towards the girls who held her before she would fall again.

Junaidu walked forward, hiding Aisha behind him. He was a big man, and so his frame could conceal Aisha, especially in the darkness. Aisha suddenly had a crazy idea. What if she exposed herself and framed Junaidu? She could tell the other terrorists that Junaidu was trying to help her escape. She squashed the thought before it was fully formed, knowing that it would mean a death sentence for her as well. So, she followed quietly.

When they got to her tent, he pushed her inside, then he yelled. *"Menene ki ke yi a nan bayan an ce ku fita?!"* - What are you doing here after being told to come out?!

Then he dragged her out and roughly pushed her toward the other girls. Aisha felt confused, but it dawned on her. Junaidu was pretending.

She suddenly started sobbing. *"Ciki na na ciwo."* - My stomach hurts. - She held her stomach and squatted.

Junaidu dragged her up and pushed her forward. *"Yarinyan nan ba ta ji!"* Junaidu slapped her, claiming she seemed to be hard of hearing. The girls made way for him to get to the soldiers, while he dragged Aisha towards them.

*"Na gan ta a cikin dakin su a kwance."* —Junaidu lied that he found her sleeping, then he nodded to them to continue their work. Aisha was both thankful for his act but was beginning to wonder why he was helping her.

After the headcount was done and all the girls were accounted for, Junaidu announced that there would be a meeting the next morning and then told them all to go to sleep.

The girls began to retire to their tents. Some of them glared at Aisha, especially her roommates. Somehow, they knew that she was the cause of the commotion.

*"Ina ki ka je? Karda ki sa mu a wahala fa!"* - Where are you going? Don't cause us more suffering! - Jamila pointed at her, while Nabila gave her an evil look. They all walked away, leaving her in the cold.

Aisha turned to see Junaidu and the other men retiring to their tents, too. At the entrance to his tent, Junaidu turned and stared at her for a short while before he entered the tent.

Aisha entered their tent, and in an outpouring of pent-up emotions, she fell to the ground and started weeping silently, deep heaves shaking her chest as she fought back the bitter frustration. She realised she was just lucky that it was Junaidu who had accosted her, even though she had no idea why he had helped her, but she was grateful. She also realised she might not be lucky the next time.

She dragged herself to her feet, dreading the rest of her days in the camp. She found a space that the girls had left for her.

It was too small for her body to fit into, but with the trouble she had caused them, it was better to make do with the little she had.

She closed her eyes, sank into a fitful sleep, and dreamt about Joshua Nduaguibe and a group of boys fighting with the Boko Haram members.

****

Aisha woke up to the sound of a gong. With her eyes still closed, she frowned at the noise. In Maiduguri, roosters were always there as natural alarms, but if a rooster was ever in camp, the kidnappers wouldn't hesitate to use it to complement their food.

Aisha opened her eyes and looked around her. The other girls were already on their feet, preparing for the day. She groaned. With the girls already going out of the tent, Aisha dragged herself up and followed them. They joined the assembly of girls who waited for Junaidu to address them. Junaidu seemed to be looking for someone because he searched the camp with his eyes. When his eyes met hers, his lips twitched. Aisha didn't understand what it meant, but she didn't really care. When everyone was gathered, Junaidu cleared his throat.

"I have noticed that some of you are beginning to grow wings. Last night, one of you was eavesdropping when my men were talking." Junaidu paused and looked at them with a dangerous demeanor.

"*Bazamu kara yin magana ba. Zamu kashe duk wanda ya yi irin abunan kuma.*" — We will not talk anymore. We will kill anyone who does the same. — Some of the girls gasped while others whispered to each other.

Aisha kept looking at Junaidu. He was serious, and she could see it. But he had saved her. Why did he save her? Everyone knew that as the leader, he was the most dangerous man in the camp. Even his gang members feared him. When Junaidu turned to look at her again, she quickly looked down at her feet.

"Some of my men have found some of you girls worthy of them. They will choose for themselves wives from you all. Stubborn girls who feel like their wings are too heavy to stay on the ground." Junaidu smirked. The place erupted in cries.

Worthy? What was Junaidu talking about? He talked like he was a saint, and the girls were devils, when in fact he and his gang were the devils. They were the ones who were cold-hearted, killing and kidnapping innocent people, and taking them away from their families. Aisha felt her anger building.

She looked up and noticed that the men were already choosing the girls they wanted. Aisha's heart skipped. She prayed that none of them would pick her. Once a girl was chosen, she would begin to cry and beg the man who had chosen her to leave her alone. After one of the ladies was slapped so hard that she fainted, the rest of the girls stopped making a fuss when chosen, choosing instead to cower in fear, crying quietly, and accepting their fate. It all made Aisha angrier. Some girls tried to hide behind others, and they only succeeded in delaying the inevitable, as it seemed the kidnappers already had their eyes on them.

She then saw one of the men walking towards her, eyes bulging with barely concealed lust. She froze as her skin crawled, but she couldn't do anything because if he chose her, she was doomed. So, she just stood, kept looking down, and waited.

The man got to her and pushed her aside. Then he grabbed Nabila. Aisha didn't realize that she was holding her breath until then. As she realised he wasn't after her, she started gasping and gulping in air. She was still trying to catch her breath when she heard Nabila's giggles.

She turned around in shock. Nabila was happy that she was picked by one of the men!? Aisha shook her head in disbelief. She watched the girl walk away with the man.

"*Innaninllahi.*" – Thank God!

"I can't believe this!"

"Chai!" Some of the girls muttered. They were obviously as shocked as Aisha was. She shook her head and looked towards Junaidu. What next?

"You can all get to your daily work." Junaidu waved them away. The girls moved to their assigned tasks. Some of them went to a small stream nearby to fetch water, some of them chopped firewood, some helped the older women prepare food, while the girls who were chosen to be wives followed or were dragged by their "husbands" to their tents. Aisha dreaded what would happen to them.

She was among the girls who were to get water from the stream, so she grabbed her bucket and got to work. They were followed by one of the men who held a gun. On their way, Aisha heard her name from behind one of the trees. She turned towards the direction of the sound and saw Junaidu.

The other girls looked at themselves and then at Aisha before settling their eyes on Junaidu.

"*Ku tafi.*" "I want Aisha to go and work somewhere else," Junaidu said and nodded to the guard.

Aisha exchanged looks with the rest of them before they left. She swallowed hard, unsure of what was to follow.

He motioned for her to follow him as he walked until they got to a spot under a large tree. Aisha looked at him, confused and worried.

"I'm supposed to be fetching water with the rest of them. I'll get into trouble if I don't."

"I know," Junaidu said and sat down on the bare ground and motioned for her to sit too.

She hesitated, then obeyed him.

Before last night, she had stayed as far away from him as possible. She had only seen him when he was addressing the girls or settling a dispute between the men. But he was beginning to give her attention, and she was very wary as to his real intentions.

"You look like my younger sister. She was really

beautiful."

Aisha turned to look at Junaidu properly. She took note of the scars that covered his face, one on his eyebrow that looked like the area was stitched, another on his cheek, close to his mouth, and the last one on his neck.

"Her name was Aisha, too." Junaid leaned on the tree and closed his eyes. Aisha's shoulders relaxed. She didn't know what to say, so she kept quiet and waited for him to say more.

"She was fifteen years old and vibrant. Fearless like you." Junaidu turned to Aisha, his lips forming a thin line.

Aisha kept quiet. It felt good to know that Junaidu thought that she was fearless. But she wasn't. She was scared all the time, and the reason why she kept doing stupid things that made him think that she was fearless was the fear itself.

"Where is she now?" Aisha asked.

"Dead. Killed by people who should have saved her." His voice was laced with anger.

"Which people?" She asked.

Junaidu opened his eyes and stood up. Aisha turned to see that the girls were on their way back, and she quickly got to her feet. She turned to Junaidu, terrified at what they would think. Junaidu obviously didn't care.

When they reached where she stood with him, he ordered her to go with them, and if she was asked why she didn't fetch the water, she should say that he ordered her to go back because she had done some work for him.

Aisha smiled in gratitude and joined the line of girls. She could feel Junaidu's eyes on her back, but she didn't turn around. Instead, she tried to answer the girls' questions as they walked back to the campground.

****

Aisha lay in the dark tent, tired and weary. Her relationship with Junaidu had gotten better, but she still tried to keep her distance. As time passed, she began to think that maybe he was not the cold-hearted monster she first thought he was. Maybe he was as much a victim as they were. She thought herself lucky to have heard some of the details of his life before Boko Haram. He had also started giving her preferential treatment; whenever he was on duty, she would relax while the other girls worked. It made them jealous.

But for a week now, she hadn't seen Junaidu. She heard that he had gone to another camp to oversee some things and make plans with their leader.

Aisha was sure that some of the girls were happy that she was working again. Especially Nabila and her gang.

She reflected on the two sides of the man. She was getting to know Junaidu, the man. But she also knew Junaidu the terrorist, who could laugh and say that there were only two options for the girls: marry his men and do whatever was demanded of them or die. But

Aisha still had that spark of defiance and hope; there must be a third option, escape, and somehow restarting her life. Aisha was determined to make her escape, and soon, too.

Over time, she had carefully noted the details in Junaidu's tales; the direction and distance from their camp to the main road, the direction of the military and their patrols, how they had planned to use the girls to get what they wanted from the government, and some of the fastest ways to escape the camp in the event of a military attack.

Aisha was thankful that Junaidu was not in camp. Since he was the only one who knew that she had tried to escape, she could do it again without the extra scrutiny of his watchful eyes, but this time she had to plan properly.

For the rest of the week, she had paid very close attention to the routines of the men and looked for gaps between their patrols. Even though she would see better during the day, it was too risky, so she settled for nighttime. She would wait till everyone was asleep and then escape. The darkness would impede her progress, but that would also make it harder for the men to track her. With the information she was able to glean from Junaidu, she should hopefully be able to locate a military patrol and show them where to find the rest of the girls.

For a moment, she thought of telling her fellow kidnappees about her plan, but she knew she couldn't. They might be too scared to pull it off with her, or worse, they might give her up, so she decided to escape alone and seek help for the rest of them.

Aisha sighed. She longed to see her father again. And Mairo. She longed to go back to the peaceful life she lived with her father. She knew the risks, she knew what would happen to her if she was caught, but if she stayed and did not try, she would be there for as long as Junaidu and his men wanted her to, or worse. Aisha shuddered at the thought.

Before sleeping, she had settled it in her heart that she would escape very soon.

In the morning, she went for her assigned chores. The

other girls were chatting and teasing each other. Aisha marvelled that they seemed to have accepted their fate and had adapted to their lives in the camp. Not her. She wasn't going to adapt to this life. There were dreams she had, goals to achieve, and people she would love to see again. She smiled at their words but kept her thoughts to herself.

When they got back to the camp, Aisha's mouth fell open at the sight that confronted them. Junaidu was standing over a girl sprawled in the middle of the campground. The girl was wailing and begging him, holding her ankle, which seemed to be broken. When she lifted her head, Aisha gasped. Her eyes were swollen and red, blood dripped from her nose and mouth, and she was covered in dirt. Aisha turned to see the men who had done that to her. The hatred in their eyes was clear as day. They tied her legs and hands and started kicking her with their large boots and whipping her.

The girl in front of Aisha whispered that the girl who was being punished had tried to escape. On hearing that, Aisha covered her mouth with her hands.

*"Ya isa haka! Sake ta"* - That's enough. Release her. - Junaidu commanded the men with whips.

The angry kidnappers released the girl, and Junaidu told her to go and get herself cleaned. When she started limping towards the tents, all eyes followed her. They all stood still and looked as she struggled to gain momentum. And then came the sound of a lone gunshot, and she was flung headfirst into the dirt, body broken like a rag doll, bleeding from a large hole in her head. In shock, Aisha turned back, and there was Junaidu with his gun raised, grey smoke drifting out of the barrel.

As the men let out a raucous cry of triumph, Aisha closed her eyes and blocked her ears with shaky hands. When she opened her eyes, she saw the girl on the ground, lifeless.

"No!" Aisha pushed the girls in front of her and ran towards the girl. She fell to her knees beside her and shook her body, asking her to wake up. When the girl did not move, Aisha, overcome with rage, stood up and started walking towards Junaidu.

One of the men raised his gun to shoot her, but Junaidu stopped him. When Aisha reached him, she tried to strike him, but he stepped forward and grabbed her by the throat.

The girls gasped. Some of them started crying louder, begging Junaidu to spare Aisha, while others kept quiet, from fear of being caught up in the beating they knew was coming.

Aisha struggled for breath, but she still tried to hit Junaidu, clenched fists flailing. He lifted her off her feet, and she started to pass out.

"You want to die?" Junaidu threw her to the ground and kicked her. With a defiant cry, she lunged forward, but he slapped her so hard she collapsed and fainted. He then ordered that she be flogged.

Junaidu's man did not hesitate. It was as if they had been waiting for an opportunity to deal with her. The whips landing with venom brought her to full consciousness, and she screamed in pain, covering her face and neck with her arms. The whips tore through her clothing, ripping flesh and drawing blood. When Aisha could no longer move, Junaidu told them to stop and ordered some girls to take her back to the tent.

They rushed forward and helped carry her inside, laying her down gingerly as she continued whimpering in pain.

"That is what will happen to anyone who tries to escape and anyone who wants to prove that she is stubborn. Now, get back to work!"

The girls all rushed back to their chores.

Aisha lay in the tent sobbing. Some of the girls tried to dress her wounds as best they could. However, some of them were vocally upset with her for daring to challenge Junaidu. She saw what happened to the other girl and still put herself in danger, so to them, she got what she deserved.

After resting for a while, Aisha turned to the food that

one of the girls kept for her. When she saw that it was stale food, she started weeping again. It was a mixture of anger, hunger, and pain. Her body shook as her voice got louder. She grabbed the plate and threw it out of the tent.

"Daddy…" She wailed and covered her face with her hands. No one came to check on her as she wailed, even though they were just outside the open doorway. And she was glad about that because all she wanted at that moment was to be left alone.

Later that day, Junaidu walked into the tent and ordered the other girls to leave. Aisha sat up but looked away. He dropped a plate of fresh food in front of her.

"Eat."

Aisha didn't want to obey him, but the smell of the food made her stomach growl. She grabbed the plate and began to eat. When she finished, she wiped her lips and looked at Junaidu.

He had a smile on his face. "Aisha, you will get yourself

killed if you don't calm down. *Ko kina so ki mutu yanzu?"*
- Do you want to die now?

*"Ba gara ma in mutu ba? Bana son wurin nan."* - Wouldn't it be better if I died? I hate this place. - Aisha glared at Junaidu. He laughed heartily, then he frowned.

"If you do not learn to behave yourself in this place, I will make life miserable for you. I'm sure you know what I can do. Maybe I have given you too much freedom, that is why you are acting like this. But not anymore."

Junaidu leaned forward and grabbed her chin, pulled her close, and looked into her eyes. "I will be the one to punish you next time if you do any stupid thing again."

Aisha watched as Junaidu stood up and walked out of the tent. Before he moved away, he ordered a girl to give Aisha some water.

Aisha collected the cup of water and thanked the girl who was already moving out of the tent. After she left, Aisha looked at her reflection in the water as she settled it in her mind that she was going to be patient and hope that help would come soon. Her father must have seen her text message. He would do his best to save her, but in the meantime, she would try not to get into trouble in the camp.

# CHAPTER SIXTEEN

It was early morning in Maiduguri, and the town was stirring, getting ready for the day's activities.

Emmanuel woke up and hurriedly got dressed for his rendezvous with Zalla. It had been four months since Aisha and the other girls had been taken by Boko Haram and one month since his desperate decision to do the unthinkable in a last-ditch effort to find his daughter. Once he had made up his mind and found a way to proceed, his life had taken on a renewed sense of purpose.

He remembered that fateful night.

As the days after Aisha's abduction turned to weeks and then to months, he had slowly sunk into depression and drink until he became a shadow of his former self. One night, drunk and broken, he had been wandering the dusty streets of Gombaru. He had sat down by a drainage channel and was weeping profusely when Zalla found him quite by chance. As he tried to console him and convince him to return home, Emmanuel, in the throes of his pain and deep grief, had blurted out:

"Ah, if I could see a way to join those bastard Boko Haram devils, I would do it! I will do anything to find my Aisha, I will even sell my soul to the devil!"

Zalla had recoiled in shock, but still helped him up and onto his motorcycle and then drove him home.

The next day, he had come back to a now sober Emmanuel, and slowly they had talked until Zalla mentioned that there might be a way to join the Boko Haram sect if Emmanuel was really serious, but warned him that it was extremely dangerous. Emmanuel had insisted that he had nothing else to live for anyway, so they shook hands in agreement, and that was that.

He still didn't know why Zalla was willing to help him, but he was grateful and needed all the help he could get. He had also stopped wondering how Zalla knew so much about the modus operandi of the terrorist group, but was afraid to ask. Again, don't look a gift horse in the mouth.

Everyone had their secrets.

Zalla got to his feet and started his motorbike as Emmanuel stepped outside. He looked him up and down and nodded. Emmanuel had let his hair and beard grow out, and he was wearing a *djellabia*.

Zalla had been on edge lately. Emmanuel assumed that it was because of the danger of their planned course of action.

"*Ina kwana, maigida.*" Zalla said, turning the motorbike so Emmanuel could get on easily.

"*Ina kwana, Zalla.*" Emmanuel replied, returning the greeting.

Emmanuel inquired about the meeting point, and Zalla seemed to appear scared. It was as if being reminded of the day's activities made the morning more dreadful. Emmanuel could sense his fear. He, too, was scared, but he hid his fear.

"We will meet someone I know," Zalla said as they rode up onto the tarred road. "His name is Aliyu. He will help us join the man who is in charge of... We join because of him." Zalla finished off with a deep sigh.

Emmanuel had never heard the man speak English. He didn't even know the man could speak English. It was both scary and remarkable. So, Zalla had always understood all the things he said when he spoke to people in English, but never said a word to him. What else was he keeping from Emmanuel?

*"Ka iya turanci shi ne ban taba jin ka ka yi ba?"* – You can speak English? I've never heard you speak it before!

It was more of an expression of surprise than it was a question. He couldn't see his face, but he sensed that Zalla smiled, even if slightly, in that moment.

"I learn English from my mallam, *Maigida.*"

Whoever Zalla's mallam was, he did a good job in teaching him. Emmanuel wanted to ask him more about himself, but felt it wasn't the right time.

Zalla had told Emmanuel that he had a friend who was a member of Boko Haram, and that was how he knew their recruitment process. When Emmanuel enquired further, Zalla told him that the man had died recently when he tried to leave the group.

"What makes you think they won't kill us also like they did to him?" Emmanuel had asked Zalla. The man just shrugged and said they had to believe in God that it wouldn't happen like that.

He didn't know a lot about Zalla, but he had grown to respect and trust him. He felt a strange bond with him that he couldn't explain. He had no choice but to trust him anyway.

"You will do what I say when we go there. You will keep quiet. I will talk to Aliyu."

Emmanuel didn't object.

"Is this Aliyu a friend of yours or a friend of your dead friend?"

"Aliyu is not my friend. He is someone I have worked

with before. He is not a good person."

"You worked with him? Where?"

"It is good if I don't tell you. Just know, he is not my friend, so he is not your friend either."

Emmanuel didn't argue with Zalla even though he wanted to pry further. What would be the big deal if he told him what kind of work they did with this Aliyu, or where they did it? It wasn't as if Emmanuel would use this information against him.

Zalla drove to a stop as they reached a group of houses that looked more like shacks on the outskirts of the town, and they got off the motorcycle. He told Emmanuel to wait there while he went in and spoke to Aliyu.

"Why can't I come with you?" Emmanuel inquired.

"It is good that you don't come. Stay here," was Zalla's nervous response.

It was obvious that he would have to comply, so he leaned on the bike as Zalla hunched his shoulders and disappeared hesitantly into a narrow pathway between two buildings.

It suddenly dawned on Emmanuel that Aliyu had to be a Boko Haram member. He wondered why he didn't figure that out earlier. It had to be. That was why Zalla was so scared.

But if Zalla had said they had worked at a particular time with Aliyu, did it mean that Zalla, too, was or had been a member of the Boko Haram sect? Emmanuel was now confused. The man looked too scared and compassionate to have been one of them. Maybe they had worked together in a time before Aliyu had been recruited. That seemed like a more logical explanation.

****

Zalla walked through the narrow, twisted paths that led to the safe houses. To outsiders, they were a group of houses made with old, corrugated sheets and wood, makeshift buildings for the very poor. But to Zalla and all who knew, this was one of the Boko Haram transit bases in Maiduguri.

It was the perfect hiding place. It was far enough from the centre of the town not to attract too much attention, but close enough to easily get in and out.

Aliyu and the group of fighters could lie low for weeks at a time while they awaited further instructions. They were a vital link in the Boko Haram organisation's operational chain, relaying information, stockpiling weapons, and hiding men in preparation for terrorist missions.

Zalla wasn't sure what Emmanuel would have made of him if he had told him that he was once a member of this deadly group, that he had killed people and destroyed homes, villages, and livelihoods. Emmanuel saw good in him just like *Shibarid* did, and he wasn't willing to jeopardise that perception. At least, not now.

As he walked between two shacks, a voice called out to him. "*Waye a gun! Tsaya in da ka ke kamin in bindige shege!*" — Who's there! Stop where you are, or I'll shoot you, you bastard!

He stopped. The voice didn't sound familiar, but Zalla

was prepared.

The person behind the voice stepped out of a dark opening with a gun pointed at Zalla. As his eyes adjusted to the splotches of light and darkness, he noticed that several other openings were also manned by hard-faced gunmen. The one who stepped out scanned Zalla from head to toe as if to determine if he was friend or foe. Zalla waited before speaking.

*"Ina neman Aliyu, Aliyu Mai Dafi."* - I am looking for Aliyu, Aliyu Mai Dafi.

The soldier was taken aback that he knew Aliyu and hesitated before asking Zalla who he was.

*"Wanene kai? Mai ka ke nema a gun Mai Dafi? Ya na sane da zuwan ka?"*

He stood quietly as the man asked question after question. He didn't tell him who he was, but he told him why he was looking for Aliyu and that Aliyu didn't know he was coming to see him today.

The man, cautious but satisfied with Zalla's response,

shouted at another man to go and inform Aliyu of Zalla's presence.

*"Wa za'a ce masa yana neman sa?"*

At this point, Zalla had to identify who he was so that the messenger could relay that information to Aliyu. He prayed that they wouldn't shoot him the moment he revealed himself to them. The truth is that he was a deserter, and deserters weren't given room to explain themselves or to justify their actions. They were killed in cold blood, just like Lado.

That day, once he discovered that Lado had been killed, he had packed his few belongings and run, leaving the body on the bed. To date, he did not know what had happened to Lado's body. He wondered if he ever got a proper burial. If they had gotten to Lado, they were surely coming for him, too, so he had to go into hiding. He was afraid of dying, but he was more afraid of dying without accomplishing anything. Lado had died because of him. He died because, with all his flaws, he was a good friend who refused to let him go his path alone. Lado had been the victim of Zalla's decision, a decision he took because he wanted to assuage his conscience. He wanted to make sure he did right by his teacher, his *Shibarid.*

He still vividly remembered the stench of burning flesh and his mallam's voice calling out his name and asking him to help rescue the other students. With a deep breath, Zalla brought himself back to the present and answered the soldier in front of him.

*"A fadi masa Zalla ne ke neman sa. A ce masa na gan sakon shi kuma na zo in kara hada hannu da 'yanuwa na."* — Tell him Zalla is looking for him. Tell him I saw his message and came to join forces with my brothers.

The soldier was taken aback by this revelation and didn't know how to respond, so he ordered the other man to get Aliyu quickly. Zalla waited with dread. If he were shot dead here, he hoped Emmanuel would hear the gunshot and escape before he, too, was killed. The man didn't deserve to die, at least, not before he found his daughter.

After a few moments, the man came back with Aliyu, a man people usually underestimated because of his lanky frame. But Zalla knew all too well that Aliyu was an extremely dangerous man.

*"Ka zo ka rungume mutuwa kenan."* Aliyu said with a sarcastic smile.

Aliyu had a flair for the dramatic. Zalla wanted to respond by saying he didn't come to 'embrace' death as Aliyu suggested, but he kept his mouth shut. He knew all too well that the wrong word could mean immediate death.

"I come to ask you for forgiveness and for help," Zalla said in English, not wanting the other soldiers to understand them.

*"Turanci?!* You want to speak to me in English? Hahaha!."

He never found out how Aliyu knew English so well, and he never had the courage to ask.

"Forgiveness, you say, and help. You should know I killed Lado, your friend."

Zalla swallowed hard and tried to keep a calm face,

even though he was terrified. "I know. That is why I come to ask for forgiveness and for help. I have made a mistake. I want to fight for Allah again."

Aliyu moved closer and looked into his eyes, trying to detect any hint of duplicity. He seemed surprised but certainly interested.

"So, you want to be recruited, or should I say re-recruited? That's bold, Zalla. Very bold."

The confusion on the faces of the other soldiers grew into discomfort, but none of them dared to challenge Aliyu.

"Tell me this, Zalla. Why should we take you back? Why not just kill you?"

This was the most critical point in the conversation, and Zalla had already thought it through: what to say to Aliyu, how to say it in a way that doesn't end with his head and Emmanuel's rolling on the ground.

"I am here with a brother who wants to use his gift to fight for Allah."

"Really? A brother, you say? And he wants to fight for the Supreme One's cause? Why didn't he come in with you then?"

"I don't want to disrespect you. If you permit, I will bring him in."

Aliyu seemed satisfied with Zalla's explanation and asked one of the soldiers to get Emmanuel from where he was waiting.

****

Emmanuel watched as a man came out of the opening through which Zalla had disappeared. On seeing the gun the man was carrying, his first thought was to flee, but he didn't hear gunshots or a struggle to indicate that Zalla had been killed, so he stilled himself.

The soldier motioned for Emmanuel to follow him and retreated into the darkness.

He didn't say a word to Emmanuel through the brief journey, and in no time, they were standing in a corridor-like pathway that had Zalla, another fighter, and a man Emmanuel recognised from Zalla's description to be Aliyu.

He didn't know whether to bow and greet or just nod. The churning in his stomach wouldn't let him breathe or think properly, so he just stood.

He remembered his training with Zalla over the last couple of weeks. He had recited several portions of the Quran and a couple of Hadiths that Zalla thought would be sufficient and necessary for this encounter and subsequent ones. They had also agreed on a new name: Bashir.

*"Ina yini, Bashir,"* the man who was Aliyu said to Emmanuel. He didn't know why the man greeted him first, but he knew well to answer immediately.

*"Ina yini, Aliyu."*

"See? He even knows my name! Zalla has said terrible things about me, I suppose?"

"Not at all, Aliyu."

"He even speaks English! Better than you even, Zalla.

I'm impressed. A lot of these nincompoops can't utter a single sentence in English."

Emmanuel was confused, but he nodded. He didn't expect this. He didn't expect Aliyu. He expected to see a tough-looking Islamic scholar who couldn't speak English, ordering people about and shouting and spewing froth in people's faces. Aliyu was not that man. He looked cultured and out of place.

"So, if I were to vouch for you two, I'll need to see some evidence that I am not vouching for people who are looking for quick and easy money. It's not a business, it's a cause to change the world."

Emmanuel wanted to burst out laughing, but he stopped himself. No matter what it was that Aliyu had in mind to ask him, he was prepared to answer the man's questions and win his approval.

****

Zalla watched as Aliyu questioned Emmanuel, who was now Bashir. They had anticipated these questions and hence had practiced the answers. So far, so good.

Emmanuel was doing well. He seemed to be performing better at answering Aliyu's questions than when they were practicing. Without warning, Aliyu changed the line of questioning.

"What do you want from this cause, Bashir?"

"I want to fight for Allah."

Aliyu chuckled. He didn't seem impressed or offended.

"No, Bashir. You don't. What do you *really* want from this cause?"

Emmanuel paused. Zalla was afraid the man might not have a response for this. He didn't prepare him for this line of questioning. He held his breath and prayed.

"I want to fight for Allah and bring the glory of the Supreme—"

"That's enough! Don't lie to me, Bashir."

Aliyu's voice was almost imploring at this point. He didn't look as if he was angry, but it felt as if he really wanted an answer Emmanuel didn't have.

"Truthfully, Allah isn't why I joined this cause. At least, not in the way that I made it seem…"

This caught Aliyu's attention and made Zalla's heart skip two beats.

"There is something else…" Emmanuel continued. "It is personal and selfish. But I think it's a good thing. I haven't had peace for a while now, ever since my wife disappeared. My life has no meaning anymore. So, every day, I think about the group and the cause. I think about what Allah wants and why he allowed this to happen to me. I came here to seek answers, to pursue something to fill the emptiness in my heart."

Emmanuel paused pensively and then continued.

"I am here to end the emptiness and void that her absence brought to my life. I tried several means of finding peace, but to no avail. After much thought, I believed this was to be the only way I could achieve that, and I'm willing to do anything, *anything*, to find peace."

A smile split Aliyu's face, and Zalla wondered if he

should take it as a good sign.

"Bashir. You're a man of many wonders. And the metaphor? Where did you learn how to speak like that? I hope you find the peace you so desire."

"I hope so."

"Well, I love your confidence. I am the first step. I have vetted you. I don't know how your rhetoric can be helpful to the cause, though, even if it's remarkable, but you, as a driver and mechanic, that's a great resource. Imamu would take you and Zalla to the training station. There, you will be taught the basics of war; how to fire a gun and cut off a man's head clean."

As they prepared to leave, Aliyu suddenly embraced Emmanuel. "Welcome to the family, brother!" he said with a broad smile.

Zalla remembered the first time he had met Aliyu. One of the students of the other Islamic school had invited them to listen to an Imam called Yusuf, who was going about preaching.

That was where they met Aliyu. He was part of

Yusuf's entourage and sat by the side studying the faces of the audience.

But that was a long time ago. Long before the girls were kidnapped, before Lado was slaughtered like a ram. Long before he joined the cause and went on his first mission, before the night that he stood idly by as his new friends torched the place he once called home, while his brothers were still in their rooms and classes, locked from the outside so they couldn't escape.

The teachings of Yusuf still rang in his ears. He could still feel the charged atmosphere during the preaching of the radical and violent message at the mosque that very day.

According to Lado, this Yusuf had been going around some northern states declaring the teachings of Allah and his prophet and converting a lot of people to the cause until he too became a believer.

The man's teachings were totally different from *Shibarid's* teachings. Where *Shibarid's* teachings spoke of love and acceptance, Yusuf's doctrines announced defiance and separation. Some in the capital attested that this new doctrine was the true doctrine of Allah, which was hidden before by the corruption of men but was now brought to the fore by the grace and mercy of Allah through his servant, Yusuf.

A lot of young people wanted to be on this side, the righteous side.

They wanted to fight as soldiers in Allah's noble war, and Yusuf's cause gave them purpose and direction.

"Zalla, you and Bashir should follow Imamu before the soldiers start the evening patrol."

Zalla snapped out of his reverie and looked in Emmanuel's direction. If the man was scared, he didn't show it one bit.

# CHAPTER SEVENTEEN

For over a week, Aisha had been almost invisible in the camp, keeping her head down, doing whatever she was asked to do, and avoiding trouble at all costs. Other times, she sat in the tent and allowed the memories of her father to overwhelm her. She would cry till she could cry no more. Her tent mates had slightly warmed up to her, but she kept to herself as much as possible. Some of them teased her for being too serious, while others tried to get her to open up to them. Aisha didn't care. Her resolve was back, bringing with it her desire to escape the horrible life in captivity, which was now greater than her fear of what would happen if she were caught. She just didn't want to spend one more day in the camp, but she knew that she must be very careful this time and plan properly.

It was another sunny day, and Aisha hated the way she had to suffer for a whole day and end up eating bad food. Aisha shook her head and walked to the wash basin. As she washed her plate, she marveled at how some of the girls had accepted their fates and adjusted to life in the camp. Some of the girls forcibly married off to the men were now behaving as if they were in normal relationships. Aisha now understood that this was their way of coping.

That morning, Junaidu left the camp again as he did occasionally. Whatever he did when he was gone, Aisha didn't care, and she was grateful that he had to go again. Seeing him around made her uneasy. She remembered the girl whom he killed because she tried to escape. She still remembered her lifeless body in the dirt, killed so callously.

That night, Aisha waited in the tent until the camp was totally silent. She had waited and waited, but she was fed up, and it had to be that night. There was a half-moon that gave just enough light to make out trees and aid her navigation. After what seemed like forever, she stood up quietly and tiptoed to the tent opening. Before she stepped out, she looked back at the sleeping girls. It was already the early hours of the morning, and the girls were deep in sleep, some of them snoring. Aisha smiled to herself. She gingerly stepped out, looked around, then checked the guard posts to be sure that the men were asleep. When she was sure that they were, she walked away without looking back.

She walked quietly into the bush and quickly made her way eastwards. She stopped occasionally to check if she was being followed and to get her bearings. The farther away from the camp she got, the more hope rose in her. Her heart swelled, filled with the thought of seeing Chief again, her best friend Mairo, who always had 'gist' for her, and even Joshua, her dream boy. As her hope rose, she began to imagine the warmth of her father's embrace.

She found a path and walked along it until she reached a fork. Heart beating fast, she took the right path on a whim. She took long strides, propelled by the fear of being caught. Sometimes, she would hear some noise and freeze. After making sure that she was safe, she would continue. When she had covered a reasonable distance, she leaned on a tree to rest. At least she had gotten to a point where it would be difficult to catch up with her, but it was getting to dawn. That was when she needed to move faster, because it would be easier to spot her in the daytime, but before she could take a step, she felt a hand cover her mouth. She tried to struggle, but another arm wrapped her in a powerful hold.

"You are trying to escape again, right? This time, I will teach you a proper lesson." Aisha's eyes widened when she realized that it was Junaidu. How did he find her!?

"Please. Don't kill me. Please!" She begged him. Junaidu spun her around, grabbed her arm, and started dragging her back towards the camp.

She started to struggle again. "I do not want to go back there! Please!" He just ignored her pleas. "Please! I won't say anything to anyone. I swear I won't. Just let me go."

"I should let you go so you can expose me and my men? You are mad!" Junaidu turned and shrieked at her. When she didn't say anything, he let go of her arm and continued moving.

Aisha sighed in defeat and followed him quietly. After walking for about an hour, she stopped. "Wait. Please, I need to pee." She said.

"You are going nowhere."

"Please, I can't hold it anymore." Aisha held her lower abdomen and squatted. Junaidu groaned.

"One minute! I give you one minute. And do it here."

"You have to turn around. Please!" Aisha begged.

When Junaidu turned around, she grabbed a rock and hit him on the head. As he fell, she took to her heels. With a rage-filled roar, Junaidu jumped up and raced after her. Aisha's heart threatened to tear out of her chest as she ran for her life. Within a short distance, Junaidu had caught up with her. He grabbed her with such force that they both fell to the ground, struggling. She fought with all her strength, but he was too strong for her and easily overpowered her, slapping her into painful submission.

When they got to the camp, it was already daylight. Junaidu dragged her to the middle of the campground. Aisha fell to her knees, crying and begging for her life. Her heart skipped when she saw her roommates tied hand and foot on the ground in front of their tent. Their mouths were gagged, and they had obviously been beaten. She realized then that they were suffering because of her.

She tried begging them with her eyes, but they looked away. Junaidu ordered the men to release the girls.

When they were untied, they cursed her and spat in her direction. One of the girls rushed towards Aisha and kicked her before any of the men could stop her. As the men dragged her away, Aisha looked to Junaidu with tears spilling down her cheeks. A sudden feeling of regret overwhelmed her. Her stubbornness was going to cost her life. When Junaidu started tying her hands and feet, she began to cry harder.

"Have mercy on me, please! Please don't kill me. I will not do it again!"

"Shut up!" Junaidu slapped her.

She didn't stop begging. She even began to beg the men and some of the girls around to help her beg Junaidu. Some of them shook their heads in pity, while others looked away with cold faces. She started struggling, and Junaidu had to request the assistance of the other men to hold her down while he tied her up.

"*Ka zana ta!*" Junaidu ordered one of the men, named Mahmood, to whip her. Aisha tried to struggle, but it was useless. The sound of the whip, ripping through her clothes and tearing her skin, mingled with her screams and filled the morning air. She wailed and begged, but he just kept whipping her.

Nobody, not even the girls, came to her rescue. It got to a point where Aisha gave up struggling. She lay there, exhausted and bleeding, as the whipping continued. When Mahmood stopped, Junaidu untied the ropes and freed her.

Aisha lay there, a pitiful sack of tattered clothes, bleeding and weeping quietly, wishing that she would just die. She couldn't move for the pain. Her back was torn open, blood seeping freely and forming a trail across the ground. The pain, the humiliation, the desperation, the helplessness—it was all too much, and she wished death would claim her now. Her mind drifted to her father, her chief, and at once a sob tore through her body, wracking her with even more agony. She knew what would happen next. Her thoughts spun with flashes of her father's loving embrace, her mother's distant yet tender gaze, and her own mischievous shenanigans with Mairo.

Her thoughts were cut short by Junaidu's voice, low and controlled, carrying a cruel calmness that was far more terrifying than a shout.

*"Ki tashi ki tafi dakin ki."* - Get up and go to your room, - Junaidu ordered.

She didn't move. She started crying again at the thought of what his words meant. She remembered all too well how he had killed that girl after telling her to go to her tent. But Junaidu had a soft spot for her, didn't he?

"*Na ce ki tashi ki tafi d'akin ki.*" - I told you to get up and go to your room - Junaidu yelled.

Aisha shook her head weakly and lay there begging and crying. Junaidu dragged her to her feet, then pushed her so she stumbled forward a few steps.

"I said that I will not spare anyone who tries to escape, but you didn't listen." Junaidu swung his gun from behind his back and raised it to his shoulder.

"Please... I don't want to die."

"You chose death." Junaidu pulled back the bolt of his AK-47 rifle, cocking the gun. Some girls began to scream, while others wailed, calling Aisha's name.

Aisha closed her eyes, resigning herself to her fate.

And then came the single gunshot, loud in its finality.

Aisha flinched, expecting the impact of the bullet slamming into her body, tearing through skin, muscle, and bone.

*Would I actually feel it? Maybe I'm already dead, cos he won't miss. Am I still alive? Why do I still feel pain all over?* As these thoughts flashed through her mind, she gingerly opened her eyes. When her eyes were fully opened, she searched her body for the bullet hole, but she didn't have any. She turned around to see Junaidu still holding his gun, but he looked as shocked as she was.

When she followed his gaze, she saw the man he was looking at. "Mallam Yusufu!" Junaidu exclaimed.

An old man stood a short distance away holding a pistol. He was flanked by several hard-looking, well-armed men. He was looking straight at Junaidu. Clearly, he had fired the shot.

Aisha had heard stories of Mallam Yusufu. He was the leader of this faction of fighters, but he left the actual physical work to the younger men due to his age.

Usually, he stayed at the main camp, and so the girls had never met him, but when the gang members wanted to make serious decisions, they sought his counsel. Aisha was surprised that he had saved her and waited alongside everyone to hear what he would say.

"*Ka da ka kashe ta.*" Mallam Yusufu stepped forward and eyed Aisha.

She was shocked that Mallam Yusufu ordered his men not to kill her. Junaidu quickly went to him and whispered something. Mallam Yusuf nodded and whispered back, and after some seconds, Junaidu turned to Aisha and smirked. Then he walked over to where Aisha stood. Aisha's eyes widened. She had no clue what was going on.

"*Ina Mahmood?*" - Where is Mahmood? - Junaidu called out.

"*Ga ni nan!*" - Here I am! - Mahmood answered and ran to him.

"*Ga matar ka. Na ba ka.*" He said to Mahmood, pointing at Aisha. Everyone gasped, including Aisha.

*Here is your wife! I give her to you.*

These words hit her harder than any beating she had received, any flogging she had endured.

Why would Junaidu do this? Did he now hate her so

much? If this was going to happen, if she was going to become anybody's wife in the camp, it should have been him. He had shown her compassion in his own way until she tried to fight him for killing one of the girls. Aisha looked from Mahmood, who had an evil grin on his face, to Junaidu and then to Mallam Yusufu. She shook her head, but she couldn't say a word.

"Go back to your work, everyone!" Junaidu ordered. The girls quickly dispersed.

Junaidu turned to Aisha. "You are lucky."

Lucky!? How was this lucky? As bad as things were, they just got so much worse. How would she survive being a "wife" to Mahmood? When Junaidu started to walk away with Mallam Yusufu, Aisha followed them.

"Please, sir. I promise to be obedient. Please don't let him take me." She begged.

When Mallam Yusufu turned and gave her a killer look, she stopped and stepped back, but Junaidu grabbed her arm and shook her hard.

"Listen to me, you brat! Don't think you are safe yet. You are only alive because of my master, but I still want to kill you."

He let her go and walked away with Mallam Yusufu.

*"Koma aikin ki."* - Go back to your work. - Mahmood said to her, walking away to join Mallam Yusufu and Junaidu.

Aisha collapsed in a heap and wept bitterly, consumed by the harshness of her reality. For a moment, she considered committing suicide. Nobody said a word to her. Even the kidnappers who would have flogged her for sitting there while the rest of the girls worked seemed not to care. After some time, Aisha rose to her feet and joined some girls doing the laundry. She could barely move, so she just tried to clean up her wounds.

"You are now a married woman, Aisha."

"I'll see how you will survive what he will do to you."

"Aisha Mahmood!" They teased her. Aisha swallowed the lump in her throat, fighting back her tears.

"What would he do to me?" She asked. The girl did not answer but smiled in a sinister way. Aisha had never wished that chores would keep increasing until that day.

When they were done with the clothes, they were called to go and have lunch before the afternoon chores. Aisha grabbed her plate and made her way to the food stand. When the woman saw her, she smiled. Aisha looked away and stretched her hands towards the woman. When she had received her portion of the food and was about to go, Mahmood walked to her, collected the plate from her hand, and put it down.

"But I'm hungry." She protested.

"*Na sani*," —I know—Mahmood replied and pulled her towards the tents. She tried to struggle but couldn't remove her hand from his vice-like grip. He took her towards the tents where the soldiers camped. He pushed her into the tent and entered behind her. Aisha saw some food and water on the mat. She didn't know when a sigh of relief escaped her lips.

"Eat." Mahmood sat at the end of the mat and rested

his rifle at his side.

Aisha hesitated at first, but when her stomach grumbled loudly, she rushed towards the plate of boiled yams and oil. When she finished eating, she turned to see Mahmood smiling at her. She stood to her feet and waited for what he would say next. Mahmood stood up and moved towards Aisha. He held the collar of her dress and tried to peep inside, but Aisha slapped his hand.

"Ouwww!" Mahmood laughed. Aisha felt stupid. Mahmoud was teasing her, but she doubted it would stop at that.

*"Ki koma aiki. Zan gan ki da dare,"* - Go back to work. I'll see you tonight. - Mahmood said as he left her and went out. The words reminded her of her new reality, and Aisha looked around the tent, trying to get her bearings and familiarise herself with her new lodgings. There were boots on the ground, and some clothes piled up on the ground at the back. Clothes that she would soon begin to wash. There was an iron box to one side. When Aisha opened the box, she released the

lid immediately and jumped at the sound of iron hitting iron.

The box contained various weapons and ammunition. Aisha opened the lid again and touched them. She had never paid much attention to guns before now. Different things crossed her mind as she looked at them. Maybe when she escaped again… she quickly squashed the thought and carried the empty plates out to wash.

****

Working through the day was difficult for Aisha. Just bending down caused her so much pain, but no one cared about her injuries, least of all Mahmood. He had asked her to dig a ditch for compost.

Aisha stared at him in disbelief.

"I can't." She begged.

"Try me." Mahmood held the shovel out to her. When Aisha hesitated, he slapped her.

"Try me again," Mahmood said. With watery eyes, she

collected the shovel and got to work. After some time, Mahmood ordered another girl to take over. It seemed this was all just to test her and assert his power over her. When the day's activities were finally over, Aisha dragged herself to her tent.

"*Ina za ki?*" —Where are you going? — Aisha flinched at the voice behind her. She suddenly remembered that Junaidu had given her to Mahmood as a wife. She humbly turned around and followed him to his tent.

When they got in, Aisha moved as far away from him as possible, filled with dread at what might come next.

Mahmood proceeded to take off his clothes, leaving his shorts. The large scar on his chest made Aisha gasp. It looked like a machete cut that had been roughly stitched. "Mark of a warrior of Allah." He said, seeing her look.

"How?" Aisha asked, afraid that her words might offend him.

"I fight for Allah's cause. And it's for Allah I got this mark. Touch it." Mahmood moved towards her.

She was repulsed by him and the scar, but she was more afraid of offending him by refusing. When she touched it, he held her hand and ran it over his chest. As he did so, he closed his eyes and let out a soft moan. Aisha, taken aback, quickly pulled her hand away.

"Why did you stop? *Ki cigaba.*" He nudged her to continue. Aisha shook her head.

His countenance suddenly changed. Mahmood was not an attractive man in the best of times. Now, with his features contorted by anger and unbridled lust, to Aisha, he looked like a fiend from hell. He released her and hurriedly took off his shorts. She gasped and covered her mouth with her hands on seeing his already erect penis. It was large and veined, pulsing like an angry beast. She had never seen a naked adult man before, and the sight frightened her to her core.

She knew about sex from Biology class and from the few naughty magazines she had seen in school, but the thought of such a large penis near her body almost made her pass out in fright. She vaguely remembered reading somewhere that the length of the average vagina was 4 inches. But this throbbing monster in front of her looked at least 8 inches. And it was thick, too thick! Aisha knelt and clasped her hands in front of her.

"Please … it's too big…" she pleaded.

Laughing, he pushed her onto the hard floor and ripped off her clothes. As her breasts spilled out, he got even more aroused and pushed her down and moved on top of her. She was assaulted by his smell, the unwashed smell of the bush, and his hot, foul breath, and she tried to fight him off.

"No! Please. Pleasssse!" She cried.

"Keep quiet before I make your life miserable!" Mahmood snarled, but she didn't stop. She kept struggling. He held her wrists above her head with his left hand and then started choking her with his right hand. Aisha struggled and fought as hard as she could, legs flailing, but he was just too strong for her, and she soon grew weak.

He separated her legs with his knees and thrust himself at her. When he couldn't penetrate, he got frustrated and slapped her hard. He then forced two fingers into her as far as he could. She cried out in pain. As she continued to struggle weakly, he replaced his fingers with the head of his penis and thrust hard. The pain was like nothing she had ever felt, and she started to scream.

'DADDYYYYYY!'

She gritted her teeth and screamed again, gasping for breath, but Mahmood didn't stop. He thrust harder and faster, grunting, his hot breath on her cheek and neck, until she thought she was going to die from the pain.

When he was done, Aisha couldn't move. She curled up on her side on the floor, crying, his semen dripping out of her, mixed with her blood.

Mahmood laughed and put on his clothes. He then lit a cigarette and stepped out of the tent. Aisha lay for what felt like forever. She lay there numb, not believing what had happened. She alternated between numbness and hatred, anger, and shame. She tried to sit up and winced at the pain. She couldn't even close her legs properly. She started to wail.

She cried until she fell into a fitful sleep. Later that night, she managed to clean herself up. When she was done, she used her dress to wrap herself up, then she lay back on the mat and closed her eyes.

****

Aisha woke up to the heat of the day. As she opened her eyes, she saw Nabila standing at the entrance of the tent.

"*Gashi ki saka.*" —Here, wear this—Nabila flung some clothes at her, laughing. Aisha looked at the clothes and then at Nabila.

"You'd better hurry up and join us to work," Nabila said to her as she walked away. Aisha touched the clothes and opened them up. A long-sleeved brown gown and a black veil. She slowly got up, put on the clothes, and covered her hair with the veil.

When she stepped outside, she saw some of the men sitting with Mahmood. They stopped chatting when they saw her and started laughing. Aisha used the veil to cover her face with just enough space for her to see where she was going. Tears of shame spilled from her eyes, but she wiped them off. When she reached the work area, some of the girls started sniggering.

"Aisha will soon be a mother." Nabila announced, and everyone laughed again. Aisha broke down into heavy sobs. She turned back towards the tents to run away from the shame, but Junaidu stood before her.

"Where do you think you are going?"

The coldness in his eyes was unmistakable. He pushed her back towards the work area. "You have work to do!" Aisha burst into tears and walked towards the girls who were washing some clothes. When she joined a girl who was rinsing some of the clothes, the girl hissed and turned away from her. Aisha looked at her for some seconds, then she started rinsing the clothes too. She kept using her veil to wipe her tears.

Later, when Aisha was alone in the tent, she lay on the mat and prayed. "God. If you are hearing me, help me. Please. I need to get out of here."

Before Aisha slept that night, she vowed that if she ever left the camp, she would do everything in her power to make them pay for what they had done to her. She only hoped that she would live to see them dead, from Junaidu to Mahmood and everyone who supported them.

For now, she would do everything to just survive.

# CHAPTER EIGHTEEN

The ride to the training camp was bumpy. The men sent by Aliyu to accompany them on the journey were mostly quiet. The silence was both welcoming and uncomfortable for Bashir. Emmanuel was getting himself comfortable in his new persona.

Bashir was a Hausa-Fulani man who was born in the capital city of Maiduguri. He grew up without a father and had to work his way through school by taking up an apprenticeship with a local automobile mechanic. Determined as he was, he concluded his education and set up his own shop where he fixed vehicles and sold spare parts. He was not fulfilled with life, and he felt he wanted to do more to show his faith, find peace and purpose, by serving Allah.

This story was becoming more real, and Emmanuel had settled himself into relating to others as Bashir—a zealot—rather than Emmanuel—a man who had lost a daughter. Since his Hausa was flawless, and he had grown his hair and beard, he blended in easily.

After leaving Maiduguri, they drove through the bush for hours, making several detours, sharp turns, and double-backs. Once the men were sure they weren't being followed, they then drove on until they arrived at their destination.

He looked at Zalla. The man looked very calm. After the encounter with Aliyu, his suspicion of Zalla had increased. No one could possibly know the intricacies of such a secretive group unless he was a member, Emmanuel thought.

*"Su waye ke tare da kai, Muntari?"* The guards at the entrance asked the men in the front seat of the bus, recognising them.

Muntari responded that they were sent by Aliyu to deliver new recruits for the cause. The guard nodded and waved them through.

It was a large dusty clearing with numerous buildings—from proper cement buildings to makeshift structures like the group of shacks back at Aliyu's hideout. There were hundreds of young men, and, to Emmanuel's surprise, lots of women too; and the women did not appear to be there against their will. And almost everybody was armed.

They parked the bus and started walking, following one of the guards. As they walked, several people turned and looked at them, especially at Zalla. They obviously recognised him but weren't very welcoming. Emmanuel wondered why but did not ask.

The guard led them to the biggest building in the middle of the clearing. This was clearly the headquarters of the base.

Emmanuel was amazed at the scale of the place and the amount of activity going on. With the place not so far away from the city, how had the military planes not spotted it before now? To his mind, the terrorists didn't seem to be doing a lot to hide their base.

*"Gambo, ka gaya wa Al-Amin wai Aliyu ya aiko da sabobin shiga,"* The guard that they came with said to another guard who was standing in front of the building.

A request to tell a certain Al-Amin that new recruits

have arrived. Emmanuel wondered who this man was. Maybe he controlled things on this side of the operation just like Aliyu controlled things on the other side.

The guard looked at them, then turned and marched into the building.

As they waited, Emmanuel marvelled again at the scale and level of organisation of the place. It was as large, if not larger, than the military base in the city. They even had military vehicles, which they had obviously stolen on previous attacks. He wondered how they got spare parts to maintain them.

His thoughts were interrupted by the arrival of the man they called Al-Amin. He was accompanied by two soldiers who looked more rugged than the ones Bashir had met previously. This man was nothing like Aliyu. He was a man hardened by war. He had a scar that ran from the top left side of his face through his left eye. Because of that, his left eye was bad. A one-eyed commander, great!

Al-Amin's voice was gruff, and he had to repeat himself for Emmanuel to understand what he was saying. He was asking his name.

"Bashir," Emmanuel answered.

He expected the man to ask his companion, Zalla, what his name was, but he didn't. Instead, he asked him why he came back after deserting.

*"Ba'a gudun aikin Allah,"* was the response Zalla gave to the man.

This confirmed Bashir's suspicions that Zalla was part of the terrorist group previously. But his response amused Emmanuel. People don't run from God's work. That was the most absurd thing he had heard throughout the day. What was surprising was that Al-Amin seemed to accept the explanation. He said that Aliyu vouching for them was enough for him. Before he sent them with one of the guards to get them settled, he turned towards Zalla and told him that if he ever deserted again, he would personally hunt him down and kill him.

That left Emmanuel with a chill, but Zalla just shrugged it off. The man kept getting stranger by the day.

"So, what do you think is next?" Emmanuel asked Zalla when they were finally alone in their assigned "quarters".

"They will do you three things. Teach you how to kill people. Teach you about Boko Haram and what they do. Teach you how to survive."

Zalla said all these without a hint of emotion. If he cared about these things, he didn't show it. He was more concerned about their sleeping quarters, which consisted of two mats spread on an otherwise bare cement floor in a small room.

"When do we start this training?"

"Not both of us, just you."

"Why just me? Didn't we come in together?"

"There is something I need to tell you, Emma—Bashir. I know these people. I know this place because

I have stayed here before."

Emmanuel felt bad that Zalla lied to him before, but was glad that he finally opened up.

"So how did you join, Zalla?"

"Not now. Not today. I will tell you another day."

Emmanuel could see that Zalla didn't want to talk, so he left it alone. "You didn't tell me. When do I start the training?"

Zalla looked at him with a hint of sympathy in his eyes and responded, "You will start when they want you to start."

****

Zalla looked at Emmanuel. Even though they had adopted the name Bashir, and he was living up to it, whenever he looked at him, he still saw Emmanuel, the husband of Zainab and the father of Aisha.

He didn't like what was about to happen to him, but it was part of the process.

He remembered the first time he arrived at this station. It was a bit more than five years ago. It wasn't as big or busy as it was now. Back then, there were no women in the station. The soldiers were responsible for their own meals. It was a new and exciting experience for him and Lado, and they welcomed the experience. Anything for the cause.

The training started on their first night. While they slept, someone poured cold water on them, and a group of soldiers started kicking and beating them. They were so startled that they didn't know where they were. First, they thought they were being attacked by outsiders, then they recognised some of the faces and thought they had done something wrong and were being punished.

At the end of the encounter, they would realize that what had happened was just the first phase of their training. They didn't die but had survived to continue the process. Al-Amin oversaw combat and warfare, while Aliyu taught them about the Cause and why they should be willing to kill and die for it.

His teachings were like Yusuf's, contrary to their *Shibarid's* teaching. It was filled with the radical doctrine of the movement and had a strong draw for the listener. Lado was more responsive, and he followed his friend.

At first, they were told that all the training was to help them protect themselves from the evil forces, the soldiers of *Shaidan*. But after Yusuf's death, the group took on a more violent approach under the new leader.

By the time they were six months into the cause, they had started attacking police stations and other security outposts. Not long after that, they started attacking churches and mosques that preached against them.

It was a righteous cause. To them. Everyone who stood in Allah's way needed to feel Allah's wrath. And they, privileged as they were, were Allah's swords of judgement. They would go wherever he led them and do whatever he asked them to do through the mouth of their leader. He was Allah's mouthpiece.

By the end of their first year, they were tasked with a great mission. It was a mission to silence one of the great oppositions to the progress of Allah's work on earth. He was an Islamic scholar who was adulterating the words of the Holy Book to suit his political agenda. He was the brother of a politician who had long used his position to influence unsuspecting Muslims wrongly.

It wouldn't take Zalla and Lado long to figure out who that was. It was Mallam Ashiru Anas Ibn Malik Mansur, their *Shibarid*. Zalla had told Lado that he couldn't do it. He had told Lado of his plan to tell their Imam the plot against his life so that he would run away before the group came to kill him.

Lado protested and told him it was a bad idea, a sin against Allah. Zalla knew it was a stupid excuse. There was no man on earth who loved Allah like his Imam. *Shibarid* would spend hours a day reciting the Quran and Hadiths, pray five times a day—he never missed a prayer—he gave alms and helped the poor, took in students, and taught them the ways of truth, settled disputes justly, and spoke out against people who wanted to twist Allah's words for their personal ambition. He did that to everyone, including his brother, Alhaji Attahiru.

For the first time since he joined the cause, he doubted if Allah was truly behind them and if their leader's voice was truly the voice of Allah.

He watched as Emmanuel bunched up some clothes and used them as a pillow. Apart from what Zalla had told him about formerly being a member of Boko Haram, the man didn't know much else. He watched as the man lay with his back to the mat and his face up, probably thinking about his daughter.

Zalla had heard the news of his wife's disappearance some months after it had happened. He wanted to come to Emmanuel's house and comfort him. That was some months after *Shibarid's* death, and he needed someone to mourn alongside. Someone who shared a connection with his Imam.

But he didn't know how to introduce himself to

Emmanuel. It was very unlikely that he would remember the wallet incident. Zalla had decided to keep his distance then.

 "What are you thinking about, Zalla?"

The question startled him because he had thought Emmanuel was sleeping.

"Many things," he replied.

Emmanuel didn't probe further as it was obvious that Zalla didn't want to talk. Not like he didn't want to talk to Emmanuel, but he didn't want to open wounds that were just beginning to close.

Zalla reached into his pocket and brought out a ring and put it on his middle finger. It had belonged to his Imam. It was the only object of his that he still had.

Just then, three fighters barged into their shack and dragged Emmanuel to his feet. He was startled and reached out to Zalla for help, but Zalla moved out of the way.

For a second, he saw the look of betrayal on

Emmanuel's face, and smiled to himself. Emmanuel was going to survive even though he would start the next day in pain.

And with that, Zalla tuned out the screams of his companion and took the makeshift rag pillow from Emmanuel's mat and lay down.

****

The men dragged Emmanuel out into the open square and started punching him and hitting him with sticks. He defended himself as best as he could, but in a very short time, he was getting dizzy from the beating. Thinking that Zalla had betrayed him, he decided to make a run for it, even though his chances of escape were zero.

As he ran, he expected to be shot, so he tried zig-zagging, but instead of hearing gunshots, he heard the men laughing, and as they laughed, they were joined by other fighters laughing uproariously! He stopped and looked around incredulously.

Oh, so this was some kind of rite of passage? Did that

mean his training had already commenced?

As he caught his breath, they grabbed him and dragged him to a pole and tied him to it, exposing his back. Zalla had told him in passing once that they would torture him as part of the training, but he had shrugged it off then. His confusion was heightened by the fact that he thought Al-Amin had cleared him.

*Why were they flexing these long cane rods and smiling at him?* He thought to himself.

The first cane landed on his back with a resounding "kpah!" and he screamed.

They methodically flogged his back, buttocks, and legs, each lash cutting into flesh with merciless precision. At first, the pain was sharp, searing, burning like fire on raw skin. But as the strikes continued, the agony dulled into something heavier, a throbbing numbness that sank deep into his bones. His body no longer knew how to scream properly—his cries came out as strangled gasps, broken groans, the sound of a man teetering between pain and unconsciousness.

Their laughter filled the air, harsh and mocking, as though his suffering was nothing more than sport to them. Between their jeers, the whips cracked again and again. They taunted him with cruel commands, their voices sneering above the sound of leather striking flesh. *"Be a man!"* one shouted, his words twisting into a laugh. *"Our fighters embrace pain!"* another added, as though the brutality were a lesson, a rite of passage, rather than pure torment.

The words stung almost as much as the lashes. His pride wrestled with his despair, and though his body was breaking, his spirit fought desperately not to collapse before them.

After about an hour, they took him back to the room where he collapsed and passed out.

****

The next morning started early with physical training. In pain, he had to join the other recruits to run, jump, crawl, and climb through an obstacle course. Then weapons training, then back to more physical training. The evenings were for religious study and indoctrination.

This process went on for weeks, and the years of physical discipline kept him in good standing. Furthermore, his skill with machines translated to an uncanny ease with the different weapons that they were trained with. In a very short time, he could disassemble an AK-47 assault rifle in less than thirty seconds.

By the third week, he was down to thirteen seconds. His targeting accuracy soon became so good that even the battle-hardened instructors were impressed, especially his ability to hit targets while running and shooting from the hip.

*"Wannan Bashir kisa ne, na rantse,"* the fighters joked.

Yes, I am a killer, Emmanuel thought as he poured himself into his training.

Over several weeks, they were taught tactics, evasion techniques, navigation, hand-to-hand combat, knife fighting, and other field craft. He quickly came to understand that the terrorists had numerous ex-soldiers and even foreign mercenaries working with them.

He quietly bided his time, obeying the instructors and earning their trust. Slowly but surely, Emmanuel was rising through the ranks, doing whatever task was placed before him—whether menial labor, drills, or mock combat—with a diligence that set him apart. All the while, only Zalla knew the truth of why he pushed himself so relentlessly.

Zalla supported him wherever he could, offering advice, sharing food, or covering for him when exhaustion threatened to betray his resolve. Yet they were careful, always careful. They could not appear too dependent on each other, nor let their bond draw suspicion. Their friendship was disguised in silence, hidden behind the mask of comradeship expected in the camp.

Soon, he was tasked to join patrols and then small forays for robberies, where a few shots into the air were all that was needed to subdue transporters and villagers who then parted with their valuables, including food and money.

While in camp, he was assigned to vehicles and weapons, cleaning and servicing them, and this he did with such dedication that he gained the respect and admiration of Al-Amin and the other leaders.

Unfortunately, his popularity also stirred envy and resentment among some of the men, most notably a zealous, battle-scarred fighter named Muktar. The man carried himself with the arrogance of one who believed brutality was the only proof of strength, and Emmanuel had quickly learned to avoid him.

He ignored Muktar as much as possible, forcing himself to focus on his true objective. Whenever the bitterness of camp life threatened to overwhelm him, the thought of his beloved daughter rose before him like a light in the darkness, fueling his resolve and keeping him moving forward.

# CHAPTER NINETEEN

Emmanuel crouched along a low cement fence near the edge of the town of Kalau with a group of about twenty fighters. They were tasked with securing the escape route for another group of fighters who had been sent to attack a police station in the town. His group was led by Al-Amin himself, while Zalla was with the first group.

They were all very tense, gripping their weapons anxiously while waiting for the outcome of the first attack. Emmanuel was worried, but thankful that he was not in the first group, as he had never killed anyone and had no intention of ever doing so.

As they watched, they saw and heard the explosions from the middle of the town signalling the commencement of the attack. The explosions were followed by concentrated rifle fire, accompanied by screams and the noise of commotion as people fled from their homes.

*"Allahu akbar!"* someone whispered behind him.

Soon, the shootings became more sporadic and started moving towards their position, as the first group started their escape, meaning they had completed their mission.

As the vehicles pulled alongside, some of them boarded the trucks while the rest got on their motorcycles, and they all headed out, shooting sporadically into the air and whooping.

On the way out, the group suddenly split into two, one group heading back towards their base and Al-Amin's group making a detour to a side street on the outskirts of the town. The vehicles came to a halt at a compound that contained a church and a single-family dwelling, and Emmanuel's heart skipped a beat as they alighted from the trucks. The area was lit by exterior lights on the house, while the street was in darkness.

Al-Amin then ordered the fighters to surround the house, which they quickly did. As Emmanuel hurried to go to the rear of the house, Al-Amin called him back to stay by his side.

"This man is a pastor, and he is preaching against

Allah! We will finish him and his family today." He said in Hausa. The words brought a chill to Emmanuel's spine as he imagined the horror that was about to take place. His dread increased when he noticed Muktar nearby, grinning.

*"FASTOR! NA SAN KANA CIKIN GIDAN NAN! KA FITO DA IYALIN KA, BA ABIN DA ZAI SAME SU!"* Al-Amin called out to the people inside. - Pastor! I know you're in the house! Come out and surrender and we will spare your family, nothing will happen to them!

No one moved. The interior of the house remained dark. Either the pastor and his family had escaped out the back before they could be surrounded, or he didn't believe Al-Amin's words. Emmanuel's heart raced in his chest.

*"FASTOR! ZAN KIRGA DAGA DAYA ZUWA BIYAR, IN BAKA FITO DA KAI DA IYALIN KA BA, ZAMU FARA HARBI MU KUMA KONE GIDAN NAN."* Al-Amin declared for the final time,

his voice rising with fury, the raw edge of anger sharpening every word.

This threat felt real. Al-Amin had assured the pastor that he would open fire if he and his family didn't come out. Al-Amin had given the man until the count of five.

*"DAYA!"* ONE! The cry rang out.

Al-Amin's count had started. There was no means of escape anymore.

*"BIYU!"*

The excitement on the faces of Muktar and his cohorts was unnerving. Sadiqu and the others did not smile even though they were ready to carry out whatever orders Al-Amin gave.

*"UKU!"*

Thunder rumbled in the distance, adding to the tension in the air.

*"HUDU!"*

Suddenly, the door was opened, and the pastor came out of the house with his hands raised. Almost on cue, it started drizzling.

*"Ina sauran? Ka fito da iyalin ka na ce, ko mu shiga ciki mu zazzage su."* - Where are the others? Bring your family out, I said, or we can go inside and hunt them down. - Al-Amin's words dripped with menace, his threat hanging heavy in the air like a blade about to fall.

"Please, spare my family!"

Muktar stepped forward and punched him hard in the stomach, and the man collapsed to his knees. A group of fighters entered the house and dragged out the man's wife and two daughters, screaming and struggling.

The wife fell to her knees, her voice breaking as she begged for mercy, tears streaming down her face. One by one, the daughters followed, dropping beside her in trembling heaps, their cries rising into the air like a chorus of despair. As Emmanuel looked at the girls, his mind went to Aisha, his daughter, and the terror that she must have felt when facing these same terrorists. Emmanuel was torn. But there was nothing he could do to help them, nothing whatsoever.

Al-Amin raised his rifle and pulled back the bolt, loading a round into the chamber. As the loud clack of the bolt slamming back filled the air, the woman and her daughters started wailing. To Emmanuel's shock, the pastor lifted both hands into the air and started thanking God for His mercies and His grace. Then he started asking God to forgive his would-be killers!

Al-Amin hesitated, taken aback by the man's actions. He had expected fear, but met calm; anger, but saw forgiveness. Emmanuel saw the confusion and hesitation and prayed he would change his mind.

The rain continued to fall, increasing in intensity and drenching all of them, but no one seemed to care. For a moment, they all stood still, awaiting the command to kill or to be set free. Muktar then let out a shout.

"ALLAHU AKBAR!"

The resulting cries and whoops from the men galvanised Al-Amin into action. He levelled his gun to shoot, and Emmanuel closed his eyes and turned away to prevent watching the horror unfold.

*"Ina so ka bude idanun ka, ka ga dukan abin da zai faru."* Al-Amin barked, his tone cutting like a whip.

The order to keep his eyes open was short and precise. The horror he was hoping to hide from was surely going to happen before his eyes. As Al-Amin turned back to execute the pastor, Muktar quickly walked over and whispered something to him. Al-Amin nodded, then motioned for Emmanuel to come closer.

*"Kai za ka aikata wannan."* - You will do this.

The words ricocheted in Emmanuel's head as the impact hit him. Me!? *Why me!?*

Emmanuel's hands shook as he raised his rifle. He looked around at the hard resolve on the faces of the men, and he quickly realised that his life was at stake if he didn't carry out the order. Muktar was already walking towards him with a devilish grin on his scarred face. The rain running down his scar made him look even more terrifying than usual.

As he got to him, Muktar grabbed Emmanuel's gun, took it from him, and handed him a long, gleaming machete and stepped back, raising the gun, but this time, pointing it at Emmanuel.

The pastor's family began to cry and beg again, but the pastor just looked at Emmanuel with what seemed like pity, then turned his head to look upwards to the heavens.

Emmanuel was in a quandary. It was either kill or be killed, he knew. But these people had never done anything to him. When he had told Zalla that he was ready to do anything and even sell his soul to the devil if it would help him get Aisha back, he never could have envisaged that this would be the cost.

He hefted the machete and looked to Al-Amin, hoping against hope that the commander would change his mind and not make him go through with the execution.

*"Me ka ke jira ne, Bashir?"* - What are you waiting for, Bashir? - Al-Amin was getting impatient.

There was no way out. He knew what Zalla would have told him to do in this situation. He would tell him to do it. He would tell him that this man and his family would still die, whether by his hand or another's. And if that happened, Al-Amin would kill him on the spot, and Aisha would definitely not get rescued. It was a lose-lose situation, and he saw no way out.

As he saw Muktar's shoulders tense in anticipation of firing, Emmanuel looked down at the pastor. The pastor simply smiled and nodded. With a soul-searing cry of pain, Emmanuel stepped forward and swung the machete.

*"Allahu Akbar!"* Emmanuel screamed as the blade sliced through the air and sank into the pastor's neck with a heavy thunk! He stood in shock, holding the machete with the blade to the man's neck. As he pulled it out, blood started spurting from the gaping hole in the side of his neck, and the body fell to the ground.

Screams of anguish filled the air as the woman and children howled in horror at the sight of the body, head dangling and blood pouring out, mixing with the rain and running down the sand in red rivulets.

The fighters jubilated with shouts of *"Allahu akbar!"* and fired their guns in the air. Muktar had relaxed and was awaiting further instructions from Al-Amin.

Emmanuel's body shook—from fear, from the cold, from the realisation of what he had done. The machete hung limply from his hand, and there was a loud ringing in his head. He had finally become Bashir. No longer an act. He was now a killer and an accepted member of the Boko Haram terrorist sect. The bile rose in his throat, and he had to struggle not to throw up.

At a nod from Al-Amin, Muktar took the machete from Bashir, and before anyone could react, he had swung the blade expertly and cut off the pastor's wife's head. The woman's body twitched on the muddied ground for a while, blood gushing out of the stump of her neck, before finally being still. He could see the horror in the older child's eyes as she used her hands to shield the eyes of her sister, and she pressed her head to her chest. Her eyes were fixed on Bashir, and instead of seeing the daughter of the pastor he had just killed, he saw the face of his beloved daughter, Aisha. His Ada.

The ringing in his head got louder and louder. It felt like his head would explode. Just when he thought he couldn't take it anymore, and he was about to scream, a burst of gunfire shattered the night, and a hail of bullets cut down half the fighters. Without warning, they were under attack by the military. Pandemonium broke out. Not knowing which direction the gunfire was coming from, the men scattered, firing in all directions.

Bashir snapped out of his inertia and ran towards the trucks and jumped in the driver's seat of the first truck he got to. As he started the truck and got moving, other fighters, including Al-Amin and Muktar, jumped into the back.

*"TAFI, MU TAFI, DA SAURI!"* – Go, let's go.

Quickly! - Al-Amin shouted as he leaned out from the back of the truck, firing wildly in return. The vehicle lurched forward, tires sending mud splattering through the air, while other fighters scrambled to climb aboard, some barely managing to grip the rails as bullets snapped through the air around them, while those already inside crouched and tried to return fire. The problem was that the military had them surrounded on three sides, so even as he drove, bullets were thudding into the truck.

As he sped down the street, he saw that the end of the street was blocked by a military truck. Reacting instinctively, he grabbed a gun from the dashboard and, with his left hand, shot out the headlights of the military truck. He then swerved the truck into an opening on their right. It was a large compound with a low mud wall. He revved the engine and drove through the rear fence, which caved under the momentum of the heavy truck. They came out on another street parallel to the one they had left. He turned the truck, and he sped towards the bush.

****

He kept going until they were in the shrubs, far from the town. Some of the remaining fighters had also succeeded in grabbing another truck and following them.

This wasn't the planned route of escape, but the army had caught them completely by surprise, and they were lucky to have escaped at all. Some of them, anyway. When they stopped to take stock of their situation, they realised that several of them were bleeding from gunshot wounds, Al-Amin being one of them. Three were dead. They were also low on ammunition and had very little food or water. This was supposed to have been a quick mission, but things had gone very wrong.

*"Bashir, ka cece mu."* – Bashir, you saved us. - Muktar said, his voice carrying a hint of awkward gratitude.

*"Nufin Allah ne,"* Bashir replied softly, deflecting the praise and giving glory to the Almighty for their escape.

They quickly bound up the injured as best they could and tried to get their bearings and decide the quickest and safest way back to their base. They had come to attack Kalau from their camp, located to the northwest, but in their escape, they had driven further eastward. Now, to return, they ran the risk of meeting mobilized military patrols on high alert and roving formations on search-and-destroy missions.

To make matters worse, the land to the north was mostly grass with very few trees, which would make it easy for military planes and attack helicopters to spot them once daylight arrived. They also could not use the radios in the truck, as they knew the military would be conducting blanket electronic surveillance of the entire area.

In addition, both vehicles had broken down, and so they had no means of movement.

The rain had stopped, but despondence hung like a gloomy cloud over the fighters as they huddled over a small fire and discussed their options.

# CHAPTER TWENTY

Al-Amin had been drifting in and out of consciousness due to blood loss. Thus, Muktar was the most senior fighter in the surviving group. However, Muktar, being uneducated, was more accustomed to taking orders than engaging in strategic thinking. So, when Bashir suggested that they take shelter in the nearby trees, he readily agreed.

Bashir was desperate. He had since come down from the adrenaline rush of the night, and he was torn with guilt. In his head, he knew that if he had not killed the pastor, he would be dead himself and never be able to rescue Aisha. But in his heart, he wondered if becoming a monster wasn't too high a price to pay and whether it could ever be worth it. All night, he had wrestled with his conscience, and yet he had no answers. He also knew that once it was daylight, the military would track them, and in their current state, the resultant battle would be very short.

He walked around to survey the surrounding area in the

moonlight. He noticed something and then had an idea. He ran back and, with a torch, inspected the damage to the trucks.

He hurried to Muktar to explain his idea. Muktar was with Al-Amin, who had regained consciousness and was able to talk feebly, propped up against a tree trunk. Bashir deduced that his wound was not as bad as he first thought.

*"Ina da ra'ayi."* – I have an idea. - Bashir said, his tone edged with urgency. As the others turned their eyes toward him, he leaned in, ready to explain.

"The soldiers will be coming after us at first light. And the ground is soft because of the rain, so they can follow our tracks easily." He was smiling.

*"Abun da ke sa ka murmushi kenan?"* – And why is that making you smile? - Muktar asked, a note of irritation sharpening his words.

*"Murmushi nake don ina son su biyo mu."* - I'm smiling because I want them to follow us. - Bashir's reply only deepened Muktar's confusion, stirring both

annoyance and unease in him. Before he could gather a response, Bashir pressed on, his eyes glinting with intent.

"If I remove the radiator from one truck, I can use it to fix the second truck. Now the ground slopes down from here, so we push the second truck down the slope and create a diversion so that when the military follows our tracks, it will lead them away."

"What about us? How do we escape?" Al-Amin interjected.

"We backtrack." Bashir answered excitedly.

"What!? We go back to the town!? *Ka na hauka ne?*" Muktar responded in anger.

"*A'a, ba ni da hauka.*" Bashir replied calmly, his steady voice a sharp contrast to Muktar's outburst.

"I am not crazy, but they won't expect us to come back to the town. Also, we will not go back all the way. We will drive on the tracks we have already made, and once we get to the main road near the town, we will follow the tarred road towards the north and escape from here. But…," he hesitated, "we have to do it now."

The plan was as audacious as it was dangerous. Al-Amin thought about it for a minute.

*"Jeka gyara motar."* Al-Amin commanded, his tone leaving no room for hesitation.

As Bashir hustled to carry out the order to try to fix the truck, he heard Al-Amin and Muktar in a heated debate, but his focus now was on making sure they escaped from the military onslaught that was sure to happen at first light.

Bashir, with the help of two men, and using the tools in the trucks, was able to remove the radiator from one truck and replace it with a new one in the second truck. He then siphoned the fuel from the first truck into the second and loaded their scant supplies into it.

They moved the wounded onto the back of the truck, including Al-Amin. Before they left, they loaded the truck with rocks to increase its mass, while Bashir used ropes to tie the steering wheel to the gear shaft, ensuring the truck would maintain its course as it rolled down the long slope. Then, reluctantly, they loaded the three dead men into the cabin and said their farewells.

*"Mu tura motar!"* - Push the truck! - Bashir shouted. The fighters heaved with all their strength, straining against the weight until, at last, the vehicle lurched forward. Momentum carried it on, gravity dragging it downhill. They watched as the truck gathered speed, their breaths held in silent prayer that the distraction would be enough to buy them precious time to escape.

*"Sauri, sauri!"* Al-Amin urged, his voice sharp with urgency. The men scrambled, piling into the truck in a rush, each heartbeat thundering with the fear of being caught. Somehow, they all assumed Bashir would be driving, and they waited for him to take his seat. Even Muktar realized that there had been a subtle shift in the power dynamics in the group, but he was silent, scowling to himself as he got into the back of the truck.

Bashir got into the driver's seat, started the truck, and

quickly headed back towards the town, being careful to drive along the tracks they had made on their way out.

He drove without headlights, using the moon as his only navigation aid. As they drew closer to the town, the tension in the truck intensified, giving way to palpable fear as the town came into view in the distance over the plain. As they reached the main road and he turned right, heading northwards, there was a collective sigh of relief. The farther northwards they got, the lighter the mood.

As daylight began to creep over the horizon, they saw a column of dust rising far behind them but going eastwards. On realizing that the military was following the tracks according to Bashir's plan, the men broke out in jubilation, and it took Al-Amin scolding them to keep their voices down.

*"Bashir ya cece mu!"* - Bashir has saved us!

The men were exuberant in their praise of Bashir. He gave a brief nod to acknowledge their gratitude but kept his eyes on the road, choosing instead to focus on getting them as far away as possible. Additionally, he knew that it would not take long for the Army to realize the ruse and expand its search parameters. He alone noticed that they were running low on fuel and that the truck was overheating.

When they stopped briefly to rest and tend the wounded, Al-Amin couldn't help but shower praise on him for his quick thinking and unorthodox tactics that saved their lives. Even Muktar now looked at him with something akin to respect.

*"Aikin Allah ne."* Bashir responded, giving the glory to God.

*"Amma akwai matsala."* He continued, looking worried.

On hearing Bashir say that they had a problem, Al-Amin beckoned him closer.

*"Menene!?"* Muktar asked.

*"Fetur ya kusa karewa, kuma* radiator *yana yoyo,"* - We're almost out of petrol, and the radiator is leaking. -

Bashir responded, this revelation turning the mood to confusion and worry.

*"Kai, wannan babbar matsala ce."* Muktar muttered, clearly at a loss as to what to do next.

*"Yaya nisa wannan zai kai mu?"* Al-Amin asked Bashir. - How far can this take us?

"Maybe another hour, maybe like fifty kilometers." That was the best guess Bashir could hazard, knowing that the radiator might fail at any time and the gasket would blow out, potentially killing the engine.

*"Sai mu ci gaba,"* Al-Amin ordered. He added, *"Allah zai yi mana hanya."* - God will make a way for us.

The men chorused *"Ameen"*

They all piled into the truck and set off again, the rising sun beating down relentlessly on them, as they bumped along the grassy Sahel.

****

They drove until the truck started spluttering. Once Bashir saw that there was no life left in the truck, he steered it towards a group of acacia trees, hoping to find some shade for themselves and camouflage of sorts for the truck. They rolled to a torturous stop, the last of the water in the radiator boiling out in violent clouds of steam.

The men remained in the truck for a short while, each man seemingly lost in his own personal version of their bleak future, before Bashir dragged himself out and looked around, hoping and praying for some kind of miracle. Luckily, the ground was hard, and so their tracks could not be followed easily, so he felt they were safe, for the time being.

However, their wounded needed urgent medical attention, and they had no food and very little water left. As the men trudged out, it was clear just how bleak their situation was. One more injured man had expired during the torturous drive, and Al-Amin was clearly getting worse. They moved him to the shade of a tree and covered him up. In desperation, the men searched for any edible fruits or leaves in the nearby shrubs but came up empty. They then turned to

Muktar for direction.

*"Muktar, me zamuyi?"* —Muktar, what do we do?

*"Zaa ku kalle mu har mu mutu ne?"* —Are you going to look at us till we die?

*"Don Allah, kar a yi magana haka."* Muktar admonished them. But even he had lost his usual bluster as it seemed that they had come to the end of the line. It was either they died of thirst and starvation, wild animals, or the military would find and kill them.

Bashir looked at the fear and lack of leadership in Muktar and realised that if he didn't do something fast, they would not make it till the next morning, and all his sacrifices would have been in vain. He quickly stepped forward to Muktar and told him that he had an idea. Muktar visibly perked up at this and pulled Bashir to the side.

Bashir's plan was simple; he would take anything the fighters could spare and walk north to try to find help. If he found help, he would come back for them, but if he didn't come back, it meant that he was dead. It was grim, and not what Muktar thought he was going to hear. He was hoping that Bashir would, as he had done twice already, come up with some very daring scheme that would somehow get them the resources they needed.

*"Me ya sa ba za mu nemi ƙauye kusa ba…"* Muktar suggested, but Bashir quickly cut him off.

"No, no, going to a nearby village would only alert the military. If I go alone and without weapons, even if they find me, I can use English and convince them that I was kidnapped, and I had escaped. If you or any of the other fighters are with me, they will not believe me."

It took a bit more, but eventually Muktar realized that they had no other remotely viable option.

*"Yan'uwa masu aminci!"* — Loyal brothers! —Muktar called to the remaining fighters as they walked back to the group.

*"Bashir… Bashir zai tafi shi kadai don neman taimako. Idan ya sami taimako, zai dawo ya same mu."*

*"Idan bai dawo ba fa?"* One of the men asked, seemingly more concerned about Bashir not coming back than about their current predicament. It appeared that Bashir had become something of a talisman for the fighters, and they were unwilling to part with his company.

*"Zan dawo. In shaa Allahu zan dawo."* Even as he spoke, trying to reassure the others with the firmness of his voice, Bashir could feel the crushing weight of reality pressing down on him. His words sounded confident, but inside him a storm raged. Every step ahead was laced with peril—if the police spotted him, there would be no chance of escape. Discovery meant death. And death meant not only the end of his mission, but also the end of any hope of saving his daughter, his Ada, whose innocent face haunted him with every heartbeat.

He waited till the worst heat of the day had passed before setting off. They bade him farewell, hugging him fiercely, knowing that the chances of meeting again were very slim. He wrapped his head and neck in a piece of cloth to protect himself from the sand and the heat. He then looked back one last time at the sorry group of men, waved them goodbye, and started walking.

****

Bashir walked all afternoon, stopping only briefly to rest. By late afternoon, the hunger and heat had begun to take their toll on him. By evening, his lungs seemed to be on fire, and his legs felt like they were made of lead. He walked until night fell, and he kept walking.

By night, his walking speed had dropped, but he trudged on, driven by the fear of failure and dying without seeing his daughter again. He walked until the moon was out, and he kept walking. He walked until his legs simply stopped moving. Overcome with thirst, hunger, and fatigue, he sat down by some shrubs and rested his head on his knees.

He was jerked into wakefulness by something tugging on his feet. He jumped up to see two wild dogs scampering away. They stopped a short distance away, their eyes glowing in the dark as they waited.

Bashir realized that they were waiting for him to die so they could feed on his corpse! He had heard that sometimes, these wild dogs would attack live animals, so he now had to stay awake for the rest of the night, knowing that they might eventually start feeding on him while he was alive.

He waited and waited, but as the long night wore on, he found it harder and harder to keep his eyes open. Whenever he jerked awake, he would find that the wild dogs had crept closer, eyes glowing, and teeth bared. He chased them away time and again, throwing pieces of rocks at them, but they kept coming back, closer and closer each time. By now, there were five of them. Maybe out of desperation, or out of hunger, or just out of the hopelessness of his situation, his fevered brain conjured up a desperate plan.

He quietly slid out his dagger and nicked the middle finger of his left hand so that it started bleeding. He then lay down on his left side with his hand stretched out, but his right hand holding the knife behind his back. He closed his eyes to just a small slit so he could see his left hand. He waited as the dogs crept closer and surrounded him, mouths open, and teeth glistening in anticipation. One bit his boots and pulled, and he did not move, pretending to be dead. Another tried to bite the back of his leg and got a chunk of his trousers. Still, he did not move. Emboldened, they crept even closer.

The boldest, or hungriest one, crept up to his hand and tried to take a bite. As its teeth closed on the hand, Bashir sprang into action. He grabbed the mouth of the wild dog with his left hand, and with his right, swung the dagger and buried it in its neck, killing it instantly. The other dogs scattered in fright.

He quickly lit a small fire over some rocks, skinned the dog, and roasted it. He threw the rest of the carcass, including the entrails, into the darkness, and immediately the other dogs pounced on it and tore it apart.

The light from the fire cast an eerie picture: a man eating a bloody, half-cooked piece of meat and a pack of wild dogs devouring the carcass of one of their kind, all the while eyeing each other in the darkness.

After that, he stayed awake until the first light of the day was peeking from the east. Using that to confirm his bearings, Bashir packed up the remnant of his roasted meat and continued north.

The encounter with the wild dogs had strengthened his resolve, and he walked with a renewed sense of purpose, the picture of his daughter filling his mind and driving him on.

****

By late morning, just before the sun reached its zenith, he stopped to rest and ate some of his stash. He had been getting dizzy from the heat and lack of water.

As he sat on the hard ground and nibbled on the meat, he thought he saw a cloud of dust in the distance, but he shook his head, and it disappeared. He put it down to heat exhaustion and continued eating. It must be a mirage, he thought.

When he got up to continue his journey, he saw it clearly this time, an unmistakable cloud of dust from the west heading his way. In fright, he hit the ground, trying to blend with the grass and avoid being detected. His first thought was that this was a military convoy sweeping the area, and knowing that the report of the attack on Kalau would have gone round, he knew that if he was found, it would surely mean death.

Then something occurred to him. If they were military on a search mission, why were they driving in a single file instead of spread out? As their path took them within a hundred meters of where he was hiding, he decided to risk peeking. He slowly raised his head, squinting through the hot afternoon haze, and his heart leapt for joy!

He jumped up, screaming, waving his hands above his head, and running towards the line of trucks. He had seen that they were not the military but Boko Haram. He kept screaming, waving, and running till one of the trucks peeled away from the convoy and headed in his direction. He stopped running and leaned over, his chest heaving from the exertion.

When the truck got close to him, someone opened the door and jumped out even before the truck came to a halt. As Bashir collapsed on his back on the grass, panting and looking at the sky, his view was filled with the smiling face of his only friend, Zalla.

****

When he came to, he was in the back of a truck and back with the convoy. They gave him water, and when he was revived, he informed them that the remainder of their group was about fifty kilometers due south, injured and without food and water, and he had continued on foot to try to find help.

The commander then ordered the convoy to head southwards to pick up the rest of Al-Amin's company of fighters. As they drove, Zalla informed Bashir of what had happened and how they came to be there.

After Zalla's company of fighters had completed the attack on the police station, they had driven out of the town and headed back to their camp as planned. Unfortunately, they had been trailed by the military, who, on discovering the camp, had sent a large contingent to attack it. They were hit from the air and land in a well-coordinated rocket and mortar attack that left the camp in chaos. Soldiers followed this in armoured personnel carriers and trucks with mounted 50-caliber machine guns, shooting everything that moved.

Out of over a thousand men, these twenty-odd men in the convoy of five trucks were the only ones that managed to escape during the confusion of the fighting, and they were on their way to join another camp of fighters that controlled territory near the border with Cameroun.

Before nightfall, they had arrived at the clutch of acacia trees where Bashir had left the remnant of his company. They found them very weak but jubilant at being rescued.

*"Bashir ya dawo."* - Bashir has come back.

*"Bashir ya sake ceton mu."* - Bashir has saved us again!

They gave them food and water, tended to the injured,

and then moved them into the trucks before heading off again.

As they drove further and further east, Bashir was relieved to have been rescued but continued to wonder about the wisdom of his quest, what it had cost him so far, and whether he had any real hope of success.

# CHAPTER TWENTY-ONE

Aisha had just finished sweeping the inside of the tent and was about to start the front when she heard a commotion from the main part of the camp. Wondering what could be going on, she joined the other women as they went towards the open ground.

They saw a convoy of trucks rush into the camp, with men running to assist the occupants. Mallam Yusufu and Junaidu led their men to greet the new arrivals as they exited the vehicles.

When Mallam Yusufu and Junaidu recognised an important-looking man, they rushed to help the men carry him into their medical tent. The other fighters followed them behind. The men from both groups greeted each other, but the mood was grim as they recognised the extent of the tragedy that they must have endured. Half the men had to be supported to get off the vehicles.

Junaidu emerged from the medical tent and issued orders to his men to intensify surveillance around the camp. He also asked them to prepare more tents to house their brothers who had just joined them, and that the women should quickly prepare food.

As she turned away to the assigned tasks, Aisha noticed one of the new men looking at her. His headcloth obscured his face, but she could see him staring intently at her. She shuddered at the thought of another one of these animals taking an interest in her, and she walked away as fast as she could without running.

She joined the women in cooking. When they were done, she hurried towards the campground to look for Mahmood with his food. She saw him amongst the men seated in a circle, eating and laughing.

He had a big plate of *waina* and *miyan gyada,* and he seemed to be enjoying the food. Aisha felt irritated about the way Mahmood ate, chewing the food with his mouth open like a goat.

Junaidu saw her looking at Mahmood with disgust, glanced at Mahmood, and laughed heartily. The men also laughed with him, except for one of them. The same man, whose face was half-covered. He neither ate his food nor did he laugh, but he stared at her with a steady gaze. Mallam Yusufu, who was sitting beside the man, hit him playfully on the shoulder.

*"Matan aure ne fa. Kuma ga maigidan ta a nan."* They all laughed when Mallam Yusufu explained to the strange man that Aisha was married.

Oh God, no! Aisha almost rolled her eyes. Mahmood was no longer laughing, and Aisha noticed that his demeanour had changed. When he turned to look at her, she looked away.

*"Ki koma aikin ki."* — Go back to your work. — Mahmood ordered. Before Aisha left, she glanced again at the man who was staring at her. Another man who seemed to be his friend was nudging him to eat.

Aisha joined some of the women to clean up after the men, then continued with the rest of their chores. She still had to wash Mahmood's clothes and clean his second pair of boots in addition to any other tasks he decided. As she had learnt the hard way, any sign of resistance was met with swift punishment.

At the end of the day, when Aisha retired to her tent, she found Mahmood already lying on the mat without a shirt. He had put on the lamp and arranged their sleeping space. As she entered, he removed his trousers and grinned at her as he lay back down and stroked his penis.

Aisha's throat tightened. She swallowed back the tears that threatened to fall from her eyes and closed the entrance of the tent. The first few weeks with Mahmood had been hell for her, but she had learnt to endure for her survival. An older woman in the camp had taken pity on her when she saw her crying bitterly at the back of the tent early one morning after another horrid night with Mahmood. She had given her a vial of shea butter to use as a lubricant when needed to reduce the pain of forced penetration.

She knew what to do, so she didn't hesitate. She quickly got the vial, applied some shea butter on her hands, and lay down beside him. As she replaced his hand with hers and stroked him up and down, he moaned and fondled her breasts through her dress. When he was well lubricated and ready, she took off her clothes and climbed on him. As he entered her, she gritted her teeth and hoped it would be over quickly. He grabbed her thighs and thrust himself in harder, faster, and faster until he erupted.

She lay on him, her face to one side, hiding her tears. When he stopped shaking, she rolled off him and got up to clean herself and put out the lamp before lying down on the far side of the room to try to sleep, hoping the darkness would somehow reduce the horror of her existence.

It was just another horrible night.

****

Aisha woke up before daybreak and sat up, looking at Mahmood. He was snoring. Several times she had considered stabbing him while she slept, but she reckoned that her chances of escaping successfully were very slim. And if they caught her, they would surely kill her. She, however, consoled herself with her imagination of him choking on his own blood while she stood above him with a bloody knife.

When she saw daylight peeking through the opening of the tent door, she went outside to start her chores for the day. Some of the girls were already coming out of their tents. Their first duty for the day was to fetch enough water for bathing and cooking. Her duties in the camp had reduced since she got "married" to Mahmood, but that was small comfort for what she had to endure in exchange.

She grabbed a bucket and joined the other girls to go to the stream. When they had made sure that all the drums were filled with water, Aisha sat on the stump of a tree to rest while the camp bustled with the preparations for breakfast.

When she lifted her head, she saw a man looking straight at her. It was the same man who had been staring at her the day before. She paused for a while and looked around. When she looked back, the man looked away and laughed with another man who was saying something to him.

She was now getting concerned. Why did he keep staring at her like this? And why was his face covered? The camp's ground was not dusty, so it couldn't be because of dust. However, there was something familiar about the man, something about the way he stood and how he moved his shoulders when he walked. She racked her brains but just couldn't place it. As she sat there pondering, Junaidu joined the man and his friend, and they walked together to the benches where the men usually sat.

Aisha noticed how the mysterious man kept throwing glances in her direction. She turned to see Mahmood walking towards the men, and she quickly stood up and walked back to the tent. With the way the strange man kept throwing glances at her, she feared that Mahmood would get upset.

She swept the tent and folded the mat, then she arranged the room and sat down to wait for breakfast. Not having much else to do, she went to the opening of the tent and peeked towards the open campground. The men were still gathered, talking.

Then Junaidu summoned the camp to all come together for an announcement. As the girls gathered, Aisha joined them but stayed behind to avoid attracting attention.

Junaidu cleared his throat.

"We have new men in our midst. *Na tabbata kun gan su.*" He started to move around. Aisha glanced at the men who stood behind Junaidu, including the mystery man.

"They are a part of us, and I want you to respect them just the way you respect us. If you don't, they will deal with you. I have given them permission." The place was quiet as he looked over the girls.

He walked towards the new men and pointed from one man to another, calling their names.

"This is Zalla." He pointed to the man beside the mystery man. Aisha barely gave him a glance. Her focus was on the mystery man.

"And this is Bashir. Bashir, the man of a thousand

talents!" Junaidu announced with a flourish. Both men shook hands and hugged each other. Junaidu obviously had a lot of respect for the man. The other men also seemed to hold him in high esteem.

Who was this man who attracted such attention? He was treated with almost as much respect as their leader, the one with the long scar across his face and one eye. The one the others called Al-Amin.

"Like I have said, obey and respect them. You can now go back to what you were doing and bring our food." Junaidu waved them away. The girls scattered towards their chores, whispering amongst themselves.

Aisha joined the kitchen crew to get the food for the men. She carried two plates and spoons and joined the line of girls serving the men. When it was her turn, she searched for which of them had not been given food yet.

Junaidu motioned for her to give one of the men, and then Bashir. Aisha handed a plate to the man, bowing down before turning to Bashir. When she stretched her hand to give him the food, their eyes met.

Something unexplainable about his eyes made Aisha's heart skip, and she released her grip on the plate before Bashir's hand had closed on it, and the plate clattered to the ground, spilling the food. Aisha's eyes widened in fear.

*"Wannan yarinyar ba wuya ta rikice, wallahi!"* — This girl gets so easily confused, I swear! — Mahmood stood up and raised his hands to hit Aisha, but Bashir jumped up and caught his hand mid-air. Bashir shook his head, and Mahmood stepped back and gave her a nasty look, then nodded to Bashir.

*"Ku yihakuri. Zan share wurin yanzu."* - Please be patient. I'll clean it up now. - She pleaded and grabbed the plate. She ran back to the kitchen and came back to clean up the mess. Then she ran to get him another plate of food. The man nodded to her and focused on his food. Aisha felt relieved. If Bashir had not stopped Mahmood, he would have beaten her mercilessly. To him, she acted as a bad servant, and it meant disrespect.

She had suffered his fast hands several times when she failed to satisfy his sexual needs or when she didn't cook according to his taste, or just whenever he was in a bad mood.

Aisha wished she could understand why something about the new man's eyes seemed so familiar to her, but try as she might, she just could not place it.

She went back to her chores and did her best to stay away from the men.

****

The evening was cool. Aisha sat on a bench in front of her tent, thinking about what she had faced since she got to the camp. When they had first arrived at this location and she had seen the living quarters assigned to the girls, she had thought then that she would not survive. Now, she was seated in front of a tent that belonged to her and her "husband".

Aisha sat outside till it was dark. Mahmood had not shown up yet, and she was beginning to wonder where he was. If she didn't look for him, he would disturb her sleep, so she went to the open ground, but she didn't see him. She asked some of the men if they had seen him, but nobody knew where he was.

Aisha was quietly grateful that she couldn't find Mahmood. She wished that he would disappear forever. She shrugged and turned towards the tent, but the sound of her name being called softly drew her attention. She turned around and searched the open space with her eyes. A man walked towards her. He had his hands in his pockets, and his face was half-covered. It was the man they called Bashir. Aisha was alarmed, but she didn't show it. God help her if Mahmood caught her with Bashir.

"Come with me. Junaidu is looking for you." Bashir turned around and kept walking. Aisha followed him without question, wondering why Junaidu was looking for her. Then she started wondering why Bashir was taking her into the bush away from the camp. She wanted to run, but she felt like her legs were being controlled by the man. When they were some distance away, Bashir stopped and faced her.

He slowly unwrapped the cloth from his head, revealing his face. Up close, Aisha recognized him instantly. Her heart lurched—she knew that face. Before she could cry out, his hand clamped firmly over her mouth. All at once, her emotions heightened, her thoughts spun in turmoil, and a sharp dizziness clouded her mind. Her vision swam; her eyes rolled back, and everything went dark.

When she came to, the world was hazy. Blinking, she saw her father kneeling beside her, his face etched with worry, his eyes glistening with tears. For a moment, she thought she was still dreaming, but as his trembling hands cupped her face, reality struck her. A sob broke from her lips, and tears spilled down uncontrollably.

They clung to each other desperately, as if afraid the other might vanish at any second. She pressed her face against his chest, hearing the ragged sound of his weeping, and her own sobs echoed his. Minutes passed before they pulled apart, still holding onto one another, eyes scanning every feature, every change time had carved.

At last, Aisha sat upright, her breath shuddering. A

thousand questions crowded her mind, but none found their way out. She could only stare at him, overwhelmed, her heart pounding with disbelief and wonder.

"How? What are you doing with them?" Aisha asked him. He paused before answering. He leaned forward and held both her hands.

"I had to do it, Aisha. I had to join them to try to find you. The soldiers were not making any move so—"

"You had to join them to save me?" Aisha could feel her throat tighten. She tried to pull her hands away, but he held on firmly. Aisha closed her eyes when he drew her into a bear hug. She held him tight and wept bitterly. She could tell he was crying too because he was shaking.

After a short while, Aisha pushed back a bit and grabbed his forearm tightly. "Chief, you have to get me out of here. We can go now." Aisha dragged him towards the woods. He dragged her back.

"Aisha. You must wait for a little while. Escaping now

will not be…”

“No, chief. We need to leave this place. You came to take me with you, didn't you?” Aisha was now shaking. She looked at him, confusion and fear written all over her face.

“I'm here to save you, Aisha, but now is the wrong time. Let me plan properly. I'm here now. I came here for you, okay? And don't worry, Mahmood and Junaidu left for another camp.”

Aisha's shoulders relaxed.

She looked at her father intently. Yes, he was the one standing in front of her, but something was different, something was missing. There was a kind of coldness, an emptiness she couldn't explain in his eyes, as if he had somehow lost his warmth. He looked at her, sensing her growing worry, and sighed.

“What happened?” She touched his hand. He told her everything that had happened. How he was beaten and arrested when he tried to get the soldiers to do their job, how he had met Zalla, who helped him get recruited by Boko Haram, and his training.

He also told her how they had made him kill innocent people. Aisha watched her father as he spoke. He looked so different, like something vital had died in him. It was sad that her father had to kill to save her. He had lost a lot because he wanted to save her. When he stopped talking, Aisha hugged him tight.

"And now you are married to Mahmood." The sadness in her father's voice was unmistakable. She broke into a heavy sob and hugged him again.

"I will get us out of here, but we need to plan well. These people do not have mercy. They will kill whoever crosses them." He stopped and looked around.

"You need to go back to your tent." He pushed her away from him.

"No, I want to stay with you." Aisha moved towards him.

"No, Aisha. You should go. If we get caught, we'll be

dead. Do not worry. I'm here for you."

Aisha kept turning back as she walked back to the tent, weeping at what life had given to her and her father. It wasn't fair, but she was glad that her father was here and planning to save her. She entered her tent with a new hope. Hope that she would soon leave the camp. Before she closed her eyes, she smiled to herself, the first smile in months.

# CHAPTER TWENTY-TWO

It had been six months since Emmanuel had seen or spoken to his Ada. The hardships of this place had changed her, forced her to grow up too fast. And now she was married to a member of the terrorist group? He shut his eyes at the thought of what she must have endured at the hands of that monster. He grunted in pent-up anger and drove his dagger hard into the top of the wooden table.

Zalla watched him quietly. He still didn't understand why Zalla was helping him, apart from the few unconvincing answers he had given in the past. There had to be a greater purpose, some reason Zalla would risk his life in this way. There had to be.

They were in the tent assigned to them. He stared at the food before him, unable to eat. All he could think about was his good fortune in getting this far and the coincidence, almost miraculous, of finding his daughter. Now he had to figure out a way to escape with her without getting caught.

He realized how much he had changed as well. Emmanuel would have been impulsive, reckless, unable to hold back his emotions. But not Bashir. Now, he knew patience, lying in wait like an adder, ready to strike at the perfect moment.

*"Gaisuwa, Bashir."* - Greetings, Bashir.

The greeting came from a member of the group passing the open entrance of the tent. Stories of his heroics had spread among the men of this company. He suspected they had been exaggerated, judging by the reverent looks the men gave him. They treated him like the hand of Allah himself, and sometimes he worried it might cause problems with Al-Amin, his leader, or worse, the leaders of the host camp.

He returned the man's greeting and waved jovially. Then he signaled to Zalla that they needed to find a private place to talk.

Zalla and Bashir walked outside the camp until they were a safe distance away, where they could speak without being overheard.

"I can't take it anymore, Zalla. How can I continue to sit by and watch that animal have his way with my daughter without doing anything?"

"We cannot fight now, Bashir. We cannot carry her and run—not today, not tomorrow. We must wait."

He hated that Zalla was right. But he also needed to do something to ease his daughter's suffering while they worked out a feasible plan for escape. He couldn't stand by as that beast continued violating her.

"Do not worry, Bashir. I will take care of it."

"How do you intend to do that, Zalla?"

"I do not know yet. But I will do something. I will find a way to save Aisha from Mahmood."

"Please do, my friend. I don't think I can trust myself not to put a bullet in that man's head the next time I see him."

"I want to shoot him too, but not today, not tomorrow. We must wait."

Zalla had a way of reassuring him even in the gloomiest moments. His words sounded certain, and his posture exuded confidence.

"I trust you to do this quickly, Zalla. Please."

"Trust me."

They were interrupted by the sound of leaves rustling as someone approached. They quickly crouched and raised their guns. After a moment, the man they called Mallam Yusufu emerged from the bushes to their right. He was the oldest member of the company, but apparently still in great physical shape. They relaxed when they saw it was him and rushed forward to greet him.

*"Bashir na Annabi. Wukar Ubangiji Allah! Na gaishe ka!"* He, too, wasn't reluctant to hurl praises at Bashir. Zalla chuckled by his side.

*Bashir of the Prophet. The sword of the Lord God. I greet you!*

So far, this man's praise was the strangest he had heard, and his friend was justified in laughing at it.

Bashir stretched his hands to greet the man as he came to where they were standing. He seemed happy to have found them, and he began to tell Bashir all the wondrous things he had heard about him.

*"Ba komai Muktar ya gaya muku za ku ji ba."* he said to the man.

He was shocked when the man told him it was Al-Amin, the leader of his company, who had been narrating the tales of his bravery. That explained why the men held him in such high regard. Al-Amin was a ferocious fighter, with a long history of daring and successful attacks. When someone like him was impressed with your performance in battle, others tended to pay attention.

The man began recounting the exploits of his group, from raids to the kidnappings of girls. He seemed intent on impressing Bashir. Instead, Bashir struggled to suppress his anger, smiling politely and offering the appropriate comments as the man spoke proudly of marrying off stubborn girls to his men, claiming it would cure them of all that "Western nonsense." At that moment, Zalla noticed Bashir's hand creeping toward the handle of his dagger and quickly intervened, preventing disaster.

Zalla asked the man to excuse them, saying they were about to return to eat. The man apologized quickly and stepped away.

Bashir felt the frustration welling up inside him again, stronger than ever before. This environment was stirring emotions he had not expected. He closed his eyes and focused on calming himself. Any rash decision or impulsive action could jeopardize their plans and ruin their chances of getting Aisha to safety.

It was difficult, but he knew he had to do it regardless. His daughter was depending on him. If she hadn't had hope before, she had it now, and he wasn't about to shatter it. Her father was here, the embodiment of light at the end of the tunnel.

****

Zalla watched as Bashir brought himself under control. The man's temper had been on the rise ever since he saw his daughter, but he had been able to control himself so far. Bashir was now a fierce warrior who did what he had to do to get what he wanted.

Zalla didn't know if this change was a good thing for the man's personality, but he knew they wouldn't have gotten here without Bashir. The other soldiers even considered him a hero-servant of Allah.

It wasn't that Zalla didn't see him as a hero; he did. But it was not in the way the others saw him or for the same reasons. Zalla's perspective of Bashir's gallantry went deeper than any of the men could comprehend. It was a knowledge that was reserved for him alone, Emmanuel's friend.

He followed Bashir as they joined the group of fighters. Al-Amin, Yusufu, and Junaidu were at the center, with Al-Amin propped up and heavily bandaged. Al-Amin smiled when he saw Bashir and waved him over.

They were planning a raid. Food supplies were running low, and they needed to replenish them.

Junaidu chose Mahmood to lead the operation, while Al-Amin picked Muktar to assist him. Zalla had assumed like the rest of the group, that Al-Amin would choose Bashir to assist Mahmood. But he didn't.

Zalla wondered why. Was Al-Amin afraid of Bashir's growing popularity among the brothers? Trying to stifle his chances of becoming even more revered? Or feeling insulted that Bashir hadn't been given the lead, seeing it as demeaning to put him in a subordinate role? Whatever the reason, Zalla was secretly relieved that Bashir wasn't part of the operation.

His thoughts, however, were interrupted by Junaidu.

*"Akwai wata wurin da zamu je kuma."*

Another mission!?

This other mission was to capture and kill some deserters from their group who had escaped a few days before. They were fifteen in number and had travelled eastward.

This time, Junaidu turned towards Bashir. The excitement among the men rose. The men, like Junaidu, felt Bashir was the right man for the job. He hadn't failed so far and had survived everything.

*"Bashir za ya shugabance wannan harin."*

The others cheered as Bashir was selected to lead the second mission.

Every fighter in the camp wanted to accompany Bashir on his mission, which caused Mahmood to frown at him. Zalla had observed the man's anger at Bashir ever since he noticed Bashir looking at his wife. He had no idea who Aisha was to Bashir, so he assumed that Bashir's interest in her was sexual.

Junaidu and Al-Amin divided the men into three groups: the first went with Mahmood and Muktar, the second with Bashir, and the third remained at the camp to keep guard.

There was murmuring among the third group. These were fighters; they wanted to be out there, making a name for themselves, not stuck guarding the camp.

But they could not disobey their leaders, so they sulked and complied. Zalla wouldn't have minded staying behind, but he couldn't leave Bashir alone in his current emotional state.

****

Early the next morning, Bashir gathered the men entrusted to him, thirty-five in total. It seemed an overwhelming force for the fifteen they were about to target.

He asked Zalla to ready their supplies and trucks, while he turned to Mallam Yusufu for an overview of the terrain and the fastest way to catch the deserters.

He was relieved about one thing: Mahmood was also heading out on a mission and wouldn't be around to harass his daughter. But Bashir knew he had to conclude his mission quickly and return before Mahmood's return. And he still had to come up with a viable plan for their escape.

Bashir split the men into five trucks and gave them instructions for the pursuit. As they drove out of the camp, he turned and saw Aisha standing with the other girls, looking at him as he was leaving. Did she think he was leaving her alone? That the glimmer of hope that came with his arrival was ebbing as he left the camp? He hoped not.

****

Zalla, Bashir, and the men headed in the direction that Mallam Yusufu had given Bashir. Zalla didn't know if they could take his word at face value, but that was the only information they had about the likely whereabouts of the deserters. The mission caused his heart to beat faster. Was it because he understood their predicament? Wasn't he too, at one point a deserter?

The group of vehicles maneuvered their way through the treacherous terrain of the eastern grasslands, away from the forests where the camp was located. Bashir was in the lead truck, while Zalla was in the second. Once they got out of the treeline, the trucks fanned out into a wide search pattern and slowed down as the spotters sought to pick up any trace of the deserters.

Zalla could hear the excitement in the voices of the men—the ones who had never been on a mission with Bashir. Zalla didn't share in their excitement. They were so close to rescuing Aisha, and he didn't want anything to happen to her father. The man had come too far and suffered too much to find his daughter, and Zalla was here to ensure he returned to the camp safely and continued with that mission.

*"Wadannan mutanen da mu ke nema; kun san su da kyau?"* Zalla asked the men in his truck, trying to find out about the deserters.

*"Wadancan 'yan iskan?"* One replied disdainfully and spat. *"Shugabansu Shuaibu amma ni ban san su sosai ba"*– Those bastards? Their leader is Shuaibu, but I don't know them very well.

Shuaibu?

Zalla once knew a Shuaibu from when he used to be an active member of the terror sect, but he did not know if it was the same person. He put it out of his mind and focused on the ground ahead, searching for any sign of the men they were pursuing.

After about three hours of searching, they found some tracks and the remains of a small campfire. From there, they narrowed their search and continued eastwards. They drove slowly so as not to raise any dust and possibly give away their approach.

As the evening fell, they came across an empty campsite with evidence of a struggle and hurried departure. There were discarded clothing and empty shell casings in the grass. Bashir detailed ten men to stay and protect their vehicles, while the rest continued on foot. He didn't want to be in a situation where they would lose a battle and then have no means of transport back to their base.

****

Bashir felt the beginnings of a plan forming in his mind as he led the men on foot through the tall grass and shrubs, moving eastward. His plan, however, depended on capturing the deserters alive. The sight of bullet casings gave him pause, as there had clearly been a gunfight. Yet the absence of dead bodies and the small amount of blood offered a glimmer of hope.

He deployed the thirty-five men into five groups, fanning out and moving stealthily as night fell. After about an hour, they spotted a cluster of fires ahead. Bashir and his men crawled on their elbows to within thirty meters of the makeshift camp.

They found a company of Nigerian Army soldiers, about twenty in number, with four vehicles, including gun trucks equipped with 50-caliber machine guns. The trucks were parked in a semi-circle facing west, and guards were posted around the perimeter. In the middle of the clearing, the deserters were tied together and forced to sit as a group. Clearly, they had been captured and were to be taken back to the military base for interrogation. Bashir took careful note of every position, then signaled his men to withdraw.

Once at a safe distance, Bashir explained his plan to the fighters and assigned their tasks. The plan was simple, and he prayed it would work. He could feel the men's excitement, including Zalla's, who smiled and nodded in affirmation.

After checking their weapons and saying a quick prayer, they set off to their assigned positions, waiting for the signal to attack.

Zalla and his group were stationed to the south of the camp, and their job was to draw out the guards and give the other fighters a chance to reach the captives. As planned, they opened fire towards the camp without particularly trying to hit any of the soldiers. Immediately, the soldiers ran towards the direction of the gunshots, took up defensive positions, and returned fire. Zalla's group fired short, controlled bursts and immediately lay flat in the tall grass. Then another group of fighters would open fire from a position to the left of the soldiers, and they would respond by rushing forward and engaging them. It was all happening so fast, the gunshots, then the change of direction, that in less than one minute, over fifteen of the soldiers had been drawn away from the camp. Those manning the mounted guns were firing blind as they could see nothing in the darkness.

"Stop firing!" One of the soldiers shouted. "You will hit our own men in the bush".

To add to the confusion, five of Bashir's men opened fire on the gun trucks from behind, forcing the remaining soldiers to take cover. All the soldiers were now trapped, taking fire from both the front and the back.

On cue, several fighters led by Bashir streamed from the bush and freed the captives, spiriting them back into the cover of the trees. As they ran, Bashir pulled the pins from several hand grenades and lobbed them into the trucks. The explosions tossed the soldiers like rag dolls.

Those who had been engaging the first group of fighters in the bush now realized their camp was under attack. Seeing the trucks explode, they ran back to assist, but by then the fighters had melted away into the darkness like ghosts.

The entire operation, from start to finish, took less than five minutes.

****

As they made their escape through the bush, several deserters struggled, trying to pull away, but Bashir and his men quickly restrained them. They dragged the mostly tired and famished men back to their staging area, where they rested briefly before heading to their vehicles.

Zalla and his men joined them at this point and conducted a headcount. All the fighters were accounted for, and the men could scarcely hide their admiration for Bashir. If they had respected him before based on the stories they had heard, now that they had seen him in action, they regarded him with awe.

Zalla then whispered something to him.

"*Ku koma manyan motoci ku jira mu.*" Bashir ordered the men.

Under normal circumstances, an order to leave him with the deserters they had gone to such lengths to capture from the military would have raised eyebrows, but this was the great Bashir! The men quickly left, leaving Bashir and Zalla with the prisoners.

Once they were out of earshot, Bashir and Zalla walked to the prisoners who were huddled together on the grass.

*"Ina Shuaibu? Shuaibu!"* Zalla called as he checked the prisoners.

*"Zalla, kai ne?"* It was one of the deserters who spoke. Bashir was surprised at this. They knew Zalla? His plan may be compromised before he even gets back to camp.

But before he could react, Zalla went to the man who called his name and embraced him warmly. Bashir and the others just watched them in silence, their expressions one of confusion.

The man turned to his men and explained that Zalla and Lado were deserters from the terrorist sect, like them. Back then, he hadn't understood their actions, but now he did and had followed their example. To Bashir's surprise, Zalla seemed like a role model to these men.

Bashir had not yet told Zalla his plan, what he intended to do with the deserters. He pulled Zalla aside and quickly explained that his goal was to use the prisoners to raise his standing with the camp leadership.

Since the deserters also wanted to put a stop to the sect's activities, they should help him rescue his daughter and destroy the camp. Yet doubts gnawed at him; some of the men might lose their lives, and he didn't want that on his conscience.

Zalla looked at the men, then back at Bashir, remaining quiet as if weighing a decision.

"Don't worry. We will take them to camp," Zalla said.

Bashir was shocked. "I thought they were your friends."

"They are. Their leader is Shuaibu. We went to school with him and Lado. I have a plan, Emmanuel."

Bashir tensed. His plan involved dragging Zalla's friends into a camp of Boko Haram fighters, the same people who punish desertion with death.

Zalla approached Shuaibu and the other prisoners, explaining the plan. They seemed apprehensive at first, but gradually agreed to go along with his proposal.

Bashir marvelled at his friend. They had indeed come a long way. Zalla still called him Emmanuel when they were alone. He didn't seem comfortable with the name Bashir, a name he himself had chosen for Emmanuel.

A short while later, Zalla came back and announced. "They have agreed to follow us back to camp."

"Zalla, what exactly did you say to these men that they had agreed to follow us to possibly their deaths?"

Zalla didn't say anything to him but just gave him a look that said, "Trust me." He trusted Zalla with his life.

And with that, they bound the men.

Zalla told Bashir that he had explained to the men that Bashir was on their side, that they, too, were working to bring down the Boko Haram sect. That seemed enough for the men.

As Bashir led the way to the trucks, he breathed the dry air and began to hope again.

# CHAPTER TWENTY-THREE

Aisha was jolted awake by the sound of jubilation in the camp. She had been in a troubled sleep filled with dreams of her father being chased by wild animals in the bush. As she sat up and got her bearings, Mahmood jumped up, grabbed his rifle, and ran out. She quickly put on her hijab, wrapped a shawl around her shoulders and joined the crowd of people in the open space.

When they got there, her eyes widened. She saw her father and Zalla walking towards Junaidu and Mallam Yusufu with some men that had their hands bound with ropes. The men with him were jumping, shouting and jubilating, talking of the speed of Bashir's attack.

Her eyes shifted as Mahmood moved to the front to see clearly. Then she saw Modibo, Ahmed and Dalhatu standing at a corner with frowns on their faces. These men were very close to Mahmood. Aisha swallowed and turned to Mahmood. It was obvious that Mahmood couldn't hide the irritation that seeing her father caused him. Aisha imagined what would happen if he found out that the Bashir was her father. She shook her head and focused on the fact that her father had returned safe and sound.

Mallam Yusufu stepped forward and embraced Bashir and Zalla. Aisha couldn't hear what they said, but the old man was obviously very happy. But Aisha didn't know what to think. Capturing the deserters and bringing them back to camp was a heroic deed to the Boko Haram soldiers, but to her, it seemed her father was condemning these men to their deaths. She looked on in fear and confusion, completely at a loss to understand what her father had become.

As Junaidu and Mallam Yusufu congratulated Bashir for a successful mission and took him away to celebrate, the rest of them dispersed and went back to bed. Aisha walked back to her tent with a very heavy heart.

****

The next morning, she noticed how the mood in the camp had changed. All the men seemed to bow their heads in respect whenever Bashir passed. Even the girls were gossiping about him, some even trying to flirt with him, which irritated Aisha. She knew her father was an attractive man, but clearly the girls just wanted to be with him because of his status in the camp. Either way, it irritated her. She frowned as she focused on her washing.

However, as Bashir's popularity increased, so did Mahmood's hatred of him, and he also grew suspicious of Aisha. He now watched her every move.

"*Ke! Zo nan.*" – You! Come here - Aisha heard Mahmood call one of the girls. She was holding a plate of food that clearly belonged to one of the men. The girl's eyes widened. She looked like she was contemplating if she should go or not.

"*Ba na ce ki zo nan ba?!*" – Didin't I ask you to come here!? - Mahmood yelled. The girl jogged to him and waited. "*Ki ba ni abincin.*" Mahmood asked for the food.

"*Mallama ne ta aike ni na ba wa Mallam Bashir.*" The girl

explained that the food was for Bashir. Aisha lifted her head to look at Mahmood's face. He looked towards Bashir and Zalla who sat at the end of the bench, talking.

"*Na ce ki bani abincin nan!*" – I told you to give me the food! - Mahmood stood up and grabbed the plate from the girl's shaky hands. The girl turned towards Bashir and Zalla and started crying. Some of Mahmood's men laughed behind him. Mahmood yelled at the girl to leave before sitting down to start eating.

She turned and saw Bashir and Zalla looking at Mahmood. Another man whispered something to Bashir, but he gestured for him to stay calm. Aisha didn't realize that she was holding her breath. The fact that her father was calm even when Mahmood challenged him gave her peace. She smiled to herself and continued her washing.

The girl fearfully went to explain to Bashir that Mahmood had collected his plate of food. Bashir sent her back to the kitchen to collect another plate of food for him. Aisha could see the relief on her face. As she was hurrying towards Bashir with another plate of food, Mahmood called her again. This time, everyone around turned to look at Mahmood. It was now clear that he was openly challenging Bashir. And that Bashir had to respond. Not responding would be a sign of weakness, which was the worst thing amongst these fighters.

*"Ba na ce ki zo nan ba?!"* Mahmood yelled. The girl turned to look at Bashir who was already rising to his feet. Aisha swallowed. She knew that her father could be short-tempered, and she was scared a fight might start. Bashir walked to Mahmood with a blank expression.

*"Na gaya wa yarinyan nan ta kawo mun abinci. Ka karɓi wanda ta kawo, kuma kana so ka sake karɓan wannan?"* - I told the girl to bring us some food. You took the first one she brought, and now you want to take this one too? – Bashir said calmly. Aisha could see that her father was trying to control his temper. He had not had problems with anyone since he came to the camp and Aisha didn't

want him to have issues with Mahmood. She wished she could do something, but she had no choice but to wait and hope that things wouldn't get worse.

Mahmood ignored Bashir and walked towards the girl. As he raised his right hand to hit her, Bashir moved forward, grabbed his arm and pulled downwards. In the same swift motion, he turned and leaned forward, throwing Mahmood into a hip toss. Mahmood flew into the air and landed hard on his back.

Mahmood jumped to his feet and pulled his dagger from its sheath, murder in his eyes.

*"Tsaya kafin ka cuci kan ka."* - Stop before you hurt yourself. - Bashir warned.

Mahmood lunged forward, the blade aimed at Bashir's stomach. Bashir dodged it. The men circled each other warily.

Mahmood lunged again. This time, Bashir sidestepped the attack and landed a heavy blow to his midsection, knocking the breath out of him. Mahmood doubled over but managed to swing the blade. Bashir leapt back, fast, but not fast enough. The blade nicked his shirt, leaving a small tear.

Aisha bit her lip, fighting the urge to scream at both men to stop. She looked at Zalla for help, but he caught her eye and slowly shook his head. She gave a small nod, understanding. Then turned her gaze back to the fight.

This time, when Mahmood charged again, Bashir caught his wrist and twisted hard. Mahmood cried out and dropped the knife. Bashir stepped behind him and locked him in a chokehold, kicking his legs out so he dropped to his knees. As Mahmood struggled, Bashir leaned in, applying more pressure to his windpipe.

Mahmood's men rushed forward, ready to intervene, but Zalla and the other fighters quickly moved to block them. Tension spiked. The whole camp was seconds away from erupting when Junaidu ran in.

*"BASHIR,* **TSAYA!"** he shouted, grabbing Bashir's arm and prying him off.

Aisha let out a breath. Finally, no one was going to die.
Mahmood staggered to his feet like he meant to

continue, but stopped when Junaidu shot him a warning glare. He paused, looked around at the watching crowd, then dusted off his clothes.

Seeing everyone still staring, he barked, "What are you looking at? Go back to what you were doing!" and stormed off toward the tents.

Aisha noticed Zalla smiling at her. She smiled back, then returned to her washing. Before continuing, she stole one last glance at her father and Junaidu walking away together. Junaidu was clearly apologizing for Mahmood's behavior. Strange.

She shrugged and went back to her task.

****

Mahmood didn't appear again for the rest of the day. To Aisha's surprise, the camp remained peaceful.

The girls had finished their chores and now lounged around, chatting, some with their "husbands," others in smaller groups. A few of the fighters lingered in conversation nearby.

Bashir, Junaidu, Zalla, and Mallam Yusufu stood

outside the main tent, talking. Zalla seemed to be leading the conversation. Aisha smiled. It was rare to see everyone in such good spirits.

Aisha glanced around and realized Mahmood wasn't the only one missing; his closest friends were also nowhere among the other fighters. That struck her as odd. Normally, she wouldn't have thought much of it, but after the fight that morning, her instincts were on high alert.

She hurried toward their tent. It was empty.

"Where could he be?" she murmured to herself, worry starting to creep in.

She stepped back outside and walked toward the other tents, checking around corners, hoping to spot Mahmood chatting with some of the men. But he was nowhere in sight.

Unsure what to do, she sighed and turned toward the campground. Just as she started to walk away, she thought she heard faint, low voices.

She stopped and tilted her head, listening.

There it was again, whispers coming from one of the tents near the back of the row.

Moving quietly, she tiptoed up to the side of the tent and peered through a small hole in the covering. Inside, Mahmood sat with three other men.

She held her breath and listened.

Mahmood's voice was low but clear: he was talking about Bashir. About how he planned to deal with him for embarrassing him.

Aisha's breath caught in her throat.

"*Ama ka tabbata Junaidu ba zai kama mu ba?*" One of Mahmood's friends was worried about being discovered by Junaidu. And Bashir was one of the most revered fighters in the camp. Yusufu and Junaidu had a lot of respect for him as well, which meant taking him out would be a massive problem.

"*Junaidu ba zai kama mu ba. Zamu kashe shi.*" Mahmood whispered angrily.

Aisha covered her mouth with her hands. Mahmood was planning to kill her father, and he was assuring the men that Junaidu wouldn't catch them.

She had heard enough. She slowly moved away from the tent and immediately went to look for her father. When she didn't see him at the campground, she stood looking around, getting quite agitated. Zalla saw her and signalled to her to wait for him. She grabbed a broom and pretended to be sweeping the ground. If anyone thought it strange, no one said anything to her. Zalla walked casually towards her, and as he passed her, she whispered fiercely.

"Mahmood and his men are planning to kill my father," she said in panic. He just nodded calmly and continued walking.

She looked at his back as he walked away, quite confused. She was sure that he had heard her, but why had he shown no reaction? She dropped the broom and went to her tent.

She couldn't afford to lose her father. Not now, not again, not when they had finally found each other, when all hope seemed lost.

****

Zalla was worried about what Aisha had just told him, even though he didn't show it. Mahmood and his men needed to be dealt with fast. He couldn't kill the man by poison; it would be too obvious. He also couldn't kill the man in broad daylight. What reason would he give for his actions?

He had a duty to protect both Aisha and her father. If anything was a source of harm, it was his responsibility to neutralise that threat. And Mahmood was a threat to them now.

His thoughts were interrupted by Mallam Yusufu.

*"Ina Bashir ya ke?"* Mallam Yusufu asked.

What did he want with Bashir? Zalla thought to himself.

*"Yana hutawa a cikin dakinsa. Mai ya faru?"* - He is resting in his room. What happened? – Zalla replied.

*"Junaidu ne ke neman sa,* "Mallam Yusufu.

Zalla was curious why Junaidu wanted to see Bashir. He reassured the old man not to worry that he would fetch Bashir and bring him to Junaidu. The man thanked Zalla and walked away, but he wasn't his usual chatty self. Something was definitely going on.

Zalla walked to Bashir's tent and found him sitting on the floor, a faraway look in his eyes. Zalla's presence snapped him out of his reverie.

"Junaidu wants to see you," Zalla said. "Do you know why?"

Bashir shook his head.

"Mallam Yusufu just told me now."

When they arrived at the main tent and joined the other men, Zalla studied Junaidu's face for any clue about the purpose of the gathering, but the man revealed nothing.

He welcomed Bashir and offered him a seat. Once Bashir was settled, Junaidu began to speak. He informed the group that Al-Amin's wounds had begun to fester and that he was being sent back to Maiduguri for proper treatment. In the meantime, his position would need to be filled.

He paused, then announced that the person Allah had chosen for the role was… Bashir.

The moment the words left his mouth, the camp erupted. Shouts of jubilation tore through the air.

Some of the girls left their chores to see what the commotion was about. A few of the soldiers lifted Bashir onto their shoulders, chanting, *"Wutar Allah! Wutar Allah!"*

Where they had gotten that nickname, *the Fire of God*, was a mystery to Zalla. He stood off to the side, smiling at the men. He noticed Junaidu smiling too.

Bashir had somehow managed to become even more popular than he already was when he arrived at the camp. Zalla welcomed the development. Bashir's growing influence would help push their plans forward, first, his own plan, and then Emmanuel's.

He hadn't told his friend about it yet, didn't want it to interfere with the plan to rescue Aisha.

He hadn't told Emmanuel a lot of things.

And time was no longer on their side.

After the noise had died down and the men started dispersing, Zalla and Bashir bid them goodnight and left. As they walked, they began to talk in whispers.

"What do you think of this, Zalla?

"It is good. Very good. People trust you. It will be easy for us to escape." Zalla said, turning around to make sure no one was eavesdropping on their conversation.

"Yes, I think so too."

"I need to tell you something. We need to finish Mahmood."

"Okay. Do you have a plan?" Emmanuel said, looking at him with expectation. "I did not have a plan before. But I think I have it now."

Bashir listened to Zalla as he highlighted the plan. It

was to convince Shuaibu, the leader of the deserters, to falsely confess that Mahmood was behind their escape because he didn't like Junaidu's leadership. It was a stretch, but Zalla seemed to have hope in the ability of the plan to deliver.

****

The next day, Bashir stood at the entrance of his tent and watched as Zalla called Muktar over and whispered something to him. Bashir was hoping that Zalla didn't intend to involve Muktar in this, but it seemed like he had.

He watched as Muktar, who was on guard duty over the deserters, whispered to Shuaibu what Zalla had told him. After a few seconds, he could see how the gravity of the situation dawned on Shuaibu, and he nodded.

Bashir didn't understand why Muktar would go along with this plan, but Zalla reassured him, explaining that the man would jump into a burning lake if it were for Bashir. Obviously, his fame was more than he realised. In addition, Muktar hated Mahmood.

It was now afternoon when Junaidu called Bashir over. He wanted them to interrogate the deserters together.

As Bashir approached, Junaidu was effusive in his praise. He commended the way Bashir had planned and executed the attack on the Nigerian Army soldiers. Most fighters would have turned back after seeing a military presence—but Bashir had attacked with what he called *the fury of Allah*, capturing all the deserters alive and bringing them back without losing a single man.

As they continued speaking in English, a question formed in Bashir's mind.

"But how were fifteen men able to escape so easily in the first place?"

The question caught Junaidu off guard. He paused for a moment, frowning.

"Hmmn. So you're thinking that…", he let the sentence trail off.

Bashir nodded. "Yes. They must have had help."

"So we have more traitors among us."

"Bring the prisoners!" Junaidu barked.

The deserters were dragged into the open square and tied to wooden stakes.

Junaidu demanded to know who their collaborator was. None of the prisoners answered. Bashir found their silence impressive, their acting was convincing. He thought, *If they had given up the name too quickly, it would've raised suspicion.*

Junaidu pressed on, even promising freedom to anyone who spoke. Still, the men remained silent. One of them spat on the ground in defiance. Junaidu responded with a vicious backhanded slap, then ordered them to be whipped.

Rods and whips cracked through the air for over an hour. Still, no one spoke.

Bashir decided it was time to escalate. He drew his dagger and held it to the throat of one of the prisoners.

"Tell us the name," he said.

He fully expected someone to speak now, but to his surprise, even under the threat of death, the men stayed silent.

He began to feel uneasy. His eyes searched for Shuaibu, trying to make eye contact, a signal to speak up now, *save at least one of your men.* But Shuaibu looked away, deliberately avoiding him.

The moment stretched. Then Junaidu spoke.

"Kill him," he ordered.

Bashir hesitated, pretending not to hear.

"I said, kill him," Junaidu repeated, more firmly.

Bashir turned to Shuaibu. "Tell us who the culprit is, or I'll slit your comrade's throat."

Shuaibu met his gaze and smiled. "Get on with it."

Bashir froze, stunned. The look in Shuaibu's eyes told him he wasn't bluffing. He meant every word.

Bashir was confused. What was going on here? He turned around and saw Junaidu waiting for him to kill the man. Having run out of options, he slit the man's throat. Blood spurted from the man's neck in an arc in a fountain of red. Bashir shifted quickly before he was bathed in it.

The death seemed to have awoken the others. Bashir took his bloody knife to the neck of the next man, and the man shivered and said he would talk. Finally! He couldn't imagine killing more of them.

*"Mahmood ya fada mana inda zamu. Ya kuma gaya mana yadda za mu tsere,"* one of the men confessed.

Junaidu stood there, shocked by the revelation. It was evident that he was trying hard to process it. While he tried to steady himself, Shuaibu began giving details about Mahmood's involvement in their operations. Only someone close to Junaidu could have known those things. Bashir wondered how Zalla got his hands on that information.

With the additional confession by Shuaibu, Junaidu

seemed convinced that they were telling the truth.

"*Kawo min Mahmood*," he ordered two men to apprehend Mahmood.

A few minutes later, the men returned with the accused and tied him alongside the deserters. When Junaidu informed him of the accusations, the man denied everything as expected. The alternative was death.

His pleas of innocence didn't move Junaidu. The order was clear: by evening, they were all to be taken outside the camp and executed.

****

That evening, Bashir, Zalla, and one other fighter led the prisoners out of the camp. Originally, Bashir had wanted only himself and Zalla to handle the execution, but Junaidu had insisted on three escorts. In the end, they compromised and agreed on bringing just one extra man.

They moved through the forest, Bashir in front, with

Zalla and the other fighter flanking the prisoners from behind. The deserters walked with their hands bound tightly behind their backs, their mouths gagged. The sun was nearly gone, and the trees were casting long, eerie shadows across the underbrush.

After about half an hour of walking, they reached a clearing Bashir deemed suitable. He signaled to Zalla and the third man to prepare.

Suddenly, Mahmood sprang at Zalla, knocking him to the ground. Somehow, he had managed to free his hands during the march.

Before anyone could react, he lunged toward Bashir, eyes wild with rage, hands curled into claws.

But Bashir didn't flinch. He fired two shots from the hip, one to Mahmood's chest, the other to his head. Mahmood crumpled instantly.

By now, Zalla had scrambled to his feet. The third fighter raised his rifle, preparing to gun down the fifteen prisoners. But before he could fire, Zalla raised his own weapon and shot him in the chest.

If anyone asked about the fighter's disappearance, Zalla had the story ready:

The man had turned on Bashir and tried to kill him. Unknown to them all, he had been working with Mahmood and had planned to free him and the deserters after killing Zalla and Bashir.

That story would hold. It had to.

With that, he and Bashir released Shuaibu and his men, showing them a hollow tree trunk where he had hidden supplies and weapons for them. He instructed them to remain nearby until they were ready for the final assault. Bashir outlined the plan, but they would have to wait till a good opportunity presented itself. They agreed that Zalla would bring them information if needed. Shuaibu nodded and shook Zalla's hand. Just as they were about to leave, Bashir asked Shauibu a question.

*"Me yasa ka bar ni in kashe ɗanuwar ka?"*

Zalla suspected that Bashir was confused about why Shuaibu allowed him to kill one of his men, and this question was a confirmation. Shuaibu looked at Bashir and told him that he knew Junaidu better than they did, that if that hadn't been done, it would have been difficult to convince Junaidu. And he also told them that the man in question was the idiot who was on sentry duty yet did not see the military until it was too late, and that led to their capture.

With that, Zalla and Bashir bade Shuaibu and the others goodbye and headed back to the camp.

# CHAPTER TWENTY-FOUR

Aisha focused on her chores, doing her best to avoid Junaidu. She knew about the plan her father and Zalla had devised to get rid of Mahmood, and she was deeply relieved. The thought that she would never have to spend another night with Mahmood filled her with cautious joy.

She struggled to hide it, keeping her face neutral as she walked back to her tent. Drawing attention to herself now could be dangerous.

But her hopes for a quiet, peaceful evening were quickly dashed.

"Aisha!" Junaidu called from across the open square.

She turned, heart sinking, and saw him seated with six other men, chatting casually. She quickly walked over.

"*Ga ta nan.*" – Here she is. - Junaidu said, gesturing toward her as she arrived.

One of the men stood up and walked over. Without a word, he reached out and touched her cheek, his gaze traveling down her body, stopping on her chest. Then he grabbed her shoulder and turned her around, inspecting her like livestock. His hand slid down her arm.

Aisha recoiled, visibly repulsed.

"*A'a, ba na so,*" - No, I don't want her. - the man muttered, pushing her face aside before turning back to his seat.

No sooner had he sat down than another man rose. His eyes were already gleaming with lust.

Hot tears of anger welled in Aisha's eyes.

Now it was clear, Junaidu intended to give her away, just like that, like an object.

She was being handled like a piece of clothing in the market, examined and dismissed at will. Aisha swallowed hard and looked down, trying to hide the storm rising inside her.

"*Ina son ta. Ka ba ni.*" the second man said. - I want her. Give her to me.

The words hit her like a slap. She staggered back, stunned, and looked at Junaidu with desperate eyes.

He met her gaze, expressionless, cold.

The first man suddenly stood again, now changing his mind. He shoved the second man, trying to claim her after all.

"*Ka bar ta, zan dauke ta.*" – Let her be, I'll have her. – he said.

"*Amma ka ce ba ka son ta. Yanzu kana son ta saboda na ce ina son ta ba? Toh ban yarda ba.*" - But you said you didn't want her. Now you want her because I said I want her? I don't agree. - The second man pushed the first one back and grabbed Aisha.

"*Mallam Junaidu, ka ba ni yarinyan nan. Zan yi dai dai da ita.*" Another man walked to Junaidu with expectant eyes. Junaidu turned to Aisha and smiled.

"Everybody wants Aisha as a wife!" Junaidu laughed.

"So how do we decide who she will marry!?" He spreads his hands, palms upwards.

*"Mallam Junaidu, mu yi kokawa sai wanda ya ci nasara ya aure ta."* Another, named Jafaru, said as he walked up to Aisha and touched her face. He was tall and muscular, with a deep X-shaped scar on his face that widened whenever he smiled.

He touched her lips and moved closer as if he wanted to kiss her. Aisha pushed him and jumped back. Jafaru laughed at her, then he turned to Junaidu and shouted, *"Wanda yake so ya yi min kokawa, ya ci gaba!"* Jafaru was challenging the men to a wrestling contest with Aisha as the prize for the winner.

Aisha thought of her father and Zalla in panic. They were supposed to be back by now. She looked towards the bush, hoping against hope that they would return and somehow save her from the madness about to unfold. What if something bad had happened to them in the forest and they never came back?

The raucous laughter of the men jolted Aisha back to

the present. The fighters were preparing for the wrestling contest now, with a growing crowd gathering to watch. Word of the challenge was spreading quickly through the camp, drawing more spectators by the second.

Even the girls had gathered, giggling among themselves, some of them, oddly, even envious of the attention Aisha was receiving.

Aisha glanced around again, heart pounding. Still no sign of her father. No Zalla either.

Panic rose in her chest. If these men finished their contest before her father returned, one of them would claim her, and by then, it might be too late for anyone to stop it. Not that it would be easy even now.

*Where were they?*

The first match began. Jafaru squared off against another man. As they grappled, Jafaru swept his right foot in a quick arc, catching his opponent's leg and sending him crashing onto his back.

A cheer erupted from the crowd. Jafaru raised both arms in triumph, grinning broadly.

*"Wanene a gaba!?"* he called out, mocking the other men.

Another man stepped forward, urging the onlookers to cheer for him.

Folding the sleeves of his shirt up to his elbows, he crouched and faced Jafaru, and they started circling each other. Jafaru lunged at the man, and he jumped back, taken a bit by surprise. Jafaru laughed uproariously, and the spectators responded in kind, jeering at his opponent. Embarrassed, the man got flustered and rushed at Jabaru. As they grappled, the man shifted his weight and grabbed Jabaru's right leg, attempting to lift him off his feet and topple him over. Jabaru responded by pushing hard against the man's shoulders, leaning forward, and bending his knee so that his entire weight was on his right leg, making it harder for the man to lift him up. As the man strained harder, he pushed his right foot forward to gain some leverage, but Jafaru seized that moment and made his move. He heaved upwards, breaking the man's grip on his leg. He followed that up by locking his left leg beside the man's outstretched foot and flipping him sideways. The man, suddenly losing balance, floundered sideways, and Jafaru pounced on him and threw him to the ground.

The crowd erupted in shouts of congratulations, praising his strength and wrestling prowess. Even Junaidu was cheering and clapping.

*"Akwai wani kuma!?"* Jafaru shouted triumphantly, fully expecting that no one would dare challenge him after seeing his power and skill. The man he had just defeated dusted himself and sulked away.

A man who had been considering taking his shot looked from Aisha to Jafaru and to the man who had just been defeated, walking away, and decided that it was not worth it. He shook his head at Junaidu, indicating that he would not contest.

"HAAARRRRR!!!" Jafaru shouted, raising both hands, fists clenched to celebrate his victory. Junaidu was clapping and walking towards him, smiling to present him with his prize.

Aisha recoiled on seeing him walk towards her. She remembered what she had endured with Mahmood, and just when it seemed her salvation had come, she was about to be thrown back into hell. Overcome by the weight of her plight, she sank to her knees and started wailing.

Junaidu laughed as he walked to her and grabbed her hand. He pulled her to her feet and started dragging her forward while some of the men joined Jafaru to congratulate him.

*"MENENE GAGGAWA?"* a voice called out from the bush, interrupting their celebrations. Junaidu stopped mid-stride and peered in the direction from which the voice came.

*"Za ku iya rike mutum na gaske?"* It was Bashir, stepping out of the shadows into the light of the fires burning in the open square. As he walked forward, he handed his gun to one of the men and started taking off his shirt. The implied taunt that Jafaru had been fighting weak men was too much for him to bear. He looked

at Junaidu and nodded.

Junaidu nodded back and released Aisha's hand.

*"Hatta Bashir mai girma shima yana son auren Aisha!"* - The great Bashir, too, wants to marry Aisha. "This Aisha must be very special."

Aisha pulled her hand back, rubbing her wrist where his grip was still hurting, as her heart almost jumped out of her chest. She could hardly contain her joy when her father emerged from the bush and challenged Jafaru. But wait, how was he planning to defeat Jafaru? The man was obviously very strong and quick and knew how to wrestle. And where was Zalla?

All these thoughts flashed through her mind as the camp was quickly divided into two groups, one supporting Jafaru and the other supporting Bashir.

"JAFARU, JAFARU!"

"BASHIR, BASHIR!" the cries rang out in the night.

The men took their positions, and the battle commenced.

****

As Bashir and Zalla approached the camp after killing Mahmood and the fighter sent with them, they heard the uproar of the wrestling match going on. They crept cautiously towards the open square, taking care to remain in the shadows. They saw Jafaru wrestling with another man and Aisha standing in the middle of the square. Immediately, Bashir and Zalla realised what was happening.

Bashir cursed under his breath. He had thought they would have more time, but it seemed fate was forcing his hand. He whispered the new plan to Zalla, who nodded and crept off silently into the night.

Bashir waited until the last possible moment before revealing himself.

*"Za ku iya rike mutum na gaske?"* he said in a loud voice as he stepped out of the darkness into the middle of the square to confront Jafaru for one last epic battle.

****

With her heart in her mouth, Aisha watched her father

wrestle with Jafaru. While the other people cheering and shouting saw it as just a friendly sparring contest, she and her father knew what was really at stake. Unfortunately, her father was not as strong as Jafaru, and after the first tangle, it became clear that he would have to change his tactics; otherwise, the match would be very short.

Bashir feinted to the right and dove to his left, trying to catch Jafaru with his right flank exposed, but like a cat, Jafaru sprang backwards out of Bashir's grasp. Jafaru laughed, waving both hands in the air to get his supporters cheering.

Bashir struggled to match his speed and stay out of his grip. The longer the match lasted, the more frustrated Jafaru became. He had expected to win easily, but Bashir was proving to be much tougher than he looked. He had no idea that the stakes were much higher for Bashir, hence he fought with the heart of a lion.

By this time, almost everyone in the camp was gathered in the square, cheering the contestants. Even

Mallam Yusufu had joined them, cheering for Bashir.

Jafaru rushed forward, trying to end the fight quickly, and attempted to grab Bashir around the chest. As his arms encircled Bashir, Bashir dropped to one knee, slipping below Jafaru's arms. In the same fluid motion, he swung his body to the side, ducking under Jafaru's outstretched arm and suddenly grabbed Jafaru from behind. Bashir quickly locked his arms on Jafaru's chest and neck, cutting off his air supply. Jafaru, being taller and stronger, tried to rise to his full height and grabbed Bashir's hands to pry them apart.

Bashir responded by using his knee to hit Jafaru in the back of his leg, forcing him down to one knee and leaning down to exert maximum leverage on his thick neck.

The crowd of onlookers erupted. "BASHIR, BASHIR, BASHIR!"

Jafaru struggled and struggled but Bashir held on tenaciously. When he realised that he could not escape, Jafaru tapped Bashir's arm, indicating surrender. However, Bashir did not release him. Jafaru tapped more insistently as he was beginning to lose consciousness, but Bashir held on.

The onlookers were now growing uneasy, as this was supposed to be a friendly sparring match, not a fight to the death. The shouting and cheering slowly reduced as the people looked from one to another questioningly. Junaidu, seeing that Bashir did not release Jafaru even after he had surrendered, stepped forward.

"*Bashir, me ka ke yi?*" He shouted. Bashir did not respond. "RELEASE HIM!" He shouted, running forward.

Just then, the night was shattered as several loud explosions shook the camp, followed by fires from the far side of the camp. There was a brief pause, then pandemonium broke out. The fighters ran for their guns and rushed towards the direction of the explosions and the fires.

Aisha ran toward her father.

Bashir released a limp Jafaru, caught Aisha in his arms,

and bolted for the nearest weapon.

Chaos erupted.

Junaidu, trying to rally his fighters, shouted commands as men scrambled in every direction. But before they could regroup, gunfire erupted from the bush, sharp, thunderous, and deadly.

In an instant, about fifteen fighters dropped to the ground.

Junaidu dropped to one knee, scanning frantically for the direction of the attack as he searched the tree line, his eyes locked on Bashir, who was running backward into the bush, dragging Aisha with him.

With a roar of fury, Junaidu raised his rifle and fired.

Aisha screamed.

The bullet tore through her shoulder, spinning her off balance. She collapsed.

Bashir turned, rage twisting his features, and fired his rifle on full automatic, sweeping across the open space. Several fighters went down, and others fled in panic.

Junaidu and Mallam Yusufu rallied the remaining men and returned fire.

Seeing a brief lull in the shooting, Junaidu charged forward, laying down suppressing fire to allow his men to scatter and flank the attackers. Some of the ambushers fell back. Others broke and ran.

Bashir dropped behind a fallen log, pulling Aisha with him. Blood soaked through her sleeve.

This wasn't how it was supposed to go.

The plan had been simple but precise: Use the wrestling match to distract the camp. Zalla would set fire to the vehicles, drawing fighters toward the carpool. Then Shuaibu and his men would open fire from the flanks. Bashir would cut off escape from the rear and extract Aisha in the chaos.

Everything had gone perfectly until now.

Aisha lay bleeding beside him, her face contorted in

pain. And instead of Junaidu's men being overwhelmed in the crossfire, Bashir was the one pinned behind cover, bullets whining past overhead.

Had Shuaibu's men lost their nerve? Or was Junaidu simply too skilled a commander?

Bashir ripped off Aisha's hijab, bunched it into a wad, and pressed it hard against her wound.

His heart thundered in his chest. He peeked over the log and saw a nightmare.

Bodies littered the open square. Flames flickered across the ground, casting long, grotesque shadows.

In the center, Junaidu and a few of his remaining men were dragging three surviving attackers across the square, beating them, kicking them, spitting curses.

As Bashir looked, he realised that one of the surviving attackers was Zalla. His heart sank as he realised that his plan had failed. As he tried to drag Aisha further into the bush, a man stepped out from behind a tree holding a rifle pointed at Aisha.

*"Yau za ku mutu ku biyu!"* - Today you will both die. - It was Jafaru with a deathly grin on his face. "Move!" he commanded.

Bashir helped Aisha to her feet, and they walked and stumbled into the square to join Zalla and the two other men, the only survivors from the group of fifteen.

Jafaru kicked Bashir, and he fell to his knees. Without her father supporting her, Aisha fell, whimpering in pain and frustration.

Junaidu walked over and hit Bashir's face with the butt of his rifle. He fell, with a cut above his eye, bleeding. Junaidu kicked him in the chest. Aisha screamed and tried to move to help her father, but Jafaru kicked her repeatedly in the stomach until she passed out from the pain.

"Tashe shi!" Junaidu ordered, and two men rushed forward to raise Bashir up. He was bleeding from his eye and holding his ribs that were on fire from the kick he had received.

"WHO ARE YOU?" Junaidu screamed at Bashir.

Bashir looked around and saw that there was no chance of escape. He shook his head in resignation and acceptance of his impending death. He looked from Aisha to Zalla and back to Aisha.

"My name is Emmanuel. Aisha is my daughter."

The Boko Haram fighters look from one to another in shock.

"So you came here and deceived us just to find her?" Junaidu asked. "You did all this…" he waved his rifle around, "just to save her?"

Emmanuel nodded, totally dejected. The pain in his head and his ribs was nothing compared to the pain of defeat, knowing that his daughter and his only friend were about to be killed because of him. He hung his head and started to weep.

Junaidu started laughing. Then he lifted his rifle and fired short bursts into the air.

"ALLAHU AKBAR! ALLAHU AKBAR," He cried

in triumph. His men echoed his cries, firing into the air as well.

He then walked over to one of the surviving deserters and shot him in the head. As his body crumpled, Junaidu turned to the other one. He recognised him and asked Mallam Yusufu to kill him. Apparently, that one was Mallam Yusufu's protege. He had been responsible for his training since he joined the terrorist group, and he betrayed Mallam Yusufu personally when he joined Shuaibu and the other deserters.

Mallam Yusufu raised his gun and shot the young man without hesitation.

Then Junaidu pointed at Zalla, then at Bashir.

"This one is for you, Bashir. Kill him yourself, or I'll kill your daughter."

Bashir froze.

He looked at his friend. The man who had stood by him through everything. The one who waited outside the school. The hospital. The police station. The one who gave him his only escape route and rode into danger by his side. The one who helped him infiltrate the terrorist group. Who followed him, risked everything, again and again, so that Emmanuel could find his daughter.

Zalla.

Bashir shook his head. His eyes brimmed with tears. He couldn't do it.

Jafaru stepped forward. He pulled a pistol from his holster, ejected the magazine, leaving only one bullet in the chamber.

He pressed it into Bashir's trembling hand.

"Do it."

Zalla's face was bloodied, bruised. Yet he looked straight at Bashir and nodded.

"Do it!" he said, his voice raspy but firm.

Emmanuel raised the pistol, his hands shaking. Then his arm dropped. Limp.

Junaidu snarled in disgust. He turned and stalked over

to where Aisha lay bleeding. He raised his rifle and pointed it at her.

Bashir shouted.

But before Junaidu could pull the trigger, Zalla spoke.

"About eighteen years ago," he began, "a boy left his mother and sister in the village after his father died. The boy came to Maiduguri. He knew no one. But he was helped by a Mallam, an Imamu."

His voice was quiet but steady. The camp fell silent.

He knew there would be no escape now. If he was going to die, he would say what needed to be said.

Zalla kept his eyes on Bashir as he continued.

"The man who helped the boy was Mallam Ashiru Mansur."

At the name, Bashir flinched.

Zalla saw it. He pressed on.

"The man was good. He taught the boy from the Holy

Book, the true way. He was patient, even when the boy and his friends were stubborn.

"They called him *Shibarid.*"

Bashir's breath caught.

Zalla's voice grew stronger now, as if each word gave him life.

"He didn't drive the boy away. Even when the other mallams mocked him, he taught about love, peace, and unity. About patience. About kindness to all people, even if they were not Muslim."

Zalla's eyes glistened.

"Other mallams didn't like him. They said his ways were weak. But *Shibarid* said, 'Let them mock. My strength is not in force. It is in truth.'"

"One day," Zalla continued, "his brother's daughter get pregnant for a Christian man. An Igbo. Her father, Alhaji Attahiru, no like it, but Mallam Ashiru told him to allow them be happy. Many people no agree with him. But they married."

"Then they came to see Mallam Ashiru—with their baby. The boy and his friends were sitting outside the gate of the Islamiyya."

Zalla paused, his eyes on Bashir.

"The couple were going, but the man forget his wallet. The boy's friends wanted to keep the money, but the boy refused. He run and gave the man back his wallet."

"The man no remember the boy. But the boy was happy."

At that moment, Emmanuel's face changed. His breath caught in his throat. Finally, he understood.

Tears welled in his eyes and ran freely down his cheeks.

"What is the meaning of all these useless stories?" Junaidu growled, impatient now. He raised his rifle again, but Mallam Yusufu held out a hand.

"Let him finish," the old man said quietly.

Zalla took a breath.

"After many years, the boy started following his Mallam's teachings. But one day, they invite him to come and listen to another preaching, in a mosque. He went there and met Yusuf."

He glanced at the men.

"He was happy. But Yusuf's teaching no be like the one of his *Shibarid*. Still, the boy joined."

"After some time, Yusuf died. Another man take his place. This new man begin to ask the boy and his friends to do bad things, kill people, bomb places."

Zalla's voice shook slightly.

"The boy no want to do it. But his friends convince him."

Silence.

"One day," he went on, "they send the boy to kill a man teaching against them. They say Allah want him dead. But it was the boy's Imam."

Zalla looked up at the sky, then back at Emmanuel.

"He no want to do it. But again… his friends convince him."

His voice dropped to almost a whisper.

"That night, they burned the place down with the students inside."

"The Imam saw the boy lighting fire to his school. The boy stood there… watching his Imam. That was the day the boy removed his gun…"

A long pause.

"…and shot his Shibarid."

Emmanuel locked eyes with Zalla. He mouthed the words, "I'm sorry." Zalla nodded and replied, "Goodbye."

"And what happened to the boy?" Junaidu asked.

"The boy leave the group with his friend. He was never the same. He could not sleep again. He will have bad dreams anytime he close his eyes. But people from the group came and killed his friend, and the boy decided to come back to pay back the evil. His friend, Lado, and his Imam, Mallam Ashiru. The boy came to revenge."

"But the boy failed because he will die now," Junaidu said, with anger in his voice, and shot Zalla.

Emmanuel screamed, raised the pistol, and shot Junaidu.

As he dropped the now-empty gun, he closed his eyes and prepared for the inevitable bullet, his heart full of regret. Choices that, if he had a second chance, he would have taken a different path. All the major decisions of his life flashed through his mind in that split second before.

Several shots rang out.

Emmanuel waited for the pain and the oblivion of death, but nothing happened. After a few seconds, he opened his eyes and looked around.

All the Boko Haram terrorists lay dead. He rushed over

to Aisha and lifted her off the ground, cradling her and weeping, as soldiers of the Nigerian military swept through the camp.

# PART FOUR:

# JUNE 2021

# EPILOGUE

Aisha walked through the dusty roads of Gombaru. Not much had changed since her last visit. It had been almost six years since she had left Nigeria, but it felt like a lifetime. She saw a group of children playing by the roadside in front of a shop. The number of shops at this intersection seemed to have increased while she was away.

She turned towards the road that led to her house. Her former house. The place where she and her father had lived. The place where her mother, Zainab, had lived for years. The place where her grandparents had lived with their children, the Nweze's residence. A place that held so many memories of pain, happiness, loss, love, family, and despair.

The new owners had repainted the walls of the house with a darker shade of the original colour. Or was it the same colour? She had forgotten. She walked towards the compound in hopes that she would recognize anyone from before. She didn't.

She wanted to knock. In her mind, she imagined that her father would open the door and welcome her with open arms, and he would tell her how much he missed her, and then she would call him 'chief.'

That he would lead her into the house, and she would see her mother seated in the living room, her old self before the gloomy days. That they would both welcome her back and tell her how lonely the house had been without her.

Before she could make up her mind to knock, a woman came out of the house. She looked at Aisha and asked her if she was looking for someone.

"Yes, please. I am looking for Mr Nweze. Emmanuel Nweze."

The woman shook her head and told Aisha that she and her family had just moved in after the COVID-19 lockdown. They were new to town.

Aisha thanked the woman and turned around and walked back towards the beginning of the street.

Aisha's mind went back to that fateful night and the rescue by the Nigerian military.

After the attack on the military team that had captured the fifteen deserters, the security forces launched a massive manhunt across the region. Quite by coincidence, they stumbled upon the battle between Bashir's men and the terrorist fighters during his attempt to rescue Aisha. The explosions Zalla had set off, and the ensuing gun battle, led the soldiers directly to the terrorists' camp.

Once rescued, the military evacuated Aisha and the other girls from the camp and transported them to a rehabilitation center in Maiduguri. Their wounds were treated at a hospital, and from there, the girls were transferred to a UN shelter for women.

At the hospital, Aisha received devastating news: she had been pregnant, but had lost the baby due to the beating she endured that final night at the terrorist camp.

What followed was a media frenzy. The rescued girls

were paraded from one photo op to another, as politicians delivered speeches and made lofty promises to stamp out terrorism. Within a week, many of the girls were reunited with their families.

But during this time, her father disappeared.

He left her a note.

In it, he explained that the military had grown suspicious, asking pointed questions about how he had managed to survive so long with the terrorists. What began as interviews had shifted into interrogations. Fearing he might be arrested and tried as a collaborator, he chose to vanish.

He told her not to worry. He urged her to focus on rebuilding her life, pursuing her education, seeking a fulfilling career, and moving forward.

She waited. For weeks, she hoped he would return or at least send another message. But nothing ever came.

Then, a few days later, two women came to visit. They introduced themselves as her grandmother and her mother's stepmother.

They had seen her story on the news. Her grandfather, Alhaji Attahiru Mansur, had been ill for some time, and they had come to convince her to return with them to come live with the family she had never known.

Life was such a strange thing. Her mother's stepmother, Radiya, later told her all that transpired when her father had met her mother, and the circumstances of Aisha's birth.

Surprisingly, she had not known any of these things before then. Aisha then understood more about her mother and how much she suffered.

She moved to live with them, completed her examinations, which had been so brutally interrupted, and proceeded to travel abroad for her university education.

She thought of all these events as she walked back to where she had left her car and driver. She then got back in the car and asked the driver to take her home.

She still believed with all her heart that her father was alive, that he was out there, as Bashir, fighting battles that only he could.

If he was truly out there, she knew it was her duty to find him and bring him home to her. He had sacrificed everything for her.

Memories of their time together came rushing back, and the tears followed, heavy, wracking sobs that she could no longer hold in. She had missed him deeply, but for years, she'd forced herself to bury the thought of him just to survive.

Now, standing here again, where it had all begun, he had quietly returned to the center of her world, and the weight of it was unbearable.

He had to come home. Back to where he belonged. Back to her. She had a plan. It would demand every ounce of strength she had.

It would require connections and resources, and it would be dangerous. Extremely dangerous.

But she wasn't afraid. Danger had never been a stranger to her. With a look of steely resolve, she began going over the plan in her mind, step by step, plotting the course to find her father and bring him back.

*Alive or dead.*

The car pulled away, disappearing into the dusty streets of Maiduguri.

*The End*

# Acknowledgements

The journey of bringing this story to life would not have been possible without the contributions of the following people, in one form or another.

My children, Eliora, MJ, and Ella. I had just put you to bed one night in 2016 and after watching yet another news article of schoolgirls being kidnapped, and I was struck by the weight of the tragedy and how powerless I would feel as a father.

To my brother and friend, Michael Afenfia, thank you for the years of encouragement to "just write it". You inspire me.

To Suleiman Ayuba, my Kaduna friend who guided me in fleshing out my story and gave me insights, local colour and contextual clarity, I say thank you for your work with the IDPs and other victims.

To my friend Tonye Iti, thank you for the numerous edits spanning several years.

To my friends Bilkisu Kure and Samuel Ejeh, thank you you for your belief in my audacity.

To Rebecca Mallum, I applaud your bravery, the unquenchable fire of your spirit in the face of unbelievable adversity that you have faced since April 2014, and how you have navigated life since then. Thank you for writing the foreword to this book.

To Justin Ijeh, Ogugua Ajayi, Dolapo Marinho, Ibiso Graham-Douglas, Rogers Ofime, Lolo Eremie, Moses Babatope, Rita Onwurah, Ijeoma Aniebo, and my other friends and professional colleagues, thank you for your kind words, which gave me the encouragement I needed to push through and finish the publishing process.

Finally, I wish to acknowledge the incredible amount of work I have had to do to get this book from just a story in my head one random night in 2016, to the book you are holding today. Going through this process has given me immense respect for people who have a career in writing. This is my first novel, but it will not be my last.

I acknowledge the trust, belief and support of my

entire family throughout this period of my life. May God bless and keep us all.

Finally, I want to thank God for life, health and a sound mind. I acknowledge Your sovereignty, oh Eternal One. All praise and honour are due to You. Be glorified in this work, and in the lives of Your people, amen!

www.ingramcontent.com/pod-product-compliance
Lightning Source LLC
Chambersburg PA
CBHW022250310726
48973CB00001B/21

9798889570071 6